David and Ameena

AMI RAO

FAIRLIGHT BOOKS

First published by Fairlight Books 2021

Fairlight Books
Summertown Pavilion, 18–24 Middle Way, Oxford, OX2 7LG

A CIP catalogue record for this book is available from the British
Library

1 2 3 4 5 6 7 8 9 10

ISBN 978-1-912054-27-5

www.fairlightbooks.com

Printed and bound in Great Britain

Designed by Nathan Burton

A painting is music you can see and music is a painting you can hear. —Miles Davis

Author's Note

While David himself is entirely imagined, virtually all of David's music in this novel is directly or indirectly inspired by the music of American jazz pianist Aaron Goldberg. Aaron's 'real' music across his six solo albums and multiple collaborative projects can be found on his website www.aarongoldberg.com. A heartfelt thanks to Aaron for his jazz – the magnificence of his art makes mine look half-good.

A number of paintings that Ameena interacts with are inspired by real works. The painting she sees on her first visit to the Suzy Lipskis Gallery is in the likeness of an untitled work by Georgiou Apostolos from 2014. The actual painting is as captivating as Suzy suggests. The enigmatic piece she views at the Met of the man without a face is based on a watercolour on YUPO called *In Shine Mirror* painted by the late George James. Ameena's own watercolour of the woman in the blue dress was inspired by a painting of a woman in a red dress called *Michelle* by Scott Burdick. In the real painting, the author was struck by the look of anticipation on the subject's face as she half-rises from her chair and the idea was to capture the emotion in that precise moment in time. Ameena thought a blue dress would create a more dramatic backdrop to the sunset-hued studio in the dilapidated apartment in New York's West Village, where she tells David to go to hell. When Ameena is in one of her scary moods, the author thinks it best not to argue.

Contents

presenting the composition

All art constantly aspires towards the condition of music.

Walter Horatio Pater

1.1

David and Ameena were two people with nothing in common except for the city that they lived in and the dream that lived in them.

It seems only fitting then that what happened to them happened, because ultimately it was the city that brought them together and the dream that tore them apart. Or maybe it was the dream that brought them together and the city that tore them apart.

But besides the city and besides the dream, no two people could have less in common than David and Ameena, if you considered the matter. And if you did consider the matter, you would realise quite quickly, and perhaps with some astonishment, all the different ways in which they were different. A thing of some wonder was that most of the ways in which David and Ameena were different happened to be phenotypical – a result, in a manner of speaking, of the accidents of birth; the remaining handful were also accidents of birth, only in a different, invisible, way, and as it turned out, happened to be the most profound things, as profound things go, that David and Ameena didn't have in common.

But all that would reveal itself later.

In a city that has grown vertically since its inception, and at one time, which was a time before David and Ameena met, boasted two of the tallest buildings in the world, scraping the sky at the imposing heights of 417 metres and 415 metres respectively, it is ironic then that David and Ameena met 55 metres below the ground, on the 1 train at the 191st Street stop at Washington Heights.

They were sitting at opposite ends of the compartment with – a rarity for this city – no one in the middle. It was quite late at night and David was returning home from a jam session with similarly musically inclined friends at a club near Yeshiva University. Ameena was returning home from a party at her editor's boyfriend's house, an event that was held rather ritualistically on the last Wednesday of every month and involved wine, which Ameena enjoyed; oysters, which she did not; fashion types, a group she felt strongly that she didn't belong to; and literary types, a group she felt, less strongly, that she did. But of course, David and Ameena didn't know all this about each other. In fact, they didn't know anything about each other. Come to think of it, they hadn't so much as noticed each other because they were both engrossed, heads down, eyes lowered, in their respective books rendering the very act of noticing a logistical improbability.

At about this time, the door from the adjoining compartment on David's end opened, and a youngish Caucasian male wearing grey sweatpants and a matching grey hoodie that obstructed most of his face – possibly by design, but possibly not – entered the space where David and Ameena sat. He stood almost exactly halfway between them, staring at the floor for a while, then turned his head in Ameena's direction and spoke in a low, gravelly voice. 'Hello beautiful,' he said, 'where are you from?'

Ameena started in her seat and looked up from her book, but then out of experience or inexperience – it could have been either – looked back down and chose to ignore him.

'Oh,' the hooded man sneered, 'you don't speak English!'

Ameena still said nothing.

David still didn't look up.

The train pulled up on 168th Street. The doors opened, and an armed policewoman walked in and through the compartment. She glanced at all three commuters nonchalantly in the manner police officers do when they are mentally evaluating you and your scope for making mischief, and satisfied with her visual assessment of the situation, left before the doors closed. Those same doors were already sliding shut when the youngish male in the grey hoodie made a sudden move towards them, twisting his body sideways to fit through the rapidly closing gap, but not before he gave Ameena another lustful look, and, curling his lips menacingly, snarled, 'Go home!'

'I am home,' Ameena said quietly, too quietly perhaps for the hooded man to hear her, but loud enough to catch David's attention. And surely enough, David looked up.

The two made eye contact.

David looked apologetic, and his eyes were bright. Ameena shrugged and her eyes were cold.

It was back to being just the two of them in the long carriage and therefore it was appropriate, David felt, to say whatever had been on his mind: 'Probably stoned,' he said matter-of-factly. 'Amazing how many crazies run rampant in this city. When a decent, solid home would do them such good. And apparently, you're the one who is supposed to go home. How illogical,' he continued with a thoughtful look on his face, 'is that logic? I mean, what I'm trying to say is that just because you're not interested in *flirting* with the kid doesn't mean you're not *home...*'

Ameena nodded at the logic of the illogical logic but said nothing.

'Or that you can't speak *English*,' David repeated, almost to himself.

'I suppose not,' Ameena replied in her perfectly *English* English, but chose not to elaborate further.

'Oh!' David exclaimed, with some surprise, possibly but not conclusively, at the perfectly English English.

And they both went back to reading their books.

At the next stop and the stop after that, the train started to fill up and David could only see Ameena if he either craned his neck all the way forward or retracted it all the way back, both of which left his neck in a distinctly uncomfortable position. And so, deciding to do neither, he simply focused on reading his book. A few pages later, he had mostly forgotten about her.

At 96th Street, a tall, incredibly beautiful man with matted hair and torn clothes entered the compartment with a money collection bowl, cleared his throat and started to sing. Only people with a fairly good knowledge of music (which David had and Ameena didn't) would have realised that not only was he singing in a voice so smooth it could well have caused the earth to slip off its axis, but he was singing a song that was known, rather definitively, to have marked the beginning of soul music. A few faces here and there looked up and started to take notice, but not that many. Which wasn't unusual given that when people who look like the man do things in public places for money, it is easier for everyone else not to notice, even in some cases when the people doing those things happen to be doing them exceptionally well.

Ten blocks down, on 86th Street, a smartly dressed white man carrying a cello on his back entered the train. A few seconds later, he closed his eyes and nodded his head and tapped his feet and clicked his fingers, as if to make sure he had placed the groove correctly in space and time, and once he had established that indeed he had, he picked up the correct note and, without missing a beat, opened his lungs to sing.

Suddenly, a hush descended.

It was an unusual occurrence you see, even for this city, in which unusual occurrences are rarely unusual. But *this* occurrence – specifically one in which at approximately a quarter past eleven at night, on the 1 downtown train, a well-groomed white man and a beautiful, homeless one just happened to be singing Ray Charles together *in the moment*, in a breathtakingly magical a cappella composition, more breathtakingly magical in fact than most people on that train would ever hear again for the rest of their lives – was extraordinarily unusual.

David and Ameena were each deeply moved.

Whether they were moved by the music itself or by the sight of so anomalous a duo creating art so sublime, it was impossible to say. But the fact remains that they were so moved that they couldn't possibly just sit there, unmoving.

A kind of curiosity gripped both at roughly the same time, and this compelled them to stand up, to facilitate a closer look at the two people responsible for the extraordinarily unusual occurrence.

And so, David stood up on his side of the compartment.

Ameena stood up on hers.

David didn't know that Ameena would stand up and Ameena didn't know that David would stand up, but when the two stood up, they realised straight away that it was the extraordinarily unusual occurrence that had elicited this response, independently, from both.

If they each had a mirror in front of their faces, they would see that despite the many different ways in which they were different, the expression on their faces was exactly the same. But they didn't have a mirror, and yet they seemed, somehow in the way that people know these things, to know this.

So, they looked at each other. Ameena nodded and David smiled.

1.2

Ameena Bano Hamid, eldest child and only daughter to Yusuf and Zoya Hamid, grew up in a moderately religious Muslim family from Lahore, by way of Pakistan International Airlines and Manchester.

She was shy but strong-willed, and as children who are born into moderately religious families often tend to be, she was also moderately religious. Until the day she wasn't.

This day came rather unexpectedly when she was eleven years old.

Ameena's parents lived in a converted split-level flat on Chapel Road – the upstairs level comprising one large and two small bedrooms and a bathroom, the downstairs level consisting of a second bathroom, the kitchen and an oddly shaped half-hexagonal room with three windows that looked out onto the street, and served as the room for everything except cooking, toileting and sleeping.

One evening, it was in this oddly shaped half-hexagonal room that something happened, something hardly unusual in itself, but one that elicited in Ameena a kind of feeling deep inside her chest that she had never experienced before.

That evening, as was their customary way of spending most evenings, her parents, her brother Kareem and his friend Faisal, who seemed to be in their house so often that Ameena had come to think of him as part of the furniture or indeed as a second brother, were sitting on the L-shaped burgundy faux leather sofa that took up most of the room. Ameena was squeezed in between her two brothers, on the long leg of the L, her parents were sitting side by side on the short leg, and they were all watching the BBC and eating her mother's special *shammi kababs* – sautéed ground mutton, tenderised and spiced with chillis, coriander and black pepper. It was here on the 8pm news – which, along with a few select cooking shows, also on the BBC, Zoya never missed, come rain, heavier rain, or typhoon – that Ameena saw an attractive blonde woman in a green dress report that earlier that afternoon a sizeable number of Palestinians, among them young children, some much younger than herself, had been shot dead by Israeli forces firing live rounds.

Nobody thought to say anything further nor to turn the TV off, despite the rather graphic nature of the footage being aired, and when she asked why what had happened had happened, her mother left to bring more *shammi kababs* from the kitchen, her father looked troubled and her eight-year-old brothers looked angry, and when she persisted with that line of questioning, everyone told her it was because that's what Jews did.

She accepted the explanation quietly if somewhat scepti-cally, but only weeks later, something else happened, something hardly unusual in itself, but one that elicited in Ameena that kind of feeling deep inside her chest that she had experienced only once before.

On this evening, they had been sitting in the same oddly shaped half-hexagonal room on the same L-shaped burgundy faux leather sofa, Ameena squeezed in between her two brothers, on the long leg of the L, her parents sitting side by side on the short leg, all watching TV and eating her mother's special *nihari* – slow-cooked shank of beef infused with curry leaves, cinnamon and cloves – when on that same infallible augur of all things bright and beautiful, the BBC, she saw the same blonde woman, looking equally attractive, this time in a blue dress, report that earlier that morning, a sizeable number of Israelis, among them little children, some much younger than herself, had been stabbed to death by Palestinian militia.

Nobody thought to say anything further nor to turn the TV off, despite the rather graphic nature of the footage being aired, and when she asked why what had happened had happened, her mother left to bring more *nihari* from the kitchen, her father looked troubled, and her brothers looked smug while they helped themselves to more rice, and when she persisted with that line of questioning, and still nobody said anything, she wondered if a little Jewish girl somewhere in the world was being told it was because that's what Muslims did.

That was the day she stopped believing in the concept of a benevolent God – although she would fully understand this only much later – because she thought if an all-powerful being such as that existed, neither would the Palestinian children have been killed by the guns, nor the Israeli ones by the knives.

And when she stopped believing, Ameena's disbelief came, not with a sense of sadness or anger or betrayal, but with the same kind of matter-of-fact acceptance that is felt when one day, a child wakes up and stops believing in Santa Claus.

I.3

David was the oldest son of a family of Ashkenazi Jews from Lithuania, by way of Vienna, Rome, Rhode Island and then eventually Manhattan Island.

His father, now dead, had been a watchmaker, fastidious in his trade with his sharp eyes and deft fingers. His mother, also dead, had been a schoolteacher, also with deft fingers that she put to a different use, for she had been a gifted pianist and the music teacher at the local school, and, on this basis, had inculcated in David and his younger brother Abraham both a love of music and a belief that education and industry alone were the twin tickets to freedom from the historical oppression of their people.

David, a quiet and sensitive boy, had taken both pieces of wisdom to heart. By the age of eight, he had sat his grade 6 piano exams, sang with a voice that made people gasp and played a medley of different instruments including saxophone, clarinet, trumpet and guitar. But like his mother, piano remained both his greatest talent and his greatest love. At school, he was a bright boy, albeit a bit aloof, often preferring to keep his own company, and yet when he chose the company of others, he found it easy, in the way that bright boys at school with consistently good grades generally do.

It was probably because of this – because David was an evolving example of his mother's precise ambition for him – that her death had been, for him, a truly terrible loss, not only because of the loss itself – her loss, the loss of the life she would have had – but also because he felt that he had lost the opportunity to show her the fully formed version of himself, of everything she would have wanted her son to be.

Many years later, David would marvel at things, at the concomitant effect of things, at how just as one stray ember sparking a forest fire could cause such devastation, so one death could lead to many deaths, not simply in a poetic sense, but in a real, literal sense.

David's parents had been childhood sweethearts, having grown up on the same street in the little town of Babtai in Lithuania, and on windless, summer days, when the windows were flung open and houseflies buzzed, the strains of Ruth's piano travelled across to Ben's bedroom and touched the softest compartments of his heart. It was significant, but not unexpected, then, when the time came, and they were finally granted the freedom to leave, that both sets of families made the collective decision to flee a home where sites of wartime massacres had become monuments, for a new land that they believed held both opportunity and redemption.

Ruth's mother had been especially persuasive on the merits of emigrating to America, backed in part by her impassioned conviction in the idea of the diaspora as fundamental to a new Jewish awareness of the world, and a new awareness of the Jews by the world.

This had caused some strain in her relationship with the others, particularly with her own husband, but the clever and artful woman that she was, she swayed them all in the end. She had a cousin, she said, who lived there, and had made some name for himself in the garment business and who, she was sure, would help set them up. And like that, albeit with some continuing resistance, pragmatism had trumped ideology.

So, David's father Ben, and David's mother Ruth, both young adults now, found themselves once again on the same street, just in a new adopted homeland, their new home now a little town in the state of Rhode Island, the town itself occupying a narrow strip of land running along the eastern bank of the Pettaquamscutt River all the way to the shore of the bay. Ben had been in love with Ruth long before he even comprehended the meaning of being in love – surviving genocide, fleeing oppression, uprooting lives, danger-fraught journeys across one wide sea and one wider ocean, all that was small fry held against the power of his passion – and so when on one September evening he proposed to her at Point Judith Lighthouse as the sky blazed and the waves crashed and all around them everything turned to gold, no one was really surprised.

David's mother died of lung cancer when David was twenty-two and Abraham was eighteen, on one of those days when the sun never set, and the night came late, one of those days in the long, languid summer that fell in between two other life events, for David had just graduated from college as spring blossomed into summer, and his brother was due to begin college, just as summer would melt into fall. The timing of these things, David would often think to himself, was one of those details, both tiny and vast, with the power to change everything, because that – the timing of his mother's death – had made the difference between the course of his brother's life and that of his own.

They hadn't caught it until it was too late; the symptoms had been subtle, easily explained away by any number of innocuous reasons, which was exactly what his mother had done for as long as she could, and so the weight loss had been attributed to cutting out sugar, the cough to her smoking, the dark circles to being kept up at night by the constant tick-tock of the multitude of clocks that inhabited the house like an army of pale-faced ghosts.

David found himself changed by his mother's disease, perhaps as we are all changed by certain events in our lives. It had caught him unawares, this possibility that he was going to lose the person who had given him life, and who would, even to that day, have easily given her own life to save his. And so, he found himself changed, and also fearful, and also shocked, not only by her death but by the rapidity with which it came. And the suddenness of it, like a truck coming off a bend in the road in the dead of the night without lights, without sound, without any warning. Just as her disease grew and spread through her body, so his terror grew and spread through his. He sat by her bedside and watched her scream in those last few months as she wafted in and out of the morphine-induced cloud of pain-numbing delirium; it was the closest he would ever get to seeing agony. And then he held her hand as he watched her die, not knowing – in the most polarising dilemma of his life – whether he was devastated or relieved.

In the days that followed, he played the piano obsessively, like a madman, for hours on end, as the black nights dissolved, and the sun rose over the Seven Hills and his fingers hurt but the notes still rang – strident and beautiful – breaking the eerie silence of the house with their intransigence to the very idea of death.

His father lasted less than a year before he suffered a stroke that came, much like madness comes, without warning out of nowhere, leaving him in a wheelchair, his limbs paralysed, his face frozen in an absurd expression of permanent surprise, eyebrows raised, eyes wide but unseeing, mouth open but unspeaking, dribbling saliva onto a cloth that the nurses changed diligently every few hours. He died in the nursing home only a couple of months later, quietly in the middle of the night, and this time for David, the relief had eclipsed almost everything else.

'Men,' David's mother's oncologist, Dr Noimark, would say, standing by the garden door with a bagel in his hand, while shiva was being sat in the living room, 'are definitely the weaker sex, David. For men, losing a partner is like losing an essential body part – a lung or a kidney or, more accurately, it is the heart I suppose – that has been cut out and taken away. And well, without an essential body part, of course, it's only a matter of time. *Women*, on the other hand, when *women* lose their husbands, it's like they get a new lease on life.' He took a bite of his bagel. 'Nice, this bagel – onion? Definitely the bolder, braver sex, young man, remember that when you find a girl of your own to marry, *women* hold the key to the box.' But what's in the box? David wondered but didn't ask.

Abraham had been most affected by their mother's death. Or as David tried to explain to their father just before he died, only because he knew he couldn't hear him and therefore couldn't possibly be saddened by it, Abe had 'become fucked in the head'. He had walked out of university after the first week, with no phone call and no letter, just got up one morning and packed his belongings and walked down the long path, lined with maple trees just beginning to blush, and out the gates. Just another truck coming off a bend on a different road. David had tried to contact him when their father had died but hadn't been able to trace him, each promising clue turning out to be yet another red herring, until the space between them was filled with a sea full of red herring, infinite and crimson and impossible to cross. The last he heard of his brother was that he was a diving instructor somewhere off the west coast of Australia. Or that he was a coke-head roaming the streets of Sydney with his electric guitar. It could be either. The only thing that seemed verifiable by mathematical triangulation was that he was still alive and that he was somewhere in Australia.

I.4

A few years after eight-year-old David had passed his grade 6 piano exams with flying colours, on a different island-kingdom across the mighty Atlantic, another eight-year-old discovered an unusual talent in an altogether different form of art.

Ameena first started doodling in the classroom out of boredom, starting in the margins of her notebook, first one line, then a curve, then a pattern, then another, then many, until the margins, first top, then bottom, then right, then left, were crammed with designs – countless crowded scenes of lines and curves and waves and spheres and teardrops. Soon, she outgrew the margins, and her patterns started to invade whatever white space they could find and Ameena began crafting entire constellations of triangles and stars floating across the pages of her ruled notebooks that were meant to be filled with letters and numbers.

When she was a little older – and a little bolder – she began to sketch picture books, telling full stories, intricate and detailed, through a spectrum of carefully constructed illustrated characters, making up these characters partly in her head and partly on paper, never knowing exactly what they were going to look like or how the story would unfold until she started sketching.

One time, her handiwork was discovered by a teacher who, suspecting something amiss, walked over from the top of the class to the back row where Ameena was seated and snatched the notebook from under Ameena's bent head, catching her unawares. When the teacher looked at the pages, sheet upon sheet upon sheet, of Ameena's notebook, she scolded her loudly for all the class to hear, albeit with a slight tremor in her voice, for she was taken aback by the child's exceptional control and finesse.

Later that week, Ameena and her mother were both summoned to the headmistress's office, and Ameena, expecting somewhat of a nasty dressing-down, was surprised that the purpose of the meeting was in fact to express to Ameena's mother that her daughter was believed to be gifted, that nobody without such a gift could possibly create art so beautiful.

The headmistress held open Ameena's notebook to reveal in one instance what appeared to be a strange sea-creature, which grew larger and larger as the pages turned, coiling and uncoiling, alive in the movement of its waving tentacles. Other creatures joined in as characters in the story, each one distinct with its own lively markings and features, creating all together some sort of mysterious underwater city with inhabitants that spoke in a visual language so compelling, it could almost be heard.

'What are you drawing here?' the headmistress asked Ameena, not unkindly.

'A magical sea.'

'What's the story about?'

'Magical sea animals.'

'I see.'

'Is this one of them?'

'Yes, a magical octopus.'

'What's he called?'

'She.'

'I beg your pardon?'

'She. It's a she. And she hasn't told me her name yet.'

'She hasn't... *who* hasn't told you her name yet?'

'The octopus. All my characters tell me their names. I start drawing them, and then they tell me what they want to look like and what they want to say and what they want to be called...

and this one hasn't told me her name yet, because *she*' – Ameena pointed her chin accusingly at the teacher – 'didn't let me finish.'

The teacher and the headmistress exchanged knowing glances, Ameena's mother looked terrified and Ameena, in the absence of pen and paper, played instead with the pleats of her grey school skirt, gathering up the material along the crease lines from both ends simultaneously, and creating, in the process, a strange protrusion between her knees.

After the meeting and for the duration of the bus ride home, Ameena's mother remained stubbornly silent, as though somehow needing silence to process what had transpired and how best to deal with it. Upon alighting at their stop, she grabbed her daughter's small wrist, and dragging her unceremoniously all the way home, announced, 'I will not tell your Abba and you will stop all this nonsense in school, and if that is an arrangement that is acceptable to you, I will buy you some painting things that you can keep in your room and do whatever you want with them in your spare time. If your marks at school do not improve, I will take it away faster than you can say Jack... uh... Jack Whatever-his-name-is... I will take it away very fast – and that will be the end of that. Do I make myself clear?'

Robinson, Ameena whispered, but in her own head. To her mother, she only nodded and nothing more was spoken of the matter.

The next evening Ameena found, placed in the centre of her bed, a large sealed box labelled 'Artist's Starter Kit', which, when she opened, she discovered to her utmost joy contained a stack of blank paper and mounting boards, a whole range of paintbrushes of different sizes and a set of thirty-six watercolours. After that, since her mother had kept up her end of the bargain, Ameena thought it only fair to keep up hers. Her performance in school steadily improved, there were no further complaints from her teachers – and that, as her mother said, would have been that, if not for a birthday lunch that Ameena was invited to, many months later, along with the rest of the girls in her class, at the house of one Sarah Adams.

This Sarah Adams boasted eyes of the bluest-blue and hair of the blondest-blonde and also a mother with the same bluest-blue eyes and the same blondest-blonde hair and also long red finger-nails who – to Ameena's amazement, because she generally associated mothers with peeling potatoes – played the harp.

'I've been invited on a play date,' Ameena informed her mother, looking up from her book cursorily, 'the whole class has. It's a lunch at Sarah's house. For her birthday.'

'What is a play date?' Ameena's mother asked.

'Lunch, Mum.'

'Well, why cannot you just say you have been invited to lunch?'

'Mum,' Ameena said with a sigh, '*really*? I mean what difference does it make what you *call* it?'

Zoya heaved her shoulders with her customary theatrical flair. 'This country! Back to front in every way! For children to play, you need to arrange a date. But for adults to marry? No, no, arranged marriage is for the backward people of the East. Here you happily arrange the play date, it must be perfect, every small detail must be carefully planned, nothing must be left to chance. But marriage? Oh, but no, *no*, you rush into marriage like headless chicken and then die-vorce, die-vorce, everywhere you turn your head, someone is dying and someone else is die-vorcing.'

Ameena slightly rolled her eyes but with her face down in her book so her mother wouldn't notice. 'Whatever. I need you to drop me at Sarah's house at noon on Saturday. Please, if you don't mind.'

It was in Sarah's house that Ameena saw what she saw, 'this Sarah' that both Ameena and her mother would always remember for entirely different reasons, for what happened happened because Ameena saw what she saw – in Sarah's house.

But first, Sarah's house! Oh, Sarah's house!

'Are you sure we are in the right place?' Ameena's mother asked as she turned into the drive, for neither of them had ever seen anything like Sarah's house except in the movies. From the imposing gunmetal electric gates to the long, winding gravelly drive, lined with tall rows of perfectly pruned conifer shrubs, to the lovely yellow brick house that sat at the end of the drive, surrounded by flowering bushes and covered in ivy that was, at that very time, beginning to turn at its tips, orange and violet and deep ruby pink with the onset of autumn... all this, and more, so when Ameena stepped out of their dusty, beat-up, embarrassingly bright-red Citroen, and took in her surroundings, it veritably took her breath away.

'What is someone like this doing in your school?' Zoya asked with a face full of bewilderment.

Ameena shrugged, but she knew it wasn't a strange question entirely, even if it came from her mother who was, in Ameena's opinion, full of strangeness, because the school consisted of people like herself, and Denise Richards, beautiful Denise Richards whose father was a Rastafarian tiler with a head full of dreadlocks, and skinny, blonde Victoria Windsor, who was named for a queen but came from a family so poor that they – all seven of them – slept in the same bed with gloves and woolly hats for half the year to keep warm.

So, she didn't know either what 'someone like this' was doing in her school, but instead of venturing a guess that was bound to burst open the infamous floodgates of Zoya's reproach, she opted for a far safer approach and simply said, 'See you later, Mum!'

'Behave yourself Ameena,' Zoya warned, 'and be careful of their things, for God's sake. I will pick you up at three o'clock as they've asked.' She reluctantly reversed the car, backing straight into a gigantic yellowing wisteria that protruded irresponsibly from one of the compound walls, unsure how her daughter would fit into whatever she had seen of Sarah Adams's world, even if only for the duration of this play date business. 'Bloody plant,' she cursed under her breath. 'Don't break anything,' she yelled out of the open window.

'I won't break anything Mum, don't *worry*!' Ameena yelled after her happily, as she waved goodbye.

But a wolf can come in sheep's clothing and destruction, sometimes, has nothing at all to do with breaking things. The trouble, you see, lay within.

From the moment she entered those heavy wooden double doors and stepped into the grand foyer with its staircase spiralling into the sky, Ameena saw walls covered with gigantic canvases of every beast and body that could be imagined. Art – everywhere, on every wall, in every room – canvases bursting with colour and movement and life, galloping horses and flowing waterfalls and lush forests and migrating animals and lovers and dancers and children eating grapes, naked people and beautiful people and beautiful naked people and stately men and blushing women and – in the dining room, directly in front of where she was seated as she graciously ate her lunch – a girl with a pearl earring.

Ameena was spellbound.

The paintings in Ameena's own modest split-level flat consisted of one framed Quranic verse and one enlarged yellowing photograph of her father's family home in Lahore, large and sprawling and as foreign to Ameena as the extended family who posed in front of it, formal and rigid in two rows, an arrangement that Ameena was convinced was the result of a mistake the photographer had made in communicating his instructions, for the seating arrangement was all backwards – the men sitting on chairs forming the front row; the women standing behind them, forming the back.

She had gone back home that afternoon, straight to her room, taken out her watercolours and brushes and started painting, as if possessed by something otherworldly. She continued like this for days, hiding the finished pieces under her bed and starting new ones, stopping only to go to school and at mealtimes when her father was home, making sure she washed off any telltale traces of paint from her fingers and her clothes, until finally, more than a week later when she was satisfied, she pulled out the lot from under her bed and examined them with a critical eye.

That night, after everyone had gone to bed, she went downstairs and, standing on a wooden chair that she carried around with her as she moved from one wall to the next, Ameena mounted her artwork with Blu-tack. After she had put the last one up, she surveyed her handiwork with pride, for the house seemed transfigured, its walls breathing new life.

When Ameena woke the next morning, she woke to a chaos never witnessed before in the Hamid household. She could hear them from her bedroom, the raised voices and the wailing – was it wailing? Was that her *mother* wailing? She crept halfway down the stairs and peeped over the narrow wooden bannister to see her father, mother and brother clustered together, arguing loudly among themselves, half in English and half in Urdu.

'It's *haram*, Abba,' her brother was saying, his face dark, like storm clouds.

Her mother, clearly the emitter of the terrible noise that had woken Ameena, appeared to be crying. 'That girl, I told that girl, whatever she must do, she must do quietly in her room. I knew it. I just knew it. From the beginning I knew that she would bring us trouble. Come on Kareem, start taking them down—'

'But, Zoya...' her father interrupted, stroking his beard, his face revealing a mixture of admiration and a kind of trepidation, 'can't you see, these paintings are marvellous!'

'Yusuf!' her mother screamed. 'Have you gone mad?'

'Mad, no. No, I've not gone mad. But you are both mad if you cannot see the talent in the child.'

'Abba, it's *shirk. Shirk* and *haram*.'

'Kareem, be quiet – did I ask your opinion?'

'No, Abba, but—'

'"No Abba but" what? Since when have you become such a good Muslim? Shut your mouth.'

'Yusuf, don't talk to my son like that. He is the only one here who upholds the values and morals of this house. That girl, did you see that painting there, near the bathroom? It's a woman with her *bum* showing. Her *bum*. Shame, *shame* on her. *Shame* on all of us. Oh, what did I do to deserve such a fate!'

Then they saw her, quiet as a mouse, crouched on the staircase.

There was a hushed silence, an awkwardness, almost a kind of shock as if they hadn't prepared themselves for the possibility that the creator of this current catastrophe might actually choose to make an appearance.

Her mother spoke first. 'Ameena!' she cried, holding her palm to her forehead dramatically. 'What have you done?'

Wordlessly, Ameena ran back up to her room and changed into her uniform, not coming out until it was a full ten minutes later than she would normally leave for school, thereby ensuring that in a family that valued both attendance and punctuality, there wouldn't be an opportunity for any further discussion around the paintings, which thankfully for everyone involved there wasn't.

When she returned from school that afternoon, she saw that all her art had been stacked outside, in a neat pile next to the recycling bin; inside the house, the Blu-tack still lay stuck to the walls in ugly blue blobs making four corners of a square, with nothing in the middle. Realising that no one else seemed to be about at the moment, Ameena went back outside and sifted through her soon-to-be-discarded artwork, picking out a single piece and carrying it unnoticed back into the house and up to her room.

After that day, Ameena never painted life.

She went full circle, her art reverting to the style of the doodle she had started with when she first discovered what power she had over a pencil. She began creating beautiful, intense abstracts, inspired by a cultural history she knew she was supposed to be a part of but didn't fully understand, only enough to know what made her parents happy and what made them ashamed. On these paintings, for the first time since she had started drawing, she signed her name – not her full name, just 'Ameena'. Then she hid them under the bed.

No one in her family ever spoke of art again.

Years later, when she moved to New York City, the single painting she had saved that day so many years ago was one of two items of sentimental value that she decided to carry with her. It was a vivid, eerily lifelike depiction of a wide-eyed child watching her mother playing the harp – bright blue eyes and pale blonde hair, the resemblance between mother and child striking – two creatures from a fantasy world, artist unknown.

1.5

David and Ameena, although they didn't know this about each other at the time, both believed to some extent in Paulo Coelho's idea of destiny, as in: if you look at the world around you with respect and attention, you will see the signs.

And therefore, when David looked at the world around him and noticed, with respect and attention both, Ameena getting off at the same stop as him, he took this as a sign. As did Ameena because a few seconds later, when David scrambled up the stairs that led from the subway station to the street, brushing past people with a series of hasty but not impolite 'excuse-me's', she considered it neither odd, nor too forward, only as if it was meant to be – a kind of serendipity.

There was something about his face and the way he was dressed that she liked. She had never before, as far as she could remember, paid any particular attention to the way a man dressed, but the way this one dressed, somehow, she liked. He had on jeans, a navy sweater and a maroon scarf, blue socks and brown shoes; the edges of his scarf, she noticed, were slightly frayed, his shoes slightly scuffed. She liked this about him, these minor flaws – it made him endearing, in an endearing kind of way. And his face, she liked his face – it was not handsome, but it wasn't *un*handsome either... there was an openness about it, strong jaw, strong nose, the hint of a dimple on his left cheek, his brown messy mop of hair, the way it fell in a curl over his forehead above his eyes, and the eyes themselves, the glimmer of something in his green-brown eyes, a kindness or a humour or a curiosity or something else she couldn't quite place. All this she liked, because all this, she thought, lent a spark to his ordinariness, a kind of unexpected impudence hidden amidst the decency.

'Hey,' he said, slightly breathlessly, when he had finally caught up to her, his body turned sideways, at a right angle to hers as they climbed the last few stairs in lockstep, 'hey, I was... we were... in the train together, all the way from uptown.'

'Hi,' she said. 'Yeah, I know.'

'And then I noticed we were both getting off at the same stop. Weird, huh?'

'Very,' she agreed, and they both stood on the street, in front of the muffin shop at the corner, where two roads met in that precise numerical way they did only in Manhattan, the breeze blowing down the avenue, or maybe it was the street, the reds and yellows of the cars thinning at that time of night, the muffin shop closed, but with its lights still on and the chairs stacked on top of the tables.

'You live around here?' he asked and there was a shyness in his eyes that she picked up on and found rather sweet.

'Yeah, just a few blocks,' she pointed, 'that way.'

'Oh,' he said, looking in the direction she was pointing. Then he nodded, hesitated a moment as if weighing in his own head if he should say whatever he was going to say next, and then he said it: 'You know... I saw you get off as I was getting off and I kind of took it as a sign. Sorry, I know that sounds kinda cheesy...'

'No, not at all.'

'Really?'

She shrugged. 'I believe in signs too.'

He looked surprised. 'You do?'

And then he said, 'I'm David, by the way.'

And she said, 'I'm Ameena.'

And he repeats it slowly, feeling the formation of the letters, the way he needs to move his mouth to say it: 'A-mee-na.'

They stand there for a moment, under the streetlight, richer in the knowledge of each other's names.

And then he says, 'Wasn't that incredible, what happened in there?'

She nods, and her eyes, he notices, are radiant. 'It was extraordinary. That'll stay with me a long time.'

'I know, right? It's like... that encompassed everything I love about New York,' he says.

'Me also.'

'Well, then we have something big in common.'

'Indeed.'

'So, are you English?'

'What makes you think I'm English?'

'Your accent? It's kind of a dead giveaway... wait, are you not English? Hang on! Are you pulling my leg?'

She starts to laugh. 'I'm pulling your leg.'

'Phew!' he says. '*Man*, I was about to turn on my back and vanish into that subway hole!'

'No, don't vanish into the subway hole, I'm quite enjoying pulling your leg,' she says, her mouth teasing into a smile that seems, to David, almost flirtatious.

His eyes widen in sudden surprise and then, as if emboldened by the boldness of the smile, he says, 'Look, I don't do this kind of thing – honestly, I haven't done anything this crazy in a while, but do you want to have dinner tomorrow? Around here somewhere? Valentino's? Do you know Valen—'

'I love Valentino's,' she says simply and sees that he is surprised, a second time, by her, and she realises that she enjoys it, his surprise of her.

'Wow! Really? Well, great... I mean, thank you. 7.30pm?'

'7.30pm. I'm only agreeing to dinner,' she says, narrowing her eyes, but for only as long as she needs to.

'Of course,' he says immediately.

And then, 'I'm not going to stop thinking of you between now and 7.30 tomorrow night. That's nearly twenty hours, which is a very long time you know...' he adds with uncharacteristic forwardness.

'Bye David.' She laughs, shaking her head.

Chutzpah, she thinks to herself, as she watches him walk away ruffling his hair with his hand. That's the word she had been looking for. He has chutzpah.

1.6

A few months after graduating from the University of Manchester – taking two buses each way to get there and back because her mother believed it was 'stupid' to live anywhere else when one's own home was so close – with a First Class honours degree in Journalism, Ameena announced without any prior warning or discussion to the effect that she was moving out of Manchester to live on her own.

Ordinarily, this would have been accepted with a kind of bittersweet feeling typical of most parents' reactions when it comes to accepting decisions that are part and parcel of their children's coming of age. Ameena's parents, like most immigrants who leave their homes, by force or else by will, in order to seek a better life elsewhere, considered themselves broad-minded and liberal-ish and valued independence as a quality to be imbued. And so, they found themselves somewhat accepting of this proposition – until, that is, Ameena announced that she was moving out of Manchester to live on her own – not in Manchester, or even in London, which to Ameena's parents seemed in itself like a foreign country, but in an actual foreign country, which happened to be the foreign-*est* country of all to them, as foreign-*ness* went.

Once the specific location of her desired destination was revealed, and the shocked whispers of the word 'America' were repeated over and often, there ensued much crying and screaming and hard words, none of which managed to convince either party to change its mind. This was followed by a period of bitter resignation combined with a kind of hope for the four months until Ameena was due to leave, in the same vein that relatives of a dying person feel while waiting for the person to die, and yet hoping there has been some mistake; that even after all that, something miraculous will happen and the person will not die but stay on.

As for Ameena, she spent most of her time in her room daydreaming about her new life, the particulars of which she revealed to no one but her closest school friend, who had not followed her on to university but had, to her great delight, been 'scouted' by a modelling agency, and now modelled for small, low-budget specialist hair and skin product companies. To this friend, Denise Richards, a half-Jamaican, half-Indian girl with enviably blemish-free skin and perfectly straight hair achieved with the assistance of the very products she modelled, Ameena divulged the details of this new life, namely that she had applied for and duly obtained a writing-related job for an up-and-coming fashion magazine located on the second floor of a building on 37th Street and Broadway. Along with the job, she had also obtained, by means of a series of classified ads, a room-mate to share a converted one-bedroom flat on a high floor in a building in Murray Hill – where exactly that was, she didn't know, just somewhere in Manhattan, that much she knew.

1.7

Valentino's was a small, family-run neighbourhood Italian restaurant with red and white checked tablecloths and black and white photographs on the walls, renowned greatly for its 'Big Mama's Meatballs', which happened to be, rather ironically, an off-menu item made famous entirely by word of mouth. Now it was, among foodies and other people with a keen interest in the affair, a matter of some debate as to whether 'Big Mama' was real, or a strategic figment of someone's imagination, for to run a profitable restaurant business in New York City, one needed both strategy and imagination. Following on from that then, a kind of decision tree ensued – meaning, if she *was* real, then was she dead or was she still 'alive-and-cooking', because despite repeated requests to meet 'Big Mama', so that one could see in the flesh this genius, this *artist* behind so divine a creation as those melt-in-the-mouth meatballs, no one to anyone's knowledge had ever set eyes on her.

As for the meatballs themselves, despite their soaring popularity – for they were a gastronomic delight of the variety that one spoke about with a kind of dreamy nostalgia many days and weeks later – they were never put on the menu. And so, the mystery deepened, the reputation spread, and Valentino's thrived, for people always have a fascination for what they cannot know.

David, taking an astute risk in that Ameena, being that she lived in the neighbourhood, would have heard of, if not tasted, this legendary Big Mama's legendary meatballs, and given that when it came to these particular meatballs, the old adage held true – for to taste them was to *love* them – had suggested Valentino's for their dinner date. And sure enough, she had replied by saying she *loved* Valentino's. Which was even more than he had hoped she would say. And so, when he left his apartment building at 7.15pm that evening, he left with a swing in his step.

It took him five minutes of walking at a fairly brisk pace to arrive at the restaurant and he whistled as he did so, a tune he had made up in his head right then, and he was happy he arrived early, simply because he had not wanted to arrive late. He checked in at the front and then sat down at the table, waiting with a mixture of anticipation and nervousness for her to arrive, and when at 7.30pm sharp, she did arrive, he felt, in that brief moment that lay suspended between when he noticed her, and she noticed him, when her dark eyes searched the space with a mixture of her own anticipation and nervousness, that she was even more beautiful than he had remembered.

Then the moment was over, and she saw him, and she smiled, and he smiled back.

What struck him first, before anything else, and with a kind of force that surprised him in its *oomph*, was her hair, which had been tied back into a ponytail the previous night, but now fell in thick, black waves all the way down to the small of her back, dense and complex and luxurious; in David's mind, a swirling river of mystery and a kind of hidden drama.

Then, as she walked towards the table, he noticed other things as well: he noticed her eyes, how dark they were, and her height, how small she was, and her figure; it was hard not to notice her figure for she was wearing a blue dress that gathered at the waist and ended below her knees, a simple elegant affair that showed what it needed to show, and no more.

'Hi,' she said, as she sat down.

'Hi...'

'Why are you looking at me like that?'

'Oh sorry, I didn't mean to... sorry, I was just... I was thinking.'

'Thinking's good. What about?'

'That you are more beautiful today than you were yesterday and how, therefore by that logic, it would be great to see you tomorrow.'

'Flatterer. Who taught you your pick-up lines?'

'No one. I came up with them myself. To impress you. Are you impressed?'

'Very,' she said, and she smiled, and he noticed in the candlelight that she had talking eyes.

When the waiter arrived a few minutes later with the wine list, David said, 'Oh, my... uh... the lady doesn't...'

Ameena said, 'I drink.'

David looked mortified at his own presumptuousness but said nothing and Ameena looked more amused than anything else and said, 'I'm not really fussed, but I have a small preference for red, especially in this place.' Then, she looked up at the waiter and as if to relieve David of any more embarrassment on her account, said, 'May I have a glass of the Malbec please?'

Which seemed to work because David quickly regained his composure and amended the order to a bottle, and then when the waiter was out of earshot, he said, 'I'm so sorry, I should have asked instead of assuming.' And she replied, 'No need to apologise at all. My parents don't drink and neither does my brother, but my great-grandmother, I'm told, drank like a fish.' Then the waiter returned with the bottle and opened it for Ameena to taste and then, that done to everyone's satisfaction, poured them their glasses and left, and when he left, she looked at David and her eyes sparkled. 'I guess,' she said, as she raised her glass, 'I take after her.'

'Cheers to that,' David said.

'Cheers to that,' she agreed.

And when, a few minutes later, they looked down at the food menus in front of them, and without even opening them both exclaimed 'Big Mama's Meatballs!' in the same breath, they laughed at the coincidence – but not really – of that, and so naturally they ordered the meatballs and also some linguini and some vegetables, all of which they partook of with great pleasure and David noted, with some relief, that Ameena seemed to enjoy her food, though why this made him relieved he wasn't quite sure.

'So, what do you do?' she asked conversationally.

'I work in branding, you know, advertising...'

'Cool...'

'...by day...'

'Uh oh. Sounds dangerous.'

He smiled. 'I play jazz by night.'

'You're a musician!'

He shrugged. She was watching him, he noticed, with a very intent expression. 'An aspiring one, I guess. Jazz is the only thing I've ever been truly passionate about. One day, I'd like to ditch everything else and just work on my music full-time... creating great music... playing with all the genius musicians out there... getting better at coming up with my own stuff, taking more risks with my instrument.'

'Wait, what instrument?'

He smiled. He had, she noticed, a deep, honest smile. 'Piano. I play piano.'

She nodded thoughtfully. 'An ad man by day, a musician by night. Interesting,' she said. Then she looked at him, and he could sense her curiosity – he had touched it, now it was unfurling.

And then, as if by some cosmic desire to prove him right, she said, 'And the ultimate ambition is?'

He laughed. 'Ha! Why not ask the hardest question upfront! The ultimate ambition... wow... okay... I guess, just to get better artistically, really. Play more, play better, work on my chops...'

'Chops?'

'Oh sorry – that's skills – the ability to improvise well.'

'And then? When you've done all that?'

'Ah, but you see, you'll never ever have done "all that". It's infinite.' He paused and his eyes widened momentarily as if he himself was marvelling at that, at the very fact that it was infinite. 'But, let's see, what else do I think about? Film scores? If that opportunity ever arose? I've always been interested in that, you know, the relationship between storytelling and music, so... coming up with the right music for the different scenes, thinking thematically about harmony and mood and things like that, that excites me.'

'Like, composing? You compose?'

He nodded. 'Yeah, but spontaneously. That's what jazz is all about. You know much about jazz?'

Ameena shook her head.

David smiled. 'We've got to change that. So, a jazz tune is literally one moment in time.' He snapped his fingers once. 'It's one of the few arts in which creation and performance happen as one, and you do this together with the people you play with, a kind of endless exploration. That aspect of jazz is what makes it magical for me, why I fell in love with it in the first place. So, yeah, all the time, all the time in my head, I'm making music.'

For a second, it was only that, an imperceptible second, she said nothing and there was between them a silence. Then she smiled, but still said nothing, and he couldn't be certain, but he thought he saw a small hint of something pass over her eyes, a shadow or a distant memory or a frisson of sadness.

But apart from those few moments of silence brought about by shyness or else the impulse one feels on a first date to create some sort of impression, hopefully good or at least not explicitly bad, so that there is, at the very least, the hint of an allusion to the second date before the first date has officially ended, they found that they could speak to each other comfortably and that the conversation mostly flowed.

This David felt, from instinct or experience or a bit of both, boded well, just like that first intimate encounter with someone, for there was infinitely more to first times in half-light than just first times in half-light. Lovemaking, to David, was a skill, a kind of alchemy that if done right, entailed an exchange of energy, a coming together that was much more powerful than the sum of its parts; it was more than just a thing people did, he viewed it almost artistically, a beautiful act of one-ness created intuitively, emotionally and freely in the dynamic plane of the present. Like jazz, in many ways. Yes, first times in half-light, David believed, could be wonderful, powerful, meaningful...

He had barely got this far in his head when he chided himself for thinking sexual thoughts so early into meeting this girl, but then, he told himself, he wasn't exactly thinking sexual thoughts about this girl, he was merely drawing a comparison between two first-time experiences, and that the point was that the conversation between himself and Ameena mostly flowed, and that this fact made him happy.

While David was thinking these thoughts, Ameena was thinking thoughts of her own, about dancers and pianists and fingers and feet. They were uneasy thoughts, not altogether pleasant and a little bit dark, and so she was more than a little relieved when David broke the silence.

'I didn't ask what you did,' he said, realising suddenly that he hadn't.

'No, you didn't,' she said affably.

'Well...?'

'We-ll... like you, I do something, and I enjoy it, sometimes more than others, but I guess that's with any job. But it's not what I *really* want to do. Speaking of ultimate ambitions and all. I mean, it's all very far-fetched and fantastical, but I have this... I don't even know what to call it! Passion? Desire? Dream? Dream, I guess, I have this dream.'

He smiled. 'Don't we all?'

'Yeah,' she said, smiling back, 'I suppose we do. Well, anyway, I work for a fashion magazine, I write for them... it's a lot of fun... but I paint... for myself... when I can... in my spare time. And like you, I'd like to do more of it. I'd like to tell stories – with my art.'

'A writer who wants to be an artist! I *knew* you were a creative type!'

'Really? How?'

'The eyes.'

Ameena obliged by rolling her eyes theatrically and they both laughed. David wanted to ask what kind of stuff she painted but also felt that this was the sort of thing that people tell you themselves when they are ready to tell you and so he thought it best to save it for the next time they met, the likelihood of which he now felt cautiously confident about.

They both declined dessert but ordered coffees and when they arrived, Ameena said, 'Isn't it always a nice surprise when the chocolate sprinkles on the cappuccino are really, really good?' And David said, 'You know what, I've never really thought about that, but you are absolutely, one thousand percent, impressively right! I guess – putting my branding hat on now – you aren't really focused on the chocolate... as long as the main event is okay, you're happy, but yes, these sprinkles *are* really, really good and it *is* nice, like... like some kind of unexpected treat.'

'Yeah...' she said, spooning some of the chocolate-dusted froth into her mouth in a way that David thought was incredibly sexy, though why spooning chocolate dusted froth into one's mouth would be sexy he didn't know, but it was the particular way in which she did it, he decided, was what made it so, '...exactly that.'

After dinner, he offered to walk her home and she said she preferred he did that another time, so they said goodbye outside the restaurant and he asked if she would like to meet again and she said yes she would like that very much, and he said that was great in a very composed manner, but privately he whooped, and then he kissed her on the cheek, just very quickly, and she left, and as David walked home he thought about Ameena and that her sort of beauty was altogether different than any of the girls he had encountered before.

Overnight, New York went, as it had started to do with alarming regularity in the past few years, from winter to summer.

Just like that.

No gradual waning of the cold air and the frost and the darkness.

No gentle waking to the song of the blackbird or the slow metallic lightening of skies.

No butterflies and no bees and no red-breasted robins with their chests puffed out.

No daffodils.

None of these things Ameena had grown up with in England.

No spring.

No prelude.

No such thing.

No, David and Ameena arrived home that night after dinner at Valentino's wearing their woolen winter coats, and left for work the following morning in short sleeves and cotton, as though they had been transported somehow, in the course of the night while they were still asleep, to a different city.

For the streets they walked on had been transformed, the same streets that for months now had been dark and grey and caked with grime now seemed alive, jumping with streaks of sunlight that made them appear cleaner and brighter and more hopeful. The streaks, golden and thick like honey, didn't stop on the streets, but climbed audaciously upwards, up people's feet and their legs and their bodies, ultimately reaching their faces, their eyes as they squinted into the sun, and the sun changed those faces, lighting them and lifting them, both the faces and the spirits within.

David and Ameena felt it too, and felt changed by it, the heat from that honey like a kind of tingling on their skin.

And with that, winter was done.

On that morning, the morning after their first date, David leaving his home, and Ameena leaving hers – though ten minutes apart, which led to them taking different trains, for the subway is efficient at that time of morning – both considered this, and believed that this also, was an unexpected treat, like a particularly nice kind of chocolate dust atop one's cappuccino.

I.8

Ameena's parents – Yusuf and Zoya – had been united by means of an arranged marriage as per the prevailing custom in Lahore at the time they got married, and still prevailing for that matter at the time Ameena would have got married had she also been in Lahore.

The marriage had been arranged by the elders of both families – specifically by Ameena's father's grandmother and Ameena's mother's grandmother, two notoriously rebellious ladies as rebellious ladies in Lahore went, in that they were the kind that drank whisky, smoked cigarettes, played cards and wore designer *shalwar kameezes* with bold and colourful prints that teetered on the edge of risqué.

By virtue of belonging to a similar socio-economic class, and thus having common friends who also belonged to that same socio-economic class, the two ladies were members of the same 'kitty party' – a monthly, women-only affair involving lunch, gin, gin rummy and gossip – and, on account of their mutual propensity to do 'naughty' things, were drawn to one another, and became over the years firm friends.

When Yusuf's grandmother then spotted Zoya – a young, slender thing with thick, black, wavy hair down to her hips, and large, kohl-lined eyes – at a wedding, and realised upon enquiring after her that she was her great friend's granddaughter, she clapped her hands and laughed in glee, for what could make an already strong friendship stronger than by cementing it with marriage.

The following month, on a Wednesday, at the kitty party hosted by one Mrs Mallik – the wife of a powerful opposition party politician – over *peas pulao* and some delightfully tender *mutton kofte* – Yusuf's grandmother proposed the match to Zoya's grandmother. Ages and qualifications were discussed and details swapped (Yusuf: 29, BA Engineering; Zoya: 21, B.Ed.) as were subtler considerations, specifically relating to the girl's ability to nurture, nourish, maintain a happy home, be of sound mind and good disposition and have the capability to take care of her future husband and all his present and future needs. Mutually satisfied with what they had gleaned about the young people, the old ladies grabbed each other's hands, kissed each other's cheeks, downed the last of their whisky-sodas and, over a particularly delicious *badam kheer* – rice pudding with almonds and raisins and spiced with saffron and cardamom – agreed it was a match.

Yusuf's parents and Zoya's parents were each separately informed of this auspicious and highly desirable proposal for their respective children's marriage. Then, Yusuf's parents informed their son and Zoya's parents informed their daughter of the fact that they were each to be imminently married to the other. That done, the *imam*, who quite propitiously happened to be a friend of both families, was consulted, and with much fanfare and celebration a date was fixed.

While all this was happening, Zoya was secretly seeing someone at the university at which she was studying to complete her B.Ed. degree. The someone she was seeing was a professor of English and Comparative Literature, and the reason it was secret was because he had a wife, three children, and was nineteen years Zoya's senior. The professor claimed he loved Zoya with a gripping, consuming passion and no longer loved his wife, and yet at the same time hadn't left his wife, although he had been promising Zoya to do so for the better part of the previous twenty-two months since their affair had begun. This seeming inability to action his words had been causing a steadily building tension in the relationship, like the pressure in a pressure cooker that builds silently but steadily, until it finds release in that first screaming whistle.

When Zoya was informed of her upcoming marriage, she arranged to meet the professor on a sultry evening at Racecourse Park, where under the shade of a peepal tree – the very type of tree where roughly around the fifth century BCE, some 1,287 kilometres away in the state of Bihar, which was in the eastern part of the neighbouring country of India, the Gautam Buddha had attained enlightenment – she informed the professor that if he didn't leave his wife by the date fixed for her marriage, he would never lay eyes on her again.

'I cannot be without you,' the professor pronounced, his voice thick with emotion.

They walked a while. The sun had set, the crowds had thinned. With darkness came a stillness and a coolness that hung above them, suspended in those evanescent moments between dusk and nightfall. Zoya shivered slightly and the professor put his arm round her as they walked past the lake and when they crossed the flower beds, suddenly everywhere was filled with the heady smell of roses. 'I know,' Zoya said and she was clear-eyed.

Possessed at once by an almost sickening desire, the professor grabbed her arm and dragged her across the grassy expanse to the far side of the park. It was cooler here, darker, dense with trees, their trunks, thick and gnarled and encircled with roots twisted together like millions of crawling snakes. Here he stopped, still holding her arm, his grip so tight, she would still see the mark of his fingers on her wrist days later.

Then, passionately, he took her against the ancient trunk of a nearby willow tree under its swooping canopy of neon green leaves, hard and deep and with a need so acute she felt powerless against its force, and then he turned her round to face him and pressed her against him, so tight as if he wished her body to be subsumed into his own.

Their goodbyes that evening were unusually brusque and almost cursory, as is often the case when lightness secretly masks heaviness; the weight from knowing what neither was brave enough to admit. Once again, the professor promised to leave his wife, but a month passed, then four, then six and the wedding date drew nearer and still he didn't.

Zoya did not tell anybody about the professor until her wedding night, when Yusuf lifted up her heavy pink and golden wedding *lehenga* and pulled down her white cotton panties and then whispered in her ear, 'I'll be gentle, I promise not to hurt you.'

At which point Zoya looked him in the eye and said, 'I am not a virgin.'

It took a long while for Yusuf to accept this truth. But he was a religious man who believed in forgiveness, and by and by he came if not to accept, then at least to forgive. For he realised that the arrangement of an arranged marriage meant that she couldn't possibly have told him any earlier and that really, if she had wanted to, she needn't have told him at all.

Many years later, a truth would dawn on Yusuf. After Ameena had been born, and then Kareem after her, and Zoya had failed to retain – three times – another child in her womb, the couple had decided there would be no more children, and thereby implicitly, no more sex. It was at this time that Yusuf would realise that Zoya had only ever loved the professor, and that love for her was like life itself – something that only happened once, and that once it was used up, it was gone.

But back then, in the weeks and months immediately following his wedding, when he had neither the benefits of experience nor maturity nor for that matter the mercifulness of lapsed time, he couldn't get himself to touch her where another man had before him. Instead, he immersed himself in work – for you've got to put the pain somewhere – and just short of a year after the wedding, was offered an entry-level consultant position in his petroleum company's UK subsidiary based in Manchester.

On that same day at the very same time that this news was being communicated to him, a bomb went off some distance away from the office building in which he worked, the power of the blast causing the door of his boss's office to shudder and shake. Along with many others, Yusuf and his boss walked up four flights to the flat cement roof to see what had happened, and in the distance, they saw a cloud of white smoke ballooning unnaturally in an otherwise cornflower-hued sky.

In the next day's *Lahore Times*, they would learn that the cloud of smoke had been caused by an explosion near the vegetable market some two miles away and had left twenty-six people dead. But they didn't know all that as they were watching the smoke-balloon billow and rise and then quietly condense and disappear from the roof terrace of their office building.

His boss broached the subject again on the stairs down from the roof.

'So, what do you think? It will be a huge growth opportunity for you. If I didn't have six children in school, and a mother-in-law who refuses to die, I would have gone myself. You are young, unencumbered – will you go?'

'No,' Yusuf replied simply, and left it at that.

This job proposition he mentioned to his wife in passing that evening while changing out of his office clothes into the loose-fitting traditional garb that he wore at home. He had historically not spoken to her much about what went on in the office, mostly because she had never expressed any real desire to know about it. Yet, this time, something made him want to tell her. So, he recounted the conversation that had transpired with his boss, ending with, 'Of course I said no.' Her reply surprised him more than anything had surprised him since the night of their wedding.

'I want to go,' she told him.

'*You* want to go? Why?'

'I think we should go, that's all.'

'So, you will be far away from the temptation of the English teacher?'

She looked at him. 'That was unnecessary,' she said coldly.

Yusuf, unable to meet her hard gaze, dropped his own. 'You are right. I am sorry. That was unnecessary, I admit, and yes, cruel. But I said no because of you.'

'Me?'

'Yes. We are comfortable here. And secure. You have help, servants – cook, driver, watchman. We have our families here, for support, and our friends, *your* friends. Our own people. We will always be second-class citizens there, minorities, outsiders, by the food that we eat, by our language, by our god, by our skin.'

He looked at her and saw that her eyes had grown a strange fire in them, specks of gold that lit up her face, and with it, the entire room.

She said, 'Think of the opportunity. For you. The freedom. For us. We can bring up our children in a world where they can dream.'

'To dream is a luxury, Zoya. You need to have other things before you can dream. Power, money, status. They will be paying me next to nothing by English standards. We will have no help. You will have to do all the housework yourself. I mean, I will help... I will try... but... I don't think you are thinking of the downsides. This is our home.' But he hesitated at the mention of children, a kind of tenderness filtering his eyes.

'Home is where you feel safe. I feel stifled here, Yusuf. Look at what happened on Ferozepur Road today. A life full of terror gives you no space to dream.'

'Zoya, I already said no.'

'Well, tomorrow morning, go say yes.'

And that's how Ameena's parents had ended up in Manchester.

Where she hadn't been particularly religious at home, in England, Ameena's mother became devout by her own standards, abdicating whisky and adopting the hijab, trading in one form of liberation for another. Ameena's father, who had considered himself only moderately religious in Lahore, found himself swept along by her newfound fervour, for it is hard for the weaker of a married couple not to be pulled towards the inclinations of the stronger, just like it is near impossible for a man in strong waters to resist being swept away with the tide.

It would be equally easy as it would be difficult to understand the reasons behind Ameena's mother's heightened faith. For it is always equally easy as it is difficult to understand what forms faith in the first place.

Perhaps it had to do with being in a land where she found there was so little of it.

Perhaps it had to do with being so far away from a land where there was too much of it, for one tends to miss what one does not have, only once it has been lost.

Or perhaps it had nothing to do with that at all.

Perhaps it had to do with what she carried around with her for years, some kind of deep, penetrating, unspeakable loss.

Perhaps it is loss that forms faith.

It would be ironic that years later, this same deep, penetrating, unspeakable loss would be exactly what would cause her daughter to lose her own faith.

Perhaps it is loss that takes faith away.

Easy come, as they say, easy go.

1.9

Ameena's room-mate was a tall, skinny girl from Pleasantville, New Jersey called Peggy Lannifer.

The day Ameena landed in America and arrived at the apartment straight from the airport, Peggy opened the door to let her in and said brusquely, 'I just want you to know I advertised for a room-mate because I needed the money and a nicer place to live in than I could afford alone. That's all there is to it. I'm not your friend. If you want friends, you'll need to look for them somewhere else. I don't do that crap, so save yourself the effort.' Ameena's smile faded but she nodded as she walked towards the smaller of the 'flex 2 beds' that Peggy informed her would be hers, dragging her heavy suitcases behind her.

She shut the bedroom door, leaning against the flimsy, carelessly painted wood with her eyes closed. She'd been holding her breath, without even realising it. She exhaled deeply, opened her eyes and looked around the room, its sparse furniture, its unfamiliar smells, and then when she sat down on the bed – her bed – she felt an acute anxiety and an aloneness and a sadness for everything she had left behind. For several minutes she sat like that, on the edge of the bed.

But then she stood up and tugged at the chain of the blind that covered her window and as she tugged down, and it rolled up, she gasped at the splendor of her own unveiling, for in front of her, so close she felt she could reach out and touch it, she saw the illuminated jagged spire of the Chrysler Building. And then the other buildings, countless buildings with no name, penetrating the midnight-blue sky, bright from the light of a thousand windows, each window telling a thousand stories. That's what Ameena saw the night she landed in America, as she gazed through the window of her tiny room – she saw a city that, like a clandestine lover, held in her bosom a million untold stories.

She took this thought with her when she went to sleep that night and somehow, despite it all, despite this... this grim room-mate-person that lived in the next room and probably slept with a gun under the pillow, it made her feel less alone.

By daylight, she was disappointed to note that the magic of the Chrysler Building had faded somewhat, just one more tall building melting into a plethora of others, chameleon-like, as if its real beauty emerged only when it lost its powers of camouflage.

But this was significant, she later realised, the dual aspect of the Chrysler Building, in her understanding of New York City, this bastion of urban modernity. Because things worked differently here than what she had been accustomed to. At home, Ameena felt, the fear came at night – the dread and the loneliness and the other innumerable diseases that linger around us, threatening, if we allow them, to afflict our minds. Night brought darkness. And it brought disquietude. But then, as it lifted, so gradually did the darkness, and by the time the sun rose in the morning, nothing seemed as bad, and the troubles of the night seemed less frightening, as if somehow the daylight had, if only temporarily, driven away the despair.

Not so in New York. New York, she would learn, was a city unlike any other, a city that wrote its own rules. New York came alive at night, alive with hope and radiance and the promise of dreams. The night lights that shimmered and danced – in the towering buildings, in the larger-than-life billboards, in the walking-talking adverts, in the entire 185,360 square feet of Times Square – all brought with them an energy and an urgency and a kind of hypnotic dreamlike beauty, and suddenly everything was possible, and you – YOU! – lay at the heart of this possibility.

But then, the night would pass, and in the morning, all of that would vanish and melt. In New York, in the cold light of day, you were indistinguishable, just like the buildings, one body among eight million others, camouflaged in order to survive. You were everybody; you were nobody.

As for Peggy, this too for Ameena was a kind of learning. A truth: human beings are varied, complex and unpredictable. They act in certain ways for certain reasons. She has read about this in books. She has studied this briefly in social science class. Anthropology it is called, all about how humans are a social tribe, how our responses to other people are deeply ingrained, how we crave or reject companionship, feel empathy, measure the emotions of friend and enemy alike, judge each other's intentions and plan strategies for personal social interactions. She has studied this, and so perhaps has Peggy, because very soon, the two women work out, anthropologically, how to stay out of each other's way.

And so, beyond the obligatory smile or the cursory 'hi,' when, despite their best efforts, they happened to find themselves in the communal spaces, no words were exchanged. The women stayed mostly in their respective bedrooms and one usually used the kitchen when the other was out, which Ameena found to her great relief was quite often the case with Peggy. She didn't know what Peggy did, but found that the other girl often left before she woke and returned after she'd gone to bed. Sometimes she would be gone for days, leaving handwritten notes on the dining table with nothing but four numerical digits in sets of two, separated by dashes, and Ameena had no idea what that meant until it dawned on her in a moment of epiphany that in America the month comes before the day, and she realised that for whatever it was worth, this was Peggy's way of informing her that she was travelling and would be back on the date mentioned on the note.

And so, like this they carried on, until that day when, thanks to a rescheduled flight, Peggy came home one day early to find Ameena in the kitchen. 'Oh hi,' Ameena said, awkwardly, overcome with a kind of extreme self-consciousness, 'I'll be done soon.'

'That smells good,' Peggy remarked, and Ameena found that she was both surprised and surprisingly pleased and it surprised her that she was pleased, that it mattered at all.

'Really?' she said cautiously. 'I've always thought of myself as quite an awful cook! If my mum was here, she'd be standing over me with her hands on her hips and a list of everything I've done wrong.'

At that, Peggy smiled. Woah, Ameena thought, it smiles? But it was the first time she properly noticed how beautiful the other girl was – fine, high cheekbones, big, green, almost doll-like eyes, and her skin, pale and clear and smooth like glass.

'It's chicken curry, my version of it at any rate. Would you like to try some?' she asked quickly, aware that she'd been openly staring.

'No thanks,' Peggy said formally, 'I wouldn't want to eat your dinner.'

'There's more than enough for two. Have some, please. I'd like that.'

And as simply as that, because sometimes in life you have to be willing to take a chance on people, over a dinner of Uncle Ben's microwaveable rice and Ameena's anglicised Pakistani chicken curry, a truce of sorts was called.

Another truth: women don't take long to share intimate details of their personal lives with each other. Men take years. Occasionally they discuss such things on the golf course. Most times they simply talk about sex in the abstract. Women, also, talk about sex, but never in the abstract, and mostly only when sex becomes perverted. To men, sex is almost never perverted. And so.

Over dinner, unprompted and perhaps for one of those anthropological reasons that are too complex to comprehend in one go – or a lifetime – Peggy disclosed to Ameena that she had been abused as a child by her stepfather, a brutish man who ended up breaking both her body and her spirit. He had started touching her, she said dispassionately, when she was three. At ten, she was giving him blow jobs, at thirteen they were having full sex. When at fifteen, she finally mustered up the courage to tell her mother, she was met by a staunch refusal to believe that any of it had happened at all. 'Instead of confronting him, my mother accused me of seducing her husband,' Peggy said with a small shrug of the shoulders, but her face, Ameena noticed, was expressionless. 'She told me that I was trying to steal him from her. Where does one even go from there? Anyway, I don't need your pity, I'm removed from all that now, I just wanted to tell you, that's all. If I've come across as some kind of cold, heartless bitch, it's not personal. I just don't... I guess I have trust issues with people. You're all bug-eyed by the way.' Embarrassed, Ameena blinked her eyes purposefully, twice, and Peggy laughed. And then Ameena laughed and after that, something between them changed.

The next night when Ameena came home from work, she found Peggy sitting on the living room sofa reading a book. As she had become accustomed to doing, Ameena nodded in acknowledgement, but continued to walk towards her own room, but then Peggy said, 'Hey, I bought this bottle of wine, if you wanted to share it with me?'

For some reason, Ameena remembered in that white-dove moment, when she nodded and smiled and saw the barely discernible hint of relief in Peggy's green eyes, the photo of the Afghan girl on the cover of the *National Geographic* all those years ago, Sharbat Gula, whose parents were killed when she was six years old during the Soviet bombing of Afghanistan. How many secrets, Ameena wondered, must she have hidden in those green eyes that had taken the world by storm? How many secrets and how much pain? And for how long?

I.10

'You. Yes, *you*, don't look so surprised, you and you and you and you and you and you.' Hershel E. Horowitz, Founder and CEO of The Witz Agency, a small, heaving man with a smooth bald head and a very pink face upon which he sported a thin, carefully manicured moustache, pointed his left index finger vigorously at the four men and two women around the table. '*You* lot are the brains of the agency. The brains. The grey matter. Up *here*...' he said, finger moving to his forehead just below a perfectly threaded left eyebrow, '...and we *need* what's up here to do what we do. And what we do,' he said, pausing dramatically, 'is branding.'

He looked around the room and, not seeing the desired impact of his words, continued with slightly – but only very slightly – less gusto.

'Now, branding is a complicated word and it's getting more complicated by the second because it faces extinction. Yes, you heard me. *Ex*tinction. Look around you. No, not around the room. At the world. Look at the world around you. Everything is the same these days – body wash is body wash is body wash and toilet paper is toilet paper is toilet paper. People aren't buying the cuddly puppy any more. No sir. They want it strong *and* gentle, hardy *and* soft, luxurious *and* cheap – puppy or no puppy.' He sighed loudly. 'It's sad. Very, *very* sad. Just plain depressing, if you ask me. I mean, there was a time not that long ago when all you needed was a cute lil' puppy to sell toilet paper. But now? Now that's just not cutting it any more. Now they want aloe vera. And they want it for free. It's doom and gloom, people, and you *see* that in our clients. The spark's gone from their eyes. And the money's gone from their wallets. Gone. Gone the way of the spark. Finished. Kaput.'

Here, Hershel surfaced for air. Gulped. Plunged back in.

'The truth is, folks, that our clients are *disillusioned*. They believe – and rightly so – that there is nothing left any more to differentiate between their product and that of the competition. This is serious stuff.' He nodded then once – seriously – and indefatigably soldiered on. 'Branding, as you all know, used to be one of a few remaining forms of product differentiation, and now it's *dying. Forever.* And clients can't cope with it. They can't cope with it because if there is nothing left any more to differentiate between their product and that of the competition, then there is nothing left any more to differentiate between *themselves* and the competition. This is an existential crisis, folks, plain and simple. No surprises here.'

He tapped his knuckles on the table twice.

'Knock, knock.

'Who's there?

'Client.

'Client, who?'

A pause.

'Get it? *Client, who.*'

Another pause.

Hershel looked around the room. Nodded solemnly, six times. Six blank faces stared back at him. Onward he went.

'And so, the mantle falls on us. It is a grave responsibility, but a vital one, and we must take it on. Because we know, *we know*, that the *reason* our clients can't cope is because they are *clients*. Clients trapped within the constraints of their own sad, uncreative little minds. That's where *we* come in. We step right into this dying, decaying, extinction-facing mess. And we' – another dramatic pause – '*rebrand* branding.'

David suppressed a yawn, then glanced around the room quickly to make sure no one had witnessed his act of insurgency. Unlikely, he thought, given how dark the room was. As a matter of fact, now that he was looking around, he noted that everybody in the room looked half-asleep. Once again, unsurprising, given the dull whirring *hrrrmmm* of the projector, combined with the low lighting, combined with how warm the room was, combined with the same schpiel they heard every Monday morning from Hershel, who, bless his heart, tried so hard to make it sound like they were all an indispensable part of some secret mission to save the planet.

David worked in advertising, or as they say, 'on Madison Avenue', for The Witz Agency, a small, privately owned branding firm fortuitously located (for the sake of its own brand) on Madison Avenue. The agency, named after its founder Hershel Horowitz was a niche but well-regarded establishment that prided itself on working with entrepreneurs and small start-ups to help build, as Hershel liked to call it (the term currently pending patent), 'disruptive brands.' Within the firm, David was part of a six-person team that was responsible for strategic planning, aka 'The Voice of the Consumer', or as their Founder and CEO so eloquently put it, 'The Brain of the Agency'. In fact, Hershel was reiterating this very sentiment at that very moment.

'...rely on you lot to come up with ideas. *You* lot – the brain of the agency. So, show me what you've got, people, show me what's inside you, inside that spectacular brain of yours. Because the brain, at the end of the day, is...'

It was David's job to study the triangular puzzle of brand–business–consumer and to put all of this understanding together to come up with inspirational creative briefs that disrupted the status quo and created 'paradigm shifts' in the way consumers viewed a product. Say, toilet paper, for example.

'Never forget this fundamental thing, guys. And gals. Not to miss the gals, ha-HAH, the *real* brains behind everything now, our gals, wouldn't you agree gentlemen?' Hershel looked around the room again and, ignoring the vague look of horror on the six faces, continued, 'Arrrhmm, so as I was saying, never forget this fundamental thing...'

David took a sip of his coffee and grimaced. One day, he thought magnanimously, one day when he had made it to the big leagues as a truly worthy musician, he would buy a new coffee machine for this place. It would be his gift. Who knows, it might even be a brand of coffee that he had personally worked on bringing to market, which would make it extra-poignant. But until then, he thought with a sigh, it would have to be burned coffee. *Actually*, burned coffee or nothing, he corrected himself, pushing away his cup and reaching instead for the jug of water in the middle of the table – one always has the choice to *not* do something. He felt his boss's eyes on him then, as he was pouring the water into his glass, watching him, betraying some kind of unreadable emotion. But what? David felt sorry for the man suddenly, almost wanting to stand up and sacrifice his own glass of water – have it, he would offer generously, you look like you need it so much more, have it, have all of it and then, you poor little sweaty man, have yourself some more. Hershel had taken out a large paisley handkerchief from his pocket and was dabbing the very top of his smooth pink scalp, from where the sweat seemed to emanate in small, shiny blobs and trickle down his face like tears. Just watching him depressed David. The conference room was stifling. Someone obviously hadn't accounted for the fact that it had gone from like thirty to ninety overnight.

Then he thought about Ameena. There was something about her, something different, something cryptic, something he couldn't quite figure out, an obscure trace of something sudden and sensual. It wasn't just that she neither looked nor spoke like anyone he'd been with before, though that was true too. It was something else. He shook his head slowly, then allowed himself a small smile. He needed to see her again. He felt intrigued by her, drawn in somehow. And yet she made him nervous, but he didn't quite understand why. It was like he wanted to get to know her, but slowly, delicately, as if there was a complexity to her that made her impossible to understand in any other way.

David stretched back into his chair and straightened his legs out, allowing him to reach for the cell phone he kept in his front trouser pocket, a tricky manoeuvre if it was to be executed without attracting undue attention. Stretch-Reach-Grasp-Done. Then, surreptitiously, like some kind of impatient schoolboy with a crush, he positioned it under the conference table and started composing a text message to Ameena.

'"What then is truth?" Nietzsche asked,' Hershel was saying, arms lifted on either side of his body, palms upward as if he was holding up the world, revealing in the process big, rapidly expanding blotches of wetness under his armpits. 'A mobile army of metaphors, metonymies, anthropomorphisms...'

1.11

Ameena worked as a features assistant at a small fashion magazine with offices on the second floor of a nineteenth-century red-and-white-striped limestone building in Midtown Manhattan.

The magazine, which Ameena had never heard of until she applied for the job and never read until after she was offered the job, positioned itself as a 'cool, sexy and pleasingly alternative voice exploring the intersection of fashion and contemporary culture'.

'Our biggest asset is our fearless pursuit of honesty,' the website boldly proclaimed. 'We stand apart because we tell the very honest and very personal stories behind brands and their makers; we uncover the personalities under the clothes.'

This had appealed to Ameena, this whole thing of uncovering the personalities under the clothes. She liked this, the titillation of the 'what lies beneath' idea. It made the work sound mysterious. And important.

On her first day at the magazine, Ameena was told that they hadn't seen the carpet for two years owing to the returns pile, so she stayed until 10pm every night until she had succeeded in emptying it entirely. She was also told that none of her predecessors had managed to make a decent cup of tea and how excited the whole team was that she was English. And so she discovered, quite quickly after she started, that her job description entailed being part journalist (9%), part writer/editor (15%) and part admin assistant (76%). She also discovered, equally quickly, that she was woefully inadequate at this final part. Walking past a Hallmark shop at the end of her first week, she almost laughed out loud at the big signage that demanded people 'don't sweat the small stuff', because perhaps the most important thing she had learned in her week-long career was that *her* boss took the small stuff really, *really*, seriously.

Whitney Kym, her editrix-in-chief, was a witty, perfectly groomed, extremely intelligent Korean-American woman who dropped movie references, casually churned out 3,000 words an hour and was obsessed with boyfriend jeans, headbands and the backstories that lay beneath the surface of the people she interacted with, wrote about, or worked with.

This last bit, Ameena had stumbled upon, first-hand.

When applying for jobs, she had written to several dozen magazines with offices in New York City. She received no reply from any but one.

This one reply came in email form, from someone called 'Whim', from which she could glean nothing at all of the sender, but as she told herself, it didn't really make a difference.

'I've seen your resumé,' Whim wrote, 'and your writing samples. They impressed me enough to grab my attention. It's clear you can write, but I get hundreds of applications from a lot of young people who can write, most of them with far more experience than you. Why not try and get a job in England? Why is it that you want to move to New York? And why us?'

Ameena emailed back that same evening.

She'd met a boy, she wrote, many years ago, at one of her parents' friends' houses where they had been invited to dinner. The boy was her age and had a congenital nerve condition and wore leg braces and crutches. He had a way about him, she continued, he held court with all the kids at that dinner party. During the course of the evening, he told them that he had received a letter from a famous doctor in New York, who said he would make the boy walk again. It is a place, the boy said (referring to New York), chin high, voice ringing with confidence, where anything is possible. It is a place of dreams.

I was ten years old, Ameena wrote, and I thought, about this boy, I thought, he can't walk, but he has dreams. Compared to him, I had everything, but I had no dreams. So, I started dreaming his dream, I dreamed he would go to New York, I dreamed he would meet this great doctor, I dreamed one day he would walk again. A few years later, we heard from our parents' mutual friends, the ones who had hosted the dinner party, that he had died from sepsis. The boy never travelled out of Manchester. There was something delusional in his ambition, but it didn't stop him from dreaming. To answer your first question, I guess I want to move to New York because it was central to the first experience of storytelling that I can remember. To answer your second question, you are really the only one who wrote back.

'You gawn completely crazy, wot?' Denise had yelled her outrage when Ameena showed her the email. 'An' this place wuz your only hope too and you screwin' it up like this. Girl, don' you learn *nothin'*? All this *history* and you learn *nothin'*! Honesty an' truthfulness, they don' get you *shit*!'

Ameena got her job offer the next day.

The letter was signed Whitney Kym.

1.12

The next time they met was on David's rooftop, the arrangements made hastily by means of a series of text messages that were only slightly flirtatious but more pragmatic than anything else, deliberately so, because it seemed presumptuous, a little bit, to David and to Ameena both, as well as slightly dangerous, to appear too keen too early on in their relationship, not really knowing with certainty what the other felt.

But then the beginning of every relationship is a leap of faith and one is always unsure, which is also the very thing that makes it exciting – the hoping, the uncertainty of not completely knowing.

David, being the man, felt it appropriate to send the first message, though Ameena, who didn't really believe in gender stereotypes of this sort, would probably have done so later that same day or the next, had he not initiated contact, for she had genuinely enjoyed his company the first time. But David, who couldn't possibly have known any of that, had sent the first text in any case, and it arrived to her in the form of a vibration on her desk, which surprised her, and also came as a sort of relief, as she was editing a particularly cumbersome piece on brogues for women.

what then is truth, nietzsche asked, the text on Ameena's phone said, making her laugh out loud.

A: 'Supposing truth is a woman?'
D: very good! didn't realise you were a writer and an artist and a
    philosopher
A: I'm not
A: That's the sum total of my knowledge of Nietzsche

D: good. i was almost not going to ask you out again

A: Oh?

D: my boss quotes nietzsche

A: Oh!

A: Sorry. I wouldn't want to remind you...

D: awful thought. stop there.

A: ...of your boss

D: no

A: No

D: but of that...

D: there's no chance

D: you're beautiful

D: and interesting...

D: and mysterious...

D: and many other things...

A: !!!

D: on which note...

A: Yes?

D: shall we meet again?

A: Yes

D: tonight?

A: Yes

D: rooftop of my building?

A: Yes

D: 9pm?

A: Yes

D: see you then

A: See you then

And then he texted her the building number and the coordinates, a very New York thing to do, she noted.

In that way, their second date was arranged.

David's building's rooftop had once been a rooftop bar, after some particularly enterprising entrepreneur had decided it would be a winning business idea to combine Manhattan views with overpriced cocktails and perhaps a bit of atmospheric music to go with it, and that had worked well for a few months and then not so well for the next few. Then to everyone's great shock, on a balmy summer's night, a red-headed girl in a red cocktail dress and high heels, also red, who may have consumed far too many of the overpriced cocktails, stepped too far back against the low cement wall and, before anyone could stop her, tumbled backwards and plummeted sixteen storeys to her tragic and untimely death. And so, the time came when the enterprising entrepreneur decided with great sadness, as well as a great hit to his finances, that the price of the cocktails, no matter how 'over' they happened to be, simply did not swallow the cost of insuring the space against any further deaths of this nature. So now it was back to being just a rooftop, without the bar.

This suited David fine because just before Ameena was due to arrive, he set up, on that rooftop, his own little bar, nothing fancy, just a chilled bottle of wine and two glasses and some cheese and crackers and a few green grapes he had picked out from the Bengali fruit-seller on the corner of 3rd Avenue earlier that evening, juicy and plump, a nice addition, he thought, lending colour and character to his platter of cheese and crackers.

Ameena arrived at two minutes past nine, straight up the elevator to the roof terrace, without a call or a text message stating that she had arrived, which David thought showed a bit of spirit on her part because it is usually expected of people to send some kind of intimation of their arrival, by way of an 'Almost there!' or 'Two minutes away!' or something to that effect, though to David, the action seemed a wasted effort, serving no practicable purpose, like many other things that people did that were also wasted efforts serving no practicable purpose, but then people did them anyway.

And so, he liked this about her, the fact that she didn't. That she may have done this, or rather not done this, not by any conscious decision-making on her part, but because in her rush (and slight nervousness) she had forgotten her phone at home, did not occur to him once, which was not unusual at all, since we often tend to believe about people what we want to believe. And it was the same way with David.

She was, he noticed – though hopefully in not too obvious a manner – wearing jeans that hugged her hips and a loose-ish V-neck t-shirt that ended just above the copper button of her jeans. The t-shirt was a deep, dark green and against her eyes and hair, which were both of the deepest, darkest brown, she conjured in his head the image of a forest, dense and shadowy and rich with the smell of pine.

He, himself, was wearing jeans and a dark grey short-sleeved t-shirt, as the night was warm, and the short sleeves, he hoped, would show off his arms that he had been spending a bit of time and effort over in the gym lately, to make them worthy of being shown off on just the kind of warm night as the one they were in.

'Hi,' she said as she walked towards him, deliberately delaying her own smile until he smiled.

'Hey,' he said, and smiled, and then she smiled too, and he offered her some wine, and she nodded, and he poured her a glass, which she took with a 'Thank you, that's lovely,' in her very lovely English way.

They stood for a while, leaning against the low cement wall, sipping their wine, looking out at the city, and he noticed how her t-shirt showed – but only when the wind blew – the shape of her breasts and the narrow curve of her waist.

'Be careful,' he said suddenly, 'don't lean too far back, someone once fell off that wall, you know.'

Her eyes widened for a tiny second, but then a small giggle escaped from her before she could hold it in. 'Sorry, sorry,' she said clapping her hand to her mouth, 'I didn't mean to laugh, I mean it's very sad, obviously, dreadful, but your face looks so solemn, it's really quite comical. Gosh, you must think I'm *terrible*. You think I'm terrible, don't you? Maybe I'd just better sit down. And you also.'

She looked at his face and her giggle grew into a peal of laughter, and he found himself infected by it and then he was laughing, and they were both laughing, uncontrollably laughing, holding their sides and wiping the tears from their eyes, enjoying their guilty pleasure in that quick, quiet moment before morality began to whisper and nag.

When they finally stopped, she sat down, and he sat down beside her, leaning against the wall, legs stretched out in front of him, then on an impulse he bent the leg that was closest to her so his knee was pressed up against his chin, and in that way, he created a space. For a moment or two, she looked up at his face with complete attention. Then she shifted her body towards him, into the space he had made, and he stretched his leg out again, around her, so she was in the triangle between his legs, her back pressed against his chest, the outside length of her legs touching the inside length of his, her feet stopping somewhere near his mid-calf, his chin resting lightly on top of her head.

They sat like that for a long time, their bodies fitting into each other, not speaking, and the silence between them was beautiful and intense.

'Do you ever,' she asked after a while, 'do you ever find yourself wondering, as you look at all these windows, what is going on in those peoples' lives?'

'No,' he said honestly, 'not really.'

'I do. And then I make up stories about them. The people I see through their windows. Their lives. I make up stories about their lives.'

She turned her face upwards to look at him. 'See, that guy there' – she pointed – 'yes, that guy sitting by the window in that redbrick building, the one with the geraniums on the windowsill, or they may be petunias, I don't know anything about flowers, they all look the same in the dark. Anyway, yes that one, that's my building. Can you see, he's working on his computer? He's a writer. Now watch, any minute now, a woman will come into sight and she will lean against his desk – ah, there you go – and she will kiss him. That's his mistress. She's called Juliette. She's French.'

David started a little. 'You know those people?'

'Of course not. I told you, I just make this stuff up.'

'He's not a writer?'

'No, he's not. I mean, he might be. He looks like he might be. But I don't know.'

'How did you know about the woman?'

'Oh, I've just been watching her... them, you know, while we've been sitting here, how she goes away and then comes back every few minutes to kiss him. It didn't seem very wife-like to me – too intense, too erotic-chemistry, though that could well be wife-like of course, and she could well be his wife. I just liked the idea that she wasn't.'

'And the building? You don't live there?'

'I do. That's my building, I live there yes. But the rest I made up.'

David felt a tinge of admiration and something else that felt distinctly like wonder, but also a kind of anxiety that he couldn't explain, but that had something, certainly, to do with how casually she lied, for after all, stories are but fiction, as are lies, with a thin line between the two that makes the one art, the other deceit.

'Do you know,' Ameena continued nonchalantly, 'on my first day of uni... first day, first class, my professor – he was this really "proper" chap, you know... very old-school, very English, lots of silver hair and tweeds and scarves, theory-head, a famous one, written lots of respectable books, *that* kind. Well, so he wanted to see where we stood as a class, what level of ability we were at, so he could set the standard, tailor his lectures accordingly etcetera. So, he asked us all to go away and write something, a short piece of fiction on this topic he gave us – I still remember it, it was about doors, we had to write about doors, literally or metaphorically, that bit was never specified, just go write five hundred or a thousand words about doors, and he asked us not to write our names on it.'

She took the last sip of her wine and held out the glass for him to refill. She had delicate arms, he noticed, smooth and shapely, small hands, long fingers, prominent veins on the underside of her narrow wrists, like tiny green rivers.

'Thank you,' she said when he had done that, and then continued, 'So then three or four days later he comes back and he starts off by saying how impressed he was with everyone's work and how we should all be proud of ourselves and blah di blah blah and then he goes on to talk about how hard it was for him to do this, but that he had picked one that stood out particularly to him, that he had enjoyed the most – and he wanted to read the beginning of it.'

She paused and inclined her head slightly. 'So, he did and then he said could the writer please identify themselves to the class. He read my story, David, and then when I raised my hand to claim it, there was this kind of shocked silence. Those faces. The look on them. I'll never forget that look. I mean, it was everybody in the class, but mostly – most strikingly – it was him.'

'But why,' David asked, 'why would that be so unbelievable?'

Ameena sighed and then took his hand and guided it, very gently, inside the V of her V-neck t-shirt, and he was astonished by the forwardness of the gesture, both astonished and touched, for it was indicative of a kind of great trust on her part that he wasn't sure what he'd done to earn.

'I don't know. It just was. It was very clear that he didn't imagine, not for one second, that anyone who looked like me or had a name that sounded like mine – some Paki girl – could have written the best story.'

'Ameena...'

But her eyes had started to flash, and he let her speak.

'David, do you know something? I'm not stupid, it's not like I've never had an awareness of my ethnicity or my religion or the way I look, but that moment was such a moment of clarity for me. It was like I learned, in that moment, for the first time in my life, that things are connected to it, to *this*' – she touched her skin – 'ability and authority and access, all of it, are connected to this.'

'Ameena?' David said with sudden, unexpected vitality.

'Mmm?'

'I want you to hear me play.'

'Me?'

'We-ell... I'd be happy if anyone did honestly, but yeah, you would be especially nice.'

'Okay.'

'Okay, you will?'

'Okay, I will.'

And with that, because never before in his life had he asked a girl to listen to him play, David felt the first stirrings of passion in his heart for this person he had only just met, who he felt like he wanted to keep meeting, whose body he was at that moment touching with the kind of intimacy that comes, even to lucky people, very rarely.

1.13

I am a Jew, son of immigrants.

As a child, David wanted to tell people this.

Also, his full name. He wanted to tell people his full name. David Greenberg. GREENBERG.

He wanted to say it aloud – to *reveal* this – to everyone he met, on the narrow, winding coastal New England streets, in the classroom, at the playground, in the corner shop where he went to buy milk, just so once it had been said, it would have been said, it would be out there, loud and clear and unambiguous; it wouldn't need to be whispered or presumed upon or thought-but-not-articulated in that part of people's brains that is reserved for things that can be thought-but-not-articulated. If he just told them, David reasoned, then they would know. And he would know they knew. And that would bring a kind of relief, a kind of opposite thing to the wariness he now constantly felt.

For David, it began with language.

At home his parents spoke to the boys in Yiddish. They talked to each other in Lithuanian in private, and in English when the boys insisted they should ('But how can you learn a language if you won't speak it?'). He and Abe spoke to each other solely in English – the kind of passionate Americanised English of boys – they talked baseball and basketball and boxing but also, because of their mother, they talked Chopin and Bach and Glenn Gould and the Gershwin brothers. At school David spoke English, but also learned French and Latin with everyone else. Every Sunday morning, David and Abe were sent to Hebrew school at the synagogue where they were taught to read and write Hebrew. Their mother spoke no Hebrew apart from a few words, but their father was conversant in Ivrit, having gone to Israel on what was intended to be a 'heritage trip' but resulted, as these things do, in something else, and he returned three years later, enriched by the gift of Taglit, to marry David's mother, quit his job in the garment factory in which his own father and Ruth's would work until they died, and declare himself 'an independent luxury watchmaker' – in that order.

And so, every Saturday at lunchtime, their father would spend forty-five minutes separately with each of his sons – never a minute less, never a minute more – teaching them how to speak Ivrit. They would read the Israeli newspapers together and engage in often passionate discussion about what was going on in the world: literature, politics, philosophy... and then the time would end, with a warning chime of a clock, too soon. For David, this was the best part of his week, but whether it was the subject matter that delighted him or the alone-time with his father, he couldn't be sure. And in this way, the boys learned to converse in Hebrew, with each other and with their father – a profound connection that came primarily from language, and this they realised and cherished dearly. But in other ways, all these tongues made David weary. How unburdensome, he would think, looking at some of the other little kids in the school playground, to only speak one language, to only speak English to everybody. How simple. How freeing.

There was a period in his early childhood when David remembers not knowing what language he was speaking even as he was speaking it – often he would start off a sentence in one language and end it in another. 'What?' his school friends would say, looking blankly at him. 'What did you just say?' And David would blink and stare back. What *had* he just said? He didn't remember. He remembered what he was trying to say, the semantics, but not *how* he'd said it, what *language* he had used to express his meaning.

And this, his own inability to differentiate between the languages, to understand the appropriateness of what got spoken where, troubled him, it made him both weary and wary.

Sometimes he felt this was why he had turned so readily to music – a kind of expression of himself outside of language. He believed earnestly that music had been given to him for a reason, that words could not possibly be the only means of man's expression, and if he wished to be understood fully, he would have to speak in this other kind of voice. Music had the same rules for everybody, African-American or European, Gentile or Jew. And he found that he succeeded in that, in understanding that even those rules were a kind of freedom, and in seeking to perfect those rules, he felt truly free. He was expressing emotion through this voice from within. He was singing through the piano! He *had* music; music was his.

And yet, greedily, he wanted language too, he wanted language to be his, just like music was his, and he deeply felt the limitations of 'proper' English as a means of his private expression. At school, he found that the teachers tried especially hard with the children of immigrants, to Americanise them – to 'civilize' them, his father would sometimes say when he was in one of his moods. 'Oh, stop it, Benjamin,' his mother would cry, 'they're only trying to get the kids to assimilate, to make them American.'

'Yes, yes, Ruthie, I know. To civilize is to Americanize and to Americanize is to civilize,' his father would retort calmly without looking up from his magnifying glass where he would be scrutinising some minor imperfection, undetectable to the human eye, in a priceless watch. And his mother would make an impatient sound and leave.

Sometimes, David's father would look up from his desk, his watches and clocks and his staking set, and proclaim loudly, 'Both of you are my favourite sons,' and you could tell he said it not only because it made their mother happy to hear it, but because he meant it with all sincerity. He loved them both equally in a way that some parents do successfully manage to love their children equally.

Children, on the other hand, are more discriminating – or perhaps more honest – than the grown-up versions of themselves, so while Abe seemed to align naturally with his father's strong ethnic identification, David saw the world through his mother's more conciliatory eyes.

To him, it was a thing of honour and a thing of dignity that at school, there were people dedicated to trying to help children from all backgrounds move forward, fit in, dream 'the dream'. It was at school that he was introduced to the pride of American literature, to novelists like Faulkner and Hemingway and Fitzgerald and – to David's great admiration – to Jewish writers like Bellow and Roth who had, over the course of their writing lives, become 'American writers'; they had earned this distinction for themselves solely by their own genius. He loved this about school, he loved that there was a core program of literary patriotism, he loved that he had teachers who took the effort to make them spell correctly and write grammatically and read good books, he loved that there was 'an American way', and that there was someone who cared enough to show it to him. Understanding what made one an 'American' – the duties and obligations that governed this identity – made David's chest swell with pride.

Abe was less interested in linguistic matters, or more broadly in any matters of the classroom. He was far more involved in the language of the street – prizefighting, craps games, graft, pop-culture slang. And, sports. Abe shone at sports. He was tall and big-built and with that came a natural athleticism. But somehow his excellence on the court or in the field or on the gridiron didn't shield him in the way David's excellence in music did, for children are as unpredictable and as fickle as they are honest. In truth, perhaps because kids like Abe were not 'expected' to be good at sports, the fact that he was *so* good – better than most of his non-Jewish classmates – was what seemed to engender, in itself, a very specific kind of hostility.

'Woah, Aby-baby you're running fast!' a boy in the playground would yell. 'But you don't need to run so fast anymore, the fire's out!' 'You're so *strong*, Abe,' another boy would shout. 'Did you run away from Belsen and hide in a gym?' And then they would make hissing noises and snigger and laugh.

Miraculously, none of this seemed to touch Abe emotionally. He was completely comfortable with his Jewishness; often David thought it was his Jewishness that gave him comfort. And so, no barb seemed sharp enough to penetrate him. On the contrary, Abraham Greenberg, naturally confident, rivalrous and often combative, seemed to gain some sort of strength of will from it, a kind of fearlessness, and the more he got taunted, the stronger and angrier he became.

But it affected David deeply.

I am a Jew, son of immigrants, he wanted to say. And my name is David Greenberg.

1.14

To Ameena's memory, her father had never been a violent man. Zoya on the other hand, when in a fit of rage, had held no qualms about smacking her or Kareem for even minor transgressions.

One time, Ameena, six years old, had been smacked for complaining that the food her mother had cooked for dinner was too 'greasy', a word she had learned from an incident at school not that long before when at lunchtime, the grease from the chips had dribbled on to their school uniforms and a classmate's mother had raved and ranted and accused the school of making her obese child obese. And so, when presented that evening with a bowl of aubergine curry swimming in some kind of mysterious orange oil, Ameena felt it would be clever to transpose the analogy from potatoes to aubergine. But no, Ameena had misjudged, and she realised very quickly after the fact that potatoes and aubergine must never be confused, and neither should her mother's cooking with that of the school cook. Also, as she had suspected before and had confirmed yet again, in her family, undue displays of cleverness were rewarded with an entirely different kind of plaudit. This time it was a single slap, quick and hard across the cheek, followed by a protracted glare of utter disbelief at the audacity of it all. 'Go up, *UP*, you ungrateful girl! Praise be to Allah, you get any food at all! When there are children, small, *small* children...' At this, Zoya raised her right hand up in the air, thumb and index finger inches apart to demonstrate exactly how small. '... starving on the streets of Africa! Greasy, she says, *greasy*. Miss

Muffet sitting on tuffet. Next time you open your mouth, you cheeky girl, you will get spiders put into it. Then you will begin to appreciate real food. Greasy!'

Her father had chosen to remain silent on the subject. Kareem had sat there, smiling smugly at her misfortune. Ameena had winced at the force of the slap but not cried, resisted saying something instructive about Africa, and run up the stairs, albeit out of defiance more than obedience. But when Kareem, upon finishing his dinner, had come upstairs and opened the door of her room just to say, 'Goodnight Miss Muffet,' with a snigger, she had gone back out and crouched at the top of the stairs unnoticed, for she was sure that now that they were alone there would be a conversation between her parents, and Ameena wanted to hear it, for she was endlessly amazed by how differently they lived compared to normal people.

'You really need to stop hitting them. It's not legal in this country,' Yusuf cautioned.

Zoya smirked. 'Legal shegal. What will they do? Report me? We were spanked as kids and we turned out alright, didn't we? The whole nation of Pakistan and that big fat country next to it, they are doing okay, aren't they, all one billion of them! Better than *these* people here, always in the loony sessions.'

Yusuf couldn't help but smile. 'I think you mean therapy.'

'You can call it what you like, fancy names, they are still loony sessions. Saw the news today? Some couple threw the nanny into garden bonfire and the man is standing there, grilling chicken to hide the smell.' Zoya stuck her hand out and rotated her wrist in front of an imaginary barbeque. 'Throwing the nanny into the bonfire! Imagine! Like she is Tandoori Chicken.'

She stopped grilling then and brought the same hand up to her forehead, making little circles with her index finger. 'Mad, all mad.'

Ameena standing at the top of the stairs felt her eyes grow wide and before the gasp of horror escaped her, she ran into her room feeling a sense of such gladness that she had a mother who slapped her when she was naughty rather than throw her into bonfires. And gladness also that they were not like normal people, for they had neither nanny nor barbeque, nor garden for that matter, in which one could grill anything, chicken or nannies, alike.

1.15

He walked her home that night, the night they met on the rooftop, a hot, still night, the air sticky with humidity and the secret intimacy of new lovers.

'Ameena,' he said as they walked past the primary school playground, its brightly painted swings and slides lying unnaturally still and silent under the honey glow of the streetlights.

'Hmm...?'

'What kind of stuff do you paint?'

'Can't tell you!'

'Oh?' he said, and held it like that, his mouth, in the shape of the 'o', and it hung suspended between them like an invisible object.

They walked some more in silence, side by side but not touching, past the little dog park with its gate padlocked several hours earlier, past the 24-hour pharmacy, past the elegant brownstones with their chandeliers on, past the pizza place, which was bustling, and the salad place, which was not.

'Only joking,' she said lightly after a bit, and just like that, the 'o' was gone. She looked at him, then hesitated. She knew Peggy was away on work, touring a paper mill in Savannah – due diligence, she had explained to Ameena, for her to be able to value the business accurately for investors – but still she hesitated. They passed a pretty white church, Greek Orthodox, David gathered from the Byzantine cross above the tower, and then next to it a redbrick building, in front of which she stopped and said, 'This is me.'

'Looks different from down here than from my rooftop,' David observed.

'Perspective,' she said, 'is a beautiful thing.'

'Isn't it just,' David agreed.

'Do you want to come upstairs?' she said, and she said it quickly as if any delay might put her in danger of changing her mind.

'I'd like that,' he replied.

'To look at my paintings, I mean.'

'Of course.'

He nodded. And then she nodded. And in that way, their meaning was clear.

David and Ameena squeezed into the elevator and stood against the back wall, their shoulders touching, not because they necessarily wanted to or didn't want to, but because it was impossible in that tiny elevator for them not to. They didn't feel the need to speak and their silence magnified the sounds of the elevator, sounds that seemed alien to Ameena, as if she'd never heard them before, but she had, of course, she just hadn't paid attention to them, the groaning and the rattling and the rumbling of the ironwork.

On fifteen, the doors heaved open, Ameena stepped out and David followed. They walked in single file, down a dimly lit corridor, passing on either side identical pale green doors, all the way to the end, then she stopped and unlocked her own pale green door. She went inside first and reached for a light switch, then motioned for David to follow her in.

'They're all in my room,' Ameena said, 'stowed away under the bed,' she added with a little laugh, 'where no one can find them. Stay here, I'll call you when I've got them out.'

Alone, David looked around the apartment. It was small, clean, distinctly female. The kitchen was painted an unusual but rather striking teal and opened out into a living area with a sofa and a TV and a small rectangular wooden table that seemed to double up as both dining table and reading desk, for in that moment, it lay strewn with books along its entire length. A large triangular-shaped glass vase sat on one edge, bursting with lilies that quite spectacularly filled the room with their fragrance. On one side of the room was a single large window with an enviably close-up view of the Chrysler Building; on the other side was a bookshelf, crammed tight with books.

David walked to the window and looked out at the city lights. The yellow globe of a full moon hung low, softening the hard lines of the buildings, bathing the night sky in thick, milky splendor. Below, on the avenue, tiny vehicles rushed along the perfectly geometric grid lines, creating continuous threads of light, red on one side, white on the other, running parallel to each other as far as David could see – all the way to the end of the earth, David thought to himself with a little smile as he turned away from the window and wandered towards the bookcase. He scanned the titles for a minute, then picked out a book that caught his attention – a collection of photographs of the Ballets Russes. It was signed, he noticed, when he opened it – 'To: *Zvyozdochka moya*' in an elegant slanting hand. It didn't say who it was from. *Zvyozdochka moya*, he mouthed the words silently. He didn't know what they meant, but he liked how they sounded, those Russian words, how they made him feel; there was a certain melancholy to the whole thing, the sound of the words, the curve of the letters. David felt unexpectedly moved, almost to tears, but he couldn't understand the reaction in himself, as inscrutable as the words themselves. He ran his thumb over the inscription slowly, feeling the slight depression in the paper where the ink had touched it and now resided in its own little valley below the surface, altering its form permanently. Then he quickly turned the page. He had just started looking at some extraordinary pictures of Nijinsky, admiring how the great dancer was able to reshape his head and neck and shoulders like that to suit his different character roles, when he looked up to see her silhouetted against the door frame of her bedroom.

'Hey,' she called softly as he glanced up at her aspect, and when she stepped forward into the light, he thought he saw something that resembled apprehension on her face. He understood that look, what solitary angst it concealed within it, for art, like music, like dance, like language, was an exposition of oneself of sorts, you put your whole self into it and then you put it out there, you put *yourself* out there, into the world.

Then she led him into her room and showed him what she had put out there, into the world.

She'd laid them out everywhere, on the floor, on her bed, leaning against the legs of the chair and the small dressing table, stood up against the windowsill against the glow of the city lights, different pieces like an entire orchestra of watercolours. His eyes swept over them, first all of them at once, taking in their collective beauty, the accumulation of gestures and textures and colours, provocative and performative all at once. Then he studied them individually, each brushstroke, a thing in itself as well as the thing it depicted. How long did he spend? How long was time when he was no longer in that room, but somewhere else, as if he'd entered the paintings, penetrated their space, penetrated *her* space, as if the room itself was a living thing, organs pulsing, alive with tension and drama – and that living thing was her.

How could this woman, he thought, this slender, small-boned woman, have this inside her – this capacity to, without *language*, without *music*, produce so much meaning?

Ameena leans against the far wall and watches him in silence as he walks around her bedroom, surveying her work, one, then another and another, his eyes narrowed in complete concentration. She watches the expression on his face change.

'Fuck,' he says finally, shaking his head in amazement.

She says nothing, only shifts her body forward so there is no longer the support of the wall. He is standing at the other end of the room, but the room is tiny, and in a few seconds she is directly in front of him. She notices the faint beads of perspiration that have formed in the smooth crevice above his upper lip.

Fifteen storeys below them, an ambulance wails.

There is an intimacy then in that moment, in the privacy of the moment, and it passes between them like a secret that has been shared and now nothing can be the same again.

'I thought I made it clear there was going to be none of that,' she says softly. Then she kisses him once. And then once again.

1.16

Paint spreading. Margins dissolving. Two colours blending into one:
Artmaking.

آرت آرت آرت آرت آرت آرت آرت آرت آرت آرت

אומנות אומנות אומנות אומנות אומנות אומנות

آرت آرت آرت آرت آرت آرت آرت آرت آرت آرت

אומנות אומנות אומנות אומנות אומנות אומנות

آرت آرت آرت آرت آرت آرت آرت آرت آرت آرت

אומנות אומנות אומנות אומנות אומנות אומנות

آرت آرت آرت آرت آرت آرت آرت آرت آرت آرت

آرت אומנות آرت אומנות آرت אומנות آرت אומנות

1.17

'I don't really want to start going around with my portfolio. If I really wanted to be discouraged, I'd start doing just that,' Ameena said to David the following morning as they rode the subway together to work.

'That's ridiculous, they're amazing.'

She rolled her eyes. 'Whatever. You asked why I haven't done anything with them. I answered.'

'Ameena, you're wasting your talent.'

'Did you know,' she said, reaching across him for a pole to hold onto, 'that most of the talent in the world goes wasted. People die with unnoticed capabilities. At this very moment, entire nations you've never heard of are wasting copious amounts of talent.'

He cocked his head in acknowledgement 'Fine. True. Very good point in fact, and I agree one hundred percent. But right now, I care about *your* talent.'

The subway door opened at Grand Central and a great throng of people squeezed and elbowed their way in. A vast nylon-clad body now stood between Ameena and the pole she'd been grasping. She let her arm drop and David picked it up casually and placed it round his waist. Another body behind her pushed hers closer to his.

She could smell the toothpaste on his breath.

'What talent?' she said, trying to focus away from her acute awareness of the proximity of their bodies in so public a place.

'Is this a British thing or an artist thing or an Ameena thing?

She laughed. 'Don't know what you're talking about.'

'No?'

She shook her head, still laughing. 'No.'

'This annoying habit of perpetual self-deprecation.'

'Look who's talking!'

'Me? I'm not self-deprecating. I'm American. And I'm a musician. And I'm fucking good.'

'You are, are you?'

'Yeah. Check your phone at noon.'

'What? This is my stop.'

'I know it's your stop. Just check your phone at noon.'

He called her phone at eleven o'clock.

'It's not noon.'

'Hello to you too!' David said in a faux-hurt voice.

'Sorry – hello. I'm just informing you that it's not noon.'

'I know it's not noon. Check your phone at noon. But listen, I've been thinking about them.'

'Whom?

'Your nipples.'

She gasped audibly into the phone.

'I'm kidding, I'm kidding. Your art.'

'You've been thinking about my art.'

'Yes.'

'That's flattering.'

'I don't flatter.'

'Sounds like flattery to me.'

'Ameena, listen, can I come by this evening and take some photographs of your work? You don't even need to be there. Just leave me with them for a bit. Go for a walk or something.'

'You're asking me to go for a walk?'

'Or something.'

'Or something?'

'Yes.'

'You're asking me to go for a walk. Or something?'

'Not really. I'm telling you.'

On the other end of the phone line, Ameena made a noise of defeat. Valiantly, she tried to refocus the conversation.

'David... I... you're not making any sense. Peggy's home tonight.'

'Okay, introduce me to the scary roomie, then leave me with her and go for a walk.'

'Stop. Listen. Seriously. I'm trying to work and you're not making any sense.'

He sighed. 'Okay, look. I don't want to raise your expectations, it could turn out to be nothing, it probably *will* turn out to be nothing, but there's this woman – Suzy Lipskis – she is... was... a friend of my mom's. Her daughter Janice and I went to school together and I basically rescued her from flunking out, freshman year of college. Long story, but Suzy owes me. She also happens to be an independent curator at a small gallery here in the city. She's a pretty daunting woman, she's Lithuanian, she may have killed her husband.'

'What?'

'I'm kidding. She lost her husband, poor thing. Heart attack. Collapsed right there, on the toilet.'

'Oh?'

'It seems to happen that way for so many people. I think it's the exertion that causes it, you know, all the...'

Ameena groaned. 'David. Please.'

'Oh sorry. Anyway, look, she's a formidable woman with strong interests and aesthetic, a kind of creative agent in her own right. She leans toward art that's not only visually beautiful but that makes some sort of political or social statement. I spoke to her about you. She wants to see your work.'

A pause. Then: 'Umm, okay, let me understand this. You spoke to someone about me without asking me first?'

'Yes.'

'How the hell could you do that?'

'Because your work is amazing.'

'David, my work is private. And *I'm* private. Ugh! This is so frustrating! You don't even know me.'

'I know you.'

'My work is private.'

'Your work is amazing.'

'You're so infuriating.'

'Are you mad at me?'

'Yes.'

'Good, check your phone at noon.'

At noon, a video message beeped its arrival on her phone. Below the video, a one-line text: i wrote this for you. it's called 'when you are near'. hope you're not mad anymore.

Ameena smiled to herself, then walked to the small conference room and shut the door. It was hot in the room. The midday sunlight blazed in through the wall of windows, casting an array of swirls and squiggles across the long rectangular table. Outside, the towers of Manhattan glistened, a sweeping iridescence of silver and blue. She crossed the room and leaned her back against the cool glass. She inhaled. Behind her, a city exhaled.

She pressed play.

Music filled the room.

David.

David on the piano.

But not David, just his fingers.

David's fingers caressing the keys... chords, notes, a tune, music, a piece of music. A piece of music, intricate and achingly erotic, she felt it wash over her, pressing down on her in an intensely physical way. She shivered despite the heat.

'I wrote this for you...'

Ameena played it again, watching his hands, the precise movement of his fingers. She felt something inside her then, a movement of her own, a flutter, a lurch, a creature come alive by those fingers that seemed to touch something within her and summon up a strange ragbag of emotions: happiness, a sudden spurt of joy, shooting up from her toes. But also, sadness, sweet, clenching sadness. And pain, exquisite pain.

And she knew at once that something like this, this bizarre, incongruous, dangerous cocktail of feelings, could only mean one thing.

You're fucking good, she wrote back, wanting to write one thing, and writing something else instead.

1.18

Three months after Ameena moved to New York, she found herself heartbroken, the breaker of her heart being a Russian-Canadian ballet dancer with floppy hair and strong arms, and ambitions to become the best male dancer in the world.

They had met at a bar; he was there with his friends, other floppy-haired, strong-armed dancers. And she was there with some of the girls from work and he had sent over a drink and looked at her with his blue eyes, looked at her so intently that she had to look away, then he had come over and asked for her number and she had given it to him and then regretted the action later. But she had been taken by his beauty, his supple beauty, his supple, white, blond beauty, unlike anything she had encountered before in such close proximity, not in any of the men she had met through her parents, their friends' sons, skinny and hairy and all so academic.

Still, she had ignored his calls and his texts at first, not from a lack of attraction, not in the slightest, but from fear and a kind of confusion in understanding what someone like him would want from someone like her. But he would send her videos of him dancing, of entrechats and jetés, his body flexible and fluid and gliding on air, and he danced beautifully, wondrously. And even though she hated herself for it, she couldn't help but watch him, surreptitiously, on her computer screen at work, his legs twisting, twisting and twirling and jumping and splitting, creating move-ment, such beautiful movement. He had pursued her relentlessly and then finally, worn out from being chased – not by him but by her own private fears – she had given in.

Talent is always sexy, someone had once told her. When anyone is that good at anything, it becomes erotic.

So, she had given in to the eroticism of his talent.

And then learned later that he was as skilled a lover as he was a dancer, that his feet were magical even when they weren't off the ground, that he had a natural rhythm in the way he moved, in the way he made her move, a rhythm and a music and a choreography and a poetry, that the openness of his body was an expression of his passion and his art and that he carried both with him into their private world. That he loved with the beautifully slow and sustained grace of the adagio. That she loved the way he loved.

He taught her about dance, the greatest dancers that ever lived, Baryshnikov and Nijinsky and Nureyev and Vasiliev. He spoke passionately about the music of dance, Tchaikovsky and *Swan Lake* and the *Nutcracker*; he showed her the movements – the precision and the discipline of the movements – the five basic positions of the feet, the shapes they made, how to watch for the shapes they made, how the position of your feet changed the whole shape of you.

She sat at her desk at work writing his name on the sides of draft articles that were waiting for her to edit. Writing his name and then her name and then a combination of their names, her first name with his last name. Followed sometimes – but not always because the dancer had said he didn't want children, that music and dance were his twin children – by their children's names, pretty names, eclectic names, a mix of Eastern and Western, just as their children would be – if he ever changed his mind – Eastern and Western, true citizens of the world.

And then, when she thought it was all only beginning, it was over. Just like that.

They'd been sitting in the bath, she was soaping his leg – that supple, lithe leg that he swung around her body, circling it like an animal – when he told her he'd met this Danish girl, that it just happened, and he thought he loved her.

She had got out of the bath then, just stood up and stepped out and then taken the toothbrush holder – a sweet ceramic thing, white with blue and yellow and green zigzag patterns – and thrown it to the floor in a rage. Somehow, she didn't know how – and even when she thought about it now, after all this time had passed, she *still* didn't know how, only that it was a sign, it had to be – a small piece of it had bounced on the side of the bathtub and ricocheted up, the jagged edge of it cutting the skin on the underside of her forearm, the fleshy bit just below the bend of her elbow. All this, as she stood there in horror, on the tiled floor of his bathroom, water dripping from her body, from her hair, while he sat there in the bath, with his impossibly toned stomach and his flaccid penis, with a matching look of horror – or maybe it was one of relief that he'd met the Danish girl, that at least she wasn't some kind of raging psychopath like this one was.

But that was the thing, Ameena thought, as the blood gushed from her arm and the water from her hair dripped directly onto it, watering down the blood into a thin, pink stream – an insult, really, the whole thing – she wasn't a psychopath. She didn't throw things. But of course, *he* didn't know that. He probably thought she'd done it on purpose, incredible narcissist that he was, he probably thought she had cut herself intentionally for him, out of love or rejection or whatever. In a principally perverse way, for Ameena had always had the capacity to see humour even in dark things, this thought made her laugh.

She exited the bathroom without bothering to close the door behind her, calmly picked up the various items of her clothing that lay strewn across his bedroom floor, then, once she was fully dressed, went back in, helped herself to his face towel and, wrapping it round her arm, said, 'Well, I don't know about the best dancer in the world, but you can sell the shit out of a partnership, that's for sure,' and left for home, people staring at her on the bus, the stolen towel now sticky and bright red, her hair still wet, still dripping on her wound.

Back in her apartment, she sat down on the bed and felt faint and wondered if she would die. She had heard of people who died from an excessive loss of blood. But then she must have fallen asleep because when she woke the next morning, the ugly cut had scabbed over, and she was not dead, only heartbroken.

He had called her later that day to ask how she was. She had called him a motherfucker – she rarely swore, she had never used that word in her life before – and told him to fuck the fucking hell off to Denmark. Or something like that. Which apparently he had done, because he didn't call to enquire after her again. Following this, Ameena became wary, and promised herself that going forward, she would never lose sight of the principles of chemistry – or was it physics, she couldn't remember – but whatever it was, it certainly betrayed biology when it declared that two similarly charged bodies attempting to come together, even under the pretext of fine and noble persuasions such as love, was likely to lead to a string of unmitigated disasters, and so when David told her that he wanted to be a composer, she found herself unable to offer words of wonder or encouragement or admiration; she found herself unable to offer any words at all.

1.19

what are you doing tonight? flashed the message on her phone.

Watching the lights of the great city, she replied truthfully.

She was lying in bed, facing the window, listening to the Fugue in G Minor by Johann Sebastian Bach – the man was a gift, David had told her, to all humanity. Now, she flipped from her side onto her back, held up the phone in front of her face, typed with her two thumbs.

A: You?

D: will pull up in cab, 20 mins, come down

A: WHAT?

D: 20 mins. don't be late

A: But where are we going?

D: cello concert. friend had 2 tix

A: Where? What time does it finish? What do I wear?

D: surprise. don't know. nothing.

A: Rubbish answer.

D: ;)

And then he was gone.

Twenty minutes later, she found herself next to David in the backseat of a yellow cab.

'Well,' she remarked, 'this was spontaneous!'

'Jazz has a way of teaching you to live in the moment,' he said with a laugh. 'You look beautiful by the way in your red dress.' Then he whispered, 'Step down from nothing, but not by a lot.'

'Stop,' she mouthed, but smiled shyly, immediately conscious of the chemistry between them, of his desire for her that he made no effort to mask.

'Can't,' he said in a grave voice, shaking his head. Ameena pursed her lips to conceal a smile and pretended to look outside her window at the great city moving backwards.

A few minutes later, David tapped on the see-through plastic partition that physically separated the front seats from the back to get the attention of SUKHWINDER SINGH AHLUWALIA, licence number 4xxxx. 'Can you go up Park, please,' David said to him through the little window. 'Sixth is always gridlocked at this time of the evening. Could have taken a left there – you missed it – oh come *on*!'

'Why,' Ameena said, turning towards him, 'genuinely why, are New Yorkers always telling taxi drivers how to drive? Why can't you just sit back and let him do his job? I wonder about this lots, you know... I've only ever seen it happen here. What is it about? Is it him? Or is it you? And can we ever know?'

At this, SUKHWINDER SINGH AHLUWALIA flips his turbaned head right round to stare at the seeker of such metaphysical truths.

'You're so Zen,' David said, smiling.

'Touché,' she replied. 'Anyway, cello concert? I thought you wanted me to listen to *you* playing *jazz*.'

'I did. I *do*! But then this came along, and I thought I'd love to take you, the cello can be magnificent if done well. And also.' He reached for her hand on the seat and put his own over it. 'Also, I was thinking, on my way here, maybe it's not such a bad thing, it kind of follows my own progression in a way; my mother played – and taught – classical music so that's what I was playing for about seven years before I came to jazz.'

'How *did* you come to jazz?'

'Ha! Good question. It's a good story actually. So, at my high school, this is in Rhode Island – I grew up in Rhode Island, I don't know if I told you that already – there was this science teacher who was a jazz bass player by night.'

'God, David, that sounds like something out of a movie!'

'No, seriously.' David nodded. 'And then, he convinced the school that he didn't want to be a science teacher any more, so he transitioned into being a full-time jazz teacher. Or rather, educator, I should say.'

David thought back, not without some amusement, to Jack Winters, the science teacher who, to the class's half-shock, half-fascination, would routinely fall asleep with both eyes open, often in the middle of his own sentence.

This unusual behaviour, which at first had been wrongly attributed to some very hip and illegal reasons, was eventually – and somewhat to the disappointment of a group of high school kids with fertile imaginations – explained away by less enthralling factors. For it was not a long time later that Mr Winters confessed to the school principal the practical impossibility of explaining the anatomy of a rat by day when he'd been up playing jazz all night.

A few weeks later, a timid-looking woman with glasses and stringy brown hair showed up to teach the science class, the music department introduced a new jazz class and the old science teacher became the new jazz teacher.

For David, it had been pure luck. One of those unexplained karmic forces that conspire to put you on a certain path for a certain reason which you do not fully understand and from which there is no turning back.

David looked outside his window.

They were driving past Columbus Circle, a shifting swirl of colour under the rainbow lights.

To Ameena, he said, 'Frankly, anyone who is willing to teach jazz to high school kids is a hero. And Jack Winters, because he had this incredible ear-based, organic ability to play the music, understood that jazz is an aural tradition and needs to be taught in that same fashion. So, I guess I was very, very fortunate to have such an excellent first teacher. Beyond my mom, I mean. So, jazz-wise, credit where credit's due, this guy was just phenomenally good at taking high school kids who had never heard a note of jazz before and turning them into, at the minimum, jazz lovers, if not more.'

'That's like a real movie scene,' Ameena said. 'It's got that sweet, wistful sentimentality to it. Tell me you don't see it!' She held her hands apart as if she was holding a banner: 'Students help teacher find true calling, spurred by a mutual love of jazz.'

David laughed as the taxi pulled up to the curb. 'Well sweet, what can I say? It's all true.'

'We are hair,' announces SUKHWINDER SINGH ALHUWALIA in a bored voice. It's been particularly dull, he thinks with disappointment, this conversation at the back, after starting out with such promise.

'Great,' David said amiably as he handed over a twenty-dollar bill, 'he says we're here, so we must be here, and in perfect time too. No, I don't need any change, you can keep that, thanks.'

Outside the taxi, he held her hand. Around them, New York City. Statues. Jumping fountains. A sea of yellow cabs. The flash of the greenback. Exquisite energy. Sinful. Sexy.

David said: 'Let's go watch this thing. Dress rehearsal. *Then* we'll go watch the real thing. Just joking – you hear that sound? That's my mother turning in her grave.'

'David!'

'I'm joking, I'm joking. It's my father.'

'You! Honestly, you're something else!'

And in that way, David revealed to Ameena two important details about himself:

1. That his parents were dead.
2. That had they been alive, they would likely have disapproved of David's proclivity for this one style of music vs. the other.

She picked up on both.

1.20

On the burgundy faux leather sofa, Ameena's father Yusuf was troubled.

These were troubled times.

Someone, he read in the newspaper that morning at the barber's shop, had raped an underage girl – a *child* for all intents and purposes – the previous day. She had been found, in the early hours of the morning, sitting on the smooth marble floor of the Arndale Centre, quivering and terrorised. Police were asking around for witnesses, anyone who may have seen something suspicious.

Please God, Yusuf found himself thinking, please don't let him be Muslim.

This wasn't an unusual thought for Yusuf to be thinking. In fact, of late, every time he read of horrendous happenings anywhere in the world, he found himself praying that the perpetrator was not Muslim, not Pakistani, not brown.

Not anyone who looked like his son.

1.21

It was intimate, far more intimate than she had expected from a venue of such eminence.

It had scale – Ameena imagined it could fit a few thousand people at capacity – and yet, the combined effects of the stage, the steeply raked stalls and the low gallery created a surprisingly personal venue, which delighted her, and she tugged at David's arm.

'I love this,' she said, looking around.

'It used to be a church,' David whispered, 'in the 1900s. And then people basically stopped going to church, so they sold it. It opened as a concert hall in the early 2000s. They did massive amounts of work on the acoustics.'

'It's wonderful,' she said, 'you feel like you can reach out and touch the instruments.'

The stage had been set up, the various instruments placed on the seats of chairs or stood up in front of them. It was amazing, Ameena thought, that in a few minutes, all those instruments would be playing at once; so many talented musicians on one stage, playing their different instruments, whatever each played best, yet all coming together as one to celebrate a single piece of music.

'I want to feel the music,' Ameena said as they took their seats, 'the way *you* feel it.'

David smiled. 'You know that Michelangelo quote, "I liberate the statue from the marble"? That's what I'm hoping they will do for us tonight, a liberation of the statue in sound. I hope we will both feel it resounding around the room!'

'And what a room!' she exclaimed, turning her head all the way round and then up towards the elaborate cathedral ceiling.

David delights from her excitement. She's infectious, he thinks, this girl is infectious.

'I know it's night-time,' he said looking up at the large multicoloured panels that rose above the balconies on each side, 'but if you come here during the day, you really appreciate the stained glass. It was designed by a Danish guy, he learned the art of stained glass while working here in New York with Tiffany.'

'Oh,' she said, 'how nice. Another Danish person bringing virtue to the world.'

'Huh?'

'Nothing. Tell me about the stage set-up.'

He looked at her curiously. 'Is this your first time? Watching an orchestra?'

She nodded, suddenly feeling inadequate, a kind of realisation that when it comes to certain experiences in life, some people are so much richer than others.

'I'm sorry,' she said, 'do you think less of me?

'No, no, not at all. I just didn't realize you were a music virgin that's all,' he said, with a twinkle in his eye.

'*Music* virgin?'

'I'm honoured that your first time is with me. I promise I'll be very giving.'

She hit him on the arm playfully. 'You're such a perv!'

He smiled, and she noticed how his dimples played on his cheeks, the left one deeper than the right. 'Haven't even gotten started...'

She waved her hand dismissively. 'Whatever.'

'I'm absolutely serious,' he said, and he looked at her and her face was boundless like the sky and her eyes were like stars.

'What do you mean?' she asked.

'You'll see,' he said. 'Actually, I take that back. Maybe you won't.'

In the darkness, everything was heightened.

The sound of her own breathing, the sound of his, the breath of the bow drawn across the strings. And the vibrations, the breath of the vibrations, as they ricocheted through her chest.

'Do me a favour?' he had said a few minutes earlier. 'Close your eyes. Don't open them till the end.'

She looked at him, her dark eyes penetrating, searching. 'What? You brought me here to see this thing, but you don't want me to see this thing? Like at all?'

'You wanted to feel the music? Then *feel* it,' he said softly. 'Suppress one sense, heighten the others. Music is a tactile experience. Emotion over perception.'

Ameena turned towards him. Then she smiled and shut her eyes as if to test it out, examine for herself if there was any truth to what he was saying. He looked at her for a long moment, sitting like that, eyes shut, lips gently parted, marvelling at the simple beauty of her face. On an impulse, he placed his palm over her eyes, the lightest touch, leaving it there for a few seconds before brushing his fingertips over her face, caressing it, his fingers moving downwards, reaching her neck, stopping only at the hollow between her collarbones.

Ameena took in a breath.

'Okay...' she said, but she opened her eyes and looked around the packed room.

'It's full,' he said as if in confirmation.

She nodded.

He held her hand. 'You can watch if you prefer to watch. Don't listen to me, do whatever you want. The beauty is in the music and all the different ways you can feel it and understand it. You'll enjoy it either way, I promise you.'

The musicians picked up their bows. A quiet descended.

Ameena felt the silence around her, the tension of it, like a rubber band stretched tight.

On the stage, she saw the woman in her black dress and her long hair, her chin tilted, her bow drawn, her thighs apart, creating a nest between her legs for the instrument to lie in. And then it snapped. The silence snapped. And the silence was accompanied, but not replaced, by something else. The sound came, deep and rich. Companion to silence, knit together, a marriage.

And Ameena. She is disarmed.

She looks at David, at the unique composition of his face, examining it, studying how his each feature exists in relation to the others. The irises of his eyes, she notices, are striking, green-gold and open and full of integrity.

He squeezes her hand and instinctively she squeezes back.

For a moment, exquisite and ephemeral, their eyes lock.

Then she shuts hers.

On stage the cellist is playing the tune in E minor. Somewhere in the room, a phone rings, then abruptly stops. Ameena shuffles lower in her seat and reclines her head, dark hair fanned out against the deep maroon velvet of the cushion. David doesn't know this at the time, but it is a vision of her that he will always remember, as if in that moment she is not real, but a kind of dream or ideal.

Almost involuntarily, he leans into her, lifting her hair up and over her shoulder, and kisses her neck, and there is a gentleness about the way he touches her, and a great yearning stirs deep within her.

'David, I just want you to know...' she starts to say, but then the moment had already glided into the next, and her voice stuck in her throat.

'I already know,' he said softly.

On stage, the orchestra burst forth in a blaze of passion. To

Ameena the sound was enormous. Everywhere. Everything. She let it flow over her and fill her, all the empty spaces within her, into those dark hollows encasing her heart, and then all the emptiness was gone, and she felt a lightness and she was rising, up, up, up.

And then they weren't in the concert hall at all, but in a darkened room with a ceiling fan and a bookshelf crammed with books and a bed with a jade-green cover and she was lying down on this bed – his bed – and she could feel the weight of him in the deep, soulful timbre of the cello, and his weight was filled with loneliness and longing.

And then they weren't in the room, but under water in a swimming pool blowing bubbles with their mouths, and they were swimming towards each other, arms outstretched, closer and closer until the tips of their fingers touched.

And then they weren't in the swimming pool, but in a wood with tall trees and the forest floor was a carpet of lavender and they were running on this carpet, running barefoot, holding hands, running towards the orange sky where the sun was flaming over the horizon.

And then they weren't in the forest, but back in the room, in the concert hall, but there was nobody else there, they were alone, just her and him, and the music. And she could feel it. The tension in the air. And the cry of the bow. And the vibrations in her ribcage. And the unexpected swell of joy that lives on the other side of the surrender.

'You okay?' she heard a voice say and it sounded so far away.

'Ameena? You okay?'

She nodded without speaking. But she took his hand and held it to her heart.

1.22

In David's apartment, very early the following morning, they were propped up in bed, reading the newspaper and drinking coffee.

'If all else fails,' Ameena said thoughtfully, looking up from the paper, 'you can become a barista...'

'Is the coffee good? Is that what you're saying?'

She smiled, a sweet sensual smile that David knew said many other things too. 'Yes. Very.' Then, turning to face him and attempting to look serious, she said, 'Okay, I have a question.'

'Anything. Aside from how I make such great coffee because that's a secret I take into the *ground*. Get it, get it?'

Ameena chuckled. 'You should be a stand-up. Ever thought of being a stand-up? You'd be a great stand-up.'

He held his palms facing upwards and then proceeded to alternately raise and lower them as if weighing something. 'Hmm,' he said thoughtfully, 'barista or comedian? Tough choice! Impossible choice! An embarrassment of riches! Which one shall it be?'

'You can do both! Do both! It'll be amazing. A funny barista. A funny Jewish barista. Just what the world needs. I mean, have you ever, in all your life, met a barista who made you laugh? The Jewish part is like a triple bonus. Like finding YHWH in your triple venti soy latte.'

He laughed, then leaned over and kissed her. 'Have you made this your life's purpose, beautiful? To find my calling? I already have a calling, remember?'

'Yes! And that's what I wanted to ask you about before you distracted me with all the coffee talk...' She sat up suddenly. 'Hey! we could call it "Jehovah Java"!'

David rolled his eyes. Ameena made a comical expression, 'Or not! Okay *listen*, so the guy who wrote that piece we listened to last night...'

'Elgar?'

'Yeah. Elgar.'

'Edward Elgar, one of your lot!'

'He's English?'

'Well, he's dead now, but he was English, yeah. 1900s. One of the greats. I believe he was knighted and everything.'

'Oh...' she said, pondering that fact.

After a few seconds, she nodded. 'Yup, that's what we do where I'm from. We take the common man and when he does something really, really good, we touch his shoulder with a sword and hey-ho! we make him royalty. Anyway, here is my question, knighted or not, you have seventy players sitting on a stage, so when he writes this stuff, how does he decide who does what?'

'Ah, my lovely, that's orchestration.'

'Umm...' Ameena frowned, looking quizzical. 'I don't want to be the girlfriend who says I don't know what you mean, but I don't know what you mean.'

David smiled. 'I don't expect you to know about orchestration, but the girlfriend part was nice to hear,' he said, and looking at him, Ameena felt herself blush.

'Right, okay,' he said, 'let's see. So orchestration basically means choosing an instrument to play each note of a piece. So for example, a piece written for piano has ten notes at a time, orchestra has seventy instruments, so if you want to orchestrate that music, you're going to have to give some of those instruments the same note, meaning you're going to *divide* up all the notes among the orchestra instruments – each of which has a different timbre – depending on which instrument you hear playing a particular note of the piece.'

The morning sun streamed in through the open window, climbing over the wall and across the ceiling like the many legs of some strange shapeshifting creature. David turned towards her and Ameena watched as the legs walked all over his face.

She could see how much he loved this, even talking about it. His eyes were animated, filled with their own light.

'Then,' David continued, 'you're going to think of lots of other music-theory type things – texture, dynamics, tempo, harmony – what's the mood you want to create – do you want drama or contemplation? Lightness or darkness? Happiness or melancholy? Or some of all of the above at different points in the composition? All these decisions to consider and the whole effect can be transformed with just minor adjustments to a single choice. Just like that, it becomes a different piece.'

She nodded and she realised then, with some instinctive certainty, that he was happiest when he spoke to her about his music and somehow to her, *this* – his being happy – mattered. 'So it's fair to say Elgar was a composer and an orchestrator?'

'Yes, and in this particular case, Elgar was self-taught. Bach – you already know I think Bach is the greatest – so for me, he was *the* master orchestrator. I think it was Stravinsky who famously said about Bach, "You can smell the resin in his violin parts, taste the reeds in the oboes..." So yeah, most great composers who write music for orchestras are magnificent orchestrators, and as they write, they can see the whole thing unfold. I've heard of some composers, you show them a sheet of music and they can hear the entire orchestra in their heads.'

'Seriously?'

'Yeah. It's incredible, I know.'

'And that's kind-of-sort-of what you want to do? But with jazz and movies?'

'In a nutshell, yeah.'

She nodded her head.

Then, to David's great amusement, in the kind of accent you'd expect to hear in a Tennessee Williams play, she said, 'Well, I do think that's swell.'

Later that morning, at work, David walked into Hershel's office and closed the door behind him. He leaned up against it, arms crossed behind his back, one leg bent, the flat of his foot pressed to the door.

'Hershel.'

'David.'

'I had an epiphany last night.'

'Uh-oh.'

'No seriously. I was with Ameena…'

'David, if I were you, I'd stop right there. This is a place of work.'

'…at a concert.'

'At a concert?'

'At a concert.'

'Who's Ameena?'

'My girl— a friend. Doesn't matter. Look, the chocolate milk client? We've been hitting a wall because we've been thinking about it wrong.'

Hershel looked at him curiously.

'What's that look?' David said.

'Nothing, go on.'

David threw him an exasperated look of his own, then continued. 'Okay, this is the thing, right? We've been driving the pitch forward on logic, and that's a perfectly viable – and valuable – way to do things. But then you know in that last meeting, we kept saying we're missing something, and we all agreed we were missing something but none of us knew what that missing something was. Well, this is the thing, I think it is missing heart. I'm not sure this pitch is about logic alone.'

He stopped. Hershel was chewing his pencil. David noticed to his amazement that he had worked his way up to about half the length of the thing.

'Can you stop doing that, it's disgusting.'

'David, do me a favour?'

'Throw the pencil away?'

'No. Don't touch my pencil but *do* please carry the fuck on. I'm listening. I wouldn't be listening if it wasn't good. But I ain't got all day, even if it's coming from our very own Messiah Ben David.'

'Haha, Hershel, that's hilarious.'

Hershel waved his hand dismissively, but David could see from the way he was sitting, leaning forward on his desk, eyes narrowed to a virtual slit, that he had the man's attention, which David knew from experience was a fickle thing. So, he ignored the urge to curse and simply continued. 'I mean, this has been said before, but the pressures of the business and this incessant desire to appear "new and shiny" often leads us to prioritize left-brain rationality over right-brain emotion. The truth is that the world's most iconic brands, from Nike to Dove to Apple to Coca-Cola, have all been built on the back of goosebumps-inducing, emotion-based advertising. Truly memorable advertising begins with one question: What do we want our consumers to *feel*?'

Hershel raised his eyebrows. 'What do we want our consumers to *feel*?'

David nodded. 'What do we want our consumers to *feel*.'

'And you got this from a concert with Mina?'

David turned to leave. 'You're welcome. And it's Ameena.'

A few hours later, in the afternoon, David and Ameena exchanged emails at work.

davidgreenberg: hi!

ahamid: Hi

davidgreenberg: so... randomly. just listened to the main theme from *the da vinci code*. same, very basic fifteen-note motif played over and over endlessly. yet thrilling due to orchestration.

ahamid: Oh yeah?

davidgreenberg: bold as brass. one tune. on a loop. like an academic exercise in development through orchestration. shows what orchestration is and why it matters, to answer your question from before.

ahamid: Hmm... trying to get head around. Sorry. Head somewhere else this morning. (Thanks muchly to you). Are you saying it is a single unremarkable tune but becomes ledge because of orchestration?

davidgreenberg: ledge?

ahamid: Yes. Ledge – legend. What better word?

davidgreenberg: ok whatever (!) well, yes. basically.

ahamid: Listen together tonight?

davidgreenberg: sure. your place or mine?

1.23

And then... Yusuf thought as he prayed together with his son facing the window, which faced east towards the Qibla...

And then, there was Kareem.

Kareem who had always been more Pakistani than a Pakistani in Pakistan. More Pakistani in his thoughts, in his tastes, in his habits, in his allegiances, in his stubborn adherence to a cultural ideal his parents had left behind a long time ago.

Kareem who, in Yusuf's mind, was full of contradictions.

Kareem, who wouldn't think twice about parking illegally in a disabled spot, but who would happily give up his seat on the bus to an ageing or less abled person.

Kareem, who against his teachers' expectations (and perhaps also their will, for Kareem was not popular with his teachers), obtained perfect grades in maths and science but failed English with equal consistency because he couldn't be bothered to read the texts – 'All these dead people,' Zoya overheard him telling Ameena one day, 'who cares about all these dead people and what they wrote?'

Kareem, who found it difficult to express his affection for his sister, but had always been fiercely protective of her, so much so that despite Ameena's heated opposition, he would sometimes take the bus all the way to her university and 'shadow' her home if it was late.

'Do you think I'm stupid,' she asked him one time, 'do you *seriously* think I don't see you sitting at the other end of the bus with that dumb cap over your face?'

'Don't know what you're on about, yo,' he replied, pretending to tie his laces.

Kareem who had, at that very moment, spun his Eminem cap back to front, his own casual way of conforming to the religious practice of wearing head garb while praying.

Kareem, whose deep confusion about un-belonging had been simmering under the surface for years, but who had lately begun asserting his place in the world with a brazenness that tore at Yusuf's heart. For Yusuf felt it sharply, this tear in his own heart, because he had not come here to this foreign land for his *children* to be torn in their hearts. No. Had he known how much distress it would cause, this disease – this dis-ease – he would not have come, not for all of Zoya's begging and pleading and illusory talk of dreams.

He looks now at the boy, his son Kareem. They have finished praying and Kareem has respectfully folded away his father's prayer mat, before putting away his own. After he has stacked them both neatly in their place, he says politely, 'I need to go out now Abba,' and when he comes down a few minutes later, donned in his 'going out clothes' – his cap turned back the right way round, a pair of baggy Levi's and those massive white sneakers and all that fake gold that brown boys his age seem to want to cover themselves in – Yusuf gapes at him until Kareem asks his father to 'quit staring like that, yo, it's freakin me out!' Technically, he doesn't *ask*; he sort of raps it out, hand gestures and all. A different boy, this one who has come down, from the one who went up.

Different…

And yet the same.

Some people, Yusuf knows, go through their whole lives living in multiple compartmentalised worlds and manage to go back and forth between them with ease. As a father, the thought is bewildering.

Yusuf sighs.

He loves Kareem. He has always loved Kareem. In fact, every time he looks at Kareem, he is filled with wonder, at how beautiful the boy is, at how *he*, Yusuf, could possibly have had anything to do with it.

So, every time he reads news like the kind he read that morning not so long ago when he was at the barber's shop getting his beard trimmed, he finds himself wondering, with anxious mind and bewildered heart, about the perpetrator of the crime: the rapist, the murderer, the robber, the terrorist. What mental affliction, he wonders, must drive someone to such horror. What abuse or abandonment or monstrous lack of love. What terrible sense of despair he must be subsumed by, someone who is capable of such inhuman acts. The someone he had read about. Someone. Someone...

Someone else's son.

1.24

Jazz, David had once mused, has a way of teaching you how to live.

Later, in the privacy of her own mind, Ameena had pondered upon that statement. It was, she felt, something one might say about a person. Inside of those words, lived love.

'I want to know... more,' Ameena remarked casually one evening. They were at David's apartment. David had been playing the piano; Ameena had been lying on the sofa, eyes closed, listening to him play. 'I want to know... you,' she said, when he was done. 'What's your story, Piano-man?'

He smiled at the nickname; she had never called him that before. 'My story? You already know my story.'

She shook her head and slightly furrowed her brows. 'Nope, I know all these disconnected bits and pieces. I want to know the complete story. Specifically, about you and jazz. How you two fell in love. The love story of David Greenberg.'

David walked over to the sofa and sat down next to her. He lifted her legs gently, placed them on his lap and smiled as her frown lines dissipated. 'The love story of David Greenberg...' He chuckled. 'Okay, Miss artist-writer, I think I can give you a pretty good story. So, you know how I told you about my high school science teacher?'

'Who became a jazz teacher?'

'Yeah. Him. Jack. So, imagine... I'm fourteen, it's my freshman year of high school, and there's this jazz class.' David smiled at the memory.

David had signed up for the class without even having heard the music. His only goal at that time had been to take a class – just not his mother's – that would give him credit for knowing how to play the piano. And playing the piano, teenage David had thought privately, was something he was pretty good at.

'You're taking the jazz class?' one of his friends had asked him at the time.

'Yeah,' he had said airily.

'Why?' his friend had asked.

'Why not?' he had replied.

The friend had smirked. 'Taught by the science teacher?'

'He's a professional bass player,' David had replied, which was the truth but also born out of some strange sense of loyalty towards someone he didn't even know yet.

Now, he said to Ameena, 'My mother taught piano at my high school, classical piano, and my dad adored her – both her and her music – so that's the kind of music I grew up with, Bach, Haydn, sometimes a bit of opera. I had no idea what improvised music was. All I knew how to do, thanks to my mother, was to convert notes on a page to sound.' He laughed. 'Basically, I was clueless.'

Ameena smiled too, at her own imagined throwback image of an adolescent David – conscientious, earnest, a bit nerdy, eager to do whatever it took to shine at school – and felt a kind of unexpected tenderness. Oh Piano-man, she thought – a tiny, private, slightly shocking thought – I may just be falling in love with you a little bit. A little bit. *May. Just.*

'So, get this,' David continued, oblivious to her private thoughts, 'you know how the other day we were talking about life being about moments, right, how chance and moments and random luck can change one's life? Well, I had a couple of these moments of my own, and one of them was that the summer before this jazz class, we all received a cassette in the mail...'

It had come through the post, a simple black audio cassette along with a little typewritten note that read: 'Summer homework for jazz students: listen to this cassette.' And David (but naturally!) had done his homework. It would be his first ever encounter with jazz.

Resting his head back on the sofa now, he caressed the arch of her right foot with his thumb, marvelling at how soft her skin was there, underneath, on the soles of her feet, one shade paler than on top.

'There were six or eight tunes on that tape,' he mused. 'I didn't know a single one, I didn't know any of the musicians, I wasn't even sure sometimes what instrument I was listening to, but none of that mattered. Once I started listening, I just couldn't stop. Jazz got me.'

He shook his head, as though marvelling at his own childhood innocence, his ignorance, at how far he had come from there.

'When the summer was over and I walked into that jazz class for the first time, I still didn't know anything about anything, but the one thing I knew, without the shadow of a doubt, was that I had fallen in love with this music. The thing was, Ameena, I didn't have a music of my own. I was kind of ambivalent to what my friends were listening to, the pop music of the day, and I also wasn't deeply passionate about the classical music that I was playing, even though I was able to appreciate its beauty on some level. But to me, that was my mother's music, music that needed a kind of solitary discipline, a different type of emotion than what I was feeling... I couldn't get myself to think of it as my music.'

Ameena nodded. 'I know what you mean. Who you are, who you *want* to be, is so important, being able to discover that for yourself. Basic existentialist creed, right?'

'Right,' David replied. 'It's a kind of freedom. And that's how I felt, that my mother's music was hers. In a way, it was also my dad's. But it wasn't mine. But *this* music hit me, moved me in a way that no music had up until that time. In fact, I would say the only thing that had moved me in a similar kind of way by that age were books, some novels that I'd read, by Bellow I think, and Faulkner and a few others – I thought of them kinda as these "stylists" you know, of American literature – but from an artistic standpoint, this was my first experience of that feeling of communion with art. And I think that was enough to give me passion to at least try to figure out the puzzle of how this music is played. But I never thought I could become good enough to make a life from it.' He looked at her pointedly. 'I guess I still don't.'

Ameena matched his gaze, copper-brown meeting green-gold. 'But that's fine,' she said. 'Actually, I like that about you.'

'You like what about me?'

'That you are still writing your story.'

1.25

The only other item of sentimental value that Ameena took with her when she left home was one of her mother's hijabs, a square piece of silk charmeuse, striking in its pattern – black with pinks and yellows and blues and greens splashed over it in abstract shapes. Something about the pattern made Ameena think of it as a work of art, created not by a single artist but by a group of artists, each holding a paintbrush dipped in different-coloured paint, then walking up to the stark black background, turn by turn – and then, a small shake of the wrists, paint spurting from brush onto blackness, altering its essence with each successive shake, each amoebic blob of paint.

An expression of collectivity. Disobedience. A kind of anarchy.

A birthday present from her father.

Ameena's mother had worn it on the day, but never again.

It fell, her mother's birthday, in the prime of the English springtime, a joyful season of new beginnings and new life, when the whiteness of winter waned, and the colours appeared and deepened, and the blackbird hopped, and the first swallows were seen, and the air grew fragrant and the whisper of something wonderful lingered.

'It's too bright for me,' Zoya said when Ameena once asked her mother why she never wore it, 'but I didn't want to hurt his feelings.'

Ameena thought it was beautiful, the idea of it, the idea of art on a cloth. In truth, the hijab had probably been made by a machine, with little care or human intervention – one of a few hundred or so pieces made on an assembly line in some factory somewhere in northern China, and then sold on by Marks and Spencer for twenty times the price – but Ameena's brain wouldn't even allow her to imagine such a possibility, let alone process it. To her, it was art. A kind of aspirational thing. Plus, it smelled of her mother. And so, when it came time for Ameena to leave, she took it with her. She took it without telling her mother; the alternative seemed pointless.

On the day of her first meeting with Suzy Lipskis, Ameena pulled this out of her cupboard and wrapped it round her neck – a scarf to go with a simple sleeveless, knee-length black dress – partly for colour and partly for luck. She stood in front of the mirror and assessed her reflection – self-assured and composed, the antithesis, in fact, of the apprehension she felt inside. How little, she thought, how little we can know about someone else just from looking at them from the outside. And yet we do this all the time, make assumptions about people based on their clothes or their shoes or how they wear their hair – how confident they are, how successful, how happy, what kind of marriage they have…

She frowned. But then, equally, she thought, the irony of the converse; you could know someone for a lifetime and still not know them at all. That was true as well… You never truly know, she concluded, with other people, if you are dealing with them or their reflections.

She took one last look at herself in the mirror before she left, straightening the scarf, dismissing with efficiency the runaway twinge of longing she felt for her mother.

The art gallery was a chic, pristine space, located discreetly on the corner of two narrow cobblestoned streets. There was something about the structure that Ameena took to straight away. A former warehouse built of concrete, it seemed to her to have the right architectural bones that shaped the ambience of viewing art, a place with the capacity to exhibit the physical experiences that are often part and parcel of visual representation. Or, as the Chinese would say, she thought approvingly, it had good *chi*. The front door pushed open easily, but when Ameena stepped inside, there seemed to be nobody about. She waited hesitantly for a few minutes by the entrance, then decided to look around. Currently on display was the work of a painter who Ameena had never heard of before – his name sounded male, Greek? She shrugged. It almost didn't matter. In art, she felt the creator was always secondary to the work, or at least that was the Barthesian way in which she thought about her own work. *This* artist, she decided as she studied his work admiringly, seemed a master of that idea; the characters on his canvases were so alive, they appeared to be painting their own abstract versions of self.

She was struck by one of the pieces in particular – a gathering of people in evening wear doing a kind of ballroom dance in the middle of someone's living room, wooden chairs with velvet cushions stacked haphazardly on sofas and tables, right side up and upside down, seemingly moved hurriedly out of the way to create floor space – a sort of stage – for the dancers. So intently was she studying the brushstrokes, how the artist had so expertly captured the detail of the grain in the wood, the distinctive texture of the upholstery, the folds in the silk dresses of the women, that she hadn't realised she was being watched.

'Captivating, yes?' A woman's sonorous voice came from behind her, and she spun round immediately so they were standing facing each other. She could feel the other woman's eyes on her, taking her in, assessing her. What would she see, Ameena wondered – reflection or reality?

As for Suzy – the observable Suzy, that is – Ameena saw in her a small, neat woman with a mane of silver hair, bright red lipstick and black-rimmed glasses. She wore large diamond solitaires on her ears, a smart black and white jacket over a tailored black skirt and a long vintage Chanel pearl necklace that looped round her neck twice.

'Yes,' Ameena replied smiling, 'completely.'

'Shall we go to my office,' Suzy said brusquely, and it was a statement, Ameena realised, not a question. Ameena followed the older woman into a small room with glass walls that looked directly onto the gallery space – she's always watching, Ameena thought to herself, from her fishbowl. Suzy pointed to a chair and gestured for Ameena to sit while she perched herself neatly on the edge of the beautiful mahogany desk that Ameena guessed was some kind of priceless antique. Wordlessly, she flicked a key on her keyboard and the computer sprang to life.

Suzy's monitor had been turned at an angle so Ameena also had a clear view of it and when she saw the screen fill with images of her work, all her art that David had so meticulously photographed, she found herself colouring, embarrassed suddenly, ashamed even, as if not just her work, but she herself was on display. She wanted to look away, overcome with a kind of nausea as Suzy zoomed in on the images one by one, but of course she couldn't without making herself look ridiculous. This was the essence of art, she knew that, one of the rare times that one got consent – the permission – to take someone else's thoughts into the private space that contain your own. Still, she found the permeability of that idea unnerving. She cleared her throat nervously.

'Why watercolour?' Suzy asked without any introduction or pleasantries.

'Oh!' Ameena said, slightly startled by the question, though she wasn't sure why – it was, under the circumstances, a perfectly natural question, and yet, there was something about its tone or in the directness of Suzy's glance that unnerved her. 'I... I don't know... I guess it's what I started with and I just feel more comfortable with a water-based medium. I've experimented with oils, but I found myself coming back to water. I enjoy its fluidity of movement, its organic flow.'

'I don't like experiment. I like fulfilment,' Suzy remarked, almost to herself. Then: 'Do you consider yourself a figurative artist?'

'I don't think of myself as figurative, no.'

'But I do.' Suzy took off her glasses – she had brown eyes, sparkling with a kind of astute intelligence – and peered into the screen. 'In your work, it's quite clear.'

'Oh?' Ameena said again, feeling flustered. 'Is it?'

'Why do you deny where you clearly shine? Is there a reason you wouldn't want to be a figurative artist?'

Poised, yet forceful – questions that insisted upon an answer. A skill, Ameena thought admiringly.

'No, no,' she faltered, 'I guess... I guess I try to represent bodies in a more abstract and performance-based way. So, you see there is no literal presence of a figure, but... perhaps... well obviously, you see it... there is a strong sense of "someone" in my work.'

Suzy peered at her, even though Ameena had dropped her own gaze. Then the gallerist opened her mouth as if to say something, but paused and appeared to change her mind, and with her eyes now back on the images, she asked coolly, 'Is your work religious?'

'No.'

'Political?'

'Isn't everything?'

Suzy nodded.

'Either we see it, or we pretend that it doesn't exist,' Ameena said but Suzy chose to ignore the comment.

She swivelled the computer back towards herself and seemed to study the images very carefully and quietly, as if she was looking for something in them, and then she turned to Ameena and without any emotion or explanation, said in her faintly Russian-inflected accent: 'I offer you a solo show at my gallery this October.'

'Gosh!' Ameena exclaimed. 'Really? I mean...'

'It was George Orwell.'

'Sorry?'

'What you said. That it is political for art not to be political. George Orwell said that. We will be in contact. You know your way out?'

'I like her,' Suzy told David later that evening over the phone. 'Your girlfriend. Her work is... luminous.'

1.26

From the outside, it looked like a blind pig straight out of the 1920s, a tiny charcoal-coloured arch-top door set into a deep russet stucco wall, a small awning above and a blackboard outside on the sidewalk indicating that tickets were $20 for the night.

Ameena furrowed her brows.

'What?' David said, looking at her. She was wearing lipstick, a deep, ruby red, and she looked very beautiful, David thought, like a character from a novel, someone marvellous and mysterious, like Anna Karenina or someone.

'Nothing, I'm just thinking that it doesn't quite look like I expected...'

'Oh? Is that good or bad?'

'Good, good. It looks... scrummy.'

'Wait – *scrummy*?'

'Yeah! Like scrumptious. Tasty.'

David chuckled. 'You English people say the weirdest things. I'm not even going to ask you to explain that! Shall we go inside?'

He knocked on the door and nodded at the man who opened it, who nodded back at David and gave a quick, barely interested glance at Ameena before letting them in. The man wore a suit, dark glasses and a navy-blue Yankees hat. This, Ameena thought to herself, must have been exactly what it was like to enter a bar during Prohibition. Inside, there was a tiny square of foyer, which led immediately to a narrow flight of stairs going down below street level. Ameena held David's hand and followed him down to enter the club's subterranean main room, a dark, plush space, suffused with the smell of whisky and adorned with mirrors and velvet and black-and-white photographs of the jazz 'greats' placed somewhat haphazardly on its exposed brick walls. It struck Ameena immediately how tiny the whole place was, how intimate, like your grandma's living room.

'Illegal,' she said suddenly. 'That's the word I was looking for, in my head – illegal. Inside and out, it looks illegal.'

David laughed out loud. 'Well,' he replied, following her eyes as she looked around, '*this* might probably be as *legal* as you're going to get outside of New Orleans. There's no fooling around here, it's the real deal. Like love,' he said, cheekily, his dimples deepening. 'And by the way, speaking of love, I worked things out with the guys so I'm playing just the first set tonight. Usually I would play all three, then we'd jam a bit, then I'd stumble home way past your bedtime in a musically induced stupor of euphoria!'

'Oof! Sounds... sexy. I think I might be jealous! Think about it, I'll *never* know what it feels like to be in a musically induced stupor of euphoria!'

David laughed.

'Why?' Ameena said.

'Why, what?

'Why are you only playing one set tonight?'

'Why? To hang out with you of course. We can watch the rest together or we can leave if you're bored.'

Ameena shook her head and smiled. 'Well, Piano-man, I can already tell you that I'm not going to be bored!'

'Come on,' he said, taking her hand, 'let me introduce you.' He led her to a group of three guys standing towards the front of the room. They were all dressed, like David, in variations of the jacket-jeans-untucked-shirt combo, and one of the guys had a hat on. A hat, *and*, she noted with some amusement, glasses with distinctively bright cobalt blue frames. They looked up as David and Ameena approached, and she noticed the particular way in which the men greeted each other, a kind of warmth, inscrutable and marvellous – it was camaraderie of course, but it was also something else, she thought, something more.

'My boys,' David said, sweeping his arm in her direction, 'this here, all the way from Manchester, England, is my friend, Ameena...'

'Hello Ameena,' the three guys chorused.

'...who has never heard jazz before!' David finished, and as if on cue the three men dropped their jaws in mock horror.

'Wait, no,' Ameena protested, 'I *have* heard jazz before, we had this "jazzathon" thing at the pub at uni sometimes...'

'...And she's never heard jazz before,' they all said almost in unison, and Ameena laughed.

'But *Manchester*,' one of the guys mused, 'a city that believes in its music.'

'I know, but,' Ameena replied, visibly embarrassed, 'my family was diff— I guess we were never exposed to... culture as such.'

'Well, miss,' the guy with the hat grinned, tipping it in her direction, 'nothing like getting an untainted perspective! Let us know what you think later. Don't hold back now!' He winked.

'I won't,' she said, grateful for how generously he had circumvented any potential ignominy over the broad, nebulous subject of her upbringing. 'Love your glasses by the way. Very fashionable.'

'Think we're about ready to go on,' one of the other guys said, motioning to the stage.

'Be right up.' David nodded before turning to face Ameena.

'They seem so nice,' she whispered to David.

'All musicians are nice,' David said, pulling her close to him, 'especially this one.' He kissed her then with a kind of unusual possessiveness, and then stepped back. 'Time to play. See you from up there, enjoy it.'

'Good luck,' Ameena said, and she felt moved by the intensity of the kiss, and by his reluctance to let her go and by what she thought she saw in his eyes, a certain conviction and with it... was it... affirmation? She couldn't be sure. Stemming from... what? Was it... it had to be... she felt, from allowing her access to this part of his life and to himself, for surely in bringing her here, he was expressing the desire to experience a kind of shared joy together with her, and she was surprised by how she felt by all this, by his willingness to offer himself up in this way – a kind of giddy, *stupid* pleasure.

Gosh Ameena, get a grip, she rebuked herself, stop behaving like a smitten teenager! She turned away from the stage and glanced around the room. The club had filled up completely with more bodies than chairs and she noticed that people who hadn't found a seat were standing towards the back of the room, leaning against walls, happy just to be there. The patrons were mostly couples or small groups of threes and fours, but she realised there were also a sizeable number of people seemingly on their own – true aficionados, she guessed – choosing to spend their evening alone, and yet not alone, listening and lingering to the great vibes they admired. David had found her a seat near the front of the room and a few minutes later when it was time, she sat down and clapped with everyone else, as the musicians took their places.

After that, she remembers what she remembers, the rest is lost in a kind of dreamlike haze. It starts with the lights, the shadows shift, the last of the claps fade, the musicians nod to a beat they haven't yet played, and the quartet begins to perform. David is on the piano, accompanied by the three men she has just met, one on the drums, one on string bass and the man with the hat, his eyes now half-closed, on tenor saxophone. But then, as soon as they start to play, the individuals melt away and four become one, then one becomes none, and all that is left is the music.

Almost instantly, the little room is transformed.

The quartet seem to travel together to some other place, but what is incredible – what Ameena can't explain – is how, in doing so, they take the room with them. Because suddenly the music is inside the room and the room is inside the music, bodies cocooned within the notes of this collective voice, intimate and compelling and metamorphic. It's as if they've made a kind of secret pact, a wordless collaboration: carry them away, they have decided implicitly among themselves – we are going to carry them away.

And Ameena is carried away.

She sits up straighter, leans forward, elbows on the table, fingers folded under her chin, rapt, as they pass solos around in what appears to be a completely arbitrary sequence. And yet there is unbelievable order and it works so beautifully, flowing with ease from one to the other, each voice speaking alone, yet drawing strength and a kind of love from the others, creating, exploring, supporting, evoking melancholy and exuberance and a kind of deep nostalgia all at once.

The room bursts into loud, appreciative applause. Ameena finds herself feeling humbled by it, and even a little bit envious, of the ability to alter the character of a room like that, to win over strangers in this way. Jazz, she thinks as she looks at the four of them, demands to be listened to.

She begins to understand then, not fully, just a glimmer, the sentiment with which the musicians greeted each other earlier. The intimacy of the wrap-the-thumbs clasped handshake, and the hug and the pat on the back, held a kind of shared pride in themselves and of each other and for their art – for why they were there, and what they were there to do. They are jazzmen – so beautiful, she thinks, the making of that identity – and the jazz she is listening to is what the four of them create together in the moment, what they bring to it, take from it, discover inside of it. An act of homage, if ever such a thing existed.

Ameena thinks of David then, of his ambition, and as she does, she notices that there are no stands on that stage or sheet music as there had been in the cello concert. It seems impossible to her, the very mechanics of it, and she makes a mental note to ask him how this is even done, this kind of extemporaneous performance, unwritten, unrehearsed, just *felt*, driven by some inner mechanism that thrills to the idea of creative exploration. And if that's the case, then she realises that he is already a composer, that they all are, in this remarkable gift they possess of spontaneously scoring music together.

He had looked up at her a few times even as he was playing, their eyes meeting in split seconds of closeness, but for the rest of the time, she knows he isn't really in the room at all, he is somewhere else, face cast in some mysterious expression, body rocking forwards and back, lost inside the music.

And then she's tapping her foot to the beat, as if it has entered her body also, found a way in through her brain and then flowed downwards to her feet and then it needs to be released, like a sort of energy, only it is no longer exactly as it had entered her body, but a transformed version of it, as if it has been changed by her, by her sensibility, changed by each person present in that room at that moment in time. This energy, she thinks, is what drives the music forward, like a kind of hope that drives us all forward, keeps us excited, greedy for more – more music, more time, more freedom, more life.

'Well?' David asked after.

'Unbelievable,' she said, shaking her head.

'Enjoyed it?'

'I loved it. I absolutely loved it. It was amazing.'

He smiled. 'I'm thrilled you enjoyed it. Well, now you know everything about me!' He looked around the room. 'This is basically what I do, what I love to do. The day job pays the bills and the night job fuels a passion.'

'Promise you'll never stop. Never ever.'

'Ha! Brought you over to the dark side already, have I?'

'Yes, in the first five seconds! I'm being serious though. This is *you*. It's what you're meant to do. Anyone can see that. And...'

'And?'

'And people eventually end up doing what they're meant to do. Well, at least that's what I believe. It takes some people a lifetime to figure out what that is. So, if you've found it already, I hope you never stop.' She shrugged.

David cocked his head slightly, then nodded. 'I like that idea, that people eventually end up doing what they're meant to do. It's a nice thought. Though you know, I'm not sure I *could* ever stop. It's like a hunger, an itch. Life without music seems almost too unbearable to contemplate.' He reached for her hand and held it, caressing the top of her palm with his thumb. 'But the main thing,' he said, 'is that you enjoyed yourself.'

'Hey,' she said suddenly, 'can I ask you something? I'm sorry if it's ignorant of me.'

'Yes of course, don't be silly.'

'So, you're playing, and there's the melody, right, and then under that, the beat. So, as a listener, I find the beat and then I hold it and I start to listen for it, but then it goes off, like I'm *here* in this one place, and then all of a sudden, I'm somewhere else. Why does it go off-beat like that?'

'Syncopation?'

'Oopsie!'

'What?'

'Not another technical term! Remember I'm the uncultured one who has never heard jazz before, never listened to an orchestra before... just like you said, the original vestal virgin if ever there was one!'

His face fell instantly. 'Ameena, I never meant it like that. I don't think of you as uncultured at all.'

But she only laughed. 'I'm pulling your leg, silly. I'm English. Every time we open our mouths, we're trying our damnedest to be funny.'

But David still looked so sorrowful that Ameena reached across and kissed him quickly on the cheek. 'I'm joking. I promise.'

She nodded as she saw the muscles on his face ease. 'I promise,' she said again with her most convincing solemn face. Then she lowered her voice conspiratorially. 'In fact, don't tell anyone but as of the last count, I have eleven unclaimed children of various ages scattered all over the British Isles.'

'Okay shut up,' he said jokingly, and his dimple gradually reappeared in a way that Ameena found incredibly attractive, 'and listen to me.'

'Listening!'

'So, in very simple terms, syncopation is a disruption of the regular flow of rhythm, a kind of deliberate shifting of the beat, so when I play, I stress the "upbeats", and to the listener, the melody feels "off" and kind of swinging – just like you said.'

'Yes, I wasn't expecting it – it threw me off.'

He shook his head. 'No, it threw you *on*!'

He stood up then and motioned towards the piano. 'Here,' he said, 'let me show you. It's easier if I just demonstrate. Walk with me to the piano for a second. Don't worry, no one will care.'

They walked to the stage and David sat down at the piano with a kind of easy elegance, Ameena noticed, a beauty of line, like it belonged there, his body, on that piano bench.

'Listen,' he said. He played a tune. 'This is Mozart.' He stopped and looked up at her, then he closed his eyes. 'Now listen. This is Thelonious Monk.' A few minutes later, he lifted his fingers off the piano and opened his eyes. 'You hear the difference?'

She smiled. 'Yes, you're right, that second tune threw me *on*!'

'Yup,' David said. 'Syncopation in music is kind of like a stylistic device in literature – humour or a twist – it lifts the writing, makes it more colourful, more imaginative. Similar kind of thing. When the rhythm gets loose, it adds depth and brightness to the music, makes it come alive. That's why jazz is so great, and so playful. And so *human* in a way, if you consider that humans are inherently unpredictable and quirky!'

'And that comes from?'

'Like its genesis, you wanna know?'

'Yeah! I'm interested.'

David laughed. 'Ameena, this can get very detailed, and I don't think you want a history lesson, but the quick answer is that syncopation came from Africa. Mainly West Africa... Senegambia, Benin, Cameroon, the Congo. And then, for historical reasons it developed in the Caribbean... Haiti, Cuba... and also simultaneously in Brazil. So, in the jazz idiom, syncopation is deep-rooted in African music, partly derived from Afro-Caribbean dance rhythms, partly from African drumming. When we go home tonight, remind me, and we can listen to some West African drummers, you'll be able to hear it rhythmically straight away. *Those* musicians might improvise for hours on end making subtle changes to the accents, and the enormous varieties of syncopation are the entire point – the thing that makes your body move and your mind enter trance.'

'So, then you'd hear syncopation in non-jazz, African-influenced music too, right?'

'Right. You'd hear it in Caribbean music... hip hop, rap... yeah, basically, all African-rooted musics... R'n'B, Michael Jackson, Stevie Wonder, soul. And in jazz, because it's improvised, and because for better or worse it's always trying to be "hip", there's syncopation going on literally every second.'

Ameena nodded. She studied David's face, how his eyebrows actually jumped as he spoke, a physical demonstration of passion, if such a thing existed.

And he looked at her, listening to him the way she was, her brown eyes wide with genuine curiosity and he felt a sudden sense of fulfilment – the joy of loving someone who gets why you love what you love.

'You should teach...' she said warmly, as they made their way back to the table together, 'you're amazing. You explain it so well.'

'It's not me. It's the music.'

Ameena nodded. 'I understand. It's so rich and varied, the story of this music... so beautiful.' She smiled then and it was disarming, both her smile and the honesty of what she said next. 'I didn't know any of that, and I bet that's not even scratching the surface. I guess it's what makes you a jazz musician, an appreciation for the history of something beyond just its practice.'

He shrugged one shoulder in that non-committal way she had learned he did when he didn't quite agree with you. 'I'm not exactly going to dispute that, but I'm not sure, you know, I don't feel like I'm at that place yet, to be able to claim true jazz musicianship status.'

She frowned. 'Which is what, exactly?'

He sighed. 'It's complicated. In music circles, we talk about soul – what kind of soul do you need to have to play jazz?'

'What kind of soul do you need to have... I love that.'

He stood up. 'I'm sorry,' he said, 'I started off saying I didn't want to give you a history lesson and I think that's exactly what I've done. Anyway, they're about to start the second set and you're supposed to say, "That handsome, dashing guy up there on the piano" – my good buddy Aaron, by the way – "is nowhere near as handsome and dashing as you, David, or as talented or gifted or comes even close to possessing enough soul to explain what it means to syncopate a rhythm..." Can I get you another drink?'

'David...?'

'Yeah?'

'I want to get out of here.'

'Are you bored?'

'No. I want to syncopate with your jazz soul.'

1.27

On an ordinary Wednesday morning at approximately 10am, a scene was unfolding in the conference room of Ameena's workplace:

'What *kind* of name is Ameena Hamid? What *kind* of question is that, Bob?' Whitney Kym was speaking across the table to Bob Hunter, Press Relations Officer for a major international fashion house. Her thin brows were so tightly drawn they seemed almost joined together in one neat, perfectly straight line.

Bob was there to discuss the specifics of an exclusive awarded to the magazine, which would cover a preview of their upcoming fall line. A few minutes earlier, Whitney had explained that given the high-profile nature of the project, she had given the brief to one of her most skilled and savvy writers.

'What's her name?' Bob had asked casually, biting into his oatmeal raisin cookie.

'Ameena Hamid,' Whitney had replied.

And Bob Hunter had spat at least a few of the raisins out.

'What kind of name is Ameena Hamid?' he had asked.

And Whitney had responded with her displeasure drawn on her forehead. And thrown the question back at him.

Slowly, Bob reached for a napkin while he collected his thoughts.

'It's just that, you know,' he said, gathering the now-moist cookie crumbs with his index finger and carefully guiding them into the mouth of the napkin that he had folded into a kind of pyramidical receptacle, 'people read you. People read *you* and buy *us*. That's the point.'

'Yes.' Whitney nodded. 'With you so far.'

'So...'

'Yes?'

'I don't want people to read you and *not* buy us. See?'

'No, actually. I do not see.'

'Well, I'll speak plainly then. The thing is, with it being written by someone so distinctly Moslem-sounding...'

'Jesus, Bob.'

'Sorry Whitney, but fashion, as you of all people know, is about perception and positioning. I mean, we are after all, the House of— well, you know who we are, brandishing the name about would be crass. The point is that we cater to, shall we say, a more *discerning* segment of society.'

'How come you don't have a problem with me?'

'Well, you run the place for starters, secondly when is the last time China attacked America on American soil and thirdly, you went to Stanford, your English is better than mine.'

'Oh, for fuck's sake, Bob, my grandparents were Korean.' Whitney tilted her head and nodded a few times. Then, with her head still tilted and a strange glint in her eyes, she said, 'You're worried about her *grammar*?'

'Well, yes, there's that. Partly. I mean, at the very least I was hoping you'd have given it to someone for whom English isn't a foreign language.'

Whitney smiled and reached for the phone in the middle of the table, pressed a button and spoke directly into the intercom. 'Ameena, can you come in here for a second please? The conference room, yes.'

Bob Hunter's face registered pure panic. His eyes grew wide, magnifying both the quantity and the quality of the lines that framed them like rays. White faces age so horribly, Whitney thought to herself, divine karma, this business of looking seventy when you're fifty.

'Uh, Whitney, what are you doing?' Bob was saying nervously.

'Dispelling your worries. Mostly.'

'Look, please, that's not necessary. I'm sure we can sort this out... between us, I mean. We are friends, after all, I've known you now, what, ten years...'

But Ameena was already at the door and Whitney motioned for her to come in.

'Ameena,' she said smoothly, 'Bob here is worried that his fall preview brief might be too much for you to handle.'

Ameena smiled. 'I assure you Mr Hunter, you have absolutely nothing to worry about. I've already started thinking about how we can play with the writing in a way that sets you instantly apart from everybody else in the space. The piece will be as sophisticated and unique as your collection.'

A somewhat shell-shocked Bob looked up at Ameena, then at Whitney and then back to Ameena again.

'You're... uh... you're English?'

'Yup,' Ameena said, her smile intact, 'like the language.'

On the same Wednesday, at evening rush hour, a scene was unfolding on the curb off the Princess Parkway–Wilbraham Road junction in Manchester:

Yusuf scratched his beard with his left hand; his right hand was steadily on the wheel. He was driving Kareem home from university where, unbeknownst to Zoya, he had been summoned to 'have a chat' with his son's academic advisor.

'The fact of the matter is, Mr Hamid,' the advisor had started to say... he pronounced the name HAM-ID like the cut of pork, followed by a short, staccato 'id', a particularly ironic Anglicism of his last name, Yusuf had always thought... 'The fact of the matter, as it were, is that it is perhaps the prerogative of young people to rally around a cause they believe in, it gives them a sense of purpose, you see – a *narrative*, so to speak. And Palestine is clearly a very important narrative for him, uh, for you all. So, I am not, as it were, entirely *un*sympathetic.

'However,' he continued, in that typically sheepish manner that English people seemed to have about them when delivering unwelcome news, 'in my position, I am forced, you see, to draw a line between the goodness of defending one's politics and having it, so to speak, dominate every minute of one's university life. Which, I'm afraid, is exactly what is happening with Kareem. He's so busy organising rallies, he has no time to turn up to class. Here is, as it were, a record of his attendance this term. You can see, of course, for yourself that...'

So preoccupied was Yusuf by this retelling of his son's latest antics that he barely registered when directly in front of him, out of nowhere, some traffic lights appeared and – a kind of double whammy – they were coloured red. Triple whammy then, when a car magicked itself out of an invisible cross road and turned right. Right, that is, onto their path.

Yusuf missed him by a whisker.

After that, everything seemed to happen very quickly. A flash of blue steel from the corner of his eye. The beep of a car horn. The screech of tyres. An invasion of the senses. Yusuf blinked.

Then he noticed the blue steel – goodness! It was a car! – pulling out in front of them, blocking their way, forcing them to veer off the road, onto the curb, and stop.

'Shit,' Kareem said, 'shit, shit, shit.'

'Oh,' Yusuf added, squinting at his son sitting next to him.

One hand, he kept on the wheel. With his free hand, he grasped at the space between them, searching for something: courage, his driver's licence, a breath-saving mint, legitimacy, the Koran, Zoya's hand, or heart, or his own. Finally, he settled for the parking brake, pulled it up with visible effort, then sighed.

Slowly, he got out from his side, shut the car door behind him carefully and walked to the front of the car. Rapidly, Kareem got out from his side, slammed his door and ran to the front of the car, so father and son arrived clockwise and anticlockwise respectively, to stand side by side. A stocky man with the body of a boxer and the face of a particularly pugnacious pug emerged from the blue steel.

'I didn't hit you, did I?' Yusuf asked anxiously.

'No...' began the man.

Yusuf let out a loud sigh of relief.

'But...'

'But what?' Kareem said.

'You...'

'You what?' Kareem said.

'Could've,' the man finished smugly.

'Oh, for FUCK—' Kareem rolled his eyes and his entire head with it.

'Yes, yes,' Yusuf interjected before Kareem could get any more in. 'I am very sorry. I should not have taken that light. Very sorry.'

'Then it's only my quick reflexes that saved the day, yeah?' the man said belligerently.

You couldn't save your cock from your fly, mate, Kareem thought.

'Lucky for all of us then, innit,' Kareem said sarcastically, 'your quick reflexes? Now, seeing as my dad's apologised already and if there's no harm done, maybe we can all just get on our way.'

The man's eyes narrowed suspiciously. '...'Ang on a forking minute, did you two swap places? Wuz that your son that wuz doing the driving?'

'Sorry?' Yusuf blinked for a second time, genuinely baffled by this Holmesian turn of events.

'Wuz that your son that wuz doing the forking driving, I said,' the man repeated, slowly and loudly like one would address a particularly obtuse child.

'Was my son...? No. Certainly not. Why would you think my son was driving?'

'Fork I know, gov? Maybe you wuz trying to protect 'im? Thinking maybe I'd take pity on you, being as you are, a man of some years, and let the two've you go, wiv no trouble from the coppers.'

'Pity? Trouble? Sir, I really don't understand. It was myself driving, I assure you.'

'Why the fork did you *both* get outta the car then?'

'Are you fucking kidd—' Kareem started to say.

Yusuf touched his son's shoulder to stop him and addressed the man directly. 'I am sorry, but I don't know what explanation I can provide for that. But what, please, would be the connec—'

'Ah-hah! No explanation. I knew it! When someone does sommink with no explanation, it's fishy, I say.' He looked at Kareem carefully. 'All you young Pakis are all the same. *Fundamental*, that's what you are. *Radical*. I mean no tits and no drink'll do that to anyone, really. But forkit, least you can do is show some forking respect for the rules and regulations of the country that's bin generous enough to take you in, yeah?'

'Areyoufuckingkiddingme?' Kareem said in one breath, his only chance, he knew, of ever finishing the sentence.

'Kareem,' Yusuf said firmly, 'I will handle this please.' He turned to the man. 'I think you will agree, sir, that all this profanity, *including* from my son' – at this point Yusuf looked sharply at Kareem – 'seems quite unnecessary. The car is not damaged, it has not even been touched.'

'But it could've bin? Yeah? Yeah? It could've, yeah?'

Yusuf sighed. 'Once again,' he said in a voice that sounded very exhausted, 'I am very sorry for the inconvenience I have caused your good self, but I assure you, it was not my son driving, but myself. Now, given it is quite late in the day and my son and I are delayed for our evening prayers, we will take our leave. I wish you a pleasant evening.'

Without waiting for a response, Yusuf turned round slowly and got into the car. Kareem reluctantly followed.

'Effing racist cunt,' Kareem said promptly as he watched the pug-faced man get into his own car – with equal reluctance it seemed – and slowly drive off.

'Kareem,' Yusuf said sternly, 'you will watch your tongue please. I am still your father.'

'My tongue? Watch *my* tongue?' Kareem said, yanking at his seatbelt and scowling. 'Abba, he insulted you! He accused us both of lying! He called me a terrorist! And best of all, nothing happened to his car!'

Yusuf sank deeper into the driver's seat gratefully, allowing his body to go completely limp. At least his seat was dependable, he thought, offering the resistance he expected, unlike everything else that seemed to be crumbling away beneath him. He stole a glance at his son, at the young, handsome face, the aquiline nose, the determined jaw that was clenched at the moment. Sometimes he wondered if Kareem wished for a different father. Someone unyielding and indestructible. Someone he could one day hope to become. A hero, basically.

But it was different, Yusuf knew, their specific situation. How to explain? His responsibilities were different. *He* had chosen this life; Kareem had simply been born into it. Two completely different things, those.

Not everyone has the luxury to don a cape. Some of us need to keep our feet planted firmly on earth so others can fly.

To that end, he said: 'I know, Kareem, but the fault was mine, and in situations like this, it's best to dissipate the situation, not aggravate it.'

Kareem still held the unfastened seatbelt in his hands. This he now let go and it whooshed back into place with a loud snap. He rotated his body so that he was now leaning against the car door, looking directly at his father with complete derision.

'In situations like this? Where we are accused of crimes we didn't commit because we happen to be brown and breathing?' he said.

Yusuf sighed. 'It is more complicated than that Kareem, you know that very well. Anyway, he didn't call you a terrorist.'

Kareem shook his head, a tiny movement. He spoke slowly and although his tone was measured, Yusuf realised, with some pain, that there could not have been a more scathing indictment of him than the words that came next.

'If it's complicated, Abba, it's because people like you don't stand up to people like them.'

There was a moment's pause, heavy, saturated with unspoken fears.

Yusuf felt disoriented, like he was losing the basic sense of his own self, like every rational mechanism in his brain had ground to a halt. Because the way in which he tried to fit into the world, the only way he had ever known, had finally been exposed – just in those words uttered by his only son – for the colossal fraud that it was.

He felt a sudden constriction in his chest.

Was this what they called a panic attack?

Then Kareem said, 'And why were you calling him sir?'

'It was the polite thing to do,' Yusuf said almost inaudibly.

'Sir? Seriously, *sir*? *Saala behnchod*, that's what he was. If this happened in Pakistan, they would have lynched him.'

As if to put force behind his words, Kareem slapped the dashboard violently with his right hand, causing his father's body to involuntarily jump. Both the action and the reaction seemed to provide a kind of release to the compressed tension inside the car.

Something in Yusuf's mind snapped back into place. He sat up straight and adjusted his rear-view mirror. He had allowed the situation to slip, but he was still the driver. He put his hands firmly on the wheel.

'But this is not Pakistan, Kareem. This is England,' he explained with a kind of simple finality. 'You were born here. Right here, in

Manchester, not in Lahore. You are as English as that man was. Just a better breed of English, I hope.'

He turned on the ignition then, very slowly, as much for signalling an end to the conversation as for getting out of there.

Kareem turned back round to face the road. Calmly and carefully, he put his seatbelt on and straightened his long legs out in front of him. There was something frightening about the extreme calmness of the gesture.

'I am Pakistani, Dad,' he said quietly. 'And unlike you, I am not ashamed to say it.'

On that same Wednesday, at approximately 6.30pm, a scene was unfolding in a little neighbourhood Vietnamese in New York City:

'I need this today,' Ameena was saying to David, about the glass of Merlot in her hands. 'I feel spent. Something weird happened at work this morning.'

'Oh yeah, tell me?'

'I will, but you said you wanted to tell me something about your day. You go first.'

'Oh, that.' David smiled. 'It's nothing exciting, just that Hershel saw your picture on my desk and asked if you were a Bollywood actress.'

'You have a picture of me on your desk?'

'Yeah. Why? Is that a bit creepy?'

'No, no, it's sweet... it's just... I mean I don't have a picture of *you* on *my* desk... Bollywood actress, my God, I don't know if that's a compliment or an insult!'

David laughed. 'I think he was just trying to say he thought you were attractive. In a typically Hershel way, I mean.'

Ameena picked up the restaurant menu and started to study it intently. 'Well, I hope you corrected him,' she said, and then tapped the cover of the menu with her fingernail. 'This thing is like ten pages long, it's a book.'

'Of course, I said you're a Pakistani writer.'

'Oh,' she said, without looking up.

'And artist.'

'Oh,' she repeated blankly.

'What?'

'Nothing,' she said, closing the menu shut.

'What?'

'Nothing. Too many options on this thing, it's exhausting.'

'Uh-oh, have I upset you? You weren't actually a Bollywood actress, were you?'

'No.'

'But as a little girl, you dreamed of being one!'

'No! Shut up!'

'Okay, okay, I was just kidding. So, what happened at work?'

'Never mind, it's boring, can you order please? Just order whatever, I'm ravenous.'

On that same Wednesday, at approximately 8pm, a scene was unfolding in the split-level flat on Chapel Road:

In a rare moment of restfulness, Zoya was sitting by the window, waiting for Yusuf and Kareem to return.

She was looking at the moon.

It was full and round that night, sitting high in the night sky like a king on his throne, casting his silver light over his land, spilling into the room, illuminating suddenly, in the deepest recesses of Zoya's mind, a certain truth.

How – this was the truth – could two children from the same parents, who shared the same blood, who grew up beneath the same roof, under the same circumstances, subjected to the same influences, turn out to be so different!

So different, in fact, that they had decided, almost as a laugh, to be everything that the other was not. One had picked one extreme, the other had picked another, and in doing so, both had demonstrated a failure to embrace what she and Yusuf had hoped to give them – a kind of middle way. This *was* a failure, surely, was it not? Or was it a failure on *her* part – and on Yusuf's, mustn't forget Yusuf's role here – to expect this of them in the first place, this kind of duality?

For a fleeting moment, Zoya empathised with her British-Pakistani children. Or was it her Pakistani-British children?

How can you be two things, when the two things you're meant to be are so far apart? Impossible! Unnatural!

No wonder they had rebelled. And in opposite ways.

Which one would the world prove wrong? Zoya wondered, for the world, she knew, is very quick to prove people wrong. Which one would win? And if one of her children won, would it mean that the other would lose?

Then a thought came to her, and a tiny ripple of fear travelled up her spine, stopping at the atlas of her neck.

But what happens, she thought, if they both lose? What will happen then?

improvising with love

Basically, and from time immemorial, we are accustomed to lying. Or to put it more virtuously and hypocritically, in short, more pleasantly: one is much more of an artist than one knows.

Friedrich Nietzsche

2.1

The next day, the rain came.

The city blackened and groaned, and the lightning split the sky above it into blocks, like giant pieces of a jigsaw puzzle that shifted and moved and joined back together again.

There was a strange faltering lightness to the darkness, a kind of suffused glow, but people still turned on their lamps and apartment windows shone like they would at night-time, even in the middle of a Saturday morning.

Ameena sat in her bedroom with the lights on and watched the rain fall, beating down steadily on the flat, tarmacked rooftops of the buildings outside. Below her at street level, the glare of headlights, the impatient blaring of horns as the traffic slowed and stalled.

How strange all the people looked, she thought as she peered down from her window, beneath the multicoloured tops of open umbrellas that obscured faces, bodies, revealing only legs, feet, so many sets of feet hopping over puddles, dancing a jig.

And then she thought how strange the rain was in this busy, impatient city, how something so basic and natural seemed to bring everything to a standstill. And how strange that at home, where it rained all the time, rain was just rain, a kind of way of life, and nobody stopped doing things because of the rain. 'Unless you're made of ice, you don't have to worry,' her father would tell them when she and Kareem would moan about the rain. 'Go out and do what you need to, you won't melt!'

And then when she thought of her father, she thought how strange it was that neither he nor her mother nor her brother ever called or wrote to ask how she was, but then, she had to admit, neither did she, only very rarely, and on the few occasions that she did write, she would get a polite reply, usually very promptly, more often than not from her brother, saying that everyone at home was okay and everyone at home hoped she was too, and she would hear it in his tone, inside the neutral typeface of the email message, all that buried hurt and bitterness, as if they were still unable to understand why she had left, and had still not forgiven her for leaving and, as if in the very act of leaving, she had betrayed not only them, but something bigger that they stood for.

And then she thought of David and how strange it was that his parents were both dead, buried somewhere under the earth of Rhode Island, side by side, their headstones turned towards the sea, and how he couldn't speak to them even if he wanted to.

And how strange that he had no idea where his brother was – how could you not know where your own brother is? How strange, she thought, that you could play together as children, as best friends, under the same roof, and then become strangers.

And how strange that all these situations that seemed to jar so strongly, that seemed to sit beside each other with such unease, could become at the same time so normalised.

And David, she thought with a faint touch of anxiety, her and David – how strange that they had only just met and yet already, even in this short time, she couldn't imagine him not being in her life. Not 'couldn't'. That was melodramatic. 'Didn't like to' – better. She *didn't like to* imagine him not being in her life. But how? How does that even happen? How does someone just cross your path one minute and become almost indispensable the next? And he? Did he feel the same way? The truth was that Ameena had never thought of herself as particularly clever or talented, or even pretty... while David...

She sighed to herself. David received a lot of female attention, she knew that. She could see it at the jazz clubs after he had finished playing, the groups of giggling girls falling over themselves to speak to him. 'Ooooh that was soooo gooood,' they'd say, making pouty lips and swooning eyes, 'I just *love* your music.' She'd asked one time, randomly, about exes, the women in his life. It was a list. He'd been honest, something he neither hid nor bragged about. She'd listened with a polite smile, pretending not to care. But she never asked again.

Now she wondered if she was on the list. Woman number whatever. 'Friend', he'd said when he had introduced her to his fellow musicians that night. Not 'girlfriend'. Just 'friend'. Funny, she hadn't thought twice about it then; now his use of this non-possessive common noun grated on her. Was she just another woman in his life? Was she the only woman in his life? Were they lovers? Did *he* consider them to be lovers? She thought so, but then again, you never really know what someone else is thinking.

She felt a tiny, terrifying twinge of fear. Not just for herself, but for the two of them, because – and she truly believed this – without relationships, you have no stories.

And so Ameena, being Ameena, picked up her phone and called him. 'Hey,' she said when he answered.

'Hey you!' David said, and she brightened immediately because she could hear it in his voice, how it pleased him to hear from her.

'What are you doing?' she asked.

'Nothing at all. What can you do in this weather... it's like Armageddon!'

'Shall we do something?'

'Like?'

'Shall we go for brunch and eat pancakes filled with lots of fat American blueberries?'

'Ameena, it's pouring!'

'I know! And it's making me restless. I thought I'd work on a painting that I started the other day – I've got to texturise it with salt and Peggy's rice and stuff,' she sighed, 'but it's all too much faff for a day like this.'

'Faff?'

'Ohhh. Let's see. Drama?'

'Faff.'

'Yeah. Faff. And I'm not feeling faffy. I'm feeling blueberry pancakes. With you!'

He laughed, and she felt the familiar shudder in her body at the sound of him, she pictured the small round of his Adam's apple moving in his throat as he spoke, she wondered if he had shaved yet that morning or if his cheeks carried the rough, rugged prickle of a day-old stubble. 'Do you want to wait a bit for the rain to stop?' he was saying, and she found herself shaking her head, feeling her own impatience stamping its tiny feet inside her. No, she didn't want to wait. She didn't want the rain to stop. She just wanted to see him. But she didn't want to tell him that.

So, she said what came easiest to her, the thing that was most familiar, because it is easy sometimes, to confuse what's familiar with what is normal. 'In Manchester,' she said, 'if we waited for the rain to stop, we'd be waiting our whole lives. We're not going to melt, let's go.'

Ten minutes later, in raincoats and umbrellas, they met at the diner round the corner from David's building, its 1950s-style neon light flashing cheerfully, despite the gloom of the day.

They laughed when they saw each other, their raincoats stuck to their clothes, the rain dripping from their hair despite all their gear, and the bell above the diner's door chimed ding-dong as David held the door open for her.

Inside there were only a smattering of people, determined to brave the weather, and they looked up and nodded purposefully at David and Ameena as they entered, as if they were all comrades in arms, who kept each other going when things were hard.

'Thanks for coming,' Ameena said, once they'd sat down. 'I'm sorry I dragged you out in this.'

'Anything to see you,' he said, and she averted her gaze.

For a few minutes they sat like that in silence, considering each other, and Ameena noticed that he hadn't, in fact, shaved, and that his face looked handsome and masculine, and she wondered, once again, how anyone could possibly be so beautiful, and she wondered also how she should respond, if she should respond at all, if she should tell him that she felt the same way too, that he had taken the words out of her mouth. Or if she should say something else. Or nothing at all.

'Oooh, coffee,' she exclaimed gratefully as the pot arrived. 'Hot and unlimited. Only in America.' She took a long, deep breath, inhaling the warm, rich aroma. 'Worth dragging you out for, no?'

'You do know,' he said nonchalantly, pouring coffee into her mug, 'that I'm in love with you, don't you?'

And as the stack of pancakes appeared before them, steam coming off the top in long lazy swirls, and as David and Ameena picked up their forks and started to eat from the same plate and Ameena felt the burst of sweetness inside her mouth as she bit into a fat American blueberry, and outside the rain came down in torrents, she found a happiness that felt almost dizzying, for if there is a more foolishly intoxicating feeling in the world than loving, it is in being loved.

And in that way the various strangenesses of the morning melted – like ice – into nothingness.

2.2

Later that same evening, David stood on the roof terrace of his building, he stood there alone, resisting the pull of a smoke. Just one drag. One long, single, tantalising drag. But this is the thing – our experiences shape us; they either give us faith or they take it away. He had vowed not to touch the stuff and he hasn't, and he won't start now.

The rain had let up, but the sky was still grey and there was no moon yet and no stars, but there was a breeze that blew up there on the top of the roof, and the breeze was cold, but still he stood there, in the open where there was nothing to shield him from the breeze. Or his own thoughts. He thought of the happiness that Ameena brought to his life. He thought of her impulsiveness, and the sudden force of her laughter, and how she reached for him, sometimes, at night, and enveloped him with her body. He thought of these things with fondness and tenderness. And then he thought of other times, different times, times that had gone by. And he contrasted these two times, this present time when he feels the need for Ameena... her companionship, her physical presence, her curiosity, her conversation... and those other times, when he had felt the threat of human connection and moved away, distanced himself from the people in his life, from closeness and feeling and touch. And words... even from words, from language, for as much as David respected the language of words, he knew that there are times when language fails us, when words are not enough, and that in each of our lives, there come these times...

Sometimes.

*

1. There's this time when the brothers are walking home from school.

'Let's go the long way,' Abe says, taking out a cigarette from his pocket.

'When did *you* start smoking?' David asks, adjusting the guitar on his back.

'This morning. C'mon.'

They walk through the woods, weaving their way in between the tall, dark green pines, sunlight streaming through the whorls of horizontal branches, shadows dancing on the floor, the air smelling fresh and new and righteously clean. It is so peaceful here, David thinks.

'Did you steal one of Mom's?' David asks, kicking a stone with his foot, then watching it roll forward and stop, before kicking it again.

When Abe doesn't reply, he says, 'She's gonna kill you.'

'What, before they kill her?' his brother quips with the cocky invincibility of a young person.

It is then that they hear it. It's a strange sound, long and plaintive, a cry, not human. It cuts through the trees and into the still air. They look at each other, then they start to sprint in the direction of the sound, the crunch of the gravel under their feet echoing around them. They come upon it suddenly, because it is silent now, but there it is, they see it, the little white rabbit, its belly stuck in the wire fence that is laid out separating the woods from someone's backyard. There is a child's playhouse, bright yellow and blue, on the other side of the fence, an empty paddling pool, a plastic bucket and spade, a couple of baseball bats. No one seems to be about.

Abe drops his cigarette stub on the ground and squashes it with the ball of his foot. He has only just learned how to do that. Gingerly, the brothers walk towards the animal. It raises its ears – bright pink velvet, pointed at the tips. But it isn't the ears that first strike David, it is the eyes, he will never forget those eyes for as long as he lives, crazed eyes, wild with terror. They are close enough to touch it now and it bares its teeth suddenly, then whimpers, as if anger is too much effort in such a moment. The two boys set about the task of setting it free, David holding the wriggling animal between his hands, Abe cutting the wire loose with his fingers. It takes much longer than they expect, but eventually the hole is wide enough and the rabbit squeals, then scampers away to freedom.

'Why are you so late?' their father asks, looking around at the clocks in the house, all perfectly synchronised, not one is even a second late. David shrugs his shoulders, Abe looks away, hiding his cut fingers in his pockets. They say nothing.

2. Another time, they are on a train home from Providence. There's been a big ball game at McCoy Stadium. The train is packed full of fans. A group of boys at the other end of the compartment are in high spirits. David recognises one of them; he is a senior at their high school. He stares at David, trying to place him in his own mind, and then his eyes flicker with recognition. A couple of minutes later, the boys start singing songs about camps and camp fires. They sing loudly and boisterously; there is feet stamping and saluting. One song finishes and they start another. When they begin a third song, David shouts across the train, 'Stop it,' he says, 'please. It's offensive.' A bespectacled man sitting across the aisle reading a newspaper looks up at David, and then looks away.

'What are you going to do about it, Jewboy?' one of the boys yells back. David looks at Abe standing beside him and he can see his face has gone all red and scrunchy, the muscles hard and tense. Hidden behind his big muscular thigh is a balled-up fist, knuckles clenched. When the doors open at the next stop, David tugs at Abe's arm and they get out. They walk home, twenty miles. Abe says nothing the whole way.

3. Their mother has a cough that will not go away. The pharmacist, a gruff fellow with beady eyes and his mother's rosary permanently peeping out of his trouser pocket, recommends some cough drops. They don't work. He recommends a syrup, thick and brown and sweet. That doesn't work either. If anything, it seems to make the cough worse. He recommends a course of antibiotics. 'Finish the dose, now,' he says with unwonted kindness, 'even if the cough goes away, be sure you finish the full dose.' But she finishes the dose and the cough doesn't go away. 'Didn't work,' she tells the pharmacist, shrugging her shoulders. 'Keeping Benji up all night, he won't say anything though, bless his sweet heart.' When the outline of her ribs starts to show through her thin summer blouses, she goes to the doctor, a jolly-looking man with big hands and rosy cheeks and a slightly breathless air about him. He runs some tests and asks her to come back. His face is not so jolly the next time around and something about his manner, the little-too-detached formality of it, sends a chill through her bones. When he tells her with serious eyes that there isn't any medicine that's going to work, she doesn't say a thing.

4. They are horsing around with their father's tools in the garage. David is trying to make a model wooden piano with strings that can play when you strike the keys. He is looking down, rapt with concentration, so he smells it and maybe he even hears it, that telltale sizzle and pop, before he sees it. But he turns around in alarm, and sees Abe standing by the closed garage door, his face frozen in an expression of horror. By his feet is a crunched-up old newspaper from which is currently erupting a small ball of flames. Beside it lies a bright orange lighter. David pushes open the garage door and then shoves Abe out before he reaches for the fire extinguisher.

The memory of what happens next is patchy, blotted out, like a thick cloud, but when it is all over, he covers the ugly black burn mark on the concrete floor with an old coir mat that says 'Home Sweet Home' in colourful letters. Later he ices the raw blistered patch on his wrist and changes into a full-sleeve shirt even though it is August and the heat that year is stifling. The next morning, he notices that the mat has been removed and the garage smells of air freshener. But whoever has done that says nothing.

5. And then, David has a girlfriend. The pharmacist's daughter. A slip of a girl with dark, curly hair and the wide blue eyes of a child. She sings and plays the piano. Very well, his mother, the piano teacher, admits begrudgingly. The girl's family are devoutly Catholic; the father will not sell condoms in his shop. Nobody has ever seen the mother; people say she is a shut-in, totally nuts, gone crazy from guilt. 'It's hereditary,' his own mother says knowingly, 'madness is. It runs in families.' But David sees a kindness in the girl he can't ignore, a kindness and a vulnerability that fills him with tenderness, a need to protect her from the madness that is her ultimate fate. One day, David finds a picture of her, the pharmacist's daughter, under the pillow of his brother's bed. David says nothing.

6. Their mother dies. Their father falls down one day, planting daffodil bulbs in the back garden. One minute he is planting bulbs, the next minute he is on the ground, his face turned sideways in the mud, his body spreadeagled on the pansy bed, squashing the pretty pink and purple petals with its weight. A neighbour hanging her clothes out to dry in her own garden peers over the low brick wall and sees his boot in the flower bed. She screams and is hysterical with emotion when she calls for the ambulance; two deaths in such proximity to each other – and more significantly, to her – is too much to take. David comes up from New York, Abe is nowhere to

be found. Their father sits in a wheelchair, blind and mute. 'I'm so sorry,' says the very young, strawberry-blonde nurse, dabbing her eyes, 'I don't know what to say.' She says nothing. David says nothing. Their father says nothing and never will.

Sometimes in life, thought David the man, there is nothing to say. Sometimes in life, thought David the musician, it needs to be played.

2.3

'He's gorgeous,' Whitney said, slipping an oyster into her mouth.

Ameena scrunched up her face in distaste.

'What?'

'That,' Ameena said, raising her chin.

'You can never be a real New Yorker if you don't like oysters, you know.'

'Ugh. No thanks. They're so slimy. Like eating slugs.'

Whitney waved her hand in the air. 'Whatever. He's gorgeous.'

Ameena turned around tentatively and looked over her shoulder at where David was standing, talking to Whitney's boyfriend and a few other people she worked with. Even as she watched, she saw him throw his head back and laugh in that beguiling manner he had, then he caught her eye and she smiled.

They were at the party that Whitney held every month, in honour of everyone who worked at the magazine – and implicitly, spouses, partners, significant (or insignificant) others – a supposed essential ritual, she felt, for people to get to know each other's 'style' outside the workplace.

Whitney's boyfriend was a paediatric cardiologist at Mount Sinai, a charming, strikingly handsome man from Brazil, who Whitney had met on a plane back from São Paulo a few years ago, and who graciously allowed the party to take place on the private rooftop terrace of his penthouse on Fort Washington Avenue, a lovely, open space with trailing wisteria sprigs and arches bright with fairy lights.

'Yeah,' Ameena said, 'he's lovely.'

'*Lovely*? Sweetie, I'm not talking about your grandma's knitting. I'm talking about that boy you walked in with. He's gorgeous.'

'Okay, he's gorgeous.'

'What does he do?'

'He works in advertising. And he's a jazz pianist. A very good one. He's kind of amazing with his fingers.'

'Oh?'

'I mean on the piano,' she said quickly as she saw Whitney's eyes start to twinkle.

'Oh,' Whitney replied with a look of exaggerated disappointment. Ameena rolled her eyes.

'You need to introduce us properly, not like that thirty-second thing you did earlier. I don't even know his full name.'

'Greenberg. David Greenberg.'

'He's Jewish?'

Ameena nodded. Whitney made big eyes.

'Oh dear.'

'I know.'

She touched Ameena's arm lightly and they walked towards the brick wall at the end of the terrace where they would be some distance away from the other guests. Then she leaned forward and rested her arms on the cool wrought-iron railing, gazing across the Hudson at the dark outline of the Palisades on the other side. For a few moments, neither of them said anything.

Still looking straight ahead, Whitney said, 'What tangled webs we weave.' Then she turned to look at Ameena. 'Who said that? Shakespeare?'

'Walter Scott.'

'How do you know everything? Quote a line from anywhere and you know it.'

'Not really.'

'Yes, really. How? As your boss I demand to know.'

Ameena smiled. 'I guess it comes from reading everything I could when I was in school, a certain British canon if you will. I read everything, then I memorised it. All of it. I was so naive, I thought if I could recite *Macbeth* backwards, I'd fit in somehow, as if *that* would make me more British.' She sighed. 'I wanted to be more British than the British.'

Whitney nodded. 'Ah yes, the old immigrant's dilemma. Like the prisoner's dilemma, except in this case, the only mind you're fucking with is your own. Anyway,' she looked in David's direction, 'so he's Jewish?'

'From head to toe.'

'Have you been disowned?'

'Haven't told them.'

'You haven't told your family?'

'It's not like I'm eloping tomorrow. We've barely started dating!'

She winked. 'Honey, you were just talking about his fingers…'

'On a *piano*, Whitney,' Ameena said, laughing.

'Whatever.' Whitney took a sip of her wine. 'What religion will you raise your kids?'

'Hmm, let's see… I haven't yet thought about what religion to raise my non-existent kids that haven't yet been created, from a man I haven't yet married. Gasp. Does that make me a bad mother?'

'Don't be facetious. It's a serious question. You'll be thinking of me when the time comes.'

'I'm sure I will,' Ameena said wryly.

'They're so similar, you know, theologically. Judaism and Islam.' Her voice trailed off. 'Don't tell anyone but I studied theology in college until junior year. I wanted to become a nun for the longest time.'

Ameena turned to her in mock horror. 'You? A nun! I haven't heard of anything more ridiculous.'

'Well, I did.'

'And then?'

'And then, like you, I discovered fingers.'

Ameena shook her head. 'You're a bad woman, Whitney, pure evil.'

She smiled at Ameena as she walked away. 'Yeah, that's why I'm not a nun. I'm your boss.'

'By the way,' Ameena said to David later, on the subway downtown, 'Whitney thinks you're gorgeous.'

'Oh yeah? And what do *you* think?'

She blushed. 'I think... it was very nice of you to come with me tonight.'

'Well, it was very nice of you to ask me to come with you tonight.'

'Hey,' she said tapping his arm playfully, changing the subject masterfully, 'so what's this thing with New Yorkers and oysters?'

2.4

A series of text messages the following morning:

A: You online?
D: hi!
A: Hi
A: Jazz question
D: yes?
A: I have…
D: sure
A: Are you really good?
D: huh?
A: I mean, do people who matter think you are?
D: good?
A: Yeah. How good are you, really? Who am I dating?
D: me
D: (hopefully)
A: Skilful evasion
D: not at all
A: Tell me?
D: at?
D: analytic philosophy?
D: discursive argument?
D: branding flavored yogurt?
D: racquet sports?
D: lovemaking?
A: Stop!

D: but i was just getting started ;)

A: At your music

D: how good am i at my music?

A: Yes

D: i don't have the answer

A: ?

D: the answer

D: is in the music

A: Ok

D: solely in the music

D: the rest...

D: it almost doesn't matter

A: What matters?

D: what matters?

A: Yes

A: What matters? A list...

A: Please

D: you're asking me...

A: Yes

D: ...what matters?

A: Yes

D: that is not a jazz question

D: that is a lying-in-bed-post-orgasm question

A: Blimey!

D: is that like, oh my?

A: Oh my!

2.5

By the following week, the heat was oppressive. As they did every year, New Yorkers celebrated the first month of summer, and then they moaned and sweated and wished someone had a dial they could use to turn it all down.

David and Ameena spent their spare time indoors with the windows open and the fans on, Ameena creating art in her apartment, David making music in his. They saw each other at night, venturing out like night birds when the darkness descended, and a breeze cooled the air and the heat disappeared into the ground in a big billow of steam, into all the millions of manholes that dotted the city streets.

It was a happy summer, that summer, with David and Ameena working towards something, both of their own, and also of their togetherness, and there was a tension in the uncertainty, and a certain excitement, but also a feeling of expectation; the kind of hope that makes us all, from time to time, feel glad to be alive.

2.6

'Do you ever feel,' Ameena remarked offhandedly when David came to sit with her between sets, 'that this isn't your music to play?'

Ameena had started watching David perform with more and more regularity. Occasionally, but not always, David would mention when he was playing and where, and occasionally, but not always, he would see Ameena in the audience. Whenever he did, however, he would – not occasionally but always – feel lifted by the sight of her, by her presence. And Ameena too – not occasionally but always – would feel glad to be there, her gladness extending from a growing love for David, but also for jazz itself, for its expression and its freedom and its power to elicit such rapture.

That night, David was playing as a stand-in for the regular pianist in a band – a trio – at a club, up in Harlem.

'*Woah*, where did that come from?' David raised his arms, palms facing forwards. On his face was a look of such complete shock that Ameena was taken aback by it.

'Sorry, did I upset you? I didn't mean to be insulting in any way.'

'Jazz is my life, Ameena.'

Anger, just a touch, but she'd never heard that before, not in him, not towards her. It felt new and strangely unsettling.

'I know, I know. I'm sorry. I just... Nothing. It was an irresponsible thing to say, I'm so sorry...'

David shook his head, brought the arms down, because it's not like she's the first person to ask that question or think it or whatever. He said, 'You know what, don't apologize. It's a fair enough thought to have. I'm just surprised it came up that's all, kinda out of the blue like that.'

'No... I was just looking at you guys up there... you know and...'

'And I'm the only white guy?'

'Well, yes.'

'White Men Can't Jazz?' David said, seeing the funny side.

'No, no, I'm sorry. I shouldn't have said anything. I don't want to have political arguments,' Ameena said, looking mortified, 'with you of all people.'

David touched her shoulder. 'Don't be silly, we're not arguing,' he said lightly, but then she saw his face grow serious. 'You know, let's say I even started to think like that.' He looked at the two musicians standing a little way in front of them, chatting casually to a couple in the audience. 'That would be my own insecurity speaking, a whole bunch of imagined issues related to how I view my jazz skills, and those guys would be the first to set me straight. *That* is my political argument. And *that* is the beauty of America, and of the black community, and of this music.'

She nodded. 'Okay,' she said clutching her glass with both hands.

'Stop looking so aghast, honestly! Put that glass down. You're gripping it so hard it's going to break. Listen, please, I've always believed, that if you think it, it's good to express it.' He shrugged. 'That way, at least there can be a conversation about it.'

'Okay,' she said again but put her drink back on the table, the dark honey-coloured liquid swimming around a single prismatic cube of ice like a miniature, undiscovered galaxy.

It's a strong drink. The higher up you go on this island, Peggy had once warned her, the stronger the drinks. They are way up in Harlem tonight and she's feeling it. Any higher and I'll be flying, she thinks dryly.

It isn't just the whisky, the whole place is oozing character. Original floors, panelled walls, small electric bulbs hanging from the ceiling in festive clusters like glowing grapes. Framing one wall, a line of tables, a threadbare maroon carpet in the centre, and along the other wall, an impressively well-stocked bar, serving, as Ameena discovered, some seriously potent alcohol. The bandstand – where the action takes place every night – sits just there in front, so there's no physical separation between the musicians and everyone else. Very democratic, Ameena thinks approvingly of the set-up, very, 'this-is-jazz'.

'Come here,' David was saying now, as he placed her sideways on his lap, with his arm round her shoulder, and he marvelled once again at how light she was, how petite. 'Serious conversation. You know how, that very first time you watched me play, we spoke about syncopation? Well, here's the other half of your history lesson. If jazz got its syncopation from ragtime and Dixieland and all the different forms of New Orleans music, it got something else from blues – its capacity to uplift you. *Listen* to jazz, there's so much of America in its origins; American culture lives *in* it. And New Orleans was where it all first came together – the blues, black church music, Caribbean music, European marching band music, piano music – all of it, to create the roots of jazz. Then it travelled and evolved, from Dixieland, through swing, through the 40s, through New York City bebop, through Coltrane, through post-bop, into the modern jazz you're listening to tonight – its history is the glory of American life! This is *African-American* music that I play, and you can't ever forget that, which doesn't mean that you can't play it – there's a difference.'

His words made her glance towards the other two musicians, who were laughing at the minute with a pretty waitress in a short dress. He's right, she thought, these are genius musicians affirming their humanity.

Ameena had met the bassist before on more than one occasion – a young, handsome Trinidadian with a great smile. David played with him regularly and often spoke about his 'support' – it's kind of like the binder in paint, it holds it all together, he'd explained. The bassist caught her eye then and flashed her that great smile. She nodded and smiled back.

The drummer, she met for the first time earlier that night, after the second set.

'You were so good,' she said appreciatively.

'*You* good too,' he replied with a wide grin, 'just *fine*.'

'Was he flirting with me?' she asked David later.

'Probably,' David laughed. 'He's ninety-four by the way.'

'Get out!'

'I'm totally serious.'

'But... how?'

He shrugged, still smiling. 'Genes, music, sex, religion, who knows!'

'Right,' David was saying now, swinging her round on his lap, so she was turned facing him, 'end of serious conversation.' He picked up the whisky glass to hand back to her, then, on a whim, examined it carefully and brought his own mouth to the exact spot where her lipstick had marked the minute geography of her lips.

He took a swig and instantly grimaced.

'Wow,' he said, 'that's a serious drink.'

'I know,' she said, tingling from the romance of what he'd just done.

And now it's like everything is fine between them and twenty minutes earlier she had just asked a question out of ignorance and he had felt the need to point that out, but she knows she had pressed a button, and the button had activated what we all have inside us, the thing that protects us, the thing that makes us want to impress other people, while really only trying to impress ourselves. But at the same time, for some reason, she doesn't feel particularly insulted by it, either by his apparent intellectual superiority or by his need to point that out. In fact, she is moved by what he is saying, both the story and the telling of it. There is nothing false about any of that. It is lovely.

He is touching her hair now, running his fingers through the individual strands, feeling their weight.

'You know, Ameena, when I listened to jazz for the first time all those years ago, I fell in love with what I was hearing without knowing anything about the musicians, their racial, ethnic, cultural backgrounds... nothing. I just felt the power of the music in some kind of elemental way. What's important, for anyone who likes to listen to this music, but particularly for me as a wannabe jazz musician, is to respect the beauty and the history of its tradition. And the soulfulness of the music itself and the magic of how it's done.'

'That much I know,' she said, sighing, 'and it's beautiful.'

'It is. It's why I fell in love with it.'

'Thank you for explaining.'

'Thank you too, for wanting to understand.'

'So,' she said, reaching for his arm that he had placed loosely round her shoulder and bringing the back of his hand to her mouth, 'speaking of how it's done, when you're up there and your eyes are closed and your mouth is open, in that oh-so-*sexy* way, what are you thinking?'

'Ameena, are you drunk?' David said, his face breaking into a smile.

'Drunk? Me? Never! Is it wrong to ask my jazz pianist lover what he's thinking when he's doing something he loves doing even more than when he's doing me?'

He shook his head, laughing now. 'Okay, you're drunk. But nope. Not wrong at all. What am I thinking? Ah, let's see. Hmm... well, if you really want to know, I am trying to, as best I can, hear and react to every single note that is being played by the bass and the drums – and myself – at every single millisecond.' He snapped his fingers twice. 'It's this kind of interpenetration... a constant conversation, you hear each other's music and you respond, so everything that I play is a reaction to everything that I just played and that everybody else is playing, *in that moment*. And that's the beauty and the challenge of this music – it pushes us, and we push it back.'

He nodded. 'Yup. Great jazz is made by multiple people playing together with that kind of necessity and mindset. So, there's no room for anything other than that.'

Then he paused and looked at her. Her mouth on the peak of his knuckles was wet and warm. 'Except *may*be, sometimes, but just very occasionally, for you.'

2.7

The place was Back Bay in Boston and fifteen-year-old David, who had taken the Peter Pan up from Rhode Island to watch a band perform at a famous jazz club that night, walked into the music section of a well-known bookshop and picked up a book called *Jazz: How to Become One of the Greats.*

He was flicking through the pages when a voice whispered softly in his ear, 'You're wastin' your money.'

David flipped round and noticed, standing behind him flicking through the pages of some other book – a recipe book, apparently of French cuisine, *Bouillabaisse: The Definitive Guide,* it said on the cover – a man in dark glasses even though, David observed, it was rather dark inside the shop.

David stopped flicking through the pages.

'Me?' he said nervously.

'Yeah! You're wastin' your money,' the man repeated, looking down at a picture of a giant orange crustacean. 'That title? That's all wrong.'

'Oh?'

'It's like this: think Miles learned to play by readin' a book?'

'No, sir.'

'Coltrane?'

'No, sir.'

'Charlie Parker?'

'No, sir.'

'By spendin' hundreds of dollars sittin' in a *class*room?'

'No, sir.'

He nodded his head vigorously. 'Right. That's right. Ain't *nobody* learned no *jazz* by readin' a book like *that*.'

Then he looked David up and down and his tone softened somewhat.

'You know what? You seem like a nice boy. Hardworkin' too. Do yourself a favour. Get outta here, go find someone who's got these tunes on a tape an' copy 'em. Listen up – ten tunes, alright: "So What", "Moanin'", "Autumn Leaves", "Blue Bossa", "Summertime", "Straight, No Chaser", "Take the A Train", "Cantaloupe Island", "Blue Train", "Freddie Freeloader". You listenin' boy?'

'Yes.'

'You got 'em? In your head, I mean?'

'I... I think so,' David sputtered.

'Good,' he said, sounding pleased to hear that. 'That's the first lesson learned already then. Now all you gotta do is find 'em. Then copy 'em. Then listen to 'em. Then listen *again*. And then *again*. Then go out an' play with other nice boys like yourself. That's how you learn *jazz*. Wanna be great? Here's a secret: The greatest *jazz* musicians are those who *produce* the best music *together*. The *bandstand* is their book. That's the secret, you can thank me later.'

It was a few weeks gone when David was back in Boston to watch another band at Wally's that he looked at the man in the dark glasses on stage and understood that he had learned one of the most valuable lessons in his jazz education from one of the greatest living percussionists of all time.

2.8

When it came to her art, Ameena liked to work in private, in solitude, but sometimes, though rarely, she let Peggy watch.

'They all look so calm,' Ameena had observed of the musicians at a classical concert that she had recently gone to with David – a friend of his was playing the piano and had invited them – 'so unperturbed, even in a hall chock-full of people. How?'

'Vodka shot,' David had replied with a straight face.

Ameena had looked at him horrified. 'No!'

David had smiled at the look on her face. 'Sometimes. Or whisky. Swig of whisky. Weed. Valium. Whatever it takes. It's psychology at the end of the day.' He tapped the side of his forehead with two fingers. 'All in the mind.'

'You too?'

'Sure, sometimes. But more these guys. It's not easy to display such spectacularly perfect technique in front of two thousand people every night. Mine's a different kind of musicianship, I don't need to achieve that level of perfection technically like these guys do, and by technically, I mean their ability to execute material perfectly at the instrument without making any mistakes and having perfect sound and never missing a note, night after night after night. Different brain-state. Make a mistake in a jazz gig, not many will notice; make one in a string quartet and everybody will.'

She had nodded. 'I'd be terrified. I'm not sure I could ever do what you guys do, put yourself out there like that – you're so… exposed! For the longest time, I never even signed my name on my artwork. Even now, I have to paint alone, and in a place where no one is watching me.'

But that wasn't entirely true because sometimes, she let Peggy watch.

It was therapeutic, Peggy had told her once, to follow the movement of the brushstrokes, that rhythm, that flow. And so, sometimes, while Ameena was painting, Peggy was allowed to stay.

She was in the middle of it now, that brushstroke. And Peggy was sitting behind her, studying, as she described to Ameena, the process of 'taking that wild leap, of creating something out of nothing'. To Ameena, it wasn't quite as mysterious as that, because more often than not, she could already see the finished product in her mind's eye. She usually worked like this, painting the painting in her head many times before she brought it to paper. Like having a baby, she often thought, it grows inside you and you nurture it and you feed it and then it grows too big to be inside you, and you feel that push, that urgency to bring it out, to give it its own life.

'I like David,' Peggy was saying. 'He's nice.'

'Yes,' Ameena said as she picked up a brush, and sketched the outline of a tree, loose and wild, 'he is.'

'What are you painting?' Peggy asked.

'I saw a girl cycling along the East River the other day, the sun was out, the river was calm, just lying there sparkling, and she had these flowers in her bicycle basket, bright red flowers. It was so striking, the red against that blue-gold backdrop. I'm trying to paint all that – the encounter – just without the girl.'

'Why won't you paint the girl?'

'Oh.' Ameena shook her head. 'It's a decision I made a long time ago. I painted all these people once, a whole set of portraits, and it was probably my best work, my most authentic expression of self...' Peggy noticed Ameena had a distant look in her eyes as if she was delving into the memory of something that had once been significant. Then she snapped back. 'But... well, it all got very complicated.' She sighed. 'So, I decided I would never paint figures again – not in the traditional form, at any rate, just go directly to the substance of the real thing. I try to make the representational subject dissolve into the brushwork.'

Peggy watches as Ameena picks up a brush, dips it in pale blue paint and brings it to the easel. At first it is just a line, delicate and flowing, then a sweep of swift, swirling brushstrokes. She mixes in another shade of blue, darker, more complex. The colours blend and follow their own laws, and the paint is allowed to work for itself. And then, it is a river. Just lying there. It is not sparkling yet, but Peggy knows it will. Soon enough, it will.

'Is he like your dad?'

'I'm sorry?'

'No, I mean people say women end up with men who are like their fathers. So I was wondering – is David like your dad?'

'Oh that,' she said, but she kept working, her eyes focused on the painting, which, she realised with sudden pride, had just started to breathe. 'I guess David can be a bit of a pacifist. My dad's a pacifist. I dread that about him, about both of them, come to think of it.'

'Why?'

'Because,' she said as she painted a building overlooking the water, its edges soft and diaphanous, 'pacifists usually end up disappointed.'

Peggy nodded. 'I know nothing about mine, except that when he was very young he served in a war he didn't believe in, and then after I was born, he had these delusions that the Vietcong were going to take us away, my mother and me, to the jungle and spray napalm on us, and so he ran away before that could happen, so he wouldn't have to face it, our burned and disfigured bodies, our pain. My mother told me that. She was more than twenty years younger than him, you know.'

Ameena said nothing. There was a disjointed rhythm in her painting.

'And then...' Peggy continued almost as if she was speaking to herself, or to the river in the painting, the one that was now sparkling, 'the one I knew was hardly a shining beacon of fatherhood.'

'You must hate him so much.'

She shrugged. 'He was a stranger.'

Ameena took her eyes off the painting and looked at Peggy, whose vivid green eyes were closed. Her face looked empty like a beautiful, abandoned house.

'But her? I hate her something awful. She was my blood.'

2.9

Desire for a city is primal.

Ameena was walking along the fancy shopfronts of Madison Avenue with its furs and its fashion. They are beautiful, these shops, beautifully designed, beautifully displayed, something to be stopped and stared at.

It was a Friday morning on her day off and she was walking like a native New Yorker would walk on a Friday morning on their day off, window shopping, people watching, revelling in the singular delights that only this City offers. Soon she would find a diner and sit at the counter and order a coffee and pull out a book from her bag and perhaps she would talk to the stranger next to her, and perhaps she wouldn't, but she would spend a few delicious hours doing some of those things that make her feel that she can do as she pleases and nobody cares. But now she was just walking. She stopped to look at a shop window, it was a jewellery shop, the window display was stunning. She stared at a necklace, a single strand of emerald-green beads with a gold and diamond clasp.

She had passed this shop before. She had admired this necklace before.

Someone brushed by her then in that instant even as she was looking at the necklace, then he was behind her, too close for comfort. Her grip on her handbag tightened and she was about to move away, but he touched her shoulders, strong hands, shifted her slightly to the right. She wanted to scream, wriggle free, but before she had a chance to react, his voice was in her ear. 'You gotta look at it like this,' he said.

And then he walked away, a tall man with a closely shaven head in a beige trench coat with a briefcase in his hand. He didn't look back and she never saw his face.

Her immediate reaction was one of outrage. But then she saw what he had done. In the reflection of herself in the window, the emerald beads hung in a perfect oval round the curve of her neck.

Later, many years in the future, when Ameena is older, as old as her mother was then or even older, she will think of this moment and remember it as a demonstration of the plurality of people and of places. Of this City in particular. Of how it is raw and real and free and indestructible, and when you are a part of it, you are all those things too. She will tell her grandchildren, who are pale-skinned with green-gold eyes and look nothing like her at all, while she is teaching them how to make the *badam kheer* that her own grandmother taught her to make, she will tell them about this City, how beneath the hardness lurks a liquid softness, thick and gooey, like the rich, sweetened almond milk in the pot they are all stirring together in her kitchen. She will tell them this, about her City and theirs, and she will tell them other things too, about love and about dreams and how you have to be clever to figure out this City and if you do, she says, allowing them to lick the wooden spatula one by one – if you do, it offers you in return, occasional spurts of unexpected generosity, which is the best kind of generosity there is.

2.10

Autumn rolled in languidly and the early mornings turned delicate and cool. In Central Park the hawthorns were covered in red berries, the sassafras bloomed yellow then red then purple. The church below Ameena's window stood stark and white, untainted by the flamboyance that surrounded it.

David took Ameena to Rhode Island for Labor Day weekend. Immediately, she felt the difference in temperature; it was much cooler here by the sea than in the city, the wind off the bay sharp and brisk, the salt air fresh and clean and briny in that typically New England way.

'Are you religious?' Ameena asked David as they walked along the jagged coastline hand in hand.

Earlier that morning, David had taken her to Point Judith Lighthouse, where his father had proposed to his mother all those years ago. They'd been so young, David said, only a pair of kids. David and Ameena stood together at the broad octagonal base of the structure and looked up to the very top.

'What?' David said, noticing the odd expression on Ameena's face.

'Nothing, it's so silly.'

'Oh, come on!'

'Nothing.'

'Ameena!'

'I'm moved that you brought me here. That's all. That's what I was thinking. You kind of make me want to cry. Okay? Told you it's stupid. Anyway,' she said a little too quickly, 'can you go up all the way to the top?'

'I wanted to bring you here,' David said, palms on her cheeks, holding her face in his hands. 'It was important to me.'

Ameena nodded.

'She was the love of his life,' David said gently. Then he changed the topic, also like Ameena, a little too quickly. 'They only recently restricted access,' he said, addressing the second part of her question, 'but even before that, you couldn't really go inside unless you were on official business, though they weren't nearly as strict back then. Dad and Mom and the coastguard's son were the same age, good friends too, so the coastguard – Sad Mr Jones – that's what we used to call him when we were little, because his lips curved downwards in that cartoony sad-faced way.' David grinned at the memory. 'Though in reality,' he continued, 'Sad Mr Jones wasn't sad at all, pretty funny guy actually, constantly cracking jokes, making people laugh. Anyway, Sad Mr Jones was only too happy to let Dad propose to her inside, so he allowed them to go all the way up the spiral staircase to the very top, to that little balcony – up there, look.' He took a step back and pointed to the top of the lighthouse. 'Just the two of them and the dome of the sky and the sound of the waves crashing on the rock face. This is the first time I've been back here since she...'

Ameena looked at David intently. She could see that this meant something to him, something serious and symbolic, and that he had been moved tremendously by the experience of showing this place to her, and she found herself even more touched by it, by his emotion, and that he would share it with her in this way, something so personal and so private.

Then they walked a while and he showed her the stretch of beach where he and his brother had run as kids under the open skies, even in the wintertime, back and forth from the foaming ocean to the shoreline, with their windblown hair and shirtless little bodies, not feeling the cold in the way little children don't feel the cold or for that matter any kind of discomfort, nor danger, nor anxiety, nor fear. How many carefree days they had spent on that beach, counting the boats, naming the rocks, not realising the significance of that place in an existential sense until they were much older, young men really. Only then would they ponder, though always separately, not daring to share such intimate thoughts even with each other lest they be deemed sentimental or soft – but what if she had said no, they would think, what would have become of us then?

'It's beautiful,' Ameena said, 'so wild and free and... well just utterly romantic. I can see why he picked this place to propose. And I can absolutely see why she said yes. I mean I'm sure she'd have said yes anywhere, but it's impossible for anyone not to, here.'

'Impossible?' David's eyes gleamed in amusement and then he threw back his head and laughed when he saw the look of alarm cross Ameena's face as she realised what she had said, what he had taken from that.

'Don't look so worried,' he said, putting his arm round her, 'I'm not going to propose to you. Not now, at any rate.'

She pushed him away playfully. 'That's not even a little bit funny.'

They walked some more along the beach, right along the water, the waves touching their toes, and they talked, and exactly how much time passed like that, just walking and talking, they didn't know, nor care. And then suddenly, in this way, she asked if he was religious.

The fog had rolled in over the bay, suddenly as it does, and you could feel the weight of it in the air, the heaviness of the fog and the salt from the sea. A colony of gulls circled, gliding on the wind. A lone fishing boat dotted the bay, hidden all this time, only coming into view now as the fog shifted and moved. The gulls squawked loudly, spotting the boat gleaming white under the white sun, swooping down noisily into its icy wake.

'No,' David replied slowly, as if he was still considering her question, 'I sort of lost my faith when my mother died.'

'In what?'

'In everything.'

A pause. Then he added quietly, 'I'm sorry. I know that must sound selfish.'

'No, not at all. I understand. Faith is fragile.'

'Are *you*?' he asked her.

'Religious?'

'Yup.'

'I don't pray,' she said.

'Well...'

'I drink. I don't fast. I don't cover my hair. I ran away from home. I'm with you.'

'Is that bad?' he asked.

'That I'm with you?'

'Yes.'

'No. Is it bad that you're with me?'

'No,' he said.

'Then we're okay...' she looked at him as if searching for something from his face, '...aren't we?'

He nodded. 'We're okay.'

'Okay,' she said.

Then, 'Can you do something for me, David?'

'You mean, besides bring you to Narragansett for the weekend so you can feel what it's like when the fog comes in and the wind makes your blood freeze?'

She laughed but he could see her eyes were serious. 'Is that the strange sensation my body is feeling? I thought it was just goosebumps from being this close to you. No, seriously, Piano-man. Can you?'

'Okay, seriously. I can. Go on.'

'Do you think we can leave religion and politics out of our relationship? It's not something I think I'm going to know how to handle.'

David nodded but he looked surprised. 'Is it that much of a big deal to you?'

'I don't think so,' she said honestly, 'but if we let it into our house, I don't know if I know how to ask it to leave.'

The wind had picked up and Ameena's hair and skirt gathered together and blew upward towards the sky. David felt a tenderness for her swell up within him, and a longing that was not sexual, only a kind of softness for the way she looked in that moment, standing bravely against the press of the wind – and for what she had said, the honesty of it. Then the screen door of the seaside diner opened as a young couple came out and David ran to hold it open before it banged shut and Ameena ran behind him, laughing, and then disappeared gratefully inside into the warmth and David followed, leaving only the last strains of their laughter lingering in the golden light.

2.11

The first time he brought it up, her reaction surprised him.

'Will you move in with me?' he asked softly on a Wednesday evening, as they sat in David's apartment and watched the lights of the city come on – rhythmically, symphonically, as if someone somewhere was carefully orchestrating the event for maximum emotional impact.

'Ameena?'

'Hmm...?'

'I asked if you would...'

'I know what you asked.'

'So?

'So... what?

'So, what do you think?'

'I don't know what I think.'

And he looked so crestfallen, and his eyes looked so sad, that she felt when she looked at him a kind of great love, and that great love compelled her to offer an explanation that she hoped would close the matter, if only temporarily, although she knew that he knew that it was just that – an explanation that she hoped would close the matter only temporarily.

'David, I need space that I can work in... this place is even smaller than mine. This thing with the gallery, it's kind of a big deal, you know. I never expected anything like this could happen to me and then *you* came into my life, and you wielded some sort of magic wand, and then, miraculously, it happened, it's *happening* – I'm *in* it now!'

'I know that Ameena, I wasn't suggesting you come here. I was… I thought… I thought we could look for a place together. I was so sure you'd want that too.'

'I love you David…' she said, and he knew she meant it, '…but you know the way I feel about my art when it's done.'

And then she noted his bafflement, and she said gently, 'Your idea as it sits in your imagination will always be superior to the actual work.'

David said nothing, but inwardly he thought, and not without some wonder, that Ameena was like an expert jazz musician. She could make something up on the spot, and then one minute later, or five seconds later, she could make something else up on the spot, and somehow – a talent – she could make both versions sound equally authentic.

2.12

The day before her debut show, Ameena went looking for sanctuary in the middle of the night. She didn't know what time it was, she hadn't checked, she just decided, lying sleeplessly in bed, that she needed to go for a walk.

She got dressed in the dark and closed the front door behind her quietly, so as not to wake David, who had stayed over, or Peggy, who always slept with the door to her bedroom open, for as she had told Ameena once in a way that made her blood run cold – some childhood fears never die but end up owning you.

Once she stepped out into the hallway, she checked the lit screen of her phone. It was nearly 2am.

There was nobody in the hallway, nobody in the elevator the whole way down, nobody in the lobby, nobody out on the street, no cars, no people. The city lay cool and black and silent. Only an occasional breeze made the leaves on the dark trees rustle.

Ameena made a left out of her building, stopping to admire, yet again, the solitary splendour of the Chrysler, piercing the night sky like a bejewelled spear. She started walking westward, past the church, past the dog park, past the beautiful, decaying brownstones. She looked up as she walked, peeking, as was her habit when she was on her own, into other people's windows, creating little imaginary worlds. She loved this about Manhattan, that you could speculate like this about the stories of strangers; it felt to her like being inside six novels at the same time, but that night, mostly all the windows she walked past were dark.

She walked to the end of the street and then considered which way to turn. She didn't have a destination in mind, she'd only wanted to be out, she'd wanted the night air. She stopped at the lights, then looked around her, hesitating to commit. From where she was standing, she could see the diner on the corner a few blocks down, its neon lights flashing, beckoning her somehow, and, thankful for some sort of waypost, she decided to walk towards it.

Over on the avenue, the rubbish collectors were out, their large truck taking up the whole width of the road. Two cars waited impatiently behind the truck, the drivers willing it to move, not daring to blow their horns at that time of night. The truck inched forward languidly. Impressive, she thought, how much rubbish this little island collected on a daily basis, how when you came out in the evenings, just as the shops were closing, you could see them, piled up on street corners, bags and bags of rubbish, and how they were all gone in the morning, like some kind of Houdini's act that happened in the middle of the night.

As she walked past, one of the men noticed her. He was whistling a tune, she recognised it – a David Bowie song, but she couldn't remember the name. 'Morning, miss,' he called out merrily as though he was completely free from worry. He did this as he hauled whole fistfuls of the black bags into the back of his truck and resumed his whistling. She returned the greeting, thinking how so much of life is pure conjecture, for no matter how many windows one stares into, one never really knows what is going on in someone else's life. Then she thought about herself, how she must look from the man's perspective, what a curious figure she must cut, a lone midnight walker in a man's too-big sweatshirt and baseball hat. An unintended endorsement for the Yankees, she realised suddenly – particularly ironic given she didn't understand the first thing about baseball despite all of David's infinitely patient attempts to enlighten her.

A few minutes later, she arrived at the diner. She peered in through the window – it looked open but empty. She was just about to walk on by when her glance fell on the laminated menu that had been wall-mounted just by the entrance. Something caught her eye. On a whim, she decided to go in.

Inside, there were two men sitting at the counter drinking beers. Neither so much as glanced in her direction. Another thing she loved about this city: nobody judged you in New York, they were too busy judging themselves.

A solitary waitress with an impressive number of tongue piercings, finished her yawn, pointed to a table and then, with a look of such extreme anguish that Ameena couldn't help but speculate on its many possible causes, asked what she wanted. Ameena ordered herself the ice cream sundae that had grabbed her fancy on the menu outside but when it came out a few minutes later (but how can anything be ready so quickly?) a tall, cheerful glass filled right to its scallop-edged brim with vanilla ice cream, smothered in sticky caramel, scattered over with nuts and topped with an unnaturally red cherry, her heart sank.

What decent girl eats a 'Crazy Caramelicious' (*despite* the name) in the middle of the night all alone in a diner?

Later, she would wonder what had prompted her to have such an abrupt change of heart. Maybe the two men had paused their conversation to stare curiously at it. But then again maybe they hadn't, maybe they had barely noticed it just like they had barely noticed her, but all the same, she felt a sudden prick of shame. She muttered something to the waitress, left some money on her table, over-tipping by an amount she could not mathematically explain, and left as quickly as she had come in.

Back on the avenue, the rubbish truck was gone, turned down some other road, carrying away unwanted remnants of someone else's life. A sort of blessing, really. A couple of cars sped by her, going about their own night-time business, but when she turned onto the street leading to her building, it was empty and so quiet she could hear the dull thud of her own footsteps. She felt uneasy suddenly – this didn't feel like New York. Where was the vibrancy that accompanied the lit-up steeple of the Chrysler Building? Where was the exuberance? Where was the dream? Ameena quickened her stride.

A sudden gust of wind blew a window shut above her, and somewhere far away she heard the sound of a dog barking. It smelled like rain, and maybe it was that, the scent of rain, that made her feel then, at that moment, the need – it was a need, precise and particular – to call her mother. She missed her mother, she realised with a kind of astonishment, and immediately, a deep feeling of melancholy filled her. She missed her mother and her father and her brother and her mother's cooking and her books and her bedroom that she had thought was small until she arrived in this city and understood the many shades of the word 'small'. She missed all that. She missed it more than ever now that she was the girl who had almost eaten an alliterated portmanteau alone in the middle of the night.

She was never going to tell David she'd done that. If he woke when she returned, she'd say she'd gone for a walk. That's all. Couldn't sleep, went for a walk.

She fished for her phone in the large, soft, fleece-lined pocket of David's sweatshirt – ah, there it was. And something else. Another rectangle, small, bright orange plastic. A lighter. A lighter? David's? But he didn't smoke? Almost involuntarily, she lit it, curling her fingers around the body, her thumb flicking the wheel, hearing the click, watching the steady blue-yellow flame. Did he? Then slowly, she released her thumb, watched the flame collapse back into the tiny, perfectly round orifice, and slipped it back into the pocket, her forehead creasing into lines she knew had no business being there. She exhaled deeply, feeling vaguely disorientated, then she looked at the time on her phone. It was a quarter to three in New York. Morning time in Manchester. They'd all be just waking up, her mum and dad still in their bedroom, talking in low voices under the heavy cotton quilt, her brother walking to the bathroom with his eyes closed, blinking incredulously into the mirror.

Tentatively she dialled the number, the only landline number in the world that she knew off by heart.

It rang a few times with no answer, then she heard a click.

'Hello?' her mother answered in her typically singsong manner. She sounded groggy, not yet awake.

Ameena said nothing.

'Hello?' Zoya said again, this time with that imperceptible touch of impatience. Ameena knew her mother hated being woken from her sleep.

Hello Mummy, Ameena wanted to say.

And then she wanted to tell her, *desperately* wanted to tell her mother about David and about New York and about her life. About her work at the magazine, and about how she was an artist now, a real artist, and how people thought her work was of some worth, and how she was having her first show tomorrow. Her first show as a real artist!

I am so proud of you, Ameena, her mother would reply, barely able to conceal her excitement. All of us! All of us are so proud of you, she would exclaim.

'Hello? Who is this please? What do you want?'

2.13

Daylight came.

In some other city, the birds chirped.

Outside the apartment, the sirens blared. Inside, the buzzer rang.

Peggy answered the door and almost keeled backwards at the sight of the pair standing in front of her.

'Sorry,' she said immediately, 'wrong apartment?'

She was just about to shut the door when one of them interjected politely.

'Howdy, miss,' he said in that charming Bill Clinton accent, 'this is apartment 15B isn't it? We tried to buzz from the street...'

'...but the intercom's broken?' finished Peggy.

He smiled and nodded. 'We're here to transport some artwork to the...' he looked down at a piece of paper in his hand '...Suzy Lipskis Gallery? Lips? Kiss?'

'Oh,' Peggy exclaimed, opening the door wider, 'right! Well then come on in.'

Ameena, lounging in the kitchen with a morning cup of Earl Grey, had caught only bits of the conversation, but knew that Suzy had arranged for packers to wrap and transport her artwork across for the show.

'Is it someone for my art?' she called.

'Uh. Yup,' Peggy replied, in what Ameena thought was a very odd voice.

She had just started to walk towards the door to introduce herself when she stopped short with her mouth open and her eyebrows raised all the way up, making her face look somewhat like a caricature of itself. With that same expression, she turned to look at Peggy, who, at that moment, was attempting to suppress a giggle with a long, endlessly troublesome cough, for standing in the entryway, looking at them with identical boyish grins, were her art packers – a duo sporting matching muscle t-shirts, blond spiky hair and faces so similar that only a mother could tell them apart.

She clamped her hand over her mouth and squeezed herself wordlessly between Peggy and the wall to give them room to pass. 'Good *Morning*,' one of them hollered cheerily as he walked past her, looking enquiringly around the apartment, then at her face. 'Bedroom?'

Ameena looked at Peggy and Peggy looked at Ameena and both girls carried an expression on their faces that told them instantly that if either one had the temerity to start laughing, neither would be able to stop.

Peggy coughed again. Ameena said, 'This way, follow me please,' in a funny high-pitched tone and led the way to her bedroom, where she had stacked all the paintings in a neat pile next to the door the night before.

Then she came back out, closed the door behind her, and instantly burst into a fit of giggles.

'Oh my GOD,' Peggy whispered, 'Tweedle*dee*!'

'Tweedle*dum*!' Ameena countered.

'Double trouble!' Peggy said, wiping her eyes.

'TWO hot!' Ameena shrieked.

And so, two genetically identical sets of exceptionally muscular arms wrapped thirty pieces of artwork expertly in bubble paper, packed them into wooden cartons and brought them to the front door and as they were leaving, the brothers smiled affably and said goodbye in that laconic southern drawl, their biceps bulging with the weight of the boxes they carried.

Then when the blond one with the spiky hair said, 'All done! Down yonder then, to Lips Kiss!' with a wide smile, and the other blond one with the spiky hair said, 'Lord willin' and the creek don't rise,' with the same wide smile, a few seconds after the first, neither could, for the life of them, understand why the tall woman with the blond hair and the short one with the dark hair were holding each other and laughing uncontrollably like a pair of giggly schoolgirls on a high.

And in this way, heralded by the sound of laughter that could be heard all the way down the hall, causing an elderly lady waiting for the elevator to adjust her hearing aid and smile, and dissolving, at the very same time, any man-made constructs that may have otherwise existed between the two room-mates, Ameena's art was transported to the gallery for her first show.

2.14

And Zoya in her bed in Manchester was lying in the deepest sleep when she was woken by a snore from Yusuf.

After that, as she lay for hours tossing and turning between the sheets, listening to this man rumble beside her, she wanted to cry from a feeling of such deep despair that she herself was shocked by its intensity.

It was a hot, muggy night. The scent of rain was thick and heady, but everything was still, and no breeze came through the windows that had been left open for precisely that purpose. Inside the little bedroom, the humidity pressed down – suffocatingly, Zoya thought as she flung the covers off her, cursed under her breath and prayed for sleep to come. She wondered who had called so early that morning, who had called and then held the line like that without speaking when she answered. Wrong number most probably, must have realised when they heard her voice that it was not the voice they had called to hear. Still, it had been strange.

Next to her, Yusuf snorted again, then turned on his side, his hand touching her leg accidentally, and she pushed it away with force and felt in that moment a kind of violent anger towards the creator of this horrible noise, this body – she couldn't think of him at that moment as her husband, or even as a person, only another body lying next to her own – that had robbed her of one of life's little remaining pleasures. She felt a sudden urge then, as she pushed away his hand, to push the whole of him off her bed, and then felt immediately guilty at the terrible thought she had just entertained, especially over something so small.

And yet it wasn't small because Zoya, now fifty-nine, knew that there comes a time in life when there is nothing, absolutely nothing, more precious than the deepest sleep.

2.15

The seasons tripped, with a gentleness and lightness often felt by young people in love. Fall mellowed into the very beginnings of winter. Once again, the city became a shifting palette of colours and shapes and light.

Ameena's debut show had taken place and everyone agreed that it had been a success on several fronts. She had sold seven paintings on opening night and another nine over the rest of the ten-day period. Ameena herself had been somewhat disappointed, feeling a kind of secret shame in taking back the fourteen unclaimed pieces, but Suzy had taken her aside and spoken to her, not unkindly but in her usual clipped, businesslike manner.

'Can I tell you a sad story?' she had said.

'No, please don't.'

'I once had an artist,' Suzy pressed on, ignoring her, 'a very promising young man. He started off as an underground graffiti artist and morphed into a painter, he was sensational, stunning – this was New York in the 80s and his work was genre-busting stuff. But we weren't able to sell anything on his first show. And I told him it was okay. It's normal in the art business. When something doesn't look like anything you already know, it's hard to recognize it as great. But he took it so badly, the failure of that debut show, he stopped painting.'

Ameena had nodded. 'That is a sad story.'

'Yes, but do you know why it is sad?'

'Because he didn't sell anything?'

'No. Because he quit.'

'Okay,' Ameena had said.

'Not okay, Ameena, not okay. I felt for him, for many years, even now when I think of him, I possess it, this feeling... in Russian, we call it *toska*, a dull ache of the soul, a longing with nothing to long for. You understand?'

'I think so.'

Suzy had sighed. 'You don't understand. Never mind. What is important is that you did wonderful. Superlative. You sold more than fifty per cent of your inventory. On your first show. That is great, an incredible achievement. So, don't sell yourself short. This is a tough game. And New York is a tough city. Which means if you want to play, *you* need to be tough. We will do another show in the spring.'

'Really?'

'Yes, really. Because I believe in your work. So, we will have another show and this time we will try and invite some important people. And you will work hard for it, harder than you have ever worked in your life. But for now, go home, celebrate, rest, relax, make love, drink wine, enjoy your success.'

There'd been an article about her in the newspaper a couple of days after the show. David had spotted it first, then Suzy had called to alert her to it and to congratulate her. 'Good press is good,' Suzy told Ameena on the phone. 'Not as good as bad press is bad, but still good. Congratulations.'

'To me,' David read aloud, 'an art lover, not a critic, her work is fabulous: it feels fresh and contemporary, with a hectic, deeply human sensibility. It's beautiful and busy, young and timeless, graphic, chaotic, arresting, rhythmic, packed with ambiguous codes; there's a questioning of identity, and an artistic engagement with life's polyrhythmic dimensions. A definite feather in the cap for Suzy Lipskis and co. – you could stand in front of an Amena Hamid painting and be fascinated for hours.'

'Wow,' David said, putting the newspaper down, 'just wow.'

'But they spelled my name wrong!' Ameena replied.

2.16

The second time he brought it up, her reaction surprised him again.

Late one night – it was a Tuesday – Ameena had been home alone working on a watercolour that wasn't quite turning out the way she saw it in her head. She stepped back and looked at it with a frown. Then she stood up on her bed and scrutinised it from there. 'Any which way you look at it,' she said aloud, 'this blows.' She wondered if she should call David over to get his opinion – he was painfully objective about her work and, she had to admit, always at least partly right. She picked up her phone and was about to call his number when she realised he was at a gig downtown that night. Where are you when I need you? she whispered into the blank phone. For a moment, she held the screen against her cheek, feeling its coolness on her skin, then put it away and decided instead to settle for a glass of water. Yup, she thought, wiping her forehead with the paint-streaked back of her palm, nothing makes panic recede faster than a glass of water. She went into the kitchen and ran the tap, waiting for the water to turn cold. She was standing like that, feeling the sensation of the running water on the tips of her fingers, like she was washing off all the anxiety, when she heard the click of the front door and Peggy walked in, looking flushed and happy.

'Oh hey!' Peggy said smiling widely. 'Didn't realize you'd be home! You painting? Can I see?'

'What are you doing?' Ameena replied, staring at Peggy's feet, at her shoes on Peggy's feet.

'What do you mean?' Peggy asked, and then, following Ameena's glance, she said, 'Oh, I just borrowed your shoes.'

'Oh, you just borrowed my shoes?'

'Ameena, you weren't home, or I'd have asked. I've borrowed your shoes lots of times before, you've never cared!' Peggy said, sounding genuinely surprised.

'Peggy, those shoes you've borrowed in the past cost £10 from a shop called Poundsmart where nothing in the entire shop costs more than ten quid – the shoes on your feet cost $400 from Barney's and were bought explicitly for my show. You should have the sense to know the difference,' Ameena snapped and then went into her bedroom, slamming the door behind her.

'I love Peggy,' she told David later that night on the phone, 'but she's got too many boundary issues. Not surprising really given all that childhood trauma. Anyway, tonight was just the final straw kinda thing, I've been thinking about this for a while, I need to move out.'

The following morning, Ameena, who usually worked through her lunch breaks at the magazine, rang David and asked if he could meet her for lunch at the café across from the advertising agency.

'It's fine,' she said coolly into the phone. 'I'm entitled to a proper lunch once in a while that doesn't involve eating a handful of nuts while staring at the computer. In any case, if Whitney paid me for all the hours I've spent working overtime, she wouldn't be able to afford me.'

'Shall I come to you?' David asked cautiously.

'No, I'm tired of everything around here. I'll take the train to you, we can go to Arabella's. I like their salads.'

And so, when he broached the subject for the second time, they were sitting at a window table at Arabella's, a bright, contemporary space done in blues and oranges and chrome and glass, directly across the street from David's work, and Ameena was toying with her arugula, staring into her laptop at the email Suzy had sent about possible themes for the next show.

'Okay,' she said distractedly, curling a few strands of long black hair around her index finger, still focused intently on her email.

'Really?' he asked, reaching across the table and rubbing his thumb on her cheek.

'Yes, sure,' she said squinting at her laptop. 'Let's shortlist some places tonight and go look at them at the weekend. Shadows? Do you think as a theme for the next show? Faith? Identity? Identity – God, I barely have my own identity figured out, my *work's* meant to have identity?'

She had dropped her finger to type something and he noticed that the strands of hair she had been playing with now fell loosely by the side of her face, a series of pretty curlicues.

'Wow, this is a change of heart... last time...'

She popped a candied pecan into her mouth and shrugged. 'Last time there was no expectation of my saying no. This time there was no expectation of my saying yes. Shit!' she swore suddenly, jumping up with a start and snapping her laptop shut.

'What?'

'I am on deadline for the magazine. I totally forgot. Piece on boyfriend jeans. Whitney's obsession.'

'Quit.'

'What?'

'Quit your job, paint full-time, move in with me.'

'...make my breakfast, massage my feet, iron my underwear?' she said, raising her eyebrows.

'I'm serious. I'll never borrow your shoes.'

'I don't know that,' she said with a wink as she walked outside and hailed a cab.

But the following Saturday, after informing Peggy (not without some guilt) that she needed a bigger workspace – no, it had nothing to do with the shoes; yes, they would obviously still be friends; yes, it had something to do with David; no, of course she wasn't sure she was ready, but who the hell ever is; yes, she was positive it wasn't the shoes – Ameena moved in with David into a small, more than slightly ramshackle two-bedroom rented apartment in a white stucco building in the West Village, a tenth-floor corner space that – its only saving grace – looked directly across onto the Hudson River through capacious New York-style windows. 'It feels like being on a boat,' Ameena said to David, as she lowered herself onto a carboard box and, crouching on all fours, pushed it towards him, sliding like a skier across the worn but still beautiful herringbone floor – 'so open, so... free.' She stood up suddenly and gazed across the water. 'My second show, Mr Greenberg, is going to be themed around Freedom and I'm going to sell out the fucking gallery.'

2.17

Reclining on the Eames lounge chair in his office – real leather, solid cherry, and one hundred percent genuine – Hershel was anxious.

The previous morning, just after he'd woken from sleep and to his acute embarrassment, he had leaked before he made it to the toilet, and then, when he managed to get to the toilet – literally sprinting from his bedroom – he had felt an uncomfortable burning sensation during the act.

Hershel didn't like that.

His father had died of prostate cancer and his uncle before him, the latter at only forty-two. Forty-two! Imagine that! When life begins at forty! Or so the Hallmark birthday cards decreed with such authority. Which meant, if one believed that kind of thing (*should* one believe that kind of thing?), that the poor man's life had ended almost as soon as it had begun.

And so, as far as Hershel was concerned, the episode from the previous morning didn't bode well.

Hershel said nothing to his wife. He had learned many years ago that it was best, as far as his wife was concerned, to keep unnecessary chit-chat to a minimum. And so, saying nothing had hardly been the result of any kind of deliberate construct; it was habit – it simply hadn't occurred to him to tell her. Instead, he went to work at the usual time and proceeded to spend the day in his office with the door closed, sitting on his prized Eames chair, which no one else was allowed to sit on – Hershel's Rules – in a kind of terrified daze.

When he returned home that evening, at the usual time, his

wife looked at his face, deathly pale and drawn, and asked while she prepped the linguine, 'What in heaven bites you?'

But he didn't reply, just poured himself a glass of whisky on ice and ate his linguine like an obedient child, even though it was over-salted, overcooked and bland. Funny, he thought, looking at his cherubic wife as she sucked the last linguine off her plate with the expertise of a native Bensonhurstite and generously helped herself to more – who would've thought an Italian couldn't cook Italian?

Hershel hardly slept a wink that night, and felt, when his sleeping wife with her unimpeachable health turned on her side to face him, a sharp, surprising envy.

The following day at the office was more or less an unhappy rerun of the previous one, spent on the Eames chair, doing no work, doing absolutely nothing, crippled by the fear of dying, until that young, unfairly handsome lady-magnet of a David had knocked on his door and shown him the revised pitch for the chocolate milk company – an argument, he explained, built on health and positive feelings rather than on cold, hard, capitalistic facts and figures.

'I'll peruse it,' Hershel said in a miserable voice, and if David had hesitated at the door, he didn't notice. For the next hour, Hershel went through the pitch dully, not because it did not merit excitement, but because his present state of mind precluded anything but malaise.

And then. And *then*, he came upon a page titled: 'How Emotions Can Make You Sick'.

'Our subjective self (David wrote) is constantly creating information molecules that control our health and psychology. In other words, our emotional selves ceaselessly produce physical changes. Ergo: can choco + milk own your emotional health?' And so on...

At which point something within Hershel's paralysed soul sparked a tiny flicker of life.

For what young David had so cleverly introduced as a conversation idea, Hershel thought, heaving himself up from the chair – designed, they said, to look like a baseball mitt, so it could fit one's body like a glove – with a vigour absent from his being for the past two days, was exactly the kick up the ass that he needed.

Because – he realised this now and the truth filled him like a warm dose of ambrosia – it was not the painful pee alone that was making him sick, it was the fear and anxiety *surrounding* the painful pee. The Event, not in its simple static state, but in all its dynamic possibilities, a kind of *projection* of sorts – what it could mean and would mean and must mean. Which was exactly the same kind of fear and anxiety he had been consumed by when he married the Italian, when (by some monstrous accident) his son was born, and when that son turned out to be gay.

Not the actual happenings per se, but the deeper significance of what The Event(s) implied. For him and to him and about him.

As in:

1. I've married a woman I don't love.
2. I've had a child I never wanted.
3. The child I never wanted from the woman I don't love has felt this palpable absence of love.

Ergo I, Hershel Eli Horowitz, am single-handedly to blame for the dubious sexual orientation of my one and only *Bubbala bambino*.

There. He had said it. He had finally fucking said it.

Hershel inhaled noisily, profoundly moved by his own remarkable display of courage.

Yes. The *projection* from each of these Events had, in sequence, caused him immense mental trauma over the course of his adult life. Unspeakable stress. He had self-destructed his own emotional health. He had allowed himself, in his own life, to be ruled by pathos – emotional appeal, *suffering*, the ancient Greeks called it.

And, incredible *putz* that he was, he was doing it to himself, once again.

What, after all, thought Hershel when he had composed himself sufficiently, was cancer of the prostate (if indeed he did have it), compared to a cancer of the mind? Peanuts! Literally!

And with that, Hershel E. Horowitz, God of Branding, felt as if the odious weight that had sat on his shoulders for nearly thirty years had finally been lifted. And by that piano-playing mensch!

The fact of the matter was that Hershel had known in his heart, even on the day he had hired David, that the boy would eventually leave, that he was much too talented a musician to stay doing *this* stuff. Yet, he had hired him because he had been too greedy not to, but had always carried, as a result of it, some small resentment towards the boy, because unlike him, when it came down to the expansive question of what one wanted to do with one's life, he, Hershel did not have choices. But at this point in time, even that could not diminish David.

For thanks to David alone, Hershel now knew with a kind of startling clarity exactly what he needed to do.

He needed to *own* his emotional health.

And he needed to do that *now*.

Own now.

(Well! And wasn't that a perfectly splendid anagram that could be put to work fairly imminently!)

But for the moment, more precious things beckoned.

Once he was sure David had left the vicinity of his office, he opened his desk drawer and pulled out his Rolodex containing the phone numbers of all his worldly contacts – there must have been hundreds of them, arranged by Sally, his secretary, in alphabetical order. Hershel, however, knew what he was looking for, and when he found it, the small rectangular, cream-coloured business card with the neat italicised print, he stopped and picked up the phone.

'Can I help you? Hold the line please,' asked/said the clipped voice of the receptionist somewhere higher up on Madison Avenue.

'Oh yes,' he replied cheerfully to no one, 'you sure can.'

And while Hershel held the phone to his ear, listening to one of those badly remixed showtunes (What was this? 'Oh, What a Beautiful Morning'? But how apt!) that are expressly chosen to be played on a loop to make one hang up the phone and give up on life altogether, he felt almost happy. Because what was it that the famous Australian writer had said? Or maybe he was English?

No one gets out alive?

That's right, Hershel thought, wanting to laugh out loud – stress-full or stress-free, *everyone always dies.*

2.18

'Mum, I've met someone.'

Ameena had agonised over this particular phone call for days now, finding every reason she could think of to put it off, but then the move had happened so suddenly, and she was living with David now and she knew no matter how bad this would be, it would be far worse, if somehow they found out in some other way, through someone else or if she herself at some point in the future inadvertently let something slip.

But still, she worried. She worried that on top of everything else that she had done or not done that had caused her parents to be disappointed in her, this would be creating for them a whole new threshold of sadness.

She knew they worried about her. We always know who worries about us. She also knew they worried about her in a completely different way than they worried about Kareem, almost in an antithetical way, as if between the two of them, neither she nor her brother had succeeded in providing a counterbalance to each other in a way that allows some parents to say with equanimity, 'At least we have one child that turned out okay...'

Finally, she decided to do it, just do it, without thinking about it too much. Rip off the Band-Aid, as 'they' said – quickest way, best way, though she knew that 'they' were always saying something to make people feel a certain delusional optimism about life, which didn't make any of what 'they' said particularly heartening at all.

She decided to call in the morning when David had gone for his run and when she knew Kareem would be at college – shit-stirrer, that's what he was, he'd only make a bad situation worse. Better to speak to her parents first.

And so...

'Mum, I've met someone,' she said, then held her breath.

'Ohhhh Ameena,' her mother was literally gurgling, 'that is *wonderful*! My *child*! My *daughter*! But, who is the boy? Is it someone we know? Is it Aunty Neelum's son?'

'Mum, I haven't met Aunty Neelum since the first week I arrived, and I haven't met her son, ever.'

'Then who?'

'Ok Ammi, I need you not to overreact. O-kay?' she said very slowly and calmly.

On the other end of the phone line, she heard a low gasp. 'Ameena, is he... is he A BLACK?'

'Dear God, Mum.'

'Ameena.' Swift and sharp. A warning.

'No! No! He's not black. Okay? Happy? Though, I'm really quite offended that you would find that problematic in any—'

'Oh God, he's a *HINDU*?'

'No! *Mum!* Listen, he's not Hindu. He's not Indian. Or Pakistani. He's American. He's... white.'

'Ohhh Christian. Thank *GOD*. That is bad, but not terrible. Terrible, but not unthinkable. Christian is still *Christian*. Confessing lies to wooden boxes and all such cuckoo business. But still, it is a religion of the book. It could be worse.' Ameena could literally see the shudder pass through her mother's body.

She sighed. 'Uh... Mum, he's not, exactly, Christian. He's Jewish.'

A strange choking sound. Then silence.

Ameena grimaced. 'Judaism is... also a religion of the book,' she ventured.

She could hear a faint crackling on the phone. Nothing else.

'Umm... so, like I was saying... David is Jewish, but he's not observant.'

'Oh, very good, very good! One un-religious Muslim and one un-religious Jew! What do you think, two bad people make one good person? Two infidels make one fidel? *Chee! Chee! Chee! Shame* on you both.'

'Mum, are you *crying*?'

'No, no, I am not crying,' she wailed. 'I am laughing. I am celebrating that my daughter has broken my heart. Ameena, they are slaughtering us in Palestine. Slaughtering us like goats and sheeps.'

'Sheep.'

'What?'

'It's sheep. Not sheeps. He's got nothing to do with Palestine. Look, let me speak to Dad.'

There was a muffled sob followed by a silence that seemed to last forever. Then Ameena heard her father's voice – soft-spoken and gentle. Calming. A waterfall gurgling over smooth rock. The same effect on her as it had always had.

'Ameena...'

'Abbu... I...'

'Ameena, I would advise you against all this. The world is not kind to those who make such choices. But you are a grown woman now, you must make your own decisions. I can only advise you and I think you already knew my feelings before you made this phone call.'

'Abbu...'

'We will speak later, Ameena, when I have thought about your situation more carefully. Please speak to your mother.'

'His parents will *hate* you,' Ameena's mother cried. She seemed to be sobbing now, loudly and openly.

'He doesn't have parents, Mum.'

At this, Zoya let out a long, doleful howl.

'Orphan! You want to marry orphan who has never been loved by parents! How will such a person love his *wife*?'

'God Ammi, his parents *died*. Can you show some compassion? Anyway, we aren't getting married. I'm just... well... I'm just dating him.'

'But, Ameena – *orphan*?' She was begging now, pleading, Ameena could hear it in her voice.

'Well, his parents won't hate me now, will they?'

'Yes, but he will make you into his dead mother. I am warning you Ameena, I know how it is with these white boys and their mothers. Joined together on the hip. Even if it is dead hip on ghost mother.'

Ameena rolled her eyes. 'Alright Ammi, I'll speak to you later, okay?'

'My grandchildren won't love me,' she howled.

'*Who*?'

'My *grandchildren* won't love me. I don't think Kareem is ever going to meet any decent girl – he is all the time with those hooligan friends of his gallivanting here and there. You were my only hope for loving grandchildren, and now even that is gone. Gone and dead. Dead, dead, everything dead. I may as well be dead too.'

'Mum. Seriously, you've got to stop this.'

'But my grandchildren...'

'Okay, I need to go to work now.'

'What is his work, this David?'

'*His* work? Oh. He works for an advertising agency...' she hesitated. 'He's also a musician, a pianist. He plays jazz.'

'Jazz?' Zoya repeated the word blankly as if she was hearing it for the first time in her life.

Ameena sucked in her breath. 'Jazz, Mum. Louis Armstrong, Miles Davis, Duke Ellington, Count Basie...'

'These are his friends? He is friends with Duke and Count?'

'Oh God, Mum. No. Forget it.'

'Okay, send me photo.'

'What?'

'Photo. PHO-TO. Are you deaf now? Send me the photo of this Jewish David.'

In New York, Ameena didn't tell David about the conversation she'd had – there hardly seemed any point. He came back from his run, energised and happy, his cheeks flushed with the early-morning cold, and they both sat down at the breakfast bar, the smell of toast and coffee in the air, and she asked about his run and he told her about bumping into their neighbour – a silver-haired woman who wrapped her dog in a tartan blanket and 'walked' him every morning at 6am in a child's pram – and she laughed and felt a great love fill up in her body for him, a kind of billowing – like she had missed her footing off a cliff and fallen into the sea and her skirt was billowing in the water, and far away the sails were billowing in the wind, and the sea itself was billowing, by the power of what she felt – for the decency of his face and the openness of his laugh and for his honesty and his earnestness and his dreams – and it filled her with a lightness and a freedom.

In Manchester, it was raining. Ameena's mother put the phone down with a weight on her heart. She felt her chest tighten, but it was not only a physical discomfort that she felt, it was something else – a precise, familiar pain she knew only too well. She knew what it was like to be in love. She knew that feeling well. And she knew another feeling. She knew what is was like when that love went away. The unbearable loneliness, the excruciating ache of separation. She knew that feeling too. She did not envy her daughter. She did not envy this boundless optimism that young people had, this exuberant belief that somehow things had changed in the world, that things would be different and better for them.

No, she did not envy that. Nor did she envy what would follow – the enormous crushing disappointment when they realised, as everyone eventually did, that nothing was different, nothing was better, everything was exactly as it had always been – and that life, in the end, when you tallied up the score, was nothing but one tremendous compromise.

2.19

The last of autumn sprinted by in blazing red and passed the baton to winter.

Winter in New York, Ameena thought to herself as she wrapped her deep purple scarf around her face so only her eyes were visible, was a different kind of entertainment altogether. Wintertime was wet in Manchester, and perennially dark, and damp and windy, and the sky turned a particular shade of very-sad-grey, and there was frost, sure, and hail and other such handouts from heaven, but all that compared to *this* was small-time, a laugh, an insult even – for this here was cold, true cold, pukka winter, where your lips turned blue (actually) and your fingers might fall off if you foolishly left your gloves in the pockets of a different coat – which authenticity didn't change the fact that she dreaded every minute of it.

Ah, but we'll always have Fifth Avenue, she thought with a smile, as she walked down the broad sidewalk, lit up like a fairyland. And then she thought – exactly as she had done the previous year around this time – that they really did buy into the spirit of the season in this place.

The shopfronts had been transformed, everywhere was covered in garlands and twinkling lights and glowing balls of glitter and snow-powdered sparkly stars. It was really quite dazzling, she decided appreciatively, and probably exactly the kind of energy recharge that she, like so many other weary people, needed, as yet another year drew to a close.

This was the thing: in America, someone always bought what someone else sold.

Ameena had spent the last four hours in the apartment, painting a piece for her next show – a painting called *The Headdress*, an idea that had gestated within her for weeks, and that she had finally been able to transfer, with some (limited, she thought) success, to paper and when it was done, she felt both joyful and drained, as if everything she had within her, she had given to the piece, and now she was empty, her reserves exhausted, a camel without water.

She needed replenishment. And so, she'd come out to seek it. Even if it was from the inhumanely cold wellspring of New York City at Christmastime.

David was at a session at a friend's place in Brooklyn. He had called her earlier to tell her that Hershel had given him the afternoon off – an uncharacteristic move that David preferred not to jeopardise by trying to question. Instead, he'd accepted the gesture gratefully, if not with some slight suspicion, called a musician friend to see if he wanted to play, and the friend had invited him over to his home. Ameena knew him, the bassist from Brooklyn, originally from St John, a highly functioning, incredibly dexterous, intuitive jazz player.

For a moment, she considered going down there to listen to them. None of the guys David played with seemed to mind the few occasions when she had tagged along, sitting on the floor of wherever they were playing, knees up under her chin, watching them, loving their music for loving's sake, but she knew David wouldn't answer his phone in the middle of a session and she didn't like showing up unannounced; a childhood habit, she had always hated being interrupted when she was focused on something, even if it was reading a book, and therefore assumed that everybody else also shared that particular preference.

And so, she decided to walk the length of Fifth Avenue instead, past the extraordinary neo-Gothic façade of St Patrick's Cathedral, past the laughing ice skaters at Rockefeller Center, past the shop windows all decked out for Christmas. It's so funny, she thought, that someone took all that trouble over shop windows, so strange that we would even think of doing something like that, dressing up buildings and windows and trees in all this tinsel and light.

She stopped outside one of the big, famous department shops, almost unrecognisable in its festive holiday makeover. Like Cinderella, she thought, in crystal slippers, all dressed up for the ball.

A group of Japanese tourists were taking pictures, their voices high-pitched, full of excitement, thrilling endlessly, it seemed, to the idea of storytelling windows.

'You're always in a hurry,' she had remarked to David all those months ago when they first met. 'Why, may I ask, are you always in a hurry?'

'I don't know,' he'd replied, bemused by the question. 'Am I? I guess it's a New York thing.'

'Well,' she had retorted adamantly. 'I love New York, but it's never going to become my thing.'

But no, she thought with a sigh. She'd been wrong. For Ameena, even in the past year, time had taken on an urgency she'd never experienced before in her life and before she even realised it, it *had* become her thing.

Cities are like that. Cities change you.

Ameena turned towards the shop then, almost on principle, as if it would be some great English betrayal if she didn't make use of this present luxury of snatched time. She pressed her nose up against the glass and peered through the shop windows, one by one. The theme for that year seemed to be snow globes, the windows all showcasing wintery scenes through the lens of these big, perfectly round spheres of glass. In the first window, two polar bears were exchanging a special moment in a celebratory high five, the second one showed a starry night set against NYC skyscrapers, a third was the elaborate set of a vintage circus, next, a woodland wonderland and then, the grand finale – Santa in a red suit inside a snow globe, looking into his own miniature storified snow globe.

It was completely mesmerising, Ameena had to admit, so detailed and ornate – and *so* imaginative, those vignettes.

She stepped back, took one last longing look at the complete display, and walked on, feeling, once again, intrigued by the very concept of window decorations, the care that went into creating those little details. There was something both baffling and beautiful about the pointlessness of it, she thought, a kind of giving in to something, like the act of a child throwing an elaborate tea party for her dolls.

She thought then of Denise Richards, her friend at home, whom she had known since she was five, whom she still kept in touch with, who seemed to be constantly in and out of love, believing everything, giving into everything.

Same sort of thing really.

Walking alongside her on the broad sidewalk, a tall lady held the stripy gloved hand of a little boy. They were both wearing woolly coats and scarves, and something about the woman, her height or maybe it was the elegant manner in which she carried her ankle-length black coat, or maybe it was just the protective way in which she held the little boy's hand, made Ameena stop and notice them.

'Mommy, is Santa just the tooth fairy dressed up like a fat man?' the boy wanted to know.

'Is Santa what? No, Jake! Santa is *not* the tooth fairy.'

He nodded. Then, 'Is Santa real? Is the tooth fairy real?'

'Yes, *of course* they're real,' his mother prevaricated with the rehearsed expertise of a parent.

Am I going to die? Ameena had asked her mother when she got her first period at thirteen. She'd been the first of her friends to get it. She'd never been told about it at home. They didn't talk about such things in her family. The birds and the bees and other such instructive material, that she found out later all her white friends had been proffered, was not something her family believed in discussing.

'Don't be so stupid Ameena,' her mother had replied impatiently, 'you're never going to die.'

On Fifth Avenue, it started to snow.

'But are they *Two. Separate. People*?' the boy persisted.

'Jake, look at that beautiful Christmas tree on the sidewalk,' his mother said, trying to change the subject, another prerequisite of effective modern-day parenting.

'That's not a Christmas tree. That's a bush with lights around it.'

Ameena stifled a laugh. How wonderful it must be, she thought, to say it exactly as it is.

The boy noticed her suddenly and she realised that she must look very odd to him, with her face all covered up in her scarf like that – a fuzzy purple head with eyes popping out like Barney!

On a whim, she unravelled her scarf, wrapping it round her neck instead, and smiled at the boy, but he only stared back at her, his eyes serious and unsmiling. She was just starting to wonder if the old 'don't talk to strangers' had evolved into 'don't even smile at strangers', and if so, how sad, even the idea of a world in which children no longer smile freely – when she saw that they were about to turn off onto one of the side streets. On an impulse she made a face. The boy made a face back. She smiled. He didn't. Standing on the street corner, waiting for her light to change, as the snowflakes – so perfectly symmetrical, they seemed almost unnatural – fell from the sky, Ameena saw the boy turn round a few more times to look at her, but he never smiled, not once. And then he didn't turn around any more.

She shrugged. Oh well, she thought, can't win 'em all.

Come to think of it, she'd never been told about her period, even *after* she had got her period that first time. She'd never, for example, been told that it would happen again, the following month and then every month after that forever and ever. Well, almost that.

She'd been told a few other things though. That first time she found the hideous brown streak on her panties, she'd been told that it was a good, normal thing to happen, and that it was part of becoming a young woman – a virtuous, responsible Muslim woman.

And so later, when Denise got it too, and then Katie after her and Roshni and Alison and Jane, she had been surprised, because she thought it was only something that happened to good *Muslim* girls, that made them turn into good Muslim women – a kind of coming of age exclusively reserved for people like her.

So then, when she got it the second time, she was convinced she was going to die. Because she'd never been told there'd be a second time. She'd only been told that she was never going to die. And even then, she hadn't believed it.

All around her, the world turned white.

2.20

'What are you working on?' Ameena asked when he got up to get a drink. David had been engrossed for hours on his piano with his headphones on and Ameena could tell there was something different about his body language – he was always so relaxed when he was working on his music. This time there was a stiffness about him, his posture, the worry lines near his eyes, the way he ran his hand through his hair repeatedly, as if he seemed troubled, anxious about something.

'Oh... stuff...' he said vaguely, filling a glass with ice up to the very top, a very American habit, she had come to realise.

'What kind of stuff?' she asked.

'Oh, it's nothing. There's this guy, Bennie, heard me play at the club the other day, wants to see some of my work...' He frowned. 'And it's hard. I'm not used to the idea that the thing I just played is worth writing down and keeping as the definitive measure of a song as opposed to the thing I might improvise five seconds later. It kinda requires an attitude that's a little different from the attitude of, okay I'm going to make up the best thing I can in the moment and then I'm going to make up something else one second later.'

'He wants to *see* your work, meaning like a tune? *Your* tune?'

David shrugged. 'Yeah.'

'That's not nothing, that's *amazing*!'

David started to pour orange juice into his glass. He had only filled about a third of it when he realised – with some surprise it seemed to Ameena – that the carton was empty. He swore softly under his breath and as Ameena watched, he crushed the empty carton, put it in the recycling bin, opened the fridge once again and, without any visible qualms, filled the rest of his glass with apple juice.

'Ameena, there have been other guys in the past... nothing's ever come of it so I'm not jumping yet. I jumped the very first time, a little too high, didn't really land on my feet...'

'But you're so talented.'

He didn't say anything for a few seconds. She noticed the faint outline of a tiny frown above his brows, a slight, imperceptible hardening of his handsome, masculine jaw. Then he took a long sip of his serendipitous fruit cocktail. It was then, in that moment of watching David perform this innocuous and irrelevant task of drinking what she imagined to be a truly awful and vile concoction, in a way that did not seem to him to be awful and vile at all, that the realisation came to Ameena that no matter how significant she was to him or what superior significance she might attain in the future, for David, in his life, she would always come second.

This realisation of Ameena's was not conscious but subliminal, happening inside of her, microscopically, and what was surprising was only that it did not, as she would have expected, terrify her or make her sad, but filled her with a sense of calm and purpose as if a great anxiety that had been stalking her all this time had now been removed.

But all this was happening on the inside. On the outside she appeared unchanged and normal, just the way she always was, even perhaps slightly on edge given what he was saying.

'Well,' he was saying, 'it makes me very happy that you think so, but the reality, as you know, is that I can't really focus on my music while coming up with tag lines for instant coffee. It can't work like this. If you have respect for the art – and I do – I'm going to have to make a choice. Talent is great, but it stops being about talent after a point and becomes about work, commitment and getting a break.'

'Yes, but I got a break.'

David flicked a curl off his forehead. His lips twitched.

'Thanks to you, of course,' she added quickly.

He shook his head. 'You know, this isn't me asking for gratitude or anything so old-fashioned but to get your first art show in a dog-eat-dog city like New York without even trying doesn't just happen. You just happened to meet me, and I just happened to know Suzy, and she just happened to own a gallery. That's a terrific number of coincidences and I've always had a view on coincidences – when you have a whole bunch of them that make something happen or not happen, *that* has a name and it's called luck.'

'Wait, what is that tone? Are you *mad* at me? For the success of the art show? Are you advocating that ridiculous romantic notion that I'm not a true artist if I don't suffer for my art?'

David smiled at her trademark excitability and shook his head. 'Not at all. I'm telling you that the plural of anecdote is not data. And I'm also telling you that first chances are rare, second ones rarer.'

He kissed her on top of her head.

'So, I guess I am telling you not to screw it up.'

2.21

'I worry about Kareem,' Yusuf said to Zoya with a sigh as he put his book down on the small metal stool that served as his bedside table. It was a book about a Formula One driver who had literally crashed and burned and then made a miraculous comeback to win. Yusuf liked survival stories.

Zoya, in a light blue cotton nightie with smocking work on the neck (bought from Marks and Spencer on Market Street but made in Pakistan – she had noted this little detail on the label with a satisfied smile), was propped up in bed next to him watching a rerun of Begum Nadiya making chilli cheese burritos. She also, liked survival stories.

'I worry about Kareem,' Yusuf said again.

'Shhh...' Zoya tapped him impatiently on the shoulder without taking her eyes off the screen. 'I'm just seeing this. Wait a minute. This is a very important part because she tells you when to put the kidney beans in. You know how my kidney beans never cook properly, little buggers, always too hard. Timing is very important. Timing makes the difference between good burrito and bad burrito.'

She peered at the TV with intense concentration. 'Aah-hah!' she said a few minutes later, banging her hand down on the mattress so hard it made Yusuf jump. Not for the first time, he regretted giving in to this latest Zoya-demand of TV-mounted-on-bedroom-wall. 'Everybody has TV in bedroom,' Zoya had grumbled. 'Even Fiza, who does my upper lip threading.' He didn't dare ask if Fiza had a Nespresso machine in her kitchen, a far more palatable room to be discussing, Yusuf thought, than bedrooms, even between ladies threading upper lips, for what was present and what was absent from one's bedroom seemed to Yusuf to be a deeply personal affair. But that irony-laden pronouncement from Zoya had finally settled the matter, for how could Fiza who threaded upper lips for a living have a TV in her bedroom when Zoya, whose upper lip it was that paid for that luxury, didn't?

And so, it had been arranged for a TV with the wingspan of a Scottish seabird, or so it felt to Yusuf, to be mounted on the thin wall that separated their bedroom from Kareem's. The deed had been done by a burly, red-headed Mancunian who identified himself on arrival by means of a laminated card he wore on a narrow blue ribbon round his thick neck, which confirmed that he was, indeed, the person authorised to mount their new TV. How, Yusuf marvelled, of all the possible professions in the world, does one come to be the person who mounts TVs in other people's bedrooms? Chance or choice? For a young, white boy, sweet and sensitive and ripe for adulthood, it seems to Yusuf, a truly depressing profession. Yusuf looked curiously at the man, still a boy really, no older than twenty. He *seemed* happy enough, very smiley – in fact, Yusuf observed, a little too smiley. At what? he wondered, because the chap could not possibly *enjoy* this job of going around mounting TVs in people's bedrooms, but Zoya had smiled back, equally delighted, but with Mr Burly, or with the TV itself or what this would mean in power terms for the future of Zoya-Fiza bedroom discussions, he couldn't be sure.

In any case, Mr Burly had been offered (on arrival and post-identification) a coffee from the Nespresso machine, something Zoya never did with anyone who was not family or close friend – 'The pods, you see, are how these people make sure they have you by your nuts, for the rest of your life,' she had announced knowledgeably on several occasions. But the Nespresso had been offered and accepted, presumably at the risk of her husband's nuts, and the

TV had been mounted – too high, Yusuf thought critically as he lay in bed craning his neck at a painfully awkward angle watching Nadiya Hussein open a can of what seemed like already softened kidney beans and add them to her pot. '*Now* I see how she does it,' Zoya was saying, slapping the bed. 'So clever she is, Nadiya. So talented. So pretty, also.'

Satisfied then with the wholesomeness of that assessment, she turned the TV off magnanimously and turned to her husband. 'Yes, what were you saying?'

'I worry about Kareem,' Yusuf said for the third time, plumping his pillow.

'So? I worry about Ameena, what's new there?'

'Zoya, I am very serious.'

'What do you think I am? Tickle-Me-Elmo-Humorous?' She shook her head disdainfully. 'Okay, what is it you are so worried about?'

'He's...'

'Not you?'

'Zoya, please.'

'Okay,' she said in a tone that Yusuf knew meant she was conceding only because she couldn't be bothered, in that moment, to belabour that particular point, a familiar battle wound they both knew she had the power to open and close at will. This time, for some reason, she had graciously decided to leave it closed. 'Then what?'

'He's too... too...'

'Too religious?' she exclaimed, her excitement starting to mount. '*Haan? Haan?* Too Pakistani? Not white enough for you?'

'You know, Zoya, we live in this country now, it's important to assimilate.'

'Yes. Assimilate. Absorb. Dissolve! Like Ameena. Irreverent girl! No God, no country, no nothing. Painting things and living with Jews! That girl has no roots.'

'Their roots are *here*, in the West. They are Western children, British children. And that Jewish David seems like a decent fellow...'

'Decent? How do you know he is decent? He is orphan and Jewish. In his condition, it is very difficult to be decent. How can anyone be decent, when you have nobody who gives you love?'

Yusuf dismissed the insight with a wave of his hand.

'Anyway, Ameena is there now,' he intoned, 'Kareem is *here*. In this country. It would do him good to recognise that instead of roaming around all the time with those elements.'

'Elements? What is this, periodic chart?'

'Tch, tch. You know what I mean. Those boys he hangs around with all the time outside the mosque. I don't like them. They have radical thoughts.'

'Well, I think it is good he has ties to his God and his homeland. There is no need to become white man because we live in white country.'

'Zoya, you are the one who wanted to come here.'

'And you are the one who didn't,' she finished triumphantly.

He closed his eyes. 'There is no point having any discussion with you.'

'Then go to sleep,' she said, turning off the light switch above her head. 'Tomorrow, I will make chilli cheese burrito. Food of Mexico. In our kitchen in Manchester. Recipe from Nadiya. That is called assimilation.'

Next door, in Kareem's room, they heard a low, dull thud. Then it was quiet.

But a few minutes later, Zoya said, 'Are you awake?'

'I am now,' Yusuf replied wryly.

But she let that pass without the temptation of biting back. Instead she said, 'If we have any trouble, Yusuf, it will be from Ameena. You mark my words.'

Next to her, Yusuf felt a tiny quiver in his heart, for Zoya's words, intended to comfort him, had only served to deepen his worries. A reminder of how little we know the people we think we know. How unqualified we are to make assumptions on their behalf. How we don't get to choose our children, just like they get scarce choice in the matter as well. And how wrong we can be to think we know how our children will act, to think we know which one of them will cause trouble. And when. And how.

2.22

He came, like trouble often does, unexpectedly and in the dark.

Ameena answered the door and returned to the dining table with an odd, blank look.

'It's your brother,' she announced.

Abraham was tall, like really tall, Ameena thought, well over six feet, with long hair and a full beard and small, strikingly green eyes. He was built as well, strong and muscular and big – just plain *big* – in exactly the kind of way that David wasn't. In fact, never in a million years would you think the two men were related – save for the dimples, but where David had what Ameena liked to call an 'aspiring dimple' on his left cheek, Abe had a pronounced set on both sides, deep and defined, that made him look, when he smiled, like a little boy.

He came holding a small canvas travel bag and nothing else, which he explained very shortly thereafter by reporting that he would be staying 'only a few days, if it's okay by you of course' – and he looked at Ameena when he said that and Ameena was grateful for it, but noted that none of the three of them chose to elaborate on what 'only a few' meant, specifically speaking.

'I thought I'd stop by,' he said, when he was seated on the living room sofa and offered a glass of wine, which he declined in favour of water; David sitting across him on the armchair, Ameena hovering around nervously, unsure of whether she should stay or she should go, what politeness demanded in a situation such as this. 'I thought I'd stop by on my way to Israel.'

Ameena sat down.

'Abe,' said David, 'if you're coming from Australia, New York isn't on the way to Israel.'

'Yes, yes, I know, but I wanted to go... home first... you know, to Rhode Island, to the... the house.'

'The house doesn't exist any more. It's a drugstore now. The garden out the front, when you turn off the main road, is the parking lot.'

'A *drug*store? Fuck me dead. Oh sorry,' he said, looking at Ameena, ''scuse my French.'

Then he laughed. 'That's kinda funny isn't it. A drugstore when ain't no drugs could save her.' He looked intently at David through those smoky green eyes, the colour of the ocean on a stormy night. 'And the path...?'

'The path to the beach is still there.'

His huge body heaved suddenly as if he had let release some kind of tightness in his chest and Ameena wondered why the continued existence of some path would cause such a reaction when the house itself – ostensibly a far more meaningful thing – had been razed to the ground.

'Gosh,' Ameena said because no one else was speaking, 'I feel like I should break out the cake and the champagne or something. How long has it been since you two have seen each other?'

'Seven years,' David said promptly. 'How did you even find out where I lived?'

'I googled you, brother.'

'You googled me?'

'Yeah. It's not hard to find someone in New York, you know. Small city. *Tiny.* The same people walking the same streets, forming the same bad habits. Pretending as if everything in the universe emanates from here. Provincial, if you ask me.'

Ameena looked down. David felt his face go very warm. 'Why are you going to Israel?'

'It would have made Dad happy.'

'You're going to Israel because it would have *made Dad happy*?'

'Yeah. I mean, I'm going to pay my respects you know, to the homeland, like you, all of you' – he waved his hand in the air somewhere in the region of Ameena's face – 'go to Palestine, don't you, on pilgrimage?'

'Mecca,' Ameena said quietly.

'Meck-huh?'

David stood up, and when Ameena glanced at him, she could see the lines appear around his mouth, the lines that barely concealed the beginnings of anger and who knew what other emotion, but she remained seated where she was and, with a small shake of her head, said calmly, 'Mecca. Muslims go to Mecca on pilgrimage. Not Palestine.'

'Oh yeah, sorry.'

'But there does exist,' she continued, 'since you brought it up, the third holiest site in Islam, on Temple Mount, in the heart of Jerusalem.'

'Right,' said David, still standing up, 'how about you and I carry on our brotherly conversation while Ameena goes to bed. She's got an early start tomorrow.'

'Oh,' said Abe, 'but I'm enjoying this so much. So, Ameena – am I saying your name right? Where you from, beyond the fancy English accent and stuff?'

'From England.'

'Haha, no, I mean, where are you really from?'

'I'm really from Manchester. Which is really in England.'

He shrugged. 'Okay,' he said agreeably. And then, 'You work on a Sunday?'

'Pardon?' Ameena asked.

'It's Saturday night. He said you had an early start. What are you, a nurse or something?'

'She's a writer. And an artist,' David said tersely before she could answer.

Abraham whistled, but his eyes, Ameena noticed, were not warm. 'Good stuff! Come to think of it, I've been sitting here admiring all this art on your walls. Of course, I didn't know it was yours. Does it mean something? Is it symbolic?'

'Hey Abe, I think Ameena can tell you the meaning of her art another time. Shall we?'

'No, no, I'd like to...' Ameena said pleasantly. 'So, I think my work is more about conveying a personal perspective rather than making some sort of specific statement – it's idiosyncratic in that sense. I would like my art to slow the viewer down, make them stop and think. In a way, the hope is to delay the moment of understanding.'

'*Personal* perspective, like how?'

He stood up, the full length of him, and walked towards a small painting blazing with bright purples and shades of green and what looked like a river of rocks snaking through the centre and disappearing off the edge, almost into the frame.

He looked at it, then he turned to look at her. 'What's the moment of understanding in this one?' There was something in his eyes then, a kind of expectant light that Ameena couldn't place, only she knew it unnerved her.

With a small, polite smile, she said, 'Well, it's what you make of it really as the beholder, but in my head, I was picturing the dry-stone walls of the North Yorkshire Moors. It is spectacular terrain, especially in the summer, covered in heather – you never know where the moors end, they seem to roll on and on and then they meet the sky.'

He nodded. 'And that one?'

'Ah, that's Rhode Island,' she said, flushing. 'Your brother took me. It's meant to be an abstraction of the lighthouse and a fishing boat on the bay, just inverted, a kind of mirror image, like you're looking down from the sky at the reflection in the water...'

'Oh...?' he said, staring at the painting, a thoughtful look on his face.

'Sorry,' she said apologetically, 'it might not seem that way to you at all. I mean, it's seascape that's much more intimately familiar to you than I could ever...'

'That's weird. To me the boat doesn't look like a boat at all, it looks like a plane... slicing through the sky... straight towards the tall building... see...'

'You little bastard!' David said, his voice shaking with rage.

Ameena took a sharp intake of breath.

Abe laughed, and his dimples deepened delightfully.

'Oh, for fuck's sakes guys, don't look so outraged, I'm only messing with ya!'

But in two strides, David was by his side, grabbing his arm and steering him forcefully into the spare room.

'Hey! *Hey*! What are you doing? Let go of me, I'm a grown man now. Fucking hell David, come *on*!'

The door to the spare room slammed shut.

Ameena put a hand to her head. She felt weary now, like a soldier who has just had his first sighting of the enemy troops and realised with a sinking heart that no matter how brave he or his man should hope to be, or how fearless, that they wouldn't stand a chance in the face of that particular enemy, that they were no match for their scale, their strength, their brutality, or their power.

She got up shakily and started to clear away the dinner that they had abandoned midway. It made her sick, the sight of the half-eaten fish on the pretty olive earthenware platter in the middle of the table, its centre bone splayed open, naked and hideous. She threw the lot in the bin, the leftover fish, the vegetables, the untouched loaf of bread that she had proudly baked herself that evening. Wasting food was something she never did, a passing down of her mother's habit, but then long-lost brothers were something that never returned unannounced either. 'Never say never, hey?' she said aloud to herself and then laughed – a thin, hollow, crazy-woman laugh.

When David came into the bedroom later – was it minutes, hours? – she was lying in bed, watching a rerun of a popular sitcom on TV. 'Hey,' she said, and she smiled because she was genuinely happy to see him.

'I've asked him to leave,' David said, his voice still ringing with anger, and Ameena realised in a moment of surprise that she'd never seen David angry before, not like this.

'No, no, don't do that. It's okay, he was joking. He said so.'

'It wasn't funny.'

'No,' she agreed, 'it wasn't. But he's your brother, and he only wants to stay a few nights and well, where else will he go at this hour?'

'Ameena, that's not your problem. I've already asked him to leave. I have no problem asking him to leave. This is your home. He has no right to insult you in your home. Hell, he has no right to insult you anywhere. But especially not in your home.'

Ameena took a deep breath. Then she nodded and smiled at an indistinct spot on the wall. 'No, it's fine,' she said quickly before she had an opportunity to change her mind, 'he can stay.'

'Are you sure?' David ventured cautiously.

'Yes,' she said with finality, 'I'm sure.'

He sat down next to her then and held her, so her face was buried, if only for a few delicious seconds, in his warmth. 'Thank you,' he said lightly, but in his voice, she heard something that sounded distinctly like respect. 'And know that I'll make it up to you.'

She freed herself of him and winked. 'I have very expensive taste, you know...' she said.

At that, he smiled but she noticed how the smile did not reach his eyes. 'Uh-oh,' he said mechanically, and then he was up and at the door. 'I'll go let him know, the spoilt brat, I'll let him know he's only staying because you let him. Be right back.'

But he wasn't right back and then Ameena switched the TV off and put out the lights and pretended that none of the words she heard from the other room, words like Muslim and Arab and terrorist, ringing clear and loud through the thin walls, had been exchanged at all, that she had imagined them, like one sometimes does when one is afraid of something that hasn't even happened.

She didn't know when David came to bed, but he was still asleep next to her in the morning when she woke, his face peaceful, his hair falling in a lazy curl over his forehead the way it did, and when she stepped out into the hallway – tiptoeing like a burglar in her own home – she realised when she peeked her head through the open doorway that the sofa-bed in the spare room had been perfectly made, the bathroom had been left spotless, and Abraham had gone.

2.23

Why, Ameena had asked him some time ago, if you came from a musical mother, didn't you become a full-time professional musician to begin with? Didn't you think, as a boy, that that's just what one does when one grows up?

David had told her that he never thought he was good enough to afford the art the respect it deserved. To many others, accustomed to a less oblique conception of work, this might have seemed an odd response, but she had only nodded. Of course, she understood.

He had lied.

Not of course, that he believed he was good enough.

Which creative person, even if considered a kind of prodigy by others, believes, in their own mind, that they are ever quite good enough? This is the maddening thing about art, though admittedly, the very thing that keeps people like David going, the substrata of dissatisfaction that hooks them like a drug, the awareness that they are trying to get somewhere they know they will never reach.

But in answer to her question, that was not, strictly, the whole truth. *That* truth lay, as it usually does, in some other obscure place.

The truth lay in history.

The truth lay in circumstance.

It lay in being the older son of nervous immigrant parents who desperately wanted him to become *somebody* so that he would fit in with *everybody*, who clung to the idea that conformity was the best antidote to bigotry, who clung to the ideal of eventual equality in an unequal world, who clung to the belief that power could be earned and shifted, who clung to the hope that economic stability would lead to respectability, which in turn would lead to the eventual demise of the ghosts of the past that had followed them around for over two thousand years like a constant darkness. Who clung to all this like a lifeline.

The truth lay in his name.

As a young boy, he didn't ever get as far as the *fear* of failure. David Greenberg could not even have imagined it.

2.24

And then... Yusuf thought, waiting for Zoya to bring him his evening tea...

And then, there was Ameena.

A strong-willed and independent girl who had always known her own mind. She had assimilated admirably into this unknown, unfamiliar Western world. In fact, it was largely on account of her misery that they had stopped their annual visits back to Pakistan. There's nothing to do here, she would complain, only grown-ups drinking tea all day long. Nobody understands my accent, they keep asking me to repeat the same thing a hundred times. Which is fine because I don't really understand anything any of *them* are saying either. I've read all the books I brought with me from home. Mum says I'm not allowed to paint here. Kareem spends all his time playing cricket with those other boys on the street outside the house and they won't let me play because I'm a girl – they even told me that, can you believe it! So *sexist*! Seriously Abba, it's so unfair. It's so hot. It's so dirty. It's so crowded. It's so lonely. It's so boring. It's so strange.

Eventually they had decided to stop going. Especially after his and Zoya's parents had died. After that, there seemed to be nothing left for them back home, barring a kind of forced sentimentality. Plus, there was always trouble at the immigration desk on the way back. And so, he and Zoya had made the joint decision one day in the taxi back from Manchester Airport after they had been detained for hours in a little windowless room for no apparent reason – when it's more trouble than it's worth, it's better to stop. So, they had stopped, and no one had been happier than Ameena. Ameena was that way. She spoke her mind. Not a girl who believed in keeping things to herself. It was good, Yusuf thought, healthy, to let it out like that. Keeping things inside could make you sick, kill you slowly. At least in her own way Ameena had figured that out.

Kareem was different. In Kareem, there was a certain unflinching loyalty. And a sense of honour. And a quiet, repressed anger if his morality stood in danger of being violated. Yusuf saw Zoya in him. That's why he loved his son the way he did. He saw the boy's mother in the boy. Mirror and reflection. All her imperfections, all her flaws. And Yusuf loved his son in spite of them. Or maybe, he thought with a small smile, it was because of them.

And Ameena. He loved his daughter with all his heart, the kind of pure, boundless love that made him want to shield her from harm, to protect her from everything, including, if it came to that, from her own destiny. Uncanny though, between his two children, she was the more unpredictable one. She could express herself easily, but you never really knew what she was going to do next, what set her off. With Kareem, he believed what he believed. It might be frightening, what he believed, but at least you knew. You never really knew what Ameena believed. If she believed in anything at all.

This happened occasionally, he knew that, even in good, decent families – one child who worships a different god, speaks in a different tongue, dances to a different beat. She had flipped around, his daughter, even in the womb, head up, legs down, ready even before birth to jump out and run away. Yes, he thought, Ameena had assimilated well into the West. But then he sighed. Too well perhaps. Which showed a different kind of naivety. Did she realise that reciting Keats and moaning about the rain was not enough to become English? He didn't think she did, the foolish girl.

He looked down at his hands folded neatly on his lap. They were large hands, the brown skin starting to wrinkle in places, dark veins rising across them, easily traced. Not quite an old man's hands. Not yet.

His mind wandered. Then there was Palestine. The asymmetric violence of it all. Only peripherally his concern until recently. World issues, he thought, the kind where you sit on a comfortable chair in your own home and make political discourse, take a moral stance, express outrage, in front of a television, in front of friends; all that takes on a different light when your own blood is involved. Then it becomes personal. Once again in the news today. More people dead. A baby, they said. A baby. And Ameena, his one precious daughter in the cave of the lion.

He shuddered.

'Zoya!' he called impatiently across the half-hexagonal room to where his wife was in the kitchen. 'What happened to my tea?'

'What happened to your tea?' she yelled back. 'Nothing happened to your tea. Tea does not happen by magic. Be patient. It is brewing.'

She arrived a few minutes later with a tray carrying two cups of tea and a plate of samosas, golden fried and crispy on the outside, stuffed with a spicy potato-pea filling on the inside.

Yusuf felt his chest brim with tenderness and pride.

'May Allah, *Subhanahu Wata'ala*, bless you, Zoya. How well you take care of me.'

Zoya sniffed. 'Nothing to do with you. My heart was craving for samosas. Remember the samosa stall on Lakshmi Chowk? Butt's? He used to fry them right there in front of you, while you waited, piping hot and fresh. That first bite. Oof! The crunch of that first bite. It gives me the goosebumps, just thinking about it.'

Yusuf smiled at the memory. Of course he remembered. Those

cool winter evenings in Lahore after the strong sun had set and the mist had crept in, standing on that dusty street corner with Zoya, under the bright fluorescent lights of the marketplace stalls, film music blaring in the background, eating hot samosas off the same plate with the silent awkwardness of newlyweds.

'Do you miss it?' he asked, softened by the hypnotic whisper of hiraeth. 'Home?'

'Home? This is home.'

'You know what I mean... do you miss Lahore? Do you ever... do you ever regret that we left?'

'No,' Zoya said firmly. 'Think of Ameena and Kareem, what kind of life they would have had there. Corruption, pollution, sanitation, every kind of shun. Whatever our problems may be here, they are small. At least here we get clean water to drink.'

He nodded. 'Clean water. Yes.'

Then he said pensively, 'Lot of problems in the world. Today's news was not good.'

Zoya nodded. 'I saw. A baby. Kareem was watching with me. When they mentioned the baby, he just got up and left. Put on his shoes and his coat. Didn't say where he was going, nothing. Just stood up and walked out.'

Yusuf shook his head. 'He cannot carry the problems of the world on his shoulders.'

'Yes, but he cannot turn a blind eye either.'

'That is a politician's job, Zoya, not Kareem's.'

But Zoya only pursed her lips and helped herself to another samosa.

Yusuf took a sip of his tea, perfectly brewed. Zoya, he thought, for all her strong opinions and quirks of passion, was a more righteous person than he. He found it easier to swallow certain things if it meant it would keep the peace. She stubbornly stood by her convictions, no matter the price to be paid.

Also, the woman knew how to make a perfect cup of tea. She had been right, he realised, he should be more patient next time while his tea was brewing.

Brewing. He considered the word. A versatile word. Equally applicable to both tea and trouble.

2.25

'Hello,' cooed the voice in her ear and she almost jumped out of her chair. David was standing behind her, his lips resting on top of her head, hands massaging her neck in light, long strokes, kneading, slowly releasing the tension in the muscles.

Hurriedly, she pulled down the lid of her laptop and swivelled her chair around, her hand brushing against the white, ceramic 'I Heart NY' coffee mug, making it spin frantically on its base.

David reached out and steadied it, but she noticed how his eyes had narrowed ever so slightly.

'Phew! Thanks,' she said, 'good save! You're up early!'

'What were you doing?' he asked pleasantly, and she noticed how his tone was that little bit too perfunctory, and inside her, she felt a dull ache somewhere in the pit of her stomach.

'Oh, nothing. Just reading the news.'

'Oh? And what's so secretive about the news that you don't want me to see it?'

She laughed, a high, false laugh.

'Don't be so silly,' she murmured, 'how can the *news* be secret?'

'That's exactly what I'm saying too.'

She sighed. 'I guess you wouldn't believe me if I said I'm having a clandestine online affair with one of the male models I interviewed for the CK briefs piece.'

He smiled but shook his head. 'Nope.'

'I'm usually a good liar.'

'You *are* usually a good liar.'

'Just not this time?'

'Nope.'

Calm. So calm. So conversational.

She took in a small, shallow breath. 'Okay, I really was reading the news.'

'Forgive me, but I feel like we've just been here thirty seconds ago?' David said, and she felt her breathing go quicker.

He hated confrontation; she knew that. Sometimes she took advantage of it, that quality in him that hated confrontation. But he was holding his ground this time, surprisingly, he was digging his heels in.

She exhaled, then looked up at him, purposefully, in the eye.

'David, I *was* reading the news, that wasn't a fiction,' she said, and then swivelled back round the other way to open her laptop. 'Breaking News', screamed the BBC headline in red and white and bold black typeface: '**Gaza's deadliest day of violence in years.**'

The thought comes to her in that moment, the particular moment that her eyes and David's converge together on that screaming headline, that the BBC and her coffee mug – the same one that David had rescued a few minutes earlier – have the same colour scheme. She finds this so ridiculous, that she would even think to link these two things, that for a second she finds herself terrified, not only of other things, of bigger and more significant things, but of herself, her own mind.

David, looking at the headline and then at Ameena, is startled by the look in her eyes. Because it isn't anger that he sees. Or sadness. It is fear.

2.26

A few hours later on that same day, Ameena was at her desk at work, in the middle of writing a column on the three things that make an 'IT' bag (simplicITy, practicalITy and universalITy) when her phone rang.

It was one of those gloomy New York days, not unusual for late January, grey and dark with great big thunderclouds of rain that had been rumbling and growling since the early morning and then in the afternoon, they had finally burst, and the rain had come, hard and relentless. A couple of girls from the office had been soaked through on their lunch break, even just from the Jewish deli two doors down, and Ameena saw them tiptoe back to their desks, carrying the white styrofoam takeaway boxes of pastrami on rye, shoes off, feet wet, the ends of their hair stuck together and dripping. Ameena didn't mind the weather so much; a part of her even privately welcomed it – it reminded her of home, that distinct smell of rain in the air, her mother rushing to shut all the windows in the house, the aroma of the hot, cardamom-flavoured milky tea that her father liked on a rainy day.

'Hello?' she said, cradling the phone between her neck and her shoulder as she typed up the last sentence of the piece.

'You buy a handbag,' she had written, 'not only thinking that you will wear it now, but also that you are going to wear it in the future and that one of your daughters will probably steal it from your closet...'

Ameena was writing not from experience but from imagination, for Zoya had carried (not 'worn') the same severe-looking black PU handbag ever since Ameena could remember.

That bags could possibly serve an *aesthetic* purpose would be inconceivable to her mother, Ameena thought as she reread her sentence – Zoya's face was her genetic gift to her daughter; handbags were meant for carrying one's keys.

'Ameena?' It was Suzy from the gallery sounding strange, kind of breathless.

'Suzy? Hi?'

'Ameena, I *managed* to get him for your next show!'

'Whom?'

'Leo Ivanov.'

A pause. Ameena uncradling the phone. Holding it in her hand. Saving the 'IT' bag piece on the computer. Turning away from the screen.

'*My* next show?'

'*Your* next show.'

'Leo Ivanov! How in the world did you manage that?'

The older woman laughed. 'I told you, work hard and good things will happen! Well, this is a good thing, a very good thing.'

'Suzy... wow! I mean, I don't know what to say, how to thank you for this!'

'Don't thank me. Just make magic. Ivanov is not only huge, he is, like we say here in America, *mega*. He may be one man, but he is a mega-man. And Ameena...'

'Yes?'

'While you make magic, remember that Ivanov makes careers.'

Ameena nodded into the phone. She understood implicitly what the other woman was trying to say, what great significance lay under her words.

Ivanov, as everyone in the business knew, was one of the most influential collectors of Ameena's style of work. So much so that along with a small and powerful coterie of others, he had managed to dictate taste through years of setting the trend and the price, with his eye – and also, his wallet. Artists died to have him at their shows, galleries hung on to his every word. This was a guy the critics followed.

'We must get this right,' Suzy was saying. 'Perfect planning, perfect execution. When can you come to the gallery? Friday?

'Yes, sure,' Ameena replied, 'of course!'

'Okay, we meet then,' Suzy said.

'Great. Have a good week,' Ameena said. '...And Suzy...' she added softly.

'Yes?'

'Thank you.'

Then, like a little girl who couldn't possibly contain all this excitement inside her without exploding, she decided to call David to share her news but instead, heard on the other end, his beautiful voice: 'You've reached David's phone...' he said, informing her of a fact that she already knew.

2.27

In the evening, when Ameena returned to the apartment, she found there was still no David. Only a handwritten note on the breakfast bar with a single long-stemmed white rose.

> *Ameena,*
> *I haven't forgotten the promise I made to you at the lighthouse, and I never will.*
> *I love you.*
> *D*
> *P.S. At Mezzrow till late, if you want to come...*

In her head, she heard her father's voice, slow and measured: 'Ameena, I would advise you against all this. The world is not kind to those who make such choices...'

Terrible handwriting, Ameena thought, staring at the note, blocking out the voice, how could anyone have such bad handwriting?

Then she tore up the note and picked up the rose, inhaling its complex, deliciously distracting fragrance.

2.28

It was several weeks later, on a bright, cold Thursday morning, that her mother called just as she was entering her office building.

It took her a few seconds to process that little event, even in itself. Her mother never called. Neither did her father for that matter. Her parents seemed trapped in a different era when it actually cost money to make international calls. In that, as in many things, they hadn't appeared to keep pace with the rest of the world. Instead they would text – sparingly and for very specific reasons – '*Ameena please can you call us when free,*' and she would call.

But no, it was definitely her mother calling.

She frowned.

She was already running late for a meeting with Whitney.

'Mum, this is a really bad time,' she began testily, feeling instantly remorseful even as the words escaped her lips.

'It is a bad time for us also, Ameena.'

Her reaction was swift. Death. When one has ageing parents and they talk of bad times, it's got to be death. She felt her pulse quicken. It never failed to amaze her how *physical* it was, this fear. Palpable and frighteningly *audible* – her heart was *thumping*. 'What do you mean – bad? Where's Dad? Are you okay?'

'Yes, we are okay.'

Relief. They aren't dead. Not yet.

'Kareem? Has something happened to Kareem?'

'Kareem is okay. But… Ameena, something happened to all of us. Few days back. We did not want to bother you. But now, we – your Abba and I – we feel you should know about it. Kareem did not want us to tell you. He tries, you know, he wants to protect you... but we felt...'

'What's going on, Mum? Can you just *tell* me what's wrong please? And for once in your life can you stop going around the whole bloody world in circles, and get to the point, it's really early in the morning and you're driving me bloody batty.'

'Ameena, don't use such language. It is not like-lady to use those words.' She sighed. 'Anyway, you have your own problems, all alone like that in crazy, foreign place.'

'You know what, Mum, I'm late for a really important meeting and I am going to hang up if you don't just tell me why you called instead of telling me why you shouldn't have called.'

A loud intake of breath. A crackle on the phone line. An immediate sense of the physical distance between them.

'They threw pig's head into the house.'

'They threw... what? *Who* did?'

'We don't know...'

'A pig's head? What do you mean, a pig's head?'

'Pig's head, Ameena. *Suar ka sir.* They wrapped it in plastic, and they threw it into the house, while Abba and Kareem were doing their evening prayers. They smashed the window. There was glass everywhere.'

Ameena felt the bile rising in her throat, bitter and acrid. She forced it down. Behind her somewhere a car beeped, setting in motion a whole sequence of beeps of varying degrees of pitch and volume, like an out-of-tune orchestra. Just another morning in Midtown. Ameena winced.

'Have you told the police?' she said raising her voice to be heard over the commotion.

'Yes, yes, police are aware.'

'And what are they saying, Mum – who did this?'

'We don't know. They don't know. They are trying to find out.

They are asking everyone if they saw something funny. Also, the butcher. They asked him because it must have come from his shop, the pig you know, the way it was cut...'

The bile. Sloshing around.

'...it was very professional. But no one is saying they saw anything.'

'Mum, this is a...' she paused before she uttered the words, as if the weight of the words demanded a pause, you couldn't possibly utter such words without pause, '...this is a hate crime.'

'Yes, yes, we know. Police people also said same thing. That is what we don't understand. Who would hate us? Your father, he is the kindest man in this place, too kind sometimes, he lets too much go, a wonderful man he is, a *good* man.'

Despite herself, Ameena smiled. Her mother had never spoken about her father in those terms before, certainly never to her.

'Ammi,' she said softly, 'were they hurt, Abba and Kareem?'

'No, they were not hurt, it was miracle they were not hurt because the glass fragments, they were everywhere. I am still finding small pieces even after I cleaned the whole area myself so many times, with Hoover, then with mop, then on hands and knees. But mentally they are very injured Ameena, this disrespect... it is...'

Her mother sighed, a kind of deep, sinking sound. A sound you make when there is no word for whatever it is that you want to express.

Ameena looked at her watch. She was ten minutes late. And somehow the lateness made her angry, as if her anger needed something normal and unremarkable for it to emerge, an irritant, irksome yet easily explainable. Like lateness. The pig's head? That wasn't explainable, no. That didn't deserve anger. What *did* it deserve?

'Mum,' she said, finally, 'we can't just let this go.'

'The insurance company will send someone to repair the window. This week they said they will try.'

Ameena shook her head impatiently. 'God Mum, I don't mean about the window! How's Dad?'

'Your Abba is very confused. He cannot understand.'

'And Kareem?'

'*Beta*, Kareem is angry. You know what he is like when it comes to anything against his family. Such a short fuse he has. Him and you both. I don't know from where you two got your quick temper, only thing you have, both of you brother and sister, in common. Anyway. I am sorry we had to tell you.'

'Don't be silly, Mum. Of course, you had to tell me. I need to go, I'll call you tonight.'

Ameena arrived, embarrassed and apologetic, nearly twenty minutes late for her meeting, but in truth, she was neither embarrassed nor apologetic. She was furious, the anger that had only minutes ago been born now taking shape, growing inside her, filling her up.

'We need to make sure,' Whitney was saying, looking around the room, but it seemed to Ameena as if she was looking only at her, 'that the designers we are showcasing are not simply hustlers for couture but real people; people of intellect, of creativity, of ambition and character.'

How, Ameena thought, how could someone be carrying a pig's head down a residential road unnoticed? How? This couldn't have been a random act of madness by a deranged person. It smelled wrong. She shook her head. No, this kind of thing was almost always premeditated and almost certainly involved more than one person.

'Ameena, are you okay?'

'Huh?'

'Are you okay?' A pointed question, razor-edged.

'Yes, yes, I'm fine, I'm great. We have a cultural role to fulfil, I totally get that. Corporate responsibility. Ethical fashion. Yes. Couldn't agree more.'

Whitney nodded and continued, but Ameena could still feel the other woman's eyes on her.

'Boys and girls,' Whitney said, 'at a time when print is seemingly waning with too many titles transitioning to digital-only, the success of fashion-based indie magazines like us needs someone like you, someone with a contemporary voice and a connection with our readers. Do I have your commitment to that idea?'

Everyone nodded.

'Ameena?' Whitney said, raising her eyebrows.

Ameena felt small suddenly, chastened, like a disruptive student in a classroom being called out for unruly behaviour. She swallowed.

'Yes, yes. Commitment. Yes, absolutely,' she said in a low, flat voice.

The editrix-in-chief showed her scepticism by only the slightest twitch of the upper lip.

When David got home that night, he found Ameena standing by the window in the dark, her face tilted downwards.

'Hey beautiful, whatcha lookin' at?'

'The car lights. White on one side. Red on the other. We've created such order in the universe. It's impressive.' She sighed, then turned round to face him, her back to the window, leaning against it, feeling the coldness of the glass through her clothes. 'I lost a glove today. I shoved the pair into my coat pockets and then my mum called and when I pulled the phone out from my pocket, one must have slipped out. On the street, just outside work. Looked for it later but of course it was gone.'

'Sorry, sweet. Hate when that happens. Better to lose both gloves than one, I've always thought. Get yourself a new pair,' he said kindly, 'nicer than the old ones.'

'Oh, and also my family's been subjected to a hate crime.'

David's face didn't change. He was so measured, she thought, always so measured in his responses to the world.

'What do you mean by *hate* crime? Are they hurt?'

She shrugged. 'Well, they're not physically hurt, but no – they're not okay. And I'm...' she shook her head, '...I'm not okay.'

'Ameena, what happened?'

'I don't want to talk about it right now, okay?'

'Okay.'

'Maybe never.'

'Okay.'

But she told him later that night. Later that night in bed, long after he had gone to sleep, she shook him awake to tell him. And then she sobbed uncontrollably, but she didn't understand, she said, she didn't understand why she was sobbing, if it was because such a thing had happened or that such a thing *could* happen or that she hadn't been there when such a thing had happened, she hadn't been there for her family.

And then he held her, just the way she was, lying there on her side, manoeuvring her body into his so there was no space between them at all, just a single, indistinguishable curve like a comma in the middle of the bed, and he comforted her, and eventually they drifted off to sleep like that, with her still shaking and with him rocking her to sleep, telling her to let it out, let it all out, because he understood, yes, he understood, and her nodding into the pillow that she had pressed her face into, because yes, *yes*, of course he did.

2.29

The bits left unspoken. The margins on a page.

The rest between notes.

The white space on a canvas.

Or

Between

Words

Stories

Histories

The pause. The breath. Caesura.

2.30

1. And then there was the time when David went to music class and a group of boys started singing 'Hey Jude' in unison and when he pretended to ignore that and walked straight to his desk, a boy who just happened to be walking past just happened to accidently move his arm in such a way that it just happened to brush against the books on David's desk, dropping them all to the floor in a big thud-thud, and when David bent down to pick them up, he saw stuck on the underside of his desk a whole lot of yellow stars with thick black lines and the word JUDE scribbled in the middle. He was thirteen, the age at which a Jewish boy officially becomes a man.

2. And then there was the time when Ameena was asked by the other little Muslim girls in school why she didn't wear the hijab, and those little Muslim girls, in turn, were asked by the non-Muslim girls why they did, and they replied that in wearing it they were being true to their faith and when Ameena came home that day and asked her mother why she didn't wear the hijab when she – her mother – did, her mother said, you can wear it when you want to, I wore it when I wanted to, not before, so would you like to wear it now, and Ameena took the choice as it was offered to her and said, no, not yet.

3. And then there was the time when David saw Abe, he was sure of it, but perhaps he wasn't so sure of it, on the road behind the school where the high stone wall blocked off any road access, and Abe was beating up a kid, it was a kid who'd yelled across the cafeteria at lunchtime that same afternoon, looking directly at

some of the other Jewish kids eating their lunch, smaller kids than Abe, not nearly as strong-boned, if anyone would like their meat roasted, and that same kid was now backed up against a wall, and he was crouching and holding his stomach and Abe – David thought it was him but he couldn't be sure – was beating the shit out of him.

4. And then there was the time when Ameena and Kareem were at a department store in Deansgate and the alarm went off and the police were in, within minutes, searching Kareem, not giving anybody else even a second glance, not even Ameena, standing there next to him, because whatever trouble looked like, Kareem was it, with his baggy shorts and his chunky gold watch and his oversized white trainers and his half shaved boy-band haircut, so they were only searching Kareem, stripping him down to his underpants, right there in the middle of the department store floor, searching, searching, then finding nothing and walking off without an apology, without looking back once, only looking annoyed, not because they had searched him and found nothing but because they had searched him and found nothing.

5. And then there was the time when David walking along the corridor at school passed by the staffroom and overheard the other teachers talking about the piano teacher and how she had spoken out against the school's 'overexuberant' celebration of Christmas and how maybe it made sense, despite her obvious talent, to get someone more broad-minded and tolerant of other religions – after all, if Christmas or its celebration offended her all that much, she might as well go to a fee-paying faith school and move her boys there while she was at it. Besides, she smoked way too much.

6. And then there was the time when Ameena and Kareem and their mum and dad were at the trendy new restaurant in town, all dressed up for the occasion, and their father placed his order and the waiter asked him to repeat it three times before Kareem said with slow, cold anger in his voice, 'What is it that you don't understand, mate?' And the waiter said jokingly, 'Why don't you do all the orders mate, because I don't speak Paki, what your dad speaks, yeah?' And Kareem banged the table with his fist and the water spilled everywhere and he called the waiter an ignorant racist fuck and a dick-shit faggot. And Zoya gasped, just a bit. And the waiter said, 'Why don't you stinking curry-faces just fuck off back to your country and clean the toilets there instead of taking our jobs and making trouble here?' And Yusuf called the manager and the angry waiter was taken away and assigned to another table and another waiter brought out their order, but Kareem was not able to eat a thing, overcome by a seething anger, and Yusuf was not able to eat a thing, overcome by shock, and Ameena was not able to eat a thing, overcome by shame about the curry-faces thing. Only Zoya ate prawn linguine (with extra chilli) all by herself because she had heard it all and frankly didn't give a damn.

7. And then there was the time when David and Ameena skipped lunch at that school friend's birthday because the food choices on offer consisted of hot dogs and pepperoni pizza and because kids' party food is kids' party food, whether in Rhode Island or in Manchester, and David didn't mind, and neither did Ameena, for why should they mind, they both thought, independently of each other, and with the Atlantic between them, why should anyone mind, when there is always cake?

David and Ameena were two people with nothing in common except for the city that they lived in and the dream that lived in them.

(You think?)

2.31

Night-time then, in Lower Manhattan; David and Ameena are in bed. David is fast asleep. Ameena is wide awake.

She had been up for most of the night, thinking about what had happened in Manchester. In her mind she replayed the conversation with her mother over and over, wondering yet again how someone could do something so principally wrong. And *why*. And the why bothered her even more than the how. She exhaled and held her palms to her temples as if, in doing so, she could squeeze the unpleasant thoughts out of her head. Then she forced her eyes shut, as tight as she could, but a few minutes later she opened them again, as wide as she could – a kind of private mutiny. Hilarious, she thought to herself, a class act, pure comedy, should sell tickets for this one-woman show.

Then she sighed. It was no good. Beauty sleep – much like its component parts – was the rare prerogative of a privileged few. Resigned then, to philosophical insomnia – surely, the worst kind of combination – Ameena turned on her back and forced herself to think about her art; a different kind of anxiety. The following evening, less than twenty-four hours away, they were going to put the art up on the walls in preparation for her second show. Restlessly, she began to think about the order in which she wanted the paintings displayed... which one should be front and centre, the very first the viewer would see? Was there a clear showstopper in the collection? Did the paintings exist in relation to each other? Or were they an entity unto themselves? Or maybe they were of a piece, telling a larger story? And so, would sequencing them in a certain way create the narrative thread that held all the individual stories together? And if this was true, how could she play with the arrangement to create an atmosphere of maximum drama?

At four in the morning she decided to give up answering the questions in her head. This was something that needed to be visualised in the actual physical space. And *felt*, she thought, sitting up in bed and placing her hand on her stomach, *here*. And so, she got dressed and left for the gallery, tiptoeing to the bedroom door, then turning round, looking at David fast asleep, looking at his shape in the darkness, then feeling for him a sudden swell of love, coming back to kiss him quickly, his forehead warm to the touch of her lips, before finally turning round and leaving.

She walked the twenty blocks to the art gallery in her boots, listening to the crunch of her footsteps on the pavement; there was still snow on the ground, and salt, coarse and pink, and the air was cold and damp, and the streets were quiet, lit only by street lamps and the headlights of the odd car that sped by – kindred New York souls, Ameena thought dryly, attempting to *carpe* the *diem*.

When she arrived at the gallery, she unlocked the door using the four-digit code Suzy gave all her artists, left her boots outside on the mat, turned on the lights and sat barefoot and cross-legged on the concrete floor, in the middle of the room. She sat like that, ankles crossed, knees up against her chest, staring at the walls, empty and glowing a bright toothpaste white, working out in her head what went where. It was Suzy's call, she knew that, but still, she thought, no harm in expressing an opinion. Suzy liked her artists to be involved – it shows that one cares, the gallerist had told her once.

At some point, Ameena shut her eyes, still arranging paintings inside her head until they all faded into a single inconsequential wash of colour, much like the stories of each of our lives collapse finally and frivolously into a single flash of bright light. When she opened her eyes again, she found herself lying on her back in the middle of two parallel beams of sunshine that streamed in through the gallery windows.

At 7.30am, she pulled the door shut behind her and left for work. At 8am, she stopped at a deli en route to buy a toothbrush, some toothpaste, a small black coffee, a plain poppy-seed bagel and a bag of unsalted almonds. At 9am, she attended a briefing meeting about the importance of surprise and joy in content. At 10am, one day too late, she started writing a piece for Whitney, entitled 'Bold Fashion for the Feminist'. At 12pm, she ate a handful of the almonds for lunch, and kept writing. At 5.30pm she wrote the last sentence of the piece and breathed a sigh of relief, but when she popped into Whitney's office to inform her that she was done, her editor's face looked so expectant that Ameena felt a moment of regret that she hadn't put more surprise or joy into it.

For a brief second, she considered taking the whole thing back and asking for more time, but on more than one occasion Whitney had made it explicitly clear that she didn't look kindly upon broken deadlines. Or bad writing, Ameena thought ruefully. But, it was done now, and she had to be at the gallery at six. Grabbing her bag and her cell phone and ignoring the ping of a new email alert on her computer, she ran out the door and down the block to catch her train.

On the way to the subway, she checked her phone – she had locked it up inside the drawer of her desk all day, like a *thirteen*-year-old with no willpower, she thought with disdain, and noticed that David had tried to call her a few times but hadn't left a message. She tried him back and he picked up on the third ring.

'Hey,' he said.

'Hi handsomeness,' she said, 'so sorry, was trying to finish up this thing for Whitney one day late and now rushing off to meet Suzy for six but I know I'll be late. So that means I'll probably be home late.' She sighed. 'When did I turn into one of those people who is always perpetually late?'

'Ha! Don't worry. It's New York. Everyone's always finding ways to buy time.'

She smiled into the phone. 'Okay, I'm at the subway, gotta go, love you.'

'Love you more. And good luck tonight.'

Ameena ran down the stairs as fast as she could, two steps at a time, and when she'd almost reached the bottom, she heard the low rumble of the approaching train.

Made it! she thought happily.

Five seconds later, she found her body dishonourably thrust against the cool metal bar of the turnstile that appeared to be refusing, like a wayward child, to give way.

'What the hell!' she said aloud.

'Please Swipe Again.' 'Please Swipe Again.' 'Insufficient Fare.' replied the turnstile.

'Fucking crap,' someone behind her cursed, not bothering, in true New York fashion, to even attempt to conceal the contempt, 'fucking dumb tourists.' Ameena didn't dare turn around to see what this indignant emitter of eloquent epithets looked like. Even to look would be to plead some sort of unspoken defence. Train crimes, she thought, infuriated with herself, this business of not knowing your own balance. Guilty as charged.

On the platform in front of her, the train rolled languidly in, the doors opened, people got out, other people got in, the doors shut, then opened, then shut, then opened, then shut, then opened – taunting, taunting, could have made it in now, or now, or now, if *only* you were better organised, it seemed to be saying – then finally the doors shut and remained shut, and the train disappeared, slithering like a metallic snake into the tunnel on the other side.

'Bloody great,' she muttered irritably, 'just bloody brilliant.'

But a few seconds later, when she went to refill her subway card at the machine, she found herself faced with something she wouldn't have expected, not then, not in a million years, not from the MTA.

How had she not noticed this before? How had she never paid attention?

Her annoyance thawed, her eyebrows came together, her dark eyes deepened, her lips curved into a tiny, incredulous smile.

Fuck, she thought, I love New York.

And then immediately, I wonder what *David* would think?

For alone, how could she answer what was being asked of her in that moment, in the underground depths of the New York City subway? How could she *possibly* answer this, the most existential question of them all?

What do you want to do, the machine was asking her: Add Value? Or Add Time?

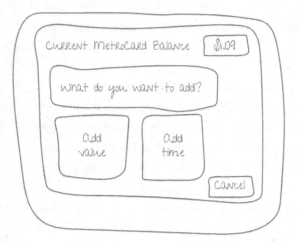

2.32

'My sons...' his mother said from the hospital bed, one of the last things she said before she found it too much effort to speak at all.

David was sitting on a chair by the window. Abe, towering over everyone else, even at eighteen, was skulking around sullenly, as he'd done ever since the jolly-looking doctor with the big hands and rosy cheeks had looked at them sadly and solemnly, and uttered the phrase, 'Not much time.'

But our father is a watchmaker, David wanted to scream, don't you get it? He *makes* time.

'My sons,' she said, this sick, frail, too-young-to-die, dying woman, in a weak voice, which like so many other things had ultimately betrayed her, 'I hope that you are kind to the world, and that the world is kind to you.'

At first David thought this was another one of her delusions. She often confused past and present in those days – morphine will do that to you, he had learned, the price of quieting pain – so he assumed that she was speaking to them in the past, as a mother of small children. It was only later that he understood that she was speaking to them in the present, as young men, as a mother of young men, and that in what she wished for them, she moved easily across the continuous spectrum of time and lifetimes. She was alluding, in that final wish for her children, not only to a future, but to a past, to a history that she had lived out with them in her own too-short life, but also to a more significant history that began long before her time and would continue long after.

For she knew, even as her own story was ending, that the bigger story can never be erased; it remains dormant within the dusty pages of history books until such time that the actions of men rouse it from its sleep.

Then, it screams.

She opened her eyes to speak. It was an effort, David could see, even that tiny movement of the lids was an enormous effort, but she made it, she opened them wide.

'Freedom,' she said, 'I wish for you...'

And David had remembered the rabbit. The eyes of the rabbit.

No, history can never be completely quietened. Not unlike a dying person's pain.

2.33

The phone on the white Formica table that sat forlornly by the entrance of the split-level flat on Chapel Road rang, shrill and loud.

Yusuf answered on the first ring. He sounded tired. And old, Ameena realised with sudden shock. That was an old man's hello.

'Abbu?'

'Ameena!' The delight. The delight that almost made her cry.

'How are... things, Daddy?'

'Things are good, fine, Ameena, not to worry. And, how are *you*, my dear?'

But before she could answer, there was a noisy screech on the phone line and she heard her mother huffing and puffing as if she had run all the way from the other end of the city – an impossibility, Ameena knew, and smiled inwardly at the thought, in spite of the grimness of their present circumstances. Zoya had always been anathema to unnecessary physical exertion of any kind; even the idea of exercise as being linked in some way to one's well-being was completely lost on her.

'Ameena?' she said, panting heavily into the receiver.

'Hi Mum...'

'Ameena, he is hiding the truth.'

'What truth?'

'Things are not good and fine. Big fat lies. They still haven't repaired the window.'

'But...' said Ameena puzzled, 'why not? It's been weeks!'

Earlier, she had stopped at the supermarket on her way home from work to pick up a few things for dinner. Now, she was walking through Madison Square Park, by the statue of Seward, best known for having purchased Alaska from Russia all those years ago for two cents per acre. It may as well be Alaska, Ameena thought wryly, groceries in one hand, phone in the other; it was bitterly cold in New York, the wind finding its way to every exposed bit of skin, chafing it, leaving its mark.

Still, their apartment was warm, she thought guiltily, warm and cosy, the heating in order, the windows intact. But, why hadn't they fixed things yet? Was the window of a style they no longer manufactured? Was the glass of a specification that took extra-long to source?

To her mother, she remarked, 'Why is it taking so long? It's probably freezing there too. Isn't it?'

'We sit upstairs. We had to cover all the furniture. The rain comes in.'

'But, I don't understand. Why hasn't it been sorted yet?'

'That is the thing your father is not telling you. There is some confusion, you see, with the insurance company. We are not covered, it seems, for terrorism.'

'*Terrorism?*'

A middle-aged man walking next to her reached for his young daughter's hand and quickened his step. Two old ladies on a park bench, gloved and mufflered, stared at her with a mixture of fear and rebuke.

She slid the grocery bag higher up on her arm and covered her mouth with her free hand.

'Mum, what are you saying?'

'I am not saying. *They* are saying. They are saying to be covered we should have been paying separate terrorism insurance policy. We have only been paying the normal home insurance, so these special cases are not covered. We never knew there was separate policy for such things. So, everyone is fighting with everyone else and the window is not fixed. I told your father, just forget it, we pay ourselves. But when has he ever listened to me? No. He likes to suffer. Every day, he is making rounds from police station to insurance company to repair shop. Every day without fail – morning he goes, evening he comes back.'

Inside her gloves, Ameena felt herself digging her nails into her palms. Movements of the body, one cannot control the movements of the body; they always speak the truth.

'And the police?'

'They are still investigating, they say. Looking into the matter. Trying their best.'

'Well, if this is deemed *terrorism*,' – she whispered the word – 'surely it should be high-priority?'

Zoya sighed. 'What else can we do Ameena? Alone, a person is invisible. They are nothing.'

2.34

The Ides of March arrived, and with it, the evening of Ameena's second show.

The paintings were on the walls, David was around somewhere, and Ameena, secretly scrunching up her toes in her very high, very expensive, very uncomfortable new shoes, was in mid-conversation with a little old lady from Greenwich, Connecticut, with false teeth, shiny black leather trousers and an only son who was a doctor-without-borders in The Gambia, when Suzy snuck up behind her and grabbed her arm with a kind of theatrical fervour.

'I'm sorry that I interrupt, Mrs Barry, but I must borrow Ameena please.'

Mrs Barry, who, by Ameena's estimation, seemed decidedly tipsy on whatever was being offered around by the waiters bearing trays, started to say something, but Suzy had already steered Ameena away.

She dragged her to a corner and, looking in the direction of a tall, balding man in a long black overcoat, whispered, 'That's him.'

Ameena followed her gaze. She tended not to be partial when it came to her work, but he was looking at one of the pieces that she had some sentimental attachment to. It was an abstraction of a flower vase David and she owned, that lived, in real life, on the windowsill of their kitchen, unbroken and happy. In the painting, it had fallen to the ground and lay shattered in fragments of red pottery, the uneven splotches of yellow and fuchsia and purple and green representing a distorted reality of the strewn petals, the scattered leaves – a kind of freeing from confinement, of living things.

'Go,' Suzy ordered.

Ameena looked at him again. He had his back to them, and yet he cut an imperious figure, tall and regal, exuding a kind of confidence that she knew came only from power.

'Go,' Suzy repeated with – Ameena noted – an almost desperate urgency.

Ameena swallowed. Then she took a deep breath, put on her most disarming smile and walked up to him, until she was standing alongside him, looking at the work she had created. She was just going to introduce herself when he turned his head sideways to look at her. He had shrewd blue eyes, she noticed, and thin, pale lips, so thin and so pale they almost melted into his face.

'It lacks authenticity.'

Ameena cocked her head slightly. Surely she'd misheard the great man.

'Sorry?' she asked in a genuinely apologetic tone, for it seemed only appropriate – after all, she was asking him to go through the effort of repeating what he had said, which she had, quite surely, misheard.

His face was turned back now, away from her, looking around the gallery, his eyes doing a practised, systematic sweep.

'Come to think of it, they all do. They all lack honesty.'

Ameena rocked backwards and found herself on the very tips of her sequinned stiletto heels – precariously – as if she had suddenly, and without warning, fallen off a mountain (though she'd never been on a mountain), as if she had drunk one tequila shot too many (though she never drank tequila), as if she'd been caught cheating in an exam (though she'd never cheated in an exam) as if what she felt – this momentary sense of delirium – was not real, but imagined, imagined in some sort of unnatural, alternate, other world.

'In what way?' she heard herself say faintly.

'There's too much going on. Too much colour, too many shapes, too much everything. Overwrought, like a Picasso that's trying too hard. You're trying too hard not to do something. Only you know what that is.' He sighed. 'But you've killed the life.'

Shame. A fog.

He paused, then looked at her pointedly. 'I wish it wasn't so, but I don't think, my dear, that you're quite ready for prime time.'

Later, she wouldn't be sure if it was the actual words or the easy matter-of-fact manner in which he said this thing, this thing that he knew – he *must* have known – was a kind of death warrant that would kill her fledgling dream, that caused something inside her to snap, but he'd barely finished his sentence when almost instantly, she felt something else, something strong and overpowering – she felt the shame melt into a bright flash of blinding anger. Who the fuck did he think he was?

'Well,' she said tersely, 'you're certainly entitled to your opinion. Art is subjective.'

'Perhaps,' he said somewhat sadly, 'but I've been in this business a long time, and I'm only telling you how it is.'

'That's only *your* opinion,' she fired back. 'It has nothing to do with the quality, meaning or significance of my work.'

He stared at her with what appeared to be a look of genuine bafflement.

'The *significance* of your work? Easy, my dear, easy! Do you know how many years I've been a collector?' But then his tone softened, 'You're still young, you have much to learn, but you're lucky, you have time on your side. You should spend it in the studio and strive to find your voice. Try and come up with something that's yours, something you have conviction in. Imitators always get found out, it's only a matter of time.'

'Imitators?' she repeated hoarsely, a barely audible whisper.

'Regrettably so. And that's perfectly natural when you try and do something before you're ready for it. You have plenty of time to get famous – I would counsel you to take that time. I'm only surprised that Suzy with all her years of experience didn't offer you the same counsel. Quite frankly, this whole thing is artistically irresponsible. There's absolutely no need to run before you can walk.'

Ameena felt the all-too-familiar rise of nausea swell up inside her, powerful, unyielding, terrifying, despite its familiarity. Her head was spinning. Or maybe it was the room. She looked around in a trance-like state and saw Suzy – multiple versions of Suzy – looking straight at her, a look of rabid concern in her eyes, she had many pairs of eyes, an incarnation of some exotic, multi-headed god. From the corner of her own eye, she saw a waiter approach, expertly balancing a tray full of champagne glasses on the under-side of his palm. He had skin the colour of hers. They made eye contact briefly, then he lowered his eyes and then he was extending the tray towards them, offering it out – a kind of munificent lord.

In front of her, somewhere beyond the amorphous throng of strangers, she saw David and Peggy standing side by side, watching her. Other people were watching her too, she felt their eyes bore into her, but what she remembers is David and Peggy. David and Peggy, Peggy and David. Blending into one, their four eyes con-verging into one single Eye of Providence, a fearful, imploring look in the Eye. Don't do it, the Eye was begging, don't do it, please don't do it.

Next to her, Ivanov extended his long, black, overcoat-covered arm towards the tray. She didn't know if it was her brain playing tricks on her, but the arm seemed to move forward in slow motion, a freakish, jerky, reptilian swaying, that made her want to scream.

And then his hand hovered above the tray.

'No!' she said, looking at the waiter, surprising herself, the word spilling out from some mysterious place inside of her. *No* – as much an order as a plea, and the brown waiter, plagued by a history of his own, unused to taking orders from someone who shared his shade of skin while the white man stood imperiously by, was confused.

But she is the artist, he thought!

And his eyes grew wide with alarm.

Torn between intuition and instruction, past and present, duty and the devil and the deep blue sea... but who are my gods? he asked himself and he shuffled his feet backwards – a *tiny* movement, a non-movement – but that was enough. Enough for everything that happened next to happen.

Ivanov, his hand having found the slender flute of the champagne glass while it was still on the tray, in the precise moment when the waiter shuffled backwards, lost his grip. The glass tipped forward, taking in its wake several of the other glasses on the tray in a perfectly orchestrated sequence of dominoes. There was the clink of glass and a loud hiss, which steadily petered out as globules of the golden liquid spilt out of the tray, drip, drip, drop, drop, the precious bubbles fizzling out, the liquid collecting on the floor in a puddle of something the exact colour and consistency of piss.

After that Ameena remembers no more except thinking that the look of outrage on the face of the white man, and the look of terror on the face of the brown one, was history on a loop. It was. It surely was.

recapitulating melodies and mistakes

*Right or wrong, it's very pleasant to break
something from time to time.*

Fyodor Dostoyevsky

3.1

That night, as a crescent moon made a yellow smudge high in the midnight sky, David told a distraught, shivering Ameena not to worry. To just go in the next morning after a full night's sleep and a calm head and tell them she was sorry. She had become overwhelmed, she had been distracted by other things on her mind, she had let her emotions get in the way of clear thinking, that of course it was all a terrible accident, she hadn't meant for it to happen like that, oh no, she was absolutely horrified that it had, she had only wanted the waiter to not interrupt that very important conversation, but still, accident or not, she would apologise profusely to Ivanov and do whatever else she had to do to make this up to everyone.

And then he said to her: My feisty angel, you need to find compromise between painting the world and living in it.

And she thought: David, sweet, wonderful David, in finding compromise, there was no one like David who was every bit as ruthlessly dedicated to his music as she was to her art, but who had, besides that, a capacity for selflessness and generosity that she knew she could spend two lifetimes trying to equal and not even come close.

3.2

'Yusuf,' said Zoya, 'I have a feeling.'

They were sitting upstairs in the bedroom, like they had done every evening for the past several weeks since 'it' happened, as they referred to the incident between themselves.

'It', like almost all historical horrors, big or small, had left for all of them an emotional residue that remained long after the actual incident was over and done with, but in this particular case, it was more than that. Emotional consequences aside, 'it' had been disastrous to the family Hamid on a very pragmatic level, in that 'it' had rendered the use of the half-hexagonal room impossible.

The thing with a room that is shaped like half a hexagon is that it remains defined by its geometry. One wall is straight, two walls are angled and everything within is built and bought and fit to accommodate. And so, when something like 'it' happens, there's no escaping the concomitant effects on the usability of the space – the pure mathematics of the shape becomes compromised – something one never pays too much attention to when buying a house, because of course, one never imagines that something like 'it' could ever happen.

But 'it' had happened.

And 'it' had happened to a family who had bought a house with a funny-shaped floorplan in a city where it rained, often and hard.

And so, despite the heavy PVC sheeting that they had dragged from the garage – it had taken all three of them plus Kareem's friend Faisal to carry it across – and duct-taped onto the window frame, when the rain came, the rain came, and well, it doesn't take 'it' to happen to realise that any act of man, no matter how heavily reinforced, is no match for an act of God, and the room and all its contents had been soaked through.

After which, Zoya had proceeded to move all the furniture to one side – for the first time in her life she was thankful there was not much of it and that the burgundy sofa expertly made to look like leather was not, in fact, leather but some man-made material of a far more durable nature. Then she covered the lot with layers of the same heavy plastic sheeting they had used on the window.

The effect, Zoya thinks every time she unlocks the front door to come back home, is a bit like walking into an abandoned house in a bad 1950s-style horror movie. Sometimes, when she is upstairs in bed and the house is still, she imagines (inspired by the same bad movie) other things too. She imagines a large, non-existent, grandfather clock striking twelve, ding-dong, ding-dong (twelve times) and then at that portentous stroke of midnight, she imagines the wind from the broken window begins to howl and the plastic covering on the furniture starts to quiver and flap and footsteps belonging to something invisible and monstrous can be heard stomping up the staircase and... well... other suspended-disbelief things like that. Zoya had always enjoyed a rather expansive imagination when it came to the supernatural.

But besides turning her house into the set of a B-grade horror movie, what upset Zoya in truly distressing ways was that because of 'it', along with the use of the room, the little time that they spent with Kareem seemed to have vanished as well.

For even though Kareem was more out than in, and spent almost all the time he was in, upstairs in his bedroom, he would still come down for meals as he had always done, ever since Zoya can remember, for no matter what they did or didn't do for the rest of the day the four of them – now the three of them – had always eaten their evening meal together on the sofa of the living room.

And now, thanks to 'it', all that had changed.

The night 'it' had happened, they had gone to sleep without dinner. First the shock of it, then deciding between themselves what to do about it, Kareem yelling and swearing and Zoya crying and Yusuf frozen in disbelief, all of them staring at the neatly severed head of the pig, not knowing what to do with it, how to get rid of it, who among the three of them would be the one to touch the thing, then Yusuf finally calling the police, and then the police taking forever to get to the scene and taking away the odious object, and then after all the questioning and the clear-up, they had been too exhausted and too sickened to eat.

The next night, at dinner time, Zoya had spread out a mat on the kitchen floor and set their plates and glasses on it. 'Like a picnic in the park,' she said brightly to Kareem when she called him down for dinner.

But he had stared at it a while and then finally said, 'This is ridiculous, I'm going to my room.' And he had done exactly that. He had helped himself to some food and taken his plate up to his room, and continued to do so ever since, and that, as far as family dinners in the Hamid household were concerned, had been that.

'What feeling?' Yusuf asked.

'Bad-luck feeling,' she replied.

He put his arm round her. 'Don't worry,' he said, 'whatever has happened has happened. It's all over now.'

But Zoya shook her head. 'No,' she said ominously, 'everyone knows. Bad luck, it comes in threes.'

3.3

When Ameena walked into the little glass office, she saw Suzy behind the desk with Luca Zima, the man who managed the gallery's accounts, a behind-the-scenes guy who Ameena had never met before but who she knew Suzy was involved with in some intimate way in her personal life, a man who was considered a savvy businessman and, behind closed doors, a sadistic brute who wouldn't hesitate to sell his mother's soul for an extra dollar, and then feel totally at ease about it.

Ameena stood by the door, unsure how to proceed, what to say, who to say it to. For one second of madness, she quite realistically pondered giving in to the temptation of turning round and running away. In as much as she had entertained no delusions of this being an easy meeting, she hadn't expected Luca to be there, and she knew what it meant, his presence in this meeting, before it had even begun; she knew how it would end.

'Are you firing me?' she asked eventually, choosing to direct her question at Suzy.

'We sold one painting. *One* painting. No one would buy anything after that... that *scene* you created,' Suzy said, looking distraught.

'I... it was an accident. It wasn't meant to happen like that... I...' Ameena started to say.

But Luca was looking at her intently and she felt herself stuck for words. He was a short, spare man with full, fleshy lips, narrow eyes and a head full of slicked-back dark hair that, when regarded in isolation, belied his years. There was something about his physicality that made Ameena cringe. He reminded her of a small, furry animal that you were inclined to pick up and then before you knew it, you had three of your fingers bitten off.

Then he spoke in low, soft tones. 'Giving an artist an exhibition is a very expensive gamble. Do you understand that, Ameena? Believing in your work is a good thing. But believing it is so good and so important that it will change the course of the gallerist's entire enterprise is egotistical and arrogant. We are not in the business of giving deference to ego. A gallery is not just a room with four walls. It represents someone's creative vision – in this case, Suzy's. And we cannot allow the future of the gallery to be jeopardized by a single artist – any single artist.'

'Suzy?' Ameena looked desperately at the older woman. 'It was the way in which he spoke to me. It was so... so... *superior*. It was like... after that, I couldn't think straight any more. He wouldn't have spoken to me like that if I was... Come on, you've got to see that! You're a woman too, you *know*.'

But Suzy only shook her head. 'There are many different ways to be a woman. Your behaviour was indefensible. I can understand you were hurt. I can understand also that you were angry. To not be hurt, to not be angry would be to not care, but this? You act like a child when you're told your painting isn't worthy to sit in the Louvre. He didn't like your work. Okay, that's not what we expected or wanted, but I would have found a way to deal with it. That is *my* job. That is *my* experience. But you! I mean, going up against Ivanov like that. Insulting him in a room full of important people. And in such a hideous manner. What were you thinking? You are, how you say... unhinged!'

'Are you firing me?' Ameena asked again and this time her voice was calm.

Suzy looked away.

Luca spoke. 'Yes, Ameena, we have decided it would be best to discontinue our relationship. Art is a business. You need to learn to treat it with the professionalism it deserves. As any gallerist can tell you, what we do is a complicated calculus, and demanding and self-centred artists are seldom worth the work. There's a very long line of talented people who would love to have an opportunity to get into an art gallery, people who are givers not takers. So, whenever you get a chance next – and I am confident that with time and maturity it will happen for you – be a giver.'

'I didn't give you a chance because your work was so great,' Suzy murmured, still looking away, as if she was speaking not to Ameena at all, but to someone else that only she could see. 'Your work was good, some of it was exceptional even, yes I won't lie, I liked your work, I thought you showed potential. But that's not why I gave you a chance.' She looked at Ameena then, and her face was sad. 'I gave you a chance because David's poor mother was my childhood friend. And you threw the chance away.'

Ameena felt her face flush and the tears appear, hot and burning, as the knot in her throat that had slowly grown larger and larger now threatened to escape. Pride dissolving into the sticky, salty, primitive language of shame. But before they had a chance to roll down her cheeks, she gathered her bag and also her phone and also what was left of her dignity and left the room.

3.4

Later that evening, when David returned home from work, he found Ameena sitting in the living room on the loveseat by the window, her small form washed in the strips of dying sunlight.

'They fired me,' she said, staring straight ahead.

'Oh Ameena,' was all he said, but his face looked stricken.

'They didn't give me a chance,' she continued, 'to do what you suggested... I tried... I tried to say it was an accident, that I don't know how it happened and it's true, I *don't*. I *don't* know how it happened. I can't remember very much, the whole evening is such a blur. All I really remember is the glasses falling and then later Peggy hugging me and saying something kind and then I was with you, here, at home. Anyway, I tried to say all that and that I was sorry... but they didn't give me a chance. In and out, it was over.'

'Baby, I'm so sorry,' David said.

'I begged. I actually begged your mother's friend for another chance. There've been some low moments in my life...' she gave a small, scornful laugh, 'but I think this just reset the bar.'

She said 'your mother's friend' in a deliberately pointed way that was not lost on David, but sensibly he chose not to indulge her by reacting. This, he believed, was not the time.

'There'll be more galleries,' he said, trying his best to sound positive, but he knew she heard it, the catch in his voice, 'this is New York City.'

'Don't you have a gig tonight?' she asked abruptly.

'Not going anywhere,' he said in a quiet, worried voice.

'I don't mean to be rude,' she said, and her own voice was listless, 'but I just want to be alone.'

David said nothing, but he walked up to where she was sitting and touched her shoulder and when she didn't react or respond or even flinch, he walked over to the kitchen and prepared a whole saddle of lamb with shallots and garlic and sprigs of rosemary, its leaves needle-like and shining silver on the underside.

When he brought it out, he noticed that Ameena hadn't stirred, neither her body, nor the expression on her face. It unnerved him, her face, in that moment, a face that had looked everywhere for the smallest sign of life, and then, not finding it, had given up.

He stood next to her, stroked her hair.

A plane cut through the sky in the distance, birdlike, the gleam of metal visible for just a few seconds in the rectangle between two buildings.

'I've made us dinner,' David said, walking back to the dining table. 'I hope you're impressed.'

'They only sold one painting,' she said, her voice empty.

There was the sound of a utensil dropping and it rang around the room, a harsh, metallic clang.

'Sorry,' he said, 'fork slipped out of my hand.'

'One painting,' she repeated vacantly as if she had barely registered the noise or the fact that he had apologised for causing it, 'they sold one painting. *One* painting.'

'Well,' he said lightly, 'one is better than none. Shall I serve you?'

'I'm not hungry.'

'Ameena, you've got to eat.'

'David, I've got to sleep,' she said.

Then she stood up, drifted zombie-like into the bedroom and shut the door behind her.

She was asleep when he got to bed, sprawled out on her stomach on top of the duvet, arms flung out like Jesus on a crucifix, all the bedroom lights still on, her face sandwiched between her own pillow and his, which she had placed on top of her head. She was wearing one of David's t-shirts and nothing else and its white oversized form swelled up around her like a cloud. On one side, it had ridden up to her waist, exposing one buttock cheek, the sight of which filled David with an intense personal shame. He shifted her body as gently as he could without disturbing her, pulled the duvet out from under her, then covered her nakedness and turned the lights out.

3.5

A day passes. Then a week.

David and Ameena dance around issues.

This is not uncommon between people and lovers.

They dance around issues because it takes two to dance, because as long as they are still involved, they retain control; they dance around issues because it is a kind of middle way, braver than running away, safer than battle; they dance around issues because burned bridges and damaged souls seem cruel and violent and impossible to repair, because the middle ground seems the way forward, and the illusion of control a salve.

They dance around issues because sometimes it just happens to be the most elegant way of doing things.

But that is the catch of course. It takes two to dance.

For a while it is good. It is a smooth dance, a waltz, travelling around the line of dance. David and Ameena become experts overnight. They waltz around the worn little apartment with its enviable river views and old-fashioned glass windows, they waltz around the living room talking about Hershel and his unexpectedly good mood, they waltz around the kitchen talking about the weather, how the winter seems interminable that year, lingering into April like an unwelcome guest, they waltz around the bedroom talking about Whitney, how she and her boyfriend are considering adopting a baby, Whitney doesn't have a uterus, you see.

Then, in the middle of a turn, Ameena announces that she has taken 'some time off work'.

'Oh,' David remarks coolly.

'Not that long ago you were suggesting I quit. Now, you seem to disapprove,' she observes.

1,2,3 (Waltz steps)

'Not at all. I'm surprised, that's all. I would have thought it would help take your mind off... other things.'

4 (Open position, open out like a book or a hinge)

'You mean,' she says, 'like an ostrich?'

5,6 (Promenade, reaching step, weight on balls of feet)

He smiles. Doesn't take the bait/lose the beat. 'You're great at your job. Just thought it would be a good thing at this time. Keep you busy.'

'I don't need to be kept busy. Don't patronise me please, David. I'm not a child.'

7,8 (Step in front of partner. Signal close.)

3.6

The following night, she is lying on the sofa in the darkened apartment when he comes home after a session, but she sits up when she hears him. The light makes her squint. She's been crying, he can see that; her eyes are swollen and puffy. She's wearing his t-shirt again.

'My mum called earlier.'

'Oh?'

'They closed the case. Insufficient evidence.'

'I'm sorry,' he says simply.

'They didn't even cover the cost of the window. Kareem got it fixed when my dad was out.'

'I'm so sorry,' he repeats, and he is genuinely sorry, but he knows how pointless they must sound, his words, how unhelpful.

She nods and disappears into the bedroom. She looks desolate, he thinks.

But a few minutes later, she comes back out. 'Where's the justice?' she demands, of the room – or the universe – and then goes back in again.

David who is a bit more well-versed in the workings of the universe, knows that those who go looking for justice find it to be an elusive thing. The kind of thing that is only truly understood by its absence, the stuff that you don't know you can't find until something much more significant is lost. The stuff that Peggy couldn't find from her own mother, Ameena couldn't find for her art, her father couldn't find from the insurance company, his mother couldn't find from life.

The stuff of blindfolded Justitia with scales and sword, painted in a pretty blue sky on the high domes of ceilings of palazzos.

The stuff of mythology.

3.7

Just ten days ago, they had been standing on a street corner speaking of joy.

David had finished playing for the night. A Saturday night. Sunday technically; it was way past midnight.

'God, David,' she had said, her face lit, beautiful, against the stream of golden car lights that were continuously moving, like a line or a kind of living thing, 'that was too good tonight.'

They'd been standing on the corner of West 4th Street trying to hail a cab.

Before them, a city lived. Walking, talking, eating, excreting, breathing, inhaling, injecting, dancing, singing, swinging, pulsing, bouncing, crying, dying, boozing, fucking, laughing, loving, living. You could see the city living. You could hear it. You could smell it. You could taste it. Or you could, as easily, miss it entirely.

Just here...

couple holding hands
dog walker
tourist with subway map
sleeping baby on daddy's chest
musician with double bass
two gay men kissing
three Italian women speaking
ambulance weaving its way through traffic
noisy siren competing with Smooth Criminal blaring from someone's red convertible

Just there...

group of half-clad teenage girls
three firemen crouching outside fire station eating pizza
half-clad girls checking them out
four boys checking out half-clad girls
whiff of chilli and cinnamon
hole-in-the-wall immigrant burrito guy with line around the corner
sound of laughter
tall, black, shaven-headed beauty turning heads
man eating ice cream cone
couple arguing loudly in foreign accent
Billie Holiday's voice floating down from open apartment window
woman with headphones
homeless guy on sidewalk with sleeping dog and 'veteran' sign
off-duty police car
another one behind it
speeding yellow cabs

Only none with their lights on.

The wind tunnelled furiously down the avenue. Bright and high and perfectly round, the library clock beheld the streets, a second moon. Ameena craned her neck forward trying to spot a free cab. She had crossed her arms around her coat and was hopping from foot to foot.

'God, it's seriously cold. No, I mean, Piano-man, *that* was some seriously good shit.'

David shivered. 'How are you wearing that tiny skirt? Here, have my scarf. Ameena, *don't* roll your eyes, I can't give you my pants can I? Yeah, that's it, wrap it around your legs. Very sexy. The music... thanks, yeah, I kind of felt it too, honestly, it was different level tonight. Josh...' David laughed, 'Josh was really grooving it... his swing, his feel, his bounce, his pulse... and Roy, I mean, Roy just owns the beat in such an intuitive way, he doesn't sound like any other drummer out there. But yeah, we had fun... finding, discovering.' He nodded. 'I felt it too, can't describe it in words, it's just the way we were playing tonight.'

'I know!' Ameena said. 'We heard it off the bandstand. We *felt* it. And you know, you never talk about yourself and I guess that's the jazz way, but the emotion and the expression, the *variety* of expression in your improvisation tonight was something else and I know enough now to tell you when it's good. *You* were amazing, and together, you guys were killing it. Fluid, like a conversation. I still don't know how you do it, you know. I mean mechanically.'

She was jumping now to keep warm, up and down, jump, jump, jump.

She looked at David quizzically. 'Okay seriously, why is everyone staring at me? Naked guy right there with a bucket on his head, speaking to himself, and they're staring at *me*? So, yeah, I'm probably still gonna be telling you this when we're both eighty, but I don't think I will ever understand how you guys play something that's not written down anywhere, no notes, no instructions, no nothing, and still make it sound this good.'

'Haha,' David said. 'You're funny. I look forward to you being eighty – will you still have a man's scarf wrapped around your legs, baby? Will you still be funny? Will you still seduce me with your good taste and eroticism? But hey, that is probably why it sounded good, the power of this music is in the making of the stuff, this idea that you listen, you imitate, you sing along with what you hear, and then you just try to play what you sing. And that we're all doing it simultaneously – Josh, Roy, me. There's a kind of organic truth to that.' He shrugged. 'Artmaking.'

'Yes! You're speaking to each other through your instruments, you say what you feel, you play what you feel. It's all feeling. That's all that remains. It's rapturous.'

David mock bowed. 'Why, thank you milady.'

'No, thank *you*. What you give to your listener is unbelievable. Something happens to me when I listen to jazz, it's beautiful, and beauty is a real thing! Your music moves me, it actually makes my body move, I just can't help it, it's like this magical involuntary thing that happens, I listen to your music and I want to extend it, in some way, in my own body... keep it going, you know? Oh my God, there are no cabs. Should I lift up my skirt and stick my leg out?'

'We'll find a cab,' David said, and she noted with some surprise how his tone had turned just that little bit serious. 'Ameena, do you know how happy it makes me that you're enjoying jazz? Jazz for jazz's sake I mean, separate from you and me. I was thinking about it the other day, that I should stop and thank you for caring about and appreciating my music and for being so curious about our art as to try and understand it. I know that it isn't only for my sake or because you feel like you've got to love what I love.'

Ameena smiled, but her words, though uttered casually, were also serious.

'It's not always obvious to me David, what makes you happy. But jazz, I know, does. Anyway, don't be so silly, you don't need to thank me. You filled my life with your music; you filled my life with you. Okay, I can't wait any longer, I'm doing this.'

Freeing herself of the scarf, she returned it to its rightful owner, looping it loosely round David's neck. She was about to move away, but David held her arm and pulled her close, bringing his lips to the hollow of her neck, where a tiny gold heart pendant sat prettily in the dip between her collarbones. His breath was uneven, and she could feel his desire, and from somewhere inside her, powerfully, her own. 'Stop doing things to me, Piano-man,' she said, 'this is not the time. Or the place. Or the temperature. But hold that thought...' She narrowed her eyes seductively, as she stepped back. And then, with her arms waving crazily in the air and one stockinged leg raised in a perfect right angle over 7th Avenue, she said thoughtfully, 'You know what, David, the greatest lesson of jazz, for me, is joy.'

Just ten days.

3.8

Time moves irreversibly forward. Sometimes we cannot help but move irreversibly backward.

And so, just ten days later, it was one of those nights, he cannot remember which one, they have all melted together into one, like multiple flavours in an ice cream cone that's started to drip, first from one side, then from another – you have to lick it, quickly, desperately, turning it round and round and round like a crazed person, just to keep it together.

'Can't you just turn that damn *light* off? I can't sleep,' she snapped, sitting up in bed suddenly, a dark fury raging in her eyes.

'Can't you just say that nicely?' he replied, but he put his book down on the side table. She could hear it in his voice and given their propinquity she could feel it, radiating from his body to her own, those silent pangs of hurt.

She slumped back with a thud as if dragged down by some invisible force and turned on her side, her back to him. 'I really don't need to say it at all. You can see I'm trying to sleep. Can't you?'

The next morning, a Sunday, she seems bright-eyed.

'Do you want omelettes for breakfast?' she asks, then rolls over, on top of him now, straddling him, sitting up, pulling her t-shirt over her head. 'Or me?'

And like that, the fight is over.

'You're still squeezing,' he says, after.

'Am I?' she asks, surprised.

Later they eat breakfast together, side by side, watching how the sunbeams make the river shine with an almost frenetic exuberance.

'I think I'm just the wrong person for this,' she says casually as she butters her toast.

'Wrong person for what?

'To be an artist. I'm the wrong person to be an artist.'

'What do you mean you're the wrong person to be an artist?' David said, and slipped headfirst into the crack.

They are elusive, these cracks, whether in people or in walls. Sometimes they come disguised, by doorframes or by desire, but look closely and you see them, the dark fissures where two bits have split, exposing what's private, what's weak. And you wonder, when you find them, you wonder where they came from, how they could appear just like that, because one minute the wall seems intact and the next, you're slipping into the crack.

'Why is this so difficult to understand?' Ameena was saying. 'I'm the wrong person to be an artist in this city at this time.' She rolled her eyes. 'Or maybe it's any city at any time. But I'm the wrong person. Wrong name, wrong colour, wrong religion, wrong sex. Wrong in every way.'

'Ameena... I—'

'No. You know what? Please don't. Please don't say whatever it was you were going to say. In fact, please just eat those excellent omelettes I made for you and don't say anything at all.'

'I was only going to say,' David continued, ignoring her, 'and it's better I say this to you than a stranger – or worse, a prospective new gallery – that I know you are stinging from what's happened to your family and I don't blame you for it – at all – but I don't think what happened at the gallery has anything to do with race or sex or religion or anything else that you seem to be hinting at. These are two unrelated incidents. Related only so much as you had one on your mind when the other happened. Terrible timing. I'll give you that. But not *everybody* is crazy. Not everybody has an agenda. The pig guy is crazy. The pig guy had an agenda. This guy? This guy just didn't like your work. Sucks. But that's the nature of what we do. Not everyone is going to like your work. It can annoy you, but you can't let it control you. It's not easy for any kind of creative. You, more than anyone else, know how long I've been trying to get someone to look at my stuff and I don't even know where to begin or if I'll be any good at it, or even, quite frankly, if it feels right creatively to be going down that path at all.' He sighed. 'It's a pretty solitary place to be, for all of us.'

Ameena pressed her lips together. Her head was starting to hurt. 'For all of *us*?'

'Yes. Us. People like us. You and me.'

'You and me? You cannot be serious!'

'I am completely serious. The world still undervalues the arts. I'm sorry but that's a fact. The vicissitudes of life are that much more unpredictable for us. It's an uphill struggle – to be *any* kind of artist. You need a break. Every successful artist has had a break and he or she will admit that openly. You might want to think you're alone because it suits you to think so at this moment. But, you're not alone. And if you're alone, I'm alone too.'

Ameena laughed.

And with her laughter, the crack was no more a crack.

'Oh,' she said at the end of the laugh. 'Oh, Oh, *Oh*! *Poor* David. Poor *Jewish* David. Trying to make it all *alone* in the world. You think I'm hinting at something? Well, how's this for a hint? *You* are trying to do what everyone else who is exactly like you has already done. In fact, there are the African-American musicians to whom this music *actually* belongs and then there's like five people remaining in the world who have done what you want to do that *aren't* like you! That's the marvellous irony of this whole thing! That you actually think you're alone. You want me to recite them back to you? The names of your idols? These people you aspire to be like, these people you want to become? Irving Berlin, Bernstein, Sondheim, Benny Goodman, Herbie Mann, Getz, Konitz, Buddy

Rich, Artie Shaw, John Zorn, Ziggy Elman, Bernard Herrmann, Zimmer, Schoenberg, Philip FUCKING Glass!'

She raised her arms in the air.

'Shall I go on?'

David's face had turned white.

But Ameena wasn't going to stop there.

She'd seen on the news the other day, while David was gigging at the Blue Note club and she was home alone, sitting on the sofa, watching TV, eating ice cream, rum and raisin, straight out of the carton, a story about a woman in Idaho who went into a blind rage and stabbed her married lover twenty-five times with an eight-inch steak knife, right there in his wife's pinewood kitchen.

This is how rage arrives, a force of nature, like a tsunami, wrathful and indiscriminate; claiming everything, sparing nothing.

So, no – Ameena wasn't going to stop, even though his face had turned white.

'Yup,' she nodded at David's white face, 'those are the people you want to become, don't you? But guess what, David? I'll let you in on a great big secret – you don't need to *become* them! You already *are* them! A whole bunch of people who look like you, who speak like you, who sound like you, who probably all fuck like you.'

He made a sound then, a tiny, strangled sound, barely audible, the kind of sound made by a small child in pain.

Ameena heard it and she took pleasure from it, from the pain she was causing him. It gave her satisfaction, a strange form of comfort, as if in hurting him she would no longer be the only one hurting.

'And you know what? Every one of those names, you taught me. *You* taught me. I may be a shitty artist and an even shittier girlfriend but at least you can't say I wasn't a fucking good student.'

3.9

Ameena's fury during those weeks! She rages at *everything*. The discoloured patch on a Pink Lady apple, the filth of the melting snow, the Chinese tourists, the sour taste of Hershey's Kisses, the long lines at the supermarket, the rats on the subway tracks, the unhelpfulness of the credit card helpline, the head cold that she can't seem to shake, the interminable wait at the doctor's office, the infrequency of the elevator, the loudness of the neighbour's dog's bark, the short lifespan of Manhattan milk...

And when there's nothing left to rage at, she still rages.

'Iva-fucking-nov,' she says, 'I wish he would die. I wish he would go somewhere and just quietly die.'

David searches everywhere for his old lighter. Finds it in the pocket of his Yankees sweatshirt. It smells of Ameena. The sweatshirt, not the lighter. Smokes three 'jazz cigarettes' back to back. Feels the panic subside. Throws away the debris. Stows away the lighter.

It helps him to pretend that these moments never happened. It is easier, sometimes, to pretend that something never happened.

3.10

Spring played truant again that year. Summer arrived. The snow melted, and the days lengthened and there was light under the dark.

Ameena emerged in this same way.

The fury ended as swiftly as it had begun. Now, she carried a moodiness that seemed to follow her at all times like a shadow attached to the bottom of her feet, but at least, David thought, she wasn't spending all her time in the bedroom with the door closed, she had brushed her hair the other day, she wasn't wearing his clothes.

While before she screamed at everyone and everything, now she would speak to him sparingly; not much, no more than a few words here and there – How are you? How was your day? Good morning, good night – uttered with a disinterest that made him wince, and he felt, in a strange and shocking way, that sometimes he preferred her storminess to this coolness. The storminess was familiar, it came with Ameena, the flip side of her passion, but this? He found that he was wary of this, this shadow, of its unfamiliar shapes, its darkness.

But he held on. Why? He would wonder years later, when he thought back to this 'phase' in their lives, why had he held on when the easiest thing for him to do would have been to cut loose and run?

'Timekeeping began with the observation of the heavens,' David's father used to say when he was teaching the boys how to tell time, 'a profound awareness of the fact that the sun sets, only to rise again.' Perhaps it was that. Hope. That silent resilience that flows through the progeny of survivors. When you come close enough to tasting death, they say, you experience the urgency to live. There is a hunger in them, in people whose people have breathed in the air at the edge of the world, a hunger and a doggedness, to never give up, to *live* – to experience life in all its whimsical incarnations to an extent that might seem foolhardy to the traditionalist, idealistic to the cynic or martyrdom to the never-oppressed. What then, in the face of all that, is a mere lovers' quarrel?

But perhaps it wasn't that at all. Perhaps it wasn't about hope or heart.

Perhaps it was jazz; the evanescent, viscerally uplifting quality of it.

Live in the moment, says jazz. And when it's gone, it's gone, let it die. And a different version will be born. So, let it go. Give it wings, set it free, let it fly. Feel the flow, start afresh, make something new, improvise, improvise, improvise. Don't look back, release yourself, just let the music be. That is the magic of it, of its existence, never constant, always changing, morphing, shifting, discovering. Being worked out in the moment. Pleasure masquerading as pain; pain masquerading as pleasure. The impermanence of both. The resilience of what endures.

You can take away our instruments, but you cannot take away our souls.

But perhaps it wasn't about jazz either.

Perhaps it was about faith.

Ameena had said about Manchester once, 'It's the only other city I love. Outsiders may not understand why, and I get that. It's wet, dark, industrial. You have to look hard to find its beauty. But it's there. I see it.'

Perhaps David saw it too. *Her* beauty. For we find beauty in everything we love. Whether in cities or in people. And when we find it, we forgive. We forgive everything of those we love.

So perhaps somewhere in him, he knew that *it was there*. Lurking beneath the shadows, surfacing gradually, like the rising sun. And perhaps he also knew that when the sun did rise, he would be there to receive its warmth and its light, because that was part of the deal wasn't it, to embrace her when she was ready to be embraced, for being without her seemed unthinkable to David. He had become acclimatised to her now – to her inquisitiveness and her passions and her vulnerabilities and her strong opinions and her fierce, protective love – and he loved her back, even for all her flaws, he loved her, for who in this world is without flaws anyway?

So, he held on. He waited, patiently and without complaint.

You cannot force someone to return, he knew that – one of the oldest laws of the universe – just like you cannot force someone to stay.

3.11

For David, the world is jazz.

Some nights ago, he'd been playing at a club he hadn't played at before when the drummer walked up to him on a break – I know a guy who knows a guy, he said with a straight face.

And David laughed, but he took down the details.

A few days later, he agreed to meet the guy, an unknown twenty-five-year-old television director about to shoot his first theatrical feature. They met at a bar on Jane Street, and over a bottle of whisky, the young film-maker said that he had listened to David's version of a classic jazz tune and he wanted a similar-sounding soundtrack for his feature debut, an interracial love story set in 1970s Harlem.

'Your music is forward-thinking, yet conscious of its roots. I've heard that tune before of course, but then I listened to you play it your way and you changed it for me. I was humming it in my sleep,' he told David after the first glass, 'so then I had to meet you.'

'I don't have a fucking clue,' he confessed after half the bottle, 'where this is going to go. It's an experiment really, but then so is life isn't it, one giant experiment? You take all these chances and you muddle through them and hope something good comes of it in the end. So, I thought, if you're up for the ride, it could be, you know, fun...'

Drawn in by the romance of the script, and also something about the director – his enthusiasm and his boyish charm – David had agreed to explore where the partnership might take them.

Those were the days when Ameena shunned his company, expressing her displeasure (Was it disgust? Disdain? Disinterest?

David found it hard to distinguish sometimes.) when he was around the apartment, as if his very presence was proving irksome to her existence.

And so, David immersed himself in his music, toiling late into the night, grateful for the work that served to fill, or at least distract from, the Ameena-shaped void in his life.

Creatively, he found the work unexpectedly gratifying. The challenge of the speed and productivity required, combined with the unpretentiousness of it all, made it surprisingly contiguous to David's improviser's temperament. At the same time as experimenting with the score – a labour-intensive, solitary task – David craved the social, almost-spiritual element that jazz offered, and he found himself at the piano almost every night. There were things about playing with other people that stirred in him an absence of self, a non-self, that he had never perhaps felt as acutely before. At the highest level, he knew bands operated subconsciously to find that singular artistic voice, and that the interaction between the different members of the band was happening at the level of the instant, much faster than the conscious mind could hope to keep up. And so, he found himself reminded – compelled to remember – that there was a great beauty in making music with other people, an act of unification, a finding of synergies, a mind-melding experience that allowed the music to be created by the product of many minds working in harmony without any awareness of self.

Ultimately, this would be what saved David, for although the culture demands of us to put all of our belief into the individual, ultimately it is always other people who save us.

3.12

It had to arrive, sooner or later, and then it did.

A magnificent summer's day. Incredible, when it happens. Incredible, every time.

On the eve of one such day, when David walked into their home, he saw her with her hair up, a bright blue apron tied round her waist, cooking in the kitchen. She hadn't stepped into the kitchen in weeks.

'Hey Piano-man,' she said brightly when she noticed him.

'Hey...' he began carefully.

Trust in the moment, one of the greatest lessons of jazz: *When in doubt, trust in the moment and go for it.*

'Man, Ameena, that smells heavenly.'

'Goat biryani. Mum makes it to celebrate things. Birthdays and Eid and exam results and things.'

She said this conversationally, cheerfully almost, and David, like a good musician, took his cue. She was offering him a chance to play; he was going to take it. Another jazz lesson. Playing with others. Remember: *they show their love for you and you show your love for them.*

He closed his eyes and inhaled deeply. 'Honestly, that must be what heaven smells like. It must! It *must* be what all the fuss is about!'

Ameena smiled. And the smile awakened in David an aching desire, a yearning for something that had been unreachable to him all these weeks. He felt it touch him, and he felt mildly annoyed by it, by this offending need he seemed to carry for her even in the most inopportune of times.

But she seemed not to notice. 'It's the spices, you see. You cook the rice with saffron and whole spices, cloves and cinnamon and cardamom – here, smell.' She crushed a small, green cardamom between her fingers and held it up, so David could breathe in its pungent, nutty aroma.

'Ummm,' he said.

'Lovely, no?' she agreed, then smelled it herself, before she threw it into the pot.

'And then,' she continued, 'I cooked the meat separately. Then I layered them, meat and rice in alternating layers, meat at the bottom, rice on top, and then I steamed the whole thing! My mother would be so proud!'

Her cheeks were flushed. She looks so youthful, David thought, so childlike.

He smiled. 'I'm sure she would.'

'Yeah man. No shortcuts. I even went to the Pakistani butcher in Little India.'

'That's actually very funny.'

'Well, considering there isn't a Little Pakistan in Manhattan, I guess that's quite a logical place for him to be. In any case, I think the Indians and the Pakistanis tend to be friends, outside of India and Pakistan, that is.'

'So, you went to the Pakistani butcher in Little India...'

'Yup. It was great fun, we spoke Urdu, he told me how happy he was to sell me his meat, then he said I reminded him of his daughter, and he gave me lunch.'

'Oh?'

She nodded. 'I offered to pay, and he said with great indignation,' – Ameena put her hands on her hips in an exaggerated mime – 'he said, would I even think of paying my own father for lunch?'

David laughed. 'Looks like you've had a good day.'

'I have.'

David caressed the top of her head, where her hair was tied up in a bun; he did this swiftly, guardedly – a door that's been opened, but only an inch. She looked up at him, and when he held her gaze, she undid it – for him – and it fell down her back in soft black waves. That yearning again.

But, 'I'm glad,' was all he said.

There was a silence then for a while, not the uneasy silence that had lingered between them these past weeks, but a different one, as if they had tacitly crossed over to the other side of the angry river – there was no wading into it, no swimming, no walking through, only leaping across. And knowing this privately, individually, they had both leapt across and found the other on the other side. And so, there were no words and no sound but for the clattering of the pot, the slow sizzle of the flame as she turned it up.

'So,' he said after a few minutes, 'if this is a celebration dish, then what are we celebrating?'

'Should we eat first?' she replied. 'It's ready...' Her eyes twinkled humorously. 'Unless you'd rather wait. For background and context...'

'Are you kidding? I would wrestle you to the ground for some of that, Miss Ameena! Context can wait.'

She laughed, and it seemed to him that she had laughed after a very long time. They sat down next to each other on the bar stools they had bought together at Bloomingdale's the weekend after they'd moved in. He'd wanted white, she'd wanted cream – it's not a footballer's house, she'd said pointedly – but they'd settled in the end for a chic, modern grey. They had placed these bar stools along the inside length of the kitchen counter, even though doing so encroached upon precious kitchen space, but it seemed worthwhile, they agreed, to do this, for it allowed them to gaze upon the river while they ate, a beautiful affair, especially in the evenings when the sun went down and the lights came on and the bridges sparkled like jewelled hoops reflected in the water like that.

Ameena served him some of the biryani and then served herself. They ate together, looking at the dark swirls of the river, rhythmic in its flow, a seemingly effortless fluid grace. Mesmerising, just to look at.

'This is just phenomenally good,' David remarked appreciatively.

'We are celebrating the fact that I *love* you,' Ameena said, answering his question from before.

Love. She said the word fiercely. And David's heart leaped. *She's back*. There was nothing unfeeling, David knew, about *his* Ameena. Ameena, like jazz: *passionate, inquisitive, emotional, intuitive, necessarily flawed, histrionic, joyful – and largely lost when translated into words.*

Not like the girl he'd been living with these past weeks, a clever impersonator, surely, a charlatan. He grimaced inwardly at the thought. No, Ameena was Ameena, in all her fullness of love and life – when Ameena hugged you, she hugged you so tight it almost hurt. He had learned this about her, that her love was as fierce as her hate.

'Okay,' he nodded, 'that's worth celebrating.'

'And...'

'And?'

'And that I'm sorry, David, for my extraordinary solipsism.'

He smiled, a small, sad smile, but he said nothing.

'And the unimaginable hurt that's caused you... it's unforgiveable...'

'It's okay,' he said.

'No,' she said, 'it's not.'

'Let's forget about it,' he said.

She shook her head, but her eyes were steady, looking straight into his – a question.

David looked directly back at her – an answer.

She nodded then, gratefully.

This is their private language, a mode of communication they have established between themselves a long time ago that helps them negotiate each other even in difficult times. They have learned the meaning of each other's faces and they need nothing more.

'And?' he prodded softly, sensing there was something else.

'And... that I called Whitney. She's happy for me to come back from my... break. I didn't think she'd be quite so generous, but...'

He nodded. 'That's great,' he said, 'that's so great.'

'And, David...'

'Yes?'

'I found someone. This guy. He curates. He's young, just starting out. Nowhere nearly as established as Suzy, not even close. There's probably no money in it at all. Or fame or any of that. But I don't need all that. The important thing is that he's willing to help me. The thing is...'

She hesitated. And when she spoke again, he felt the catch in her voice pull at his heart.

'...I want to start painting again.'

He nodded. He understood how hard this whole ordeal had been for her, how it took a certain honesty for her to have said what she said, even to herself.

'I know,' he said, 'I know you do.'

Their sex that night was serious and intense. At one point he stopped moving and just looked at her, his face so close above hers. 'Wow,' he said with genuine wonder. 'Wow. I'd almost forgotten how beautiful you are.' At another point later on, she gripped his shoulder blades and let out a low, raspy moan. Her eyelids fluttered, and her face changed. He knew that face. He knew all her faces.

After they had finished, she had fallen asleep almost instantly. And now she was lying there next to him, flat on her back, arms outstretched on either side of her body, face serene, those same eyes closed shut. It made him feel almost guilty, looking at her that way, watching her small face, her chest moving peacefully in tune with the shallow, steady breaths, a kind of survivor's guilt, a realisation that when a certain type of hand is dealt, some of us fold quicker than others.

3.13

There is a particular memory from Ameena's childhood that holds for
her a certain significance. It is one of her earliest lucid memories, its
meaning as clear and as convincing to her adult self as it was unsettling
and ambiguous to her child one; an example, she considers, as good
as any, of the futility of hindsight – that infuriating, retrospective
habit of the mind which allows us to uselessly understand now what
would have benefited us to understand then.

In this memory, she is very young, a little girl, but she can't
remember how old she is, she can't remember exactly. It is morning
time. She is upstairs in her bedroom in the house on Chapel Road.
The walls are painted pink, the exact shade of itch-relieving calamine.
Apart from the colour, itself an indulgence, the walls are bare – posters
of pop idols or movie stars are frowned upon by her mother. Ameena
is standing facing the small oval mirror that hangs at a crooked angle
on the wall above a clever Ikea creation meant for small spaces –
dressing table and study desk rolled into one. Her mother is getting
her dressed for school. She is already in her uniform – pleated grey
skirt, red t-shirt, grey socks up to her knees. Her mother is braiding
her hair in front of the oval mirror; two fat braids that fall all the way
to her waist, tied at their ends with plain black elastic. She remembers
that, and also that it was raining heavily, she remembers that too, she
remembers it clearly, a kind of psychedelic haze outside her window
blocking out all the familiar discernible shapes.

'What day is it today, Ammi?' she asked.

'Day? Today is Tuesday, naturally,' Zoya replied, suppressing
a yawn.

Ameena nodded. 'On Tuesdays,' she enquired, 'do I stay for a half day or a full day?'

'Full day,' her mother replied, 'Tuesday is full day. Every Tuesday is full day. You already know this.'

'Am I having lunch there?' Ameena asked.

'Yes, of course,' Zoya said tetchily. 'What is it with all these twenty million questions so early in the morning? Today is Tuesday, every Tuesday is full day, and you will have lunch in school, like you always do every full-day Tuesday.'

And with that final, unambiguous confirmation, to Zoya's bewilderment, Ameena burst into tears.

Hai Allah, Zoya thought. This country has finally done her in.

To Ameena, she said, 'Is it the English cook?'

Ameena shook her head. Zoya ploughed on.

'No? Not frightful English cook dishing up the lunch? Then what? You going hungry? Not enough gruel? Stingy? No? The other way around – too much? Too much shepherd's pie? Wanton wastefulness? No? Tch tch tch. The food itself then. I knew it. Enough to break the sturdiest of stomachs. What is the matter with the food? Tell me. Too soggy? Too salty? Too bland? Too British?'

But Ameena, still sobbing, shook her head each time.

Eventually, after what seemed to Zoya to be a tiresome eternity, in between the whimpering and the sobbing and the gasping for air, together they discovered the root of Ameena's deep sorrow.

There was a new system in place at school. The children were required to put on red aprons at lunchtime. Ameena didn't know how to put hers on and she was too self-conscious to ask for help. Nobody wore an apron in her house; what would the other girls think of her? Of her family?

The red apron terrified her.

Othering: A phobia.

3.14

City nights.

David doing what David does best.

Ameena sitting as close to the front as she can, listening with her eyes closed, chin cupped, swaying, tapping her feet.

The sparkle was back in her eyes, David noticed, as she opened them momentarily to look at him, at his fingers dancing over the keys, the fire that he had found himself so irresistibly drawn to, even in that first instant on the train.

And Ameena?

Ameena feels, as she watches David on the piano, his head thrown back, his mouth open, his eyes closed, shrouded in some unknowable emotion, that he is playing this song just for her. He is playing a tune called 'The Wind in the Night'. The male character is the Wind, the female character is the Night; she knows this because he has introduced the song to the audience in this way.

This much and nothing more.

But Ameena knows there is more. She can hear him do it, in the shapes he makes. He is expressing something through the piano, some voice from within, pristine and particular, and she can sense it in the atmosphere, how the room has been shifted slightly by it.

She had always been moved by the way he played, but there was a certain intimacy he shared with his music that night – a kind of protracted lovemaking – and she marvelled at it, at how that intimacy transferred from artist to art to audience, she felt this connection, and she knew that everyone else in that room was probably feeling it too. This was more than a performance, she realised, this was a going-through.

'You were magnificent,' she told him when it was over, 'simply sublime.'

'It was a love song,' David said softly, 'about a couple that has broken up after a long relationship and they have to divide up their shared belongings. It was a song I needed to play.'

She understood, then, how close to the end he must have felt they had come – she knows the performance couldn't have been that good without it. David, in playing the tune that night, had felt the power of his own music, it had opened a path to his subconscious, and he had submitted, because of them – because of *her* – to a kind of total body experience of the song. Ameena, in listening, had felt it too. And clearly so had David's bandmates, the same three guys she had met the very first time she'd heard him play. The contribution to the song had been total – the piano had told the story of the man's heartache; the saxophone had conveyed the woman's. The bass had supported their two voices, subtly and brilliantly, expressing the pain of the separation, the physical act of moving out. The drums had joined in then, bold with the promise of hope, and then all four had come together to speak of the new beginning that comes after every end, a kind of affirmation of life. Their music that night had been swinging and emotional and steeped in a bluesy feel so deep it reached her toes.

The kitchen clock ticked to half past midnight when they got back home.

'Do you remember,' she said suddenly, as she pulled off her heels right there in the entryway and walked barefoot into the living room, 'do you remember the story that Suzy told me? About that painter of hers, who quit?'

'Yeah,' David said, 'the graffiti guy? I think so.'

Ameena sat down on the sofa with her legs outstretched and started to take her bra off, reaching under her dress to unhook it, then slipping the straps off her shoulders one by one.

'I looked up her artist list the other night. That guy didn't just quit painting. He died of a heroin overdose.'

'Oh?'

'He quit quit.'

'That's horrible, Ameena, but I'm sure there must have been loads of other issues there. Some kind of profound internal conflict. You don't just kill yourself over...'

Ameena stood up then suddenly, while he was still speaking, an unusual look on her face, a kind of determination, he thought, but also pride and maybe a little fear, and walked wordlessly towards the bedroom.

'Where are you going?' he said, but she didn't respond nor stop nor turn around. She didn't close the bedroom door behind her, however, leaving it open, so he could come in if he wished or not, if he didn't – that decision, she thought, was his and not hers. Then, she opened her closet and rummaged through her clothes until she found her mother's hijab, and underneath it – shielding it from prying eyes – the watercolour, the only other relic of love that she had carried with her from home, and in a moment of such clarity that she knew it had to mean something, that it couldn't possibly not mean anything, she pulled out the painting and looked at it, at the pale face of Sarah Adams and the blue eyes staring back at her.

'Who's that girl?' David asked quietly from somewhere behind her.

'That girl,' Ameena replied, 'is the reason I started painting.'

3.15

The air softened and the dust settled. The heat descended in waves over the city. David and Ameena found themselves on a creative crest.

Ameena had converted the small spare bedroom that she and David shared as a workspace into a proper creative studio. She changed the lighting and repainted the room and rearranged the furniture with the care and detail with which he imagined some women would design nurseries.

She knew David liked to work facing the window, and so she positioned his piano like that, up against the wall so the sky seemed to begin where his piano ended. On a little desk next to it, she set his headphones and the composition paper and pencils he worked with, as well as the tattered poetry books he liked to have at hand while he worked on his music, an old superstition.

Angled against the back wall, she created her own workspace, her papers and mounts and her watercolours and her medley of painting aids – sticks, palette knives, cling film, kitchen towels, toothbrushes, masking tape, grains of rice... so the light coming in from the window was always tempered when it hit her easel, no matter how bright the day.

The curator of the new gallery, an unusual and instinctive man of Haitian descent, had gently encouraged her to experiment with her painting style. 'We can't choose what we want to be; we have to accept who we are. If you're shying away from something to protect someone else, you're more often than not trying to protect yourself,' he had said gently, and Ameena had both grasped his meaning and been amazed by how quickly he had discerned something in her that had taken her this long to fully understand in herself.

At the magazine, things were busy. Whitney and her boyfriend had finally found their baby girl after months of searching and mounds of paperwork. 'You wouldn't think there are 150 million orphans around the world, with what they put you through,' Whitney said dryly, when she brought the baby – Lucy – into work one day and watched her being passed around with more tenderness than Ameena could have imagined Whitney was capable of. With the change in Whitney's personal life, Ameena had taken on more editorial responsibility without an official pay rise or promotion, but David didn't hear her complain once.

At David's own workplace, Hershel seemed a different man, calm, relaxed and filled with a renewed zest for life, but no one knew why. David had unexpectedly been offered a generous pay rise and an increase in his holiday entitlement ('for your jazz shtick'), but again no one knew why. That all of these developments were connected in some way seemed reasonable, but not verifiable. Rumour had it that Hershel had got a divorce. Or that he had reconciled with his estranged son. Maybe both. Or neither. That's the problem with rumours.

Outside of work, David played jazz every chance he got. 'It keeps me going,' he remarked to Ameena, 'it sustains me, like lifeblood.' And with whatever spare time he found, he dedicated to making his own music with a happy but cautious optimism given the development on the film-scoring front.

Ameena had become comfortable painting with David in the room. Where before she felt the need to work in complete isolation, now she welcomed David working alongside her, his very presence offering her a kind of muse. 'Your music takes my mind to a different place,' she told him. 'It helps me to not overthink. I find myself just going along with it, and it's beautiful, allowing for the surprises and incidental happenings that sit at the heart of a water-based piece. Like the characters in a story create the narrative, so those initial brushstrokes shape the painting. For the first time in years, David, I don't feel like I'm fighting something, or wrangling with that tremendous anxiety that used to grip me if the finished product was different from the idea I had in my head. I feel – free. It's showing in the work, the artistic process is so fluid that the effort feels in some way hidden... like a performance... like one of yours.'

As for David, he loved having Ameena as his first listener. He would put together several pieces of music, different sections of the score, then improvise over them and play them to Ameena. He found that she was an honest critic of his work, as he was of hers, and they valued this about each other greatly. One time, he put together a tune mixing himself and Charlie Parker's 'Perhaps', playing the melody one quarter note apart in the right and left hand. She put her brush down and listened to it with her eyes closed, head nodding, fingers and feet tapping. 'It's your mother,' she said to him when it was over. 'That was a thing alive – her spirit lives on in your music.'

All in all, for David and Ameena, you could say that things were slowly beginning to get back to normal.

3.16

The illuminated hands of the beautiful antique clock that once belonged to David's father and now graced her bedside table, told her that it was nearly two in the morning when he crept into bed.

'How do you sleep so little and go to work the next morning?' she asked, stifling a yawn. David had been sitting in on sessions, playing nearly every night for the past few weeks, driven by a certain courage and also a certain stubbornness that she picked up on, and understood was necessary. He didn't talk about it too much, but Ameena knew he was at a crossroads in his creative life; if he was considering giving up his day job to become a full-time professional musician – perhaps the most significant decision of his life yet – playing as much as he could was something he needed to do. You need conviction to own your truth; she knew that, from her own experience.

'So sorry sweet – didn't mean to wake you,' he said snuggling under the covers. 'Ah you're so lovely and warm.'

'But how?'

'Again, please?'

'How do you sleep so little and go to work the next morning?'

'I'm a cat.'

'I prefer dogs.'

'Okay, for you, I can be a jazz dog. But only for you.'

She laughed and propped herself up on an elbow, wide awake now.

'I went to the Met today after work.'

'Oh ya?'

'It was a revelation.'

He chuckled. 'I'm sure they'd be delighted to hear that – how so?'

'So, you know, I never really went to museums growing up.' She sighed. 'I guess I didn't follow a lot of these intellectual pursuits growing up. Anyway, today, when I was there, I realised that so much of the work I loved best wasn't by someone who had necessarily studied art or art history or had a string of degrees or qualifications from fancy places or anything... they were just inspired by the work of other artists or sometimes even just by life.'

David nodded. 'Yes of course! That's the beautiful thing about art. You can be a genius without formal education. It doesn't hurt to have it of course, but above everything, it's emotional integrity that makes great art.'

'Yes! Exactly. So, listen!' she said, and even in the dark, he could see her face inside his head, how delightfully animated it became when she was excited about something. 'I went to the Met to see this special exhibition they had on, called *The Artist's Artist*, and I stopped in front of this painting – it was like the tenth or eleventh work down the row, and it was a portrait of the artist's father. And David! I found my feet were rooted to the floor, I couldn't move – I was transfixed by it. It was a painting of a man sitting on a chair and the man had no face.'

'That's pretty cool,' David said, nodding, 'I like that.'

'You see what he did, right? He skipped what was perishable and went straight to the essence of the man. It was so simple, so basic, nothing big or flashy or elaborate. And yet, there was something about it that kept me there the whole time. All the time I had budgeted for the whole exhibition, I stood and stared at that one painting. And then, after I finally walked away from it, my whole point of view changed. Everything I saw was transformed in my brain into a painted surface; I looked at people and they transformed into portraits, I looked at shapes and they transformed into stories. But David – everything, everything had a distinct physical presence. Everything had life.'

She lay down on her stomach and turned her head to face him.

'He said to me,' and David knew she was speaking of the Haitian curator, 'sometimes you're so keen to paint a flower accurately, you become tight and literal. He was right. A bunch of tulips can convey the same sense of drama as a face – if you get it right, the anticipation is so intense, a box of emotions ready to explode at any moment. The painting of the man with no face proves that! I need to trust my heart more. Ivanov was not a complete cunt.'

David, wisely, said nothing.

'Just a partial cunt,' she said with a smile that made David's eyes shine with amusement.

'Say it again?'

'What?'

'That word. Say it again, ten times, slow.'

She tapped him playfully on the arm. 'Shut *up*.'

He laughed. 'Fine, I'll shut up. Go on.'

'So, I went back,' she continued, 'the museum was closing, they were shepherding people out, but I couldn't leave without looking at it again. That face without a face. I wanted to understand how all of it was even possible. It reminded me of something I haven't painted yet.'

3.17

The summer stretched out the daylight, elongating it like Nefertiti's neck, shifting the balance between light and dark, trapping people into the smug illusion of expanded time.

Ameena left work on one of these summer evenings, when the air was hot and sticky and the light lingered for much longer than expected, and she wandered into a second-hand bookshop, one of those monuments of pleasure she knew were getting rarer and rarer, even in New York.

There she spent a few blissful hours lost in the sweet surprise of discovery, and when finally she left and began walking the city blocks towards home, lighter both of wallet and of heart, it had turned into one of those warm summer nights that almost never happened in England.

She would read one of them that very evening, she decided happily as she stepped out of the elevator, one of her new old books, pre-owned and pre-loved, with its smell of aged paper and its unknown author who had probably spent an entire lifetime writing about people who didn't exist and who no one remembered. She would read this with a glass of wine, with the apartment windows open, with the sounds of the city carrying in the breeze, with Ella on the stereo...

But when Ameena leaned forward to unlock the door, she jerked her head back in surprise, for from inside her home – surely it wasn't from inside her head – she could hear the unmistakeable notes of Ella's distinctive voice.

She smiled. She hadn't expected David to be home.

'Hello!' she called warmly. 'This is a nice surprise!'

He had been sitting on the sofa, reading; he looked up now as she walked in. 'You look so beautiful,' he said with a kind of marvel in his voice.

'I do?'

'Yeah.' He nodded. 'Always. But particularly this evening.'

She shook her head. 'You're so lovely, David, the things you say. Do you know that? *And* do you know, I was walking home with exactly Ella on my mind! Let me get out of these clothes, be right there.'

She was halfway through changing out of her work clothes when her phone rang. She frowned, but with one leg out of her grey silk trousers she hopped towards where she had placed her phone, face down, on the bedside table and her frown deepened when she flipped it round and saw the number on the display.

'Mum?'

'They can't find him,' Ameena's mother said, in a hoarse whisper.

'What? Whom? Wait, isn't it like the middle of the night for you?'

'They can't find Kareem,' her mother repeated, louder now, but blank, eerily emotionless.

'What do you mean, *they* can't find him? *Who* can't find him?' Ameena asked as she sat down on the edge of the bed and yanked the trousers off her other leg with her free hand.

'The police. They can't find him.'

Ameena covered her mouth, not letting the sound escape, more for her mother's sake than her own. 'The police? Mum, what's going on?'

David had come in and he stood by the door, a concerned look on his face, but she barely registered his presence. Or maybe she did register his presence and then gestured for him to leave, or maybe he decided to leave on his own because a few minutes later, he went back outside, closing the bedroom door behind him. She heard the squeak of the door hinges, the click of the latch, his footsteps as he walked away. Everything sounded amplified.

Inside the bedroom, Ameena rubbed her forehead with the tips of her fingers.

'Mum? What's going on?' she repeated purposefully, forcing herself to keep calm.

'We won't know till we find him.'

'Have you looked in Faisal's house?'

'They can't find Faisal either. Both are gone.'

'Gone? What do you mean, gone? They've got to be somewhere, haven't they? I mean they couldn't have vanished into thin air! Have you asked at the mosque?'

'Yes. Nobody knows anything, or they don't want to say. Ameena, I'm scared.'

'Don't be silly. He's probably gone to the Arena or wherever to watch football or music or boxing or whatever those boys do when they're all together.'

A long pause. And then Zoya said quietly, 'No... no... I think something bad has happened.'

And then Ameena knew; some part of her already knew.

'Mum, what are you not telling me?'

'Nothing. You don't worry. I will call you tomorrow,' her mother said and then she hung up without saying goodbye.

Ameena stood up and slowly walked out to the living room in her underclothes. Then she looked at David and frowned.

'I think my brother's done something terrible,' she said.

3.18

Three days. Five. Eight. Ameena spoke to her mother daily, but no one had heard anything more about the missing boys; the police were involved, her mother reported, they had a search underway, but so far they'd come up with nothing. Later, Ameena confided to David that she felt her parents were hiding something from her, only she didn't dare imagine what.

She tried to keep herself busy, spending long hours in the office, or in the studio, painting. On David's insistence, she went out a few nights with her friends from work, but despite a brave front, she carried an anxiety inside her those days, an edginess that made her jump every time her phone would ring or beep or flash. She barely slept, lying awake at night, wondering where her brother might be, what terrible fate may have befallen him, her mind wandering to innumerable dark places, until finally sleep would come and cover her like a blanket, uncoupling her, at least temporarily, from her own thoughts. And so, when she heard David's voice – uncharacteristically loud and unnaturally irate – in the darkest alcoves of her mind, she thought at first that it was a dream.

'Okay, what's this?' David was saying loudly, walking into the bedroom, waking her up. She opened her eyes. He was holding it in his hands.

'Ummm... what?' she murmured sleepily. 'Oh, hi... Yahrzeit candle... for your mum.'

'Ameena, are you kidding?' he retorted angrily. 'You know I'm not... I haven't... I don't *do* this kind of *thing*.'

But then he looked at her face, propped up on the pillow, her eyes heavy with sleep. She didn't speak. She didn't get up. She just lay there looking very sad, and he sighed.

'Oh God, I'm sorry,' he said. 'It's just... I walked into the apartment and I haven't been sleeping enough with this crazy double life and I was so tired, and it was dark, and I saw it burning there and it made it all come back, you know... all the memories, her face, the instant she... went someplace else. It made everything very real again. Sometimes, it's just easier when it's not, you know, real.'

'I'm sorry,' she said in a small voice, covering her face with her hands, 'I should have asked you first. I... well, I knew what date it was today... and... I heard you play the other night and you were better than ever, and I thought, God, classical or jazz, on the piano, that's as good as it gets, she'd have been so proud of you... and I... I had my own family on my mind, but I mean I can't presume to understand what it must feel like to lose a parent... I'm so sorry.'

'Aaah... come here,' he said, and in two strides he was sitting on the bed next to her. 'This stuff is complex, Ameena, and uber-multilayered. A man's feelings when it comes to his dead mother. Mixed with a discussion on classical music vs. jazz. Mixed with the phases of Jewish bereavement. Twelve PhDs worth of analysis right there. Not solveable by Yahrzeit candle, really.'

'I'm sorry,' she said again, burying her head in his chest.

'Don't worry, sweet,' he said, drawing her into him and caressing the back of her neck, 'you meant well. Anyway, luckily for you and unluckily for me, I find it impossible to stay mad at you for too long.' Then he pulled away slightly, so he could look at her. 'Where did you even find that?'

'The Judaica store.'

'The *Judaica* store?'

'Yeah. I think they all thought I was Jewish. I kind of played along...'

David looked at her questioningly. 'Played along? Like how, exactly?'

'Well, for some reason they thought I was from Israel.' She shrugged. 'I don't know why. The accent maybe. But I didn't really correct them. So then, I created this elaborate story. I said I came here, to this country, for love. For you. They were all very moved.'

David opened his mouth. Then closed it. Then opened it again. His eyes widened in a sudden flare of emotion. Then he threw back his head and laughed.

3.19

'Hi Sally,' David said genially into the speakerphone on his desk, 'what's up?'

'Oh, nothing – your girlfriend's here.' The office secretary lowered her voice into a conspiratorial hush. 'You didn't tell me she was so *attractive*.'

'Ameena? Ameena's *here*?' David asked, surprised, picking up the receiver. He hadn't really taken Ameena to be the surprise-giving type. In fact, it was quite the opposite with her; she liked things to be planned, she always planned – meticulously most of the time.

'Yes,' Sally whispered, 'she was *standing* right here in front of me. I asked her to take a seat while I called your office. So, now, she's *sitting* right here in front of me. God David, you really didn't tell me she was so…'

'Attractive… yes, yes, you said that. Okay, I'll be there in five minutes, I just need to get this pitch across to Hershel before he starts to moan again.'

'Oh yeah. Hershel's moany voice. Always a treat, that.'

'Yup, like Halloween candy. We've had a surprisingly long run without hearing it though, haven't we? Almost scared to breathe around him, lest the spell gets broken. Right, see you shortly. Offer her a coffee or something. She likes it hot.'

'Ooh, *David!*'

'Her coffee, Sally, her coffee. She likes her coffee hot.'

David smiled as he put the receiver down, although he was still slightly perplexed that Ameena hadn't mentioned anything about visiting. He looked at the watch on his wrist – one of his father's old treasures, a rare piece that he'd been told was worth a lot, though he would never think of selling it, no that seemed totally wrong, immoral even, like peddling his father's memories. It was five thirty in the evening. He wondered if he could go over the Burt Teabags pitch with Hershel and then just call it a day, leave with Ameena, get a drink by the river, make an evening of it.

It was more than an hour later when David emerged from Hershel's office. They had conferenced in the client, a young, particularly offensive trust-fund type named Burt Davies, over the phone and gone through the presentation together – a proposal outlining what they believed was a novel approach to marketing stringless tea bags. But what David had hoped would be no more than a quick progress check rapidly went sideways...

'It's all wrong, guys,' Burt whined in his objectionably nasal voice, 'just horribly wrong. I mean, we don't want them to think, "That's nice. That would be *nice* to have." This isn't a new food processor. This is not *nice*. This is a *breakthrough*! This is about us being environmentally forward and socially conscious. This is about bigger things. Think of all the good this will do to the environment. We are actively combatting global warming here. I mean, *fuck*! I mean, booyah! And well, I don't get any of that from what you've put together. The problem is, and it's a big one – your services are not exactly *in*expensive. Like, basically, what I'm saying is that you're gouging my eyes out. Well, let me tell you, that *this*, whatever it is you're trying to sell me, isn't worth a bag of stale bagels. No disrespect.'

David, who felt more than slightly sceptical about the general idea of teabags being 'booyah' – strings or no strings – drummed his fingers on his knee and wondered if he had ever encountered anyone, *anyone*, more pompous than Burt Teabags. But *Hershel* – Hershel, who ordinarily would have cried (actually) at the mere thought of losing a client – got on the speakerphone and cleared his throat in a way that made David grimace.

Then, in a display of such anti-Hershelesque sangfroid as seen never before, he said, 'You see, the thing is, Burt, how I see it, is that we are small, dedicated bunch of people who eschew ego, melodrama and individual agendas in favour of openness, collaboration and the greater good, so if you feel someone else can do a better job...'

And David, full of horror at Hershel's obvious recklessness, for the client was lazy, boorish and unintelligent, surely, but business was business and you never drove away business no matter how lazy, boorish and unintelligent the business may be, felt the need to overrule Hershel on this matter. And so, out of a sense of loyalty to Hershel – who had gone loopy clearly, totally bonkers – rather than any kind of goodwill for the client, he clapped his palm on Hershel's mouth, and while Hershel gurgled and gulped, he said into the phone, '...you should wait until you see what we came up with just this morning. Is what Hershel means to say.'

David then spent several minutes trying to appease the client enough to at least temporarily get rid of him. He spent another several minutes trying to assure Hershel that *he* needn't trouble himself any more with the stringless teabags – 'I've got this one, trust me' – and only when he saw that Hershel had finally stopped looking so hopelessly loopy did David leave the office, but all that had taken much longer than he expected and when he got to reception, he realised that there was no one sitting in the waiting area and that Sally was giving him a particularly apologetic apologetic look.

'She's gone,' Sally said, as if to expound upon her particularly apologetic apologetic look.

'Fuck. When?'

'I'm sorry David, but I didn't even see her leave. She didn't say she was leaving or anything. One minute she was there and the next, she was gone.'

'Oh boy, I'm in a whole lot of trouble I think.'

Sally snorted. 'Well, it's a bit harsh if you ask me, to show up without telling you and then get upset when you can't get out of work immediately. I mean this *is* your workplace.'

David laughed. 'Thank you Sally, I appreciate the moral support.' Then he ran his fingers through his hair and sighed. 'Well, I'd better go try and fix this.'

'This is the problem with these exotic types,' he could hear Sally muttering to herself as he stepped into the elevator, 'so high and mighty...'

It was close to seven in the evening when David arrived home, the mirrored panes of glass on the tall buildings reflecting the light up and down the gridded streets, giving the city the hazy, somewhat wistful look of an overexposed photograph.

'Hel-looo?' he called melodiously as he walked into the apartment. 'Ameena?'

Ameena's keys were on the little wooden plank immediately to the right of the entrance that served as their console table – a rectangular piece of heart pine they had found together on a recent trip to Vermont, on a walk through the woods, lying on the ground, stupendous in its colouring and its large, unevenly split knots. In a moment of sentimentality, David had picked it up and carved their names on it, and then of course they had to bring it home and give it legs, and now they used it as a console table on which they placed their keys and sundries.

He placed his keys next to hers and wandered in quietly in case she might be on the phone; perhaps there had been news for her from home. But she wasn't in the bedroom and David found her instead in the studio that was at that moment bathed in a floating tangerine glow. Ameena was kneeling on the floor with earphones on, painting a large sheet of paper with broad, furious brushstrokes. The image, which to David's quick glance seemed almost complete, was that of a young woman in a vivid blue dress, framed by the violet-hued evening light, rising from a chair, her face captured in a split second of anticipation. The artist herself, he noticed, was wearing ankle-length jeans and a white ribbed sleeveless vest, and with her hair tied up in a bandana, an accidental streak of blue paint on her left cheek and that characteristic look of intensity in her eyes, she conjured up a vision that made him want to lift her off the ground and kiss her mouth.

Ah, but would she kiss him back? He pondered it for a second – it was hard to tell these things with women. It was hard to tell anything with women. She hadn't even noticed him come in. But maybe when she did... Wait, was it wrong of him to be wondering such things when she was clearly angry with him? Was it utterly idiotic? Was he such a complete fool?

But she did that to him, he realised, she could do that to him by doing nothing at all. She was doing it now. Driving him to distraction. Reducing him to a creature with only two functioning organs, both of which were thinking about her face and how it changed sometimes when he touched her, how her lips parted and her eyelids trembled and her eyes rolled back all the way into them, moments before she was going to come. *That*. Her pleasure-face.

And then she moved her real-life face slightly and noticed him. He smiled. Ameena pulled off her earphones slowly, first one, then the other, and the rocky, slightly unstable tones of Nina Simone filled the room. Still unspeaking, she leaned over him, her back arched like a cat, her body brushing his ever so slightly to reach the stereo, and then turned the sound off abruptly. 'Mississippi Goddam' cut to silence.

'Fuck you,' she said with a cold, quiet, deliberateness.

'Ameena, I'm so sorry you had to leave like that.'

'Huh?'

'I'm so sorry you had to wait so long, I had to do this damn pitch for Hershel and—'

'David, I just happened to be two blocks from you, I wrapped up an interview early with a buyer, I was right there, I thought I'd surprise you, say hi, it wasn't a big deal. You were busy, that's cool.'

'Okay?' he said, confused.

'I don't give a fuck about waiting.'

'You don't?'

'No!' she said incredulously as if she could hardly believe the exchange that was taking place between them.

'So... so, why are you mad then?' he asked, brows furrowed.

She made an exasperated noise and then – 'David, *you* bought the painting and put it in your *office?*'

It took him a few minutes to grasp what she was saying and then it came to him, exactly what was going to happen. It was going to be all wrong what was going to happen, but it was going to happen anyway.

He braced himself.

'You bought the painting and put it in your office,' she repeated, a confirmation this time.

The painting. Fuck. Fuck. *Fuck*. The painting. Hershel had insisted it be hung 'front and centre', and like a moron, he had agreed, been flattered even, and so it had been hung at reception, on the wall directly in front of where she would have been sitting waiting for him. David swore silently. This whole thing was his fault of course, the flip side to his prized in-the-moment existence, this chronic failure to anticipate how the future might unfold. The painting. Of course, she had seen the painting.

And now, this.

'Okay, hang on,' he ventured valiantly, 'which part of that is bad? That I bought the painting or that I put it in my office?'

Ameena pulled the bandana off her head with a quiet forcefulness, and her hair, her magnificent mane of hair fell around her shoulders, catching the sun in a cascade of angry red tangles, framing her face like an aura, making it glow in that light, a kind of beautiful accident of place and time.

David looked at her, at her impossible, ravishing, rageful beauty, and he felt completely helpless.

'Ameena... I...'

But she tilted her chin, gave him a slow, sardonic smile.

'Just when I thought we were back on track,' she said, shaking her head in disbelief. 'How could you?'

'Ameena, I *was* only trying—'

'Please don't tell me you were trying to help,' she said firmly. 'Please. Please don't do that.'

'But Ameena, I *was* only trying to help.'

'David,' she replied, her eyes steely, 'go to hell.'

The next morning when the alarm rang, shrill and terrible, jolting them both out of sleep, Ameena didn't bring up their fight from the previous evening or the fact that she had told him to go to hell. Nor did she expound upon where she herself had gone after that, for David, half-asleep in their bed, had reached across for her several times in the middle of the night, and had found only her absence. Several hours later, in the brand spanking newness of the morning, he thought, wherever she'd been, it was clearly to someplace nicer than hell, because the blackness was gone from her mood and she seemed relaxed and happy.

'Peggy's seeing someone. I've suspected it for months, but she finally admitted it last night. He's an economist at the Bank of New York. One of those cerebral types. The four of us are having dinner next weekend. That new fish place on Mercer and Prince. Okay with you?'

'Sure,' David said, and the painting never came up again.

3.20

By the end of the following week, it cooled down, the burning heat giving way to a glorious mix of sunshine and breeze, drawing people out of air-conditioned buildings and into the world, like a kind of exodus.

David decided, on Ameena's behalf, to join in.

She was still visibly distraught over the events in Manchester, about which they had not received any news. He had asked her several times if she wanted to go back for a few days – at least, he said, that would make her feel like she was there – but every time he suggested it, she only shook her head.

In many ways, David felt helpless. There was very little he could provide by way of answers or reassurance. Instead, he tried to focus on the ordinary things, be present for her in small ways, keep her busy, distract her. He knew it helped when they were out. Back at the apartment, enclosed within those walls, she fretted even more, staring blankly at the TV, barely eating or sleeping, pacing up and down, checking her phone constantly, reading impassioned articles about the breakdown in Middle East peace talks, first on the BBC, then on Fox News, then asking him how an objective thing such as news could in reality be so subjective, then analysing the names of the reporters, scrutinising their photographs, then tiring of that and checking her phone again, her anxiety only deepening with each passing moment of silence. And so, as soon as David 'revolved' himself out of the glass doors of the Witz Agency and felt the surprising freshness of the air on his face, he called her at work, asked if she wanted to meet, take advantage of the weather, go for a walk, get something to eat, take the scenic route home.

Thankfully, Ameena had agreed. She was getting more and more unpredictable these days, David felt. One minute she'd act completely normal, another minute something would suddenly set her off. He sighed inwardly. All this stuff was tough on her, it *must* be, but damn it, it was tough on him too. But even as the thought left his mind, he rebuked himself. It wasn't a competition. It's never a competition. But still… it wasn't easy. He pushed away the thought and tried to think of happy things: this balmy breeze, Central Park at dusk, a tune he'd been working on, her eyes, the way she walked into a room…

It was still light at half past six when they entered the park, hand in hand, enjoying the cool of the evening wash over them. They walked along the path, past the Dairy, then turned into the Mall, lined with rows of towering American elms, their handsome foliage forming a lush cathedral-like canopy above the pathway.

There was beauty in that half-light.

'Hey,' Ameena said, as they strolled down the walkway past the imposing figures of Shakespeare, then Walter Scott, then Robert Burns, characters who David knew were very much a part of Ameena's childhood and education, all protagonists of a certain British canon that she had longed to feel a part of.

'Hey, so what's the deal with the path?'

'The what?'

'The path. The path that leads from your old house to the beach.'

'Oh that.'

'Yeah. I've wondered about it ever since Abe… ever since that night, he seemed very affected by it. *This* path,' she stopped and twirled around on her toes – rather expertly, David noted, like a spinning ballerina, 'reminded me of that one.'

He nodded. 'Ah, okay.'

'Well?'

He shrugged. 'It's nothing.'

'Oh, come on, tell me.'

'Let's sit down for a bit,' David said, and they found an empty bench by the side of the lake, the bright blue paint peeling off its wooden arms and rails, lending it a sweet, melancholic beauty. On the bench next to them, a little boy was playing with his dog. David and Ameena sat for a while, side by side, watching the duo.

Nothing followed.

Ameena waited, accepting his silence, but linked her arm in his.

David leaned forward on the bench, his eyes trailing the dog.

A game was being played. The boy threw the ball into the lake and the dog scrambled after it, wading expertly into the water. Once retrieved, he carried it in his mouth back to the boy, dropping it triumphantly at his feet, shaking the droplets off himself, spraying water everywhere. The boy laughed, patted the dog, picked up the ball, threw it into the water again. Back and forth this cycle went, neither boy nor beast tiring of repeating their little game endlessly.

'What can I tell you?' David said after a while. 'There's nothing to say. It's just this dumb thing from when Abe and I were kids.' He looked at Ameena and his face, she thought, displayed no emotion at all. 'My mother would wake every morning, early, before any of the rest of us, and she'd take the path down from behind the back garden to the beach and she'd go for a walk by herself, along the water. It was a sandy path, just a small, narrow thing, forsythia bushes on either side – they'd bloom bright yellow in the spring – she would walk down that path every morning and she would leave her footprints in the sand. Then later, Abe and I would wake, and Abe would climb up the bunk bed – I slept on the top one – and we could look clear out our window and we'd spot her walking, the waves touching her toes. She was always happiest there, by the sea. Then we'd go get her. We played this game you know, on that path, the sand was always damp that time of the morning, wet from the spray of the waves, and we'd step in her footprints, so our prints were inside her prints, all along the path, and then we'd run to her and she'd open her arms wide and she'd hold us, both of us at the same time, just the three of us on that long stretch of ragged coastline. And then we'd all come back home together, Abe and I on either side of her, all of us holding hands, and get ready for school. "One day," she would tell us every morning, "one day your footprints will be bigger than mine. One day, I'll be putting my feet into the shape left by yours." We did this every day, virtually every single day that I can remember.'

He paused. 'Even when she was very sick, Abe and I would support her out, down that path, to the beach and she'd just sit there and stare out at the ocean.'

Ameena blinked away the tears that she realised had pooled in her eyes. David looked away.

The last of the light began to fade; shadows came out to play.

The boy threw the ball. Too far out this time. The dog stared at the lake, then at the boy, and again at the lake, wagging his tail, unsure of what he was meant to do. 'Come on Chewbacca,' the boy called, 'let's go home.'

But Chewbacca didn't want to go home. He looked up at his little master longingly, tongue hanging out. More, he was saying, come on, more. 'The ball's gone, buddy,' the boy said, opening out his hands, palms facing upwards, 'it's lost.' Chewbacca howled. 'Don't be sad, Chewy,' the boy said, 'it's only a ball! Come on, let's go!'

The boy walked past them. Chewy reluctantly followed. David petted the dog as it crossed the bench and was rewarded with a very wet lick on his nose. Ameena laughed.

'There you go, he's forgotten all about the ball now,' she said.

David smiled, but his smile was sad. 'Tricky, huh, the concept of loss,' he said, shaking his head. 'Even for a dog.'

After that, there was a silence between them, total and tender. The lovers' covenant, inviolable like an old-fashioned wedding vow. Ameena touched his face, tracing the outline of his jaw with her finger.

It was completely dark now, the sky above them midnight-blue and sprinkled with stars. This is one of the few places in the city where, if you look at the sky, you can still see the stars.

'She died in the summer,' David continued in the same, expressionless voice, 'and the following spring, the forsythia bloomed, it seemed to me at the time, with even greater vigour than usual, as if they were turning their yellow heads towards the ocean and screaming at the waves in a kind of beautiful, indignant horror. But the path, *her* path, looked more beautiful than ever, blanketed in yellow like that.'

'Why didn't you tell me any of this before?' she said gently.

He looked at her then. 'It's silly. Kids' stuff. But that's why that silly little path meant so much to Abe.'

'It's a beautiful story.'

'I know, baby,' he said dully, 'but with a terrible ending.'

3.21

Precisely five days later, her phone rang.

Nearly three weeks now, since it had all started. Ameena's mother called to say that they had found Kareem, that he and Faisal had been found living in a friend's place in Bordesley Green.

Ameena felt, on hearing this news, a surge of relief, more than anything else, but she also felt a vague sliver of fear, and also anger, unbridled anger directed at her brother, for what he had made them all go through. Come to think of it, she felt both in equal proportions, gratitude and outrage, a desire to hug him as well as slap him across his face, all at once.

'Oh Mum, thank goodness!' Ameena exclaimed. 'What in the world was he thinking?'

'No, no, there is no goodness in this Ameena, no goodness at all.' She hesitated. 'Kareem is in jail.'

Ameena felt her body stiffen. The fear. She now understood the fear. It was no longer a sliver.

'In jail? For what?'

'He took someone's car – that Jim Jones. Faisal and him and God-only-knows who else. They took – *stole*' – Zoya whispered the word – 'his car. Then they smashed it. They broke all the windows, they used a rod or something, who knows what they used but whatever they used they used it very well because they destroyed the whole bloody car. Your brother has been arrested. For theft and destruction of property.'

'What? But why? Why would he do that? Who is Jim Jones?'

'Jim, Jim, that *Jim* Jones. You know! Jumbo or Jimbo or

something they call him, with the yellow hair and pimples everywhere. You know, *Jim* Jones! Lives at the end of the road in ugly house, just opposite to the bus stop. *He* threw pig's head into our house. It was him. Butcher told police, then they questioned him, and he made confession. Kareem...' she sighed, 'Kareem must have found out earlier somehow.'

Ameena groaned. 'Oh my God, this is just crazy. I don't even know where to start to make sense of it.'

'But the Jimbo dropped the charges. Some deal he made with police people. Your Abba and I are going now to bring your brother home.'

'Can I speak to Kareem when he's home, please Mum? Can you have him ring me – I need to speak to him.'

Her mother hesitated.

'Ameena, also...'

'There's an also?'

'The boy. The friend's house they were staying in, the Birmingham one, they're saying... they're saying that the boy has got links to some groups.'

'Links? What kind of links? What do you mean, links? What do you mean, groups? What groups? What are you saying?'

'I am not saying. *They* are saying.'

'Mum, this is all too much for me,' Ameena said, feeling a pressure building in her head that emanated from somewhere behind her eyes and made her want to scream. Or sob. Loudly and noisily. She didn't do either. Instead she said, very calmly: 'Please just call me when I can speak to Kareem.' She hung up then, as quickly as she could. After that, she sat on the edge of the bed, arms crossed, clutching her body, and waited. Waited until she stopped shaking, waited for the panic to wear off, waited for the fear to collapse back into the sliver she knew she could handle.

It wasn't until two days later, when she could no longer bear to look David in the eye and keep lying, when she told him that yes, she had heard from home.

'They found him,' she said. 'He was in Birmingham. They put him in jail, he vandalised the neighbour's car for the pig thing, the guy confessed to doing it.'

'Oh Ameena…'

'Yup.'

'How long are they keeping him?'

'No, he's out. The guy's not pressing charges if we don't. My dad said the police don't really seem to care if no one else does.'

'Well, *that's* good.'

She shrugged. 'I guess. I spoke to Kareem. He seemed really shaken up.' She shook her head. 'I guess jail will do that to you, he said he's never been more scared in all his life.'

'This is all so awful, but hopefully it's taught him not to do it again.'

'Taught whom?'

David looked surprised. 'Your brother, of course.'

'Excuse me?'

'It's a tough lesson for a kid, but at least he won't do it again.'

Ameena raised her eyebrows. *His* eyebrows, she noticed, were unraised. His face betrayed no emotion. It was relaxed and handsome. For some reason, the fact of this made her suddenly angry; that he could look handsome even as he was saying what he had just said seemed unnatural, indecent.

She took a breath.

'David, he didn't start this. Of course, it's not the right way to respond, but he was reacting to something horrific that someone did to *us*.'

'It doesn't work that way.'

'What do you mean?'

'Well, these things are hugely complex, Ameena. As you know.'

'As I know? I'm sorry, but I *don't* think I know.'

'Well, if you're going to look at who started what, your neighbour didn't start it either, this whole mess started with 9/11.'

'What does 9/11 have to do with my family?'

'What did those families have to do with your people?'

Ameena gasped – a sharp, strangled gasp. Horror. Hurt. Betrayal. Big things crammed into a little sound.

But David looked even more horrified.

'Sorry, I'm sorry Ameena, I didn't mean that. I didn't mean to say it... like that... I'm so sorry, my sweet.'

He took one step towards her.

But she stepped back from him, and her eyes were down, and her hand was up, palm facing him, fingers together, and like that, she stood before him, her body itself a symbol – a punctuation mark – its meaning so clear and unambiguous that David could not dare exonerate himself by pleading any transatlantic ignorance of language.

3.22

'I'm going to the gallery this evening,' she announced tersely the next day. 'And then I'm going to Manchester. I'm booked out of Kennedy tomorrow.'

He nodded.

'Do you want me to come with you?' he asked after a pause.

'No,' she said.

He nodded. 'They don't know, do they? About me.'

She turned to him in surprise. 'David, are you really making this about you?'

'It's about us, Ameena. It was always about us.'

She laughed scornfully.

'Oh, they know about you, David. I told them a long time ago. I told them even though I knew it would cause them sadness. I wonder if you would have told *your* parents about me if they were alive, if you'd ever have had the courage to tell them that their devoted little Jewish son was dating some Muslim girl.'

'Ameena...'

'No, you don't have to answer that. It doesn't matter. I'm going home.'

'Okay,' he said. 'That's probably a wise decision. You should.'

'I should what?' she said, shocked.

'Go home,' he said quietly.

And just like that, with the unthinking utterance of those two words, David and Ameena came full circle.

3.23

In Lahore, where people still got their clothes made by a tailor, Ameena remembers going to the textile shop with her mother and her aunties.

Ameena had never seen a shop like that before; Manchester didn't have them, these brightly lit, cavernous spaces with floor-to-ceiling vertical shelves, on which they stacked, side by side, thick towering slabs of a dizzying array of fabrics of all colours and textures and weight. There must have been hundreds, *thousands*, of those rolls of fabric inside a single shop.

'Aunty Sadia wants to buy some silk,' Zoya explained to Ameena, 'for Zeenat's engagement, you see.'

The system was simple. You'd point to whatever fabric you wanted to see up close, however many samples you wanted to see, and the man would pull out the rolls and unfurl them on the counter in front of you, reams and reams of silk, one on top of the other, each one a different colour, and as they unravelled and swam on the flat surface, they would catch the light, and shimmer and shine.

Ameena remembered this when she looked out of her window on the day she left for Manchester, at the river shimmering in the early evening light.

It is the last thing she remembers before she picks up her small suitcase and heads downstairs to find a taxi.

She wonders if things will ever be the same again.

Not because of the sorrow she feels when she thinks about her little brother, how in the eyes of the world, he had been marked – they had all been marked. Or how even in her own mind, he could no longer be a boy, how with a single swift action, the threshold into manhood had been crossed.

But it wasn't that. That was distressing, but it wasn't the cause of her anxiety.

Nor also, the painful ache inside her when she wonders how her mother must feel, or worse her father, a man who had lived his own life by his principles, who had tried to instil that same ethic in his children – 'Your birth does not automatically make you a person,' he would tell them repeatedly, 'you need to *teach* yourself how to become one.' Ameena feels it acutely, a helplessness, when she thinks of her parents, the sense of loss they must feel, the disillusionment, the shame. (But in whom? In Kareem? In her? In themselves? In the community? In the country they called home? Or in the one they had left behind? Or in both? In everything.)

But even that, she can cope with.

What she cannot live with, what she finds incomprehensible is something else. On her mind, in her brain, gnawing at her heart is only one person. Not her brother or her mother or her father, but David. Something had changed between them that evening. But it wasn't, as David would always believe, it wasn't because Ameena had taken David's allegiance for granted and had felt betrayed – stranded – when she realised that loving someone does not mean always agreeing with them. That wasn't it.

No, it was because they had said things that had recast the moulds they had created of each other in their own minds. Identities of goodness and virtue and infallibility, like a child creates of an idol, fossilised over years, sacred and specific. God, we are all so naive, she realises with sudden horror, naive over and over again. And even when we know this, even when we *know* that this ancient circular loop of naivety only serves to deepen the illusions and ensnare us into believing only what we want to believe, we still foolishly fall into its trap. This, she thinks, this failure of the human mind to break out of these illusory patterns even when we see them – almost as if we crave the suffering we know it will bring – remains, despite its infinite capacity for freedom, one of its most crippling limitations.

For otherwise, how could he have uttered those words, and how could she have not seen them coming?

Because the thing with words, the really tricky thing, is that once they've been spoken, they can be forgiven, they can be forgotten, dulled with time and tricks and the foibles of memory, but they cannot, not ever, no matter how much you try, become unspoken. In fact, she reasons, it must go even further than that. To utter words that carried such power, that had the ability to cut so deep, one must, *surely*, have been thinking them for a very long time before gathering up the courage to actually speak them. *Saying* those things, in Ameena's mind, wasn't the deathblow; the deathblow was *thinking* those things. Yes, that was it. *That*, to Ameena, was the truly heartbreaking thing; the fact that someone you loved had thought such thoughts about you all along.

It is a sadness she feels she can drown in.

In the fabric store, once you'd made your selection, the man would take a pair of giant scissors, cut off the length you wanted, fold it into a neat square and put it in a bag for you to take home. Your very own piece of shimmer.

When she looked outside the window of their home on the day she was leaving, she wished she could take a piece of the river with her, the river when it looked like this, restful and still and shimmering like silk.

3.24

While Ameena was on her flight to Manchester, David drove up to Rhode Island.

He arrived late in the afternoon, checked into his hotel, and spent the rest of the evening at a piano bar where he had often played in his summers home from college. It was a place of comfort for him and of belonging, where he recognised the smells and the rhythms, and the faces he knew he would find, old faces, familiar faces, friendly faces, the kinds of faces owned by people with whom David understood implicitly that you could pick up where you left off, no matter how long ago you'd gone or why, who welcomed you back without question or judgement, as if you hadn't gone away at all.

Earlier that day, on the way to the bar, David had driven past the large chain drugstore where his house once stood. The road still sloped upward gently and then fell downward steeply, the incline disproportionate, cruelly deceptive, surprising first-time drivers into desperately scrambling for their brakes. Years ago, his mother had joined a neighbourhood campaign to get some sort of road sign put up on the brow of the hill. There was no funding, they'd written back politely. Money was scarce, reserved for more pressing causes. There are always more pressing causes, his father had remarked wryly.

There was a sign now, David noticed, a yellow diamond-shaped lollipop with the image of a car tipped precariously on the base of an inverted triangle.

On a whim, he decided to park up and go inside. The parking lot was in front, where the small, thriving fore garden used to be, where rows of petunias once bloomed among the lilies and bushes of dwarf rhododendron lined the fence flowering a bright shocking pink in the springtime. All that was gone now, the area covered in asphalt, marked with neat white and yellow pavement markings. Behind the drugstore was the road that ran parallel to the beach along the coastline, and cutting across it, leading straight onto the stretch of beach, was the path.

David sat inside the car for a few minutes, his hands on the wheel, thinking about his childhood home, how memories attach to a physical structure, like barnacles to a rock – it was easier, he knew from experience, to break the rock than to pry the barnacle off.

A black Honda Civic hatchback pulled up next to him with an elderly couple inside. David smiled at how the man got out first, then went round to hold the door open for his wife. When he got out of his own car, the old lady looked at him curiously and whispered something to her husband, who seemed to have trouble hearing her. David followed the couple into the store wondering if they might have been friends with his parents. Or maybe they were just sizing him up, wondering what business someone in a rented car with New York plates had in their little town.

Inside, the air conditioner was turned up, uncomfortably high. David wandered through the maze of aisles marvelling at how things had changed in this tiny coastal village, at how much more was available now, things that not so long ago people asked friends to bring home from visits to the city; all that was here now, under this single freezing roof. David didn't need anything from the drugstore, but he was inside now, so he picked up an electric toothbrush and a hairbrush that was 'guaranteed to add shine'. But when he lined up at the checkout, he saw standing at the till, eyes down, scanning items from somebody's shopping basket, a woman who used to be a girl he had dated in high school, not looking much older really, in her bubblegum-blue drugstore uniform with the little white collar and white strips on her short sleeves and a white belt tied neatly round her slim waist.

He looked at her small frame, her narrow shoulders, her long neck, the glint of the small gold cross she still wore round it, the shock of dark curls on her head. She glanced up suddenly at the customer she was serving; she was done scanning, the customer reached into his back pocket for his wallet, said something David couldn't hear; he saw the girl smile, say something back.

She looked tired, David thought, but still beautiful, there had always been a fragility about her, a person always on the verge of breaking. He felt something looking at her, a kind of stirring inside of him. He stepped out of the line and leaving the two items he had picked up on a shelf where they didn't belong, he slipped out of the store.

The following morning, David went for a walk on the beach. He rose early, before the sun, and drove straight down, arriving, as he had hoped, at a time when the sand and the sea and the rocks were his alone, before the rest of the world woke to claim its share.

He had thought about her again, the girl in the drugstore, briefly in his hotel room, just before he had fallen asleep, but then when he woke in the morning, it was gone. I believe in the idea that we all have two stories and that one of them is personal, Ameena once told him, and the personal is what's true, and what's real. More real than anything public. For some reason thinking of the girl made him think of that, though he wasn't sure why.

He walked the long stretch of sandy beach, his feet making soft, impermanent prints on the sand, his presence forcing the resting gulls out of their reverie and into the sun-spangled sky with loud protesting squawks. The beach ended at a cliff and David climbed the rocks, wet with moss and spray, with the easy expertise of a man who has climbed that treacherous terrain more times than he cares to remember. Some while later, at the point where the bay came in, he stopped, and watched the gentle ebb and flow of the water below him, forming a sort of inlet, a rock pool. They used to play here as kids, Abe and him and the other little kids from school, in this exact spot, the shallow pool teeming with creatures that would appear like a miracle, and then vanish with the tide – he and the other children would wade in with their swimming shorts, the water up to their knees, and play at being fishermen, catching crabs and bristle worms and whelks with their little hand nets. David marvelled at the memory, at how vivid it still was.

He found a flattened bit of rock and sat down, his legs dangling off the cliff edge, the rock pool below him. Funny, he thought, how the memories of happiness, forgotten in the blur of life, could sharpen again, so quickly, so crisply, when you returned to the place where those memories were born. Same for sadness, those memories of sadness. That was true too.

Classical Sufi scholars, Ameena had said in that same conversation about the two stories, believe that there are two intersecting notions of transcendence. One is to gaze out at the universe and to consider that whatever you see reflects what you are. The other one is to look inside yourself and recognise that the universe is present in you.

'Hello David,' a soft voice called next to him, startling him. He hadn't heard anyone approach.

'Oh hey,' he said, surprised by her, by how the essential loveliness of her face remained unchanged even after all these years.

'I saw you,' she said, 'at the store yesterday, you didn't see me. I asked around later, after my shift was done, they said you were staying at the hotel. This morning I thought, if you hadn't left town yet, that you might be here.'

'How would you know that?'

'When you know someone, David, you know someone.'

She looked away. The wind had picked up and she pulled her yellow cardigan closer around her thin body. David noted again how tired she looked.

'Can I sit down?' she asked.

'Yes, yes, of course, sorry,' David said, shifting slightly to one side to make room for her.

She sat down next to him on the rock, her hands on either side of her, palms facing down. He noticed how small her hands were, how pale.

'I'm sorry about your mom,' she said after a while.

'Thank you,' David replied.

She chuckled suddenly, and her face lit up, a sudden ping of memory. 'She never liked me, you know, your mom. But whether it was me or my religion she felt such distaste for, I don't know.'

David laughed. 'Don't be silly,' he lied, 'she liked you fine.' It struck him how familiar he felt with her, how *safe*. The sensation of walking back into one's home after a long trip away, of sleeping on one's own bed. He had not expected that feeling so many years later.

'Oh please, I may have been young, but I'm not stupid. You always know when someone doesn't like you! Anyway, it doesn't matter. She was a good person and she had real magic in her fingers – the best piano teacher the school could have had.'

David smiled. 'Do you still sing?'

He remembered even now how sweet her voice used to be, how they would often sing together, David and the girl – how his mother would begrudgingly admit how perfectly suited they sounded, at least vocally, if not in any other way.

She laughed, a sad little laugh. 'Not in years,' she said softly. 'One needs a reason to sing. Anyway, how have you been? Are you still in New York?'

He nodded. 'I've been okay, thanks. Pretty good actually. I work in an ad agency. Branding stuff, you know, consumer goods and things. I get to play music. Jazz. Nothing big, just little gigs, here and there. Not as much as I'd like, but still, it's something. I get to play with some really great guys. I'm working on writing my own stuff. I'm seeing someone... she's incredible.'

'Wow, that's great!' she said. 'I'm really happy for you.'

There was something about the way she said it, the way she nodded and her smile and how her body shifted away ever so slightly, that he knew she meant it, she wasn't just saying it, as people do. 'And you?' he said. 'How have you been?'

She didn't answer straight away, looked out at the waves. The tide was coming in now. In the distance they could see the moored sailboats bob up and down in the wind, their tall masts glinting in the morning light.

'Jazz...' she said softly after a while, 'that passion never died, huh?'

'Nope,' David replied, shaking his head, 'that passion never died.'

She put her small hands together on her lap and looked down at them.

They sat like that for a long time listening to the sound of the sea-foam wearing down the rock edge bit by bit, stripping layer after layer, reducing it over years and years, patiently, persistently, to grains of sand, to insignificance.

'Ya well,' she said finally, 'what can I tell you? You went to college, I went to Boston. I waited some tables, worked some bars, fell into the wrong company. It spiralled down fast, David, much faster than you can imagine. I went to rehab...'

She hesitated. 'Abe came to visit me there.'

'*Abe* did?'

'David, it wasn't like that... well, not exactly...'

David shook his head, his face half scornful, half pitying. 'That little shit. Everything I had, he wanted.'

She touched his hand. 'David no, it's not what you think. He was there, that's all, he was there for me.' She swallowed as though there was something lodged in her throat, something hard and unforgiving. 'Then, I met someone. In rehab. He used to call me his guardian angel, said I saved his soul. Said other things too. Swept me off my feet.'

She clasped her fingers together on her lap, so hard, David noticed, that her nails made little red streaks on the backs of her hands.

'God, I was so stupid. We got out the same time. We made promises. He stayed clean for three months, maybe less. He was stealing money from me and I didn't even know it. Then one day, he took everything I had, wiped me clean and left. I was eight months pregnant.'

'Shit,' David said, 'I don't know what to say... that's just terrible.'

She shrugged slightly, as if to admit that there was nothing really that one could say.

'I have a child who is autistic,' she said, 'he's six. Look.' She fished a battered phone out of the pocket of her dress and held it in front of him. 'That's my Adam,' she said, smiling at the picture of a little boy with a dark storm of unruly curls and deep blue eyes.

'He looks just like you,' David said.

'Everyone says that,' she said proudly.

Then she added softly, 'He doesn't sleep very well, doesn't like the dark. So, I stay up with him most nights. We talk.'

'I'm sorry, Abby.'

'Don't be. I love him so, so much, sometimes I feel I can hardly breathe.'

'No, I mean. I'm sorry about... I'm just sorry. That's all.'

She dismissed that with a quick shake of her dark curls.

'You do what you have to in life, you make provisions.'

The wind was gusty now, the masts of the sailboats dancing gaily in their moored posts. Stomp, jump, boogie-woogie. Far away in the marina, the screen door of the diner slammed shut.

'He plays the piano,' she continued, 'he's got a real gift. Your mother would have been happy to hear him.'

You little girl, David thought, you poor little girl.

'That's great that he does that, that you spotted that gift in him,' he said.

She straightened up suddenly and clapped her hands together, a look of unbidden joy on her face.

'Will you listen to him play?'

'I really need to get back to New York, Abby.'

'David, please?'

3.25

'I just wanted to hurt him because he hurt us.'

She nodded. Perched like that on the edge of his bed, with his thick, glossy black hair falling over his eyes, she noticed how guileless he looked, still a boy.

'I understand that,' she said, 'we all feel like that sometimes. I have a list of people I want to hurt because they hurt me. But you can't go around doing things just because you want to. What happened was bad.'

He looked down. 'I wanted to kill him. I just didn't know how to do it. If I'd have known how to do it, I'd have done it.'

She didn't say anything.

'Does having bad thoughts make you a bad person?' he asked.

'I don't know,' she answered truthfully.

Kareem rubbed his index finger over a pattern on the bedspread as if he was trying to scrub it off.

Then he looked up at his sister. 'Well, I'm glad you're here,' he said.

'Ameena Hamid! How could you not think of telling us you were coming?' her mother asked indignantly when Ameena showed up at the door earlier that day, dragging her suitcase behind her.

'I didn't want you to cook five hundred different things on my account,' Ameena replied laughing, hugging her. 'Hi Mum, it's so, so, *so* good to see you.'

'Your father will be happy you are here,' Zoya said, wiping her eyes.

'Where is David?' her father asked, appearing at the doorway, his eyes searching the area behind Ameena as if David was hiding there, ready to jump out and surprise them all.

Ameena realised with some shock that he looked old, much older than she remembered, much older than she would have imagined he *could* look. How did he get so old so fast? He had lost weight, his hair seemed to have thinned and his shoulders drooped in a way she didn't remember. And his eyes, in his eyes she saw that the light had gone out. Where was the energetic, idealistic man of her childhood? Where was the man driven by some insatiable need to always do good, to keep everyone happy all the time? Where was her father? And who was this, in his place?

Later, she asked her mother if her father was sick.

'Sick? I don't think so, why?'

'He looks so frail.'

'He is broken.'

Ameena's mother said this gently, with certainty, but not anger.

And Ameena looked away because she felt the tears fill her eyes for this person, this imposter, this tired old man, with a son who had in one moment of weakness done exactly what the man had spent his entire life convincing others that people like him didn't do.

'Where's David?' her father had asked again once she'd come inside.

'David?' Ameena repeated, looking baffled.

'Yes, where is he?'

'David isn't here. Why would you think David would be here?'

'Your Ammi and I were looking forward to meeting him,' Ameena's father replied pleasantly.

And again, she saw in his eyes the enormous fatigue of a man who has tried and tried and can try no more.

She looked around the room they were standing in, the odd-shaped room she knew so well and loved so much. It appeared exactly the same to her as it always had, the burgundy sofa in its usual place in front of the telly, the windows intact, but she knows it has undergone a drastic transformation in her absence. Like a person, she thinks, who has a horrific accident and then gets fixed up and looks to the outside world, like the same person. Only he knows, the person himself, and the select few who are privy to his private trauma – the doctor, the family, the lover – how he has changed, how he can never be the same.

'Where's Kareem?' she asked.

Her father looked away. Her mother nodded towards the stairs. 'Must be upstairs. He sits upstairs a lot. Bedroom door closed. Earphones on. Listening to the "Deaf Leopard". First, there were no earphones. Then I told him we will all go deaf like the leopard. So now there are the earphones.'

Ameena had knocked on his door before she opened it.

'Mum, I've *told* you not to *barge* into my room...' he started to say, then looked up. 'Oh, hey!' he said, removing his earphones, trying his best to sound nonchalant. 'It's you!'

Then they held each other, as much for gladness as for comfort and a kind of sanity: 'It's you,' the hug seemed to say, 'despite everything, despite this crazy messed-up world, it's still you – and you, to me, are love.'

They didn't look like brother and sister, even when they were holding each other, their bodies linked together like that. Ameena, with her racially ambiguous looks, had spent most of her life indulging people who found it amusing to guess at her 'true ethnicity'– Lebanese, Mexican, Italian, Indian, Colombian, she'd heard it all; it never bothered her, she had come to accept her abstractness as a mildly amusing reality. Her bother, on the other hand, looked unmistakeably the way he was 'supposed' to look, and with that came other things, things she couldn't fully comprehend about the world and how it reacted to certain people because they looked a certain way. She only knew what she had seen, and she had seen with her brother that ever since he was twelve or thirteen, he was always being stopped by one authority or another for something or the other. She knew this, and she knew subliminally the difference between the two of them – somehow she had managed to cheat the system; he had been caught in it. Neither had planned it that way. How exhausting it must be, she realised now with sudden surprise, having to constantly defend yourself, not because of your actions but because your physical reality dictates how other people respond to you.

'How are you?' she said, pulling away reluctantly, ruffling his hair.

'I'm okay,' he said looking down, 'been better, but could be worse.' Then he looked up at her, met her gaze and held it. Their eyes were exactly the same, the singular feature they shared; their father's eyes. 'I'm sorry,' he said.

And then he had told her about wanting to kill some man whom she didn't even know, and who didn't know her, who lived down the road, and who had, for a reason she couldn't comprehend, put himself through the trouble of going to a butcher's shop and paying someone to sever the head off an animal and then lugging that grotesque cellophane-wrapped thing back out, only to later throw it into someone else's living room.

'I'm sorry,' he said again, his voice catching, 'the disrespect to Abba. I couldn't stand it.'

'I know,' she replied, feeling for the first time, the sense of responsibility, the *weight* of the responsibility one feels for one's family, no matter how fraught or fragile the relationship. Why you want to love someone who loves them and kill someone who hurts them.

'How's your boyfriend?' Kareem asked abruptly. 'Didn't he come?'

'God, why is everyone asking the same question? Isn't it enough that I'm here?'

'Yeah sure,' Kareem said nonchalantly, 'but would have been nice to meet him.'

'Really?'

'Sure.'

'I thought you disapproved.'

'I haven't even met him, why would I disapprove?'

'Because... well, you know.'

'Because he's not Muslim? Oh, come on, sis! Dad's Muslim and look how it turned out for *her*.' He cocked his head toward the door to his room as if to indicate that whoever he was referring to was outside.

'Kareem!'

But he only shrugged. 'Well, it's true. You know it is. She knows what he likes for breakfast, but I reckon it's not exactly Guy Fawkes night in that bedroom. Like, I mean – ever.'

'I can't discuss this.'

But before Ameena left to go back to New York, her mother pulled her aside.

'Tell me something, Ameena, your Jewish David, does he snore?' Zoya asked.

'What? Mum, honestly! What kind of a question is that?'

But Zoya tugged urgently at her arm. 'Ameena, tell me.'

'No, Mum, he doesn't! God, this family hasn't changed a bit...' The next day, her father pulled her aside.

'Regarding your... situation. I told you I would think about it, and I have. The world will go about its business, Ameena. And we must go about ours. If he makes you happy, if you love each other, I have no objections.' Yusuf sighed. 'I could never make your mother feel that way for me. I want it to be different for you.'

And once again, for the second time in four days, she thought of the sheer force of that responsibility for those people who share your blood. Why you want to love someone who loves them and kill someone who doesn't.

3.26

He can see she is online. 'Online' it says so clearly, and he's waiting for her to write, but she's not. Writing to him at least. And then the thought that she is writing to someone else drives him crazy. It's only been three days.

D: are you online?

D: hey?

D: i can see you're online…

D: ameena?

A: David

D: hey sweet! ♡

A: Hi

D: how's everyone there?

A: Crazy

A: As ever. I now know why I left

D: but, they're ok?

A: Thx. They're ok. Slowly getting back to normal…

A: Whatever normal is any more. Mum asked me if you snore

D: huh?

A: Exactly

D: i'm not

A: You're not what? Normal?

D: ok. i'm not ok

D: without you

A: It's late. Knackered

D: come back

A: Jetlagged

A: But!!!

D: knackered? what means?

A: Tired means

D: come back home

D: please

D: but?

A: Yes!!! But!!!

D: but, what?

A: 'Go home'

A: you said

A: 'Come back home'

A: you said

A: You also confused by that...

A: Or just me?

D: ameena

A: David

D: i'm sorry

A: I'm sorry too

A: But where are we going...

A: ...two sorrys later?

D: going crazy

A: Please don't

D: messing up

A: Don't. Please. Please don't mess up

D: can't do anything

A: I'm going to sleep now

D: without you

A: I'm sure that's not true

D: can't think

A: Stoppit

D: can't play

A: Don't you dare. Don't you DARE go there. Goodbye

D: wait. don't go. we miss you

A: Goodnight. It's 1 in the morning!

A: Who's we?

D: new york misses you. jazz too. me three

A: Nite, Piano-man

D: ameena?

D: baby, don't go…

She's offline now.

Online again.

A: FYI

A: Home day after tomorrow

D: really? hurrah!

D: which flight?

D: can't stop smiling

Offline.

D: are you listening?

D: painting?

D: dreaming?

D: i'm still smiling…

D: i'm singing a tune

D: 'isn't she lovely'

D: might go try and play it

D: on the mason & hamlin

D: 1932

D: hey?

D: goodnight sweet ♡

D: ♡ ♡ ♡ ♡ ♡ ♡

3.27

As far as love went – Ameena mused in the fourth hour of her seven-hour LHR–JFK flight, after they had been offered drinks (which everyone wanted), food (which some people wanted), duty free (which no one wanted) – her father had a funny way of showing it. Especially when it came to her brother. This had been true from the very beginning, she realised, ever since she and Kareem were children.

The saddest thing, Ameena thought, was not that their father didn't love Kareem. Because everyone who knew Yusuf knew he did. The saddest thing was Kareem's inability to reach it. At the heart of this curious tragedy, she decided, lay the fact that Yusuf's love, the kind he reserved especially for his son, had always had an aspirational quality to it. It was love not in the present tense, nor in the simple future tense, but in a kind of future conditional, a perpetual state of becoming: if you do 'x', you *just might* receive 'y'.

It almost didn't matter what the 'x' was, whether it was Kareem's performance in class, on the cricket pitch, his manner of practising their faith or the style in which he cut (or didn't cut) his hair; there was endlessly, it seemed, a kind of deficit in their father's mind where Kareem was concerned, a space between what his son had done, and then – miles above it – what he believed his son was capable of doing.

And even *that*, even that belief remained a kind of endless shifting of the goalposts, illusory, unreachable.

Years ago, Ameena remembered as she stretched uncomfortably in her tiny airline seat, leaning towards the window, as far away as possible from the man next to her (Irish, over-friendly, drunk), she and Kareem – they must have been twelve and nine – had gone with their father to some kind of county fair; they had spent the entire day with him, the only one in her life when the three of them were together, she doesn't remember any others like it. And on this day, Kareem had tried his hand at all the games – duck hooking and tin throwing and rope climbing and darts – and, somehow, it had been his lucky day; almost everything he had played at, he had won. *She* hadn't even wanted to attempt any, for Ameena had from a very early age found the prospect of losing almost unbearable, but she had cheered her brother on enthusiastically and been so excited, both excited *and* proud, when he had won. And yet she noticed, even at that age, that their father had remained impassive through it all, not hesitating to pay for the games, no, not even a bit, but equally, expressing no trace of emotion when his son had ended up with his arms full of cheap stuffed-toy prizes. She had noticed this, and she had also noticed Kareem's eyes, the hurt he carried in his eyes that evening.

And then, she noticed after that, it wasn't only on that evening, but constantly, that he carried that same hurt in his eyes, only she hadn't noticed before, like we don't often notice the things that don't affect us directly, not from a lack of caring, but from not needing in one's own self-contained, limited worldview to notice such things.

But on that day – the only day in her life that she had spent together with her father and her brother – she had noticed it, and it had caused, inside her, a hurt, a physical hurt like she was being squeezed round her chest by an invisible band. She understood then, that her physical hurt was linked in some way to her brother's emotional hurt and that the hurt, their two-together hurt, was the realisation that to Kareem, his father's love was unreachable.

That same day at the fair, just before they were leaving for home she had asked for some popcorn, and their father had bought some for her at once, a tubful big enough to bury her small face in. But

when Kareem had asked for candy floss, he had been refused it –
too much sugar was bad for the brain, Yusuf had declared. And
like this, they had continued for most of their lives: Ameena had
received popcorn, Kareem had been denied candy floss. Instead,
he had received other things she hadn't, in the day-to-day thrum
of life – a harsher tone, a tighter voice, a shorter fuse, all things
presumably, that were good for the brain.

And yet, and *yet*, despite this, despite years of Yusuf–Kareem
conflict surrounding:

- rogue cricket balls on the stairs
- angry red circles in notebooks, rugby shoes in the kitchen,
  dirty clothes in the bathroom sink, bits of food in the
  crevices of sofas
- stern meetings with teachers about bringing 'outside
  literature' to class
- stern meetings with different teachers about the use of
  'unrepeatable language' in the playground
- the routine, un-permissioned disappearance of Yusuf's car
- unironed shirts, unclipped nails, dirty ears
- reading the bloody dead Shakespeare already
- (Yusuf's mortal fear-list) the religious zeal, the identity
  politics, the jihadi leanings, the poor choice of friends, the
  stubborn, monomaniacal interpretation of ideology
- (Yusuf's begrudging acceptance-list) the gold watches, the
  logoed clothes, the distasteful slang, the hair-raising, soul-
  destroying, deafening music from that spotted cat group…

Yes. And yet.

Despite all of Kareem's perceived shortcomings that had caused
Yusuf so much private angst, if a certain choice was ever demanded
of him (although he would die before he admitted it publicly),
Ameena knew, the way a child knows these things about a parent,
that *their father loved him more.*

When Ameena was in Manchester, her mother told her about the day they had gone to bring Kareem home from 'that place' – she refused to use the word – about how she had jumped out of the car and hugged him right there on the street, from relief more than anything else, but that Yusuf had not expressed any emotion nor uttered any words on the entire journey home. And then once they were home, with the front door shut, he had struck his son, for the first time in his life, violently across his face.

'I do not want to hear anything ever again,' he had said, 'that makes me ashamed to call you my son.'

And Kareem had not said a word, only stood there bent over from the waist by the force of the blow, the palm of his hand on his cheek where he had been struck, the tears streaming down his face.

'You will do nothing like this again, is that clear? Not in my name and not in His name,' their father had said, pointing to the sky, and then walked away.

'I have never seen Yusuf like that,' her mother confided in her. 'That kind of anger in a man.'

But then, she continued, late at night, after Kareem had fallen asleep, Yusuf had gone to his son's room and sat down on the bed beside him and looked at him the way he did when Kareem was a little boy, with awe and with wonder, looked at him for a long time, and run his fingers through his hair and kissed his face where he had slapped him, and when she walked past the room, Ameena's mother reported, he was crying, crying openly without embarrassment or shame, and begging his sleeping son for forgiveness. 'I'm sorry, I'm sorry, I'm sorry,' he was saying, over and over and over again.

3.28

There he is at the arrivals gate, standing there, standing out, like he always did to her, even among the crush of people, in his jeans and his checked shirt and his jumper and that hair and that grin and those dimples and a great big sign that reads 'WELCOME HOME' in his terrible handwriting, and she feels herself feeling it, spontaneously, powerfully.

Deep inside her chest.

A figure eight.

Flitter Flutter.

Flip Flop.

The flight pattern of a butterfly.

Erratic. Evolutionary.

She doesn't know what it is, whether it is the handwriting or the hair or the grin or the dimples or all of it, all that makes him what he is, but Ameena realises, in that particular moment of seeing him, something about herself – a truth – and it is that she loves him. She loves him so much that she finds the idea of life without him unimaginable, and perhaps this is one of the side effects of love, up there with dizziness, insomnia and irregular heartbeats, never mentioned – but should be – with cautionary signs on the tin, this particular kind of lack of imagination.

Nevertheless, she feels it and then she finds herself running to him, abandoning her suitcase in the middle of the busy arrivals hall, not caring about, not even *noticing*, the annoyance of the other passengers who have to stop mid-stride and negotiate their own luggage around hers, but running, actually running, a rhythm in the soles of her feet, a rhythm she cannot control. And him, marvelling at how magnificent she is in the cream-coloured overcoat that dramatises the colour of her eyes, catching his breath for a second, then catching her, drawing her into his arms, delaying it by four full beats for no good reason, but then lifting her off the ground, her arms round his neck, her legs wrapped round his waist, in front of those same strangers, melting their annoyance, making them smile. Americans are soft like that.

'Hi,' she says, 'I'm so happy to see you.'

And he knows that she means it, that she doesn't do anything without a reason, or say anything she doesn't mean, that she has always been her own thing, so strong in her flavour and her power and her energy. And he is glad that he came, that he surprised her in this way.

'God, I missed you,' he says, looking at her, wanting to preserve this image of her face forever.

And she?

She pulls her face back and contemplates his, and imagines then, in that New York minute, that if her face is the moon, then his is the sun, whose light lights hers.

3.29

Ameena saw her school friend Denise briefly when she was in Manchester.

They'd kept in touch over this time that Ameena had been away, but when Denise answered the door, Ameena wasn't expecting to see the unmistakeable round swell of her stomach.

'You're pregnant?' she asked incredulously.

'Yeah,' Denise said, laughing happily, holding the round thing from the bottom with both her hands as if, if she were to let go, it might have bounced right off her skinny frame.

She was wearing a long, loose-fitting dress in a bright yellow print. She looked like a queen, Ameena thought, with her full lips and her almond eyes and her hair tied up at the very top of her head in a small bun.

'You didn't tell me?'

'I wanted to surprise you, love,' Denise replied affably, 'I would have, obviously, if you weren't coming. It's only just gone four months. No one knows except, you know, family...'

'Who?' Ameena asked.

'Pete,' she whispered the name although it was just the two of them.

'Pete?' Ameena Gasped. '*Peter Martin?*' Because she knew that Peter Martin and Sarah Adams – with the blue-blue eyes and the blond-blond hair – belonged to similar families, the kind of family that had art on their walls and kept fruit bowls on their kitchen counters and holidayed together somewhere in France.

Denise's family did not holiday in France. Denise still lived with her parents in the council block they had always lived in, facing the main power station, a ten-minute walk from the school where Ameena and she had first met. Ameena looked around the flat she had spent so much of her own childhood in, a small, boxy space divided into rooms by way of flimsy makeshift walls. On the windowsill over the sink, there was a new addition – some kind of green plant, sturdy enough to survive in low light. But besides the plant, they were alone.

Denise giggled and nodded happily. She was, Ameena noticed, wearing pearl drops in her ears. Her skin, which had always been smooth and fresh and enviably blemish-free, bloomed even more than Ameena could recall. Her way of speaking too had changed – no dropped 'g's', no slurred syllables, no trace of the familiar Indo-Carribean rhythm in her speech. In fact, she sounded remarkably like the white, middle-aged English teacher who had once taught them the 'proper' way to speak.

Ameena marvelled at this side of her friend. Denise never wore jewellery. Denise never giggled. Denise never paid attention to enunciation.

Denise was terrible and beautiful and wild.

Denise was going to be a mother?

They had met, Denise and her, on the first day of school, walking through the tarmacked path of the schoolyard, each holding their respective mother's hand, and they had stared at each other, in the way that children do when, for whatever reason, they find themselves attracted to some latent quality in another child. And then, after the mothers had left – Ameena's reluctantly, Denise's gratefully – one of them had spoken to the other, neither remembers who had taken that first brave step, but that had then opened up the way to a firm and loyal friendship for the next thirteen years.

Although they had never discussed such things explicitly, Ameena knew that she had been protected many times over those thirteen years because of that first tentative hello on the school playground, for Denise from the very beginning had been a force to reckon with. She was feral, quick to hit back, unafraid to use filthy language that would stun her would-be foes into a kind of shocked silence. The girls didn't come near her, the boys didn't dare take her on, even the teachers were afraid of this dazzling, sharp-tongued thing, who wore her working-class roots on her bi-racial face like it was some rare and precious gift.

That was the thing, Denise had never needed jewellery.

'I'm really sorry about what happened to your brother,' Denise was saying. 'We heard...'

'Thanks,' Ameena sighed, 'but I'd rather talk about you.'

Denise nodded. 'Sit, sit,' she said, 'can I get you some juice? Ribena? Oh, it's pouring outside, I didn't even realise. Tea?'

Then she said dreamily, before Ameena could answer, 'We're going to get married, after the baby comes, you know, when I can fit into a proper dress again. And after that I'm going to keep modelling. Pete likes me modelling,' she explained shyly. 'He says we will get a nanny for the baby, like someone with proper qualifications, from one of those nanny agencies. He had one himself. A Nigerian nanny. Retired now, but they're still close.'

'And your folks?' Ameena asked, more interested in grappling with the present than in Denise's bold vision of a future that was yet to materialise.

'My folks,' she replied, 'are terrified.'

'And his?'

'Oh yes,' she said, 'they're terrified too.'

'And you?' Ameena asked gently.

'You know me, girl!' Denise said, chin up bravely. 'I'm not afraid of anything.'

Ameena nodded, not in understanding exactly, but in a kind of acceptance, as if she had just become aware of a big and significant ignorance inside her, for otherwise, how could she not have suspected earlier that this was exactly how Denise would have ended up.

3.30

The morning Ameena is due to return to New York, David thinks of a question she has asked of him before.

'What matters?' she had asked. An impossible question. But now, he takes a crack at it.

What matters? The (evolving) list of David Greenberg. In no particular order:

Jazz

Honesty

Miles Davis

America

The band

Democracy

The smell of her

The taste of her

Listening

Her paintings

Her painting-face

The piano

History

Johann Sebastian Bach

The Holocaust

Forgiveness

Freedom

Art

Expression

Art as an expression of freedom

Ruthie Greenberg (the memory of)
Slavery
The Path
Zen
Her hair
Literature
Inclusivity
Her pleasure-face
Studying her pleasure-face
Balance
Spirituality
One-ness
The Art of Fugue
The Art of Improvisation
The Art of Lovemaking
The Art of Ameena

3.31

'Take me home,' she says as they leave the airport building and then she wants to cry, and she doesn't. But David does, she sees the mist in his green-brown eyes and she pretends not to notice, and she says nothing.

They hold hands in the backseat of a yellow cab, the windows open, their faces exposed to the brittle October breeze, not speaking.

Not needing to speak.

Not needing the need to speak.

They are familiar with this feeling, attuned to these private silences that only they share.

She can hear her suitcase sliding around in the boot.

The taxi driver swerves to change lanes, too quick, no blinker, no brakes, swears loudly, she falls sideways into David but when she tries to straighten up, he grips her arm, holds her back. Stay like that, his body tells hers.

And then a while later, when they come off a curve on the road, they spot it at the same time, that first glimpse of the skyline, as they rattle and jolt in the beat-up yellow cab.

He squeezes her hand. She shakes her head in wonderment.

Manhattan gleams in brazen glory like some great and magical city, its buildings washed in the glow of the afternoon sun, thousands of twinkling mirrors floating in the sky, and just in beholding it, their touching bodies tingle.

'New York,' she says simply, and the name is full of meaning.

The car next to them beeps loudly. A spate of angry beeps follow.

The sun is so bright that the driver has to put his visor down and he grumbles in a language that only she understands. But he keeps driving, dangerously fast, and as they come closer and closer, the buildings appear taller and grander. She notices how when the sun hits them at a certain angle, their edifices glitter and wink; shards of glass planted at different depths, like wildflowers in a field.

Then the cab makes a turn and the skyline is temporarily lost.

3.32

In Manchester, it is night-time.

Kareem steps out of his room furtively, then looks around, his eyes adjusting slowly to the darkness. Even through the closed door of his parents' bedroom, he can hear his father's loud rhythmic snoring.

He pauses, then, satisfied that he will not be intercepted, he tiptoes softly down the stairs.

He is barefoot. In his arms, he carries an object, smooth flat metal.

When he gets to the bottom of the stairs, he lays the object down carefully on the pale Oriental runner that adorns the entrance of the house – a gift from his grandmother, all the way from a factory in Lahore where he knows tiny, dexterous fingers have woven those colourful silk threads together.

He uses both hands to unlatch the front door, but still it creaks, too loudly for his comfort, and he freezes, the door half open.

Any minute now, he imagines the lights coming on upstairs, voices heavy with sleep, switching quickly to panic when the eyes that belong to those voices see him, catch him red-handed like that. He would not be able to explain himself.

But there is no sound from anywhere.

With the door half ajar, he creeps back into the house for the object and then, carrying it in his arms, he steps out into the night, pulling the door shut behind him silently, awkwardly, using his elbows.

It is a still, dark night. No moon, no stars. Far away he can hear the yippy bark of a fox.

Kareem lets himself into the garage; it is soundproofed – the previous tenant was a drummer who used the space as a studio, and Kareem knows no noise will travel from here into the house; he and his mates have put this to the test many times.

But his heart is beating too fast, and in his hurry he slams the garage door right onto his hand. He jerks back but it is only reflex, triggered instinctively, and he is surprised that he feels nothing, only a dull numbness somewhere in the tips of his fingers.

Once he is safely inside, his pupils trace the outline of the red Citroen AX that his father insists on parking inside the garage after what his son has done to someone else's car. Kareem unlocks it and watches as it comes to life, headlights almost blinding him temporarily, the omniscient eyes of some divine being.

He blinks once, then he bends down and places the object on the concrete floor of the garage, directly behind the front right wheel of the car. He does this carefully, methodically, then he stands up and surveys his handiwork – placement, he knows, will be key. Satisfied, he gets into the driver's seat and starts the ignition, cringing at its loudness. He reverses backwards, slowly and deliberately, just enough for the front wheel to drive over the object, just enough for him to hear the unmistakeable crunch of metal underneath him. He stops the car and glances in his rear-view mirror – he is inches away from the back wall of the garage. Then he drives forwards, the same tiny motion, feeling the wheel go over the object and then off it, listening again for that muffled grinding sound.

Backwards and forwards, forwards and backwards he goes. He does this fifteen times to a count. Then he turns off the engine and gets out.

He bends down to look under the car and is pleased with what he finds. Slowly and systematically, he gathers up the mangled remains of his laptop and puts them into an empty rubbish bag he has left there earlier in the day. Then he leaves the garage, and after looking around to make sure there is no one in sight, he shoves the bag at the bottom of the already full rubbish bin that he knows is emptied every Tuesday morning at eight.

He has already acquired a shiny new laptop that is, at this moment, hidden away under his bed, bought from the money he has made by waiting tables at Salim's curry house in Rusholme every evening after lectures. A new laptop identical to his old one, but with an unused, unsullied hard drive, its memory wiped clean before it had even arrived at the store he has bought it from. This new machine has no trace of what his fingers have typed or where is his mind has strayed or what history he has cached. So now, there is no way for anyone to ever know what he has thought or how often, how many times he has looked up 'ways to make a home-made bomb' or 'ways to blow up a car' or 'ways to kill a man'.

Does thinking bad thoughts make you a bad person? he had asked his sister.

I don't know, she had replied.

But he knew. He knew. He knew. He knew.

He knew, and the computer had known.

But now the computer is lying dead and disembodied at the bottom of the rubbish bin, millions of mutilated pieces of plastic and metal and secrets that can never be pieced together again. Kareem allows himself a small satisfied smile at the thought of that.

Back in his bathroom, when he turns on the light he notices the exposed flesh on his index finger where the nail has come clean off.

He turns on the tap.

And he waits for the pain to come.

3.33

In Tel Aviv, Abe is smoking a joint.

Next to him, lying asleep on the bed, is a beautiful girl.

Both the bedroom that he is in, and the bed that he is currently sitting on the edge of, as he smokes the joint, belong to the sleeping girl.

In front of him, facing where he is sitting, are glass doors that lead out onto a pretty terracotta terrace adorned with hanging pots of pink geranium.

In front of the terrace lies the shimmering sweep of the Mediterranean Sea, flat, glistening like a gold coin.

He thinks about the girl. He thinks about her tenderly. He has only known her a few weeks...

He meets her one dusty afternoon haggling for watermelons at the Shuk Ha'Carmel and is struck by how relentless she is in her negotiations. The vendor pleads penury, eight children and a cruel, penny-pinching wife, but no, the girl will not budge on her price and eventually the vendor throws up his arms dramatically and gives in, still grumbling about the heartlessness of all womenkind.

His father's early dedication to schooling him in Ivrit means that Abe can speak the language falteringly, but the girl speaks with the rapidity and fluency of a native speaker and much of what she says is lost on him; he only knows that she is in possession of three watermelons that she has obtained at a price of her asking, and he is impressed by her resolve.

There is something else about her that holds him there, as he stands hidden in the shadows, face half-obscured by the bunches of hanging apples and grapes. Maybe it is the way her hair falls over her shoulders and down her back, in iridescent rivulets. Maybe it is the expert way she holds those watermelons, the way she balances them in her arms, against her chest, close to her body like she is protecting them, now that they are hers.

She turns to him then, aware, if not of him specifically, then only of his large presence, but whatever it is, him or his shadow, it irks her, and she says in Hebrew, her dark eyes flashing, 'Do you think this is some kind of show? What are you staring at?'

Or at least that is what he hopes she says.

And he replies, but in English, because he cannot trust his Hebrew, not at this moment, for the stakes are too high and he feels unarmed, vulnerable: 'At you. You are beautiful.'

She cocks her head back then, dismissively, and says, 'American', in a tone of such contempt that Abe feels not indignation, but a kind of obligation towards his entire country and all its inhabitant countrymen. He has no choice now, he thinks, but to partake of some worthy cause on their collective behalf, so that he, single-handedly, can rid them of her contempt forevermore.

And so, he comes out of the shadows and offers heroically, 'Shall I hold your melons?'

It is unsurprising then when she looks at him with even greater contempt and, meeting his gaze directly, forces a smile and says, 'No.'

But he follows her anyway, subtly he had thought, but midway she turns round and says, 'If you're going to follow me, you may as well help me with these. You look as strong as a donkey anyway. Here.' And he stands by stupidly speechless, as she places the watermelons in his outstretched arms.

He walks ten steps behind her for the rest of the way, both out of respect and because he physically cannot keep up with her with the weight in his arms, although he realises with a tinge of admiration that she seemed to have managed all that way with no problem at all.

Walking like that, with her leading the way, never looking over her shoulder once, they enter the peaceful haven of Neve Tzedek and approach an apartment block with a handsome white façade, in front of which she stops, then finally turns around and invites him up for a glass of pomegranate juice in exchange for his load.

He accepts gratefully.

The following week, she travels with him to Jerusalem.

They travel like that, for ten days, like pilgrims, although she has lived in Israel her whole life.

Her family was killed, she tells him, eight years ago by a stray bomb that blew up the car they were sitting in, ready to attend a wedding. They had been waiting for her, she explains, in the car, her parents and her younger twin brothers, she was still in the house because she couldn't find the shoes she was meant to wear with her dress, and by the time she found the shoes and came out, the car was no longer a car and the people in it were no longer people.

'Saved by fashion,' she quips, and she speaks dispassionately as if she feels nothing, no sorrow, no pain.

'Do you hate them?' he asks, horrified.

'No,' she says after a while. 'Because I don't know who "them" is. Anyway, if I hate them, it means they still control me. I don't want them to control me.' She looks at him, her face changes. 'This is a different war, *Chamor*. In this war, there is no good and no bad, there is only perspective.'

She calls him *Chamor*, the Hebrew word for donkey. 'My name is Abraham,' he protests, but she will not stop. He calls her *Yaffa*, the word for beautiful. He doesn't know her real name, she won't tell him.

'According to Kabbalah,' she tells him one night, after he has been inside her, 'within the soul of every individual is a hidden part of God that is waiting to be revealed, and the whole revelation of light or fulfilment, happiness, joy, peace... is of our doing. Our actions can reveal or conceal that light. That light sits in our potential.'

He kisses her face then, and her neck, and he feels her body rise. He shudders.

He has fallen for her.

Walking back from the Western Wall one morning, he feels a great sense of unease caused by their momentary gender-based separation.

That evening, they light candles and drink wine and he tells her what he's told no one before her. He tells her about the streets. The streets of Sydney and the streets of Bangkok and the streets of Mumbai, these streets that come to life when darkness falls.

He shows her the knife wound, soft and rubbery, raised slightly over the muscles of his hard, flat stomach. Curved like a sceptre. She feels it, first with her fingers, then with her tongue.

'I lost control,' he says. 'After my mother died, I lost control of my life.'

'Then claim it back,' she replies.

He laughs. 'It's not so easy. Everything is not so easy as you make it out to be.'

'Yes,' she says simply, 'it is.'

He cups her small face in his large hands, holds it like that for a long time.

'What's your name?' he begs. 'Please tell me.'

'Sarai,' she says. Wife of Abraham.

Two hours after Kareem falls asleep in his bed in Manchester, having disposed of the last remaining vestige of his conscience, Abe wakes up in the bedroom in Israel next to this reminder of his own.

He looks at the sleeping girl next to him, her long, lush hair splayed across the pillow, jet black and glossy, the scattered plumage of a raven. Her face, her distinct cheekbones, the small barely discernible hump at the bridge of her nose that she's ruefully told him she hates, her pink lips. Her skin, young and taut and olive-coloured. The umber, oval mole that sits on the soft ripe swell of her left breast, that rises and falls every time she breathes as if it has a life of its own, as if it too is breathing.

He looks at her a long time. Then he kisses her mouth gently, only a caress, and she stirs.

Outside, the sky is cloudless and very blue. The sun has risen already and makes shadows of dark orange on the tiles. Sometimes they go out onto the terrace, the girl and him, as soon as they wake, and the tiles feel deliriously warm under their bare feet.

The definition of a false life, she once told him, is when your source of happiness is external. The day will come, *Chamor*, when you will find that the source of real fulfilment and happiness is internal.

When she opens her eyes, he says, 'I'm sorry. But I know you will understand.'

He has been thinking of these words all night, the right words, the right way to say them, but despite the preparation, he hadn't counted on how difficult the real thing would be and his voice is heavy with sadness.

She shakes her head. She doesn't know what he means. He can see it, the confusion in her dark eyes, and for a moment, it is only a moment, he wavers.

But then he says, 'I've got to go.'

And she knows then from his face that he means forever.

Still she asks, 'Go where?'

'Someone is waiting for me,' he says.

And she feels her head spin, like she is dizzy, like the air supply to her brain has been cut off.

'Who is waiting for you?' she asks.

'There's a little boy,' he tells her, 'in a little town by the sea.'

3.34

In New York, it has just gone midnight.

David and Ameena are home, sitting on the loveseat by the window. She sits leaning into him, in the way they like to sit together on that loveseat, her head on his chest, her legs stretched out, sandwiched between his. Billie Holiday croons on the radio. Delicate, soulful. Timeless. Outside, the Hudson shimmies in disco lights. A lone boat cruises by, casting a trail of golden light in its wake.

'I'll be seeing you...'

'David,' she says suddenly, tilting her face up towards him, 'your jumper has a snag.'

He is wearing a thin wool sweater that she had bought for him, a rich, beautiful royal blue; they had shopped for it together, he had tried it on and she'd insisted on buying it for him – I want to, she'd said, the colour suits you so much.

It seems such a long time ago.

David looks down and sure enough there is the offending rip, he can see it, just below where it sits on his chest, front and centre, not somewhere discreet like the edge of a sleeve, and yet it had slipped by unnoticed until she pointed it out.

Ameena stares at it, at the spot where his body must have brushed against something and the jumper must have pulled, breaking the delicate fibres holding it together, causing the knit to come undone. It is only little right now, barely noticeable unless you know it is there. But she knows it is there, that is the problem, and now he does too, and it seems to stare back at her defiantly, the snag, those tiny stray strands of wool hanging limp and loose in a small, unnatural loop. Like a noose, she thinks. A miniature noose splayed and splintered and frayed along the edges, the fibres dangling like so many unresolved stories.

Stories of people and nations and lovers and land. Of Zoya. Of Yusuf. Of Ben and Ruth. Of Kareem. Of Abe. Of Sarai. Of Abby. Of Hershel. Of Peggy and Whitney and Denise Richards. Of Israel and Palestine. Of Jew. Of Muslim. Of David and Ameena.

Still, it is harmless, for the moment. Not nearly big enough for a human head. Nor a human finger, for that matter. But in time, she knows, it would become obvious, catching the eye of strangers on the street. The loop would pull further, grow bigger. More threads would come undone, get entangled, things would start to unravel, a hole would form.

And Ameena, realising this, feels what? What does she feel? Guilt? But you don't feel guilt over a snag in a jumper that you didn't cause. She wants to say something then, but she doesn't. She doesn't tell him – *cannot* tell him – that the dancer had called some time ago, that she had taken his call, that she had seen him in his hotel room the night she was meant to be at the gallery, that she had done that out of loneliness or despair or spite or else out of something entirely different, she doesn't really know herself.

And he cannot tell her, not about Narragansett, not about that afternoon in the little white cottage by the bay, not about Abigail Williams, not about how he had touched her, how gently, how carefully, because he didn't dare be the one who finally broke her, no, the responsibility would be too much, not about how he had loved her that afternoon in her tiny bedroom, with the windows flung open and the wind off the bay and the taste of the sea on her skin and the sounds of the piano from the other side of the thin wall played with a terrific frenzy by an autistic child.

'I didn't even notice it,' he says.

'Shall I fix it?' she asks.

Acknowledgements

Thanks to...

My family-my loves, for reminding me what's important in life.

The incredible team at Fairlight for putting their faith into my writing, especially to Urška Vidoni for crafting this into an infinitely better book.

My first readers, Elizabeth Dawson and Scott Livingstone, for making me feel that I wrote this thing for you. Geoffrey Horton for being my Nabokovian re-reader. Anyone who is familiar with Nabokov's practice will understand the extent of my gratitude. My friends, for imparting the kind of cultural wisdom that is not available in a classroom: Sadia Hamid. Sabahat Gurdezi. Sadaf Khan. Brett and Yael Rhode. Ruth Arron.

Jim Lawless for your loyalty, your friendship and your Beethoven (but Bach is still the greatest!).

John Thangaraj for everything advertising. Holly Drewett and Megan O'Rourke for so much of the art. My son's music teacher, Rob Parton, for all the unofficial lessons in music theory.

Special thanks to David Bolchover, whose profound understanding of Jewishness is truly astounding and for your capacity to share a small slice of that with me.

Jazz pianist extraordinaire, Aaron Goldberg, for your deep passion for and knowledge of your art and for so generously indulging my curiosity of it. But most of all for your musicianship which is sensational and pushed me over the edge.

Buried somewhere in this novel are a string of words that go like this: '...if her face is the moon, then his is the sun, whose light, lights hers...' My dearest Sid, thank you for everything, for without you, there'd be no light.

About the Author

Ami is a British-American writer who was born in Calcutta, India and has lived and worked in New York City, London, Paris, San Francisco and Los Angeles. Ami has a BA in English Literature and Economics from Ohio Wesleyan University and an MBA from Harvard Business School. When she is not reading, writing, cooking, eating, sailing or dancing she can be found listening to jazz, her 'one great unrequited love'.

Ami has mentored girls of colour for the past twelve years, especially those from problematic family backgrounds. Her mentoring efforts include a keen emphasis on the merits of reading and education.

Ami co-wrote a memoir, *Centaur*, which was published in 2017. The book won the General Outstanding Sports Book of the Year Award 2018 and it was shortlisted for the William Hill Sports Book of the Year 2017.

Fairlight Books

JAC SHREEVES-LEE

Broadwater

*This farm, these people, these blocks, these
roads are my home.*

Welcome to Broadwater Farm, one of the most well-known
housing estates in Britain. A place where post-war dreams
of concrete utopia ended in riots, violence and sub-standard
housing.

In this collection, Tottenham-born Jac Shreeves-Lee gives voice
to the people of Broadwater Farm. With evocative language
and raw storytelling, she compassionately portrays their
shared sense of community. A community with a rich cultural
heritage, comprising over forty nationalities, generations old.

> '*This new collection of site-specific stories by
> Jac Shreeves-Lee redresses the balance by virtue of
> the warmth of her narrative voice and the spirit,
> pluck and humanity of her characters.*'
> —Onjali Q. Raúf, activist and
> author of *The Boy at the Back of the Class*

HELEN STANCEY

Relative Secrets

Mary has a secret that she mustn't tell. But in a care home, with her mind wandering, she's starting to slip up. Clearing out her grandmother's old room, Lucy finds something hidden that wasn't supposed to be found – a locket sheltering a shameful family secret.

She can't tell her mother. Not with their father gone, one brother absent and another acting up. Her mother was struggling with her mental health just a few years ago. Lucy will have to make sense of it all herself.

In a beautifully told drama of family secrets, Helen Stancey once again picks through the everyday of life to uncover poetry, pain and ultimately love.

Praise for Helen Stancey's writing:

'In the poised assurance of its writing...one has a sense of a writer gifted with an instinctive sense of how to tell a story.'
—The Spectator

'Writing so accomplished...'
—The Tablet